THE
RAGING
ONES

THE
RAGING
ONES

KRISTA & BECCA
RITCHIE

WEDNESDAY BOOKS
NEW YORK

THE RAGING ONES. Copyright © 2018 by K. B. Ritchie. All rights reserved. Printed in the United States of America. For information, address St. Martin's Press, 175 Fifth Avenue, New York, N.Y. 10010.

www.wednesdaybooks.com
www.stmartins.com

Designed by Devan Norman

Map illustration by Rhys Davies

Library of Congress Cataloging-in-Publication Data

Names: Ritchie, Krista, author. | Ritchie, Becca, author.
Title: The raging ones / Krista Ritchie & Becca Ritchie.
Description: First edition. | New York : Wednesday Books, 2018. | Summary: In 3525, with the threat of people learning they have dodged their deathdays, three teenagers must flee their planet to survive.
Identifiers: LCCN 2018002455 | ISBN 9781250128713 (hardcover) | ISBN 9781250128720 (ebook)
Subjects: | CYAC: Science fiction. | Death—Fiction. | Survival—Fiction. | Love—Fiction.
Classification: LCC PZ7.1.R5756 Rag 2018 | DDC [Fic]—dc23
LC record available at https://lccn.loc.gov/2018002455

Our books may be purchased in bulk for promotional, educational, or business use. Please contact your local bookseller or the Macmillan Corporate and Premium Sales Department at 1-800-221-7945, extension 5442, or by email at MacmillanSpecialMarkets@macmillan.com.

First Edition: August 2018

10 9 8 7 6 5 4 3 2 1

For Mom
You are our hero in high heels

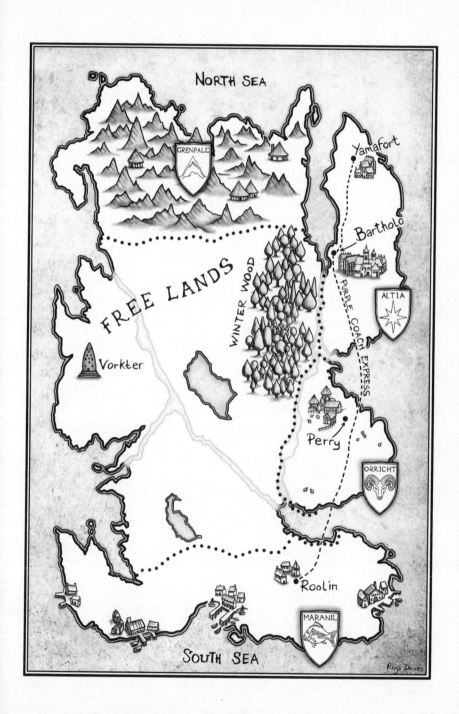

PROLOGUE

Court

I hurry.

I hurry across Bartholo's busiest and iciest city sidewalk. With assured, honest steps, I weave between young and old. My long wool overcoat flaps behind me, black scarf snug across my neck. I look forward. I look ahead.

Swiftly, I move.

I brush arms with an elderly woman in fur, and my fingers nimbly descend into her handbag. They return to my wool coat just as I pass. I lift my collar, shielding the raw, relentless breeze.

I hurry between two men in tuxedos, and I blend in. Air dignified, my black two-piece suit is ironed flat. My hands leave my sides. Gliding as fast and inconceivable as the wind. Leather wallets from their pockets to mine.

I squeeze through in haste.

From the littlest girl on the city street in braids and fur mittens, to the aging man bracing his weight on a cane—I dance around them. I dance with them.

The thief's dance is an old trick, performed around an unsuspecting, oblivious audience.

If I told you in this moment that I'm the enemy—I will not save the day, I will not change the world for the better, that this is not what will happen—will you believe me?

Try to.

Because I will lie and I'll steal more than I'll give, and this truth will hold until the very end. Remember this.

I am the enemy.

PART
One

Do not go gentle into that good night.
—DYLAN THOMAS

ONE

Franny

On the cobblestone walk of a city sheathed in ice and snow, I slam my frostbitten fist against a Plexiglas cashier window. "Excuse me!" I call out for assistance that never arrives. Five minutes till closing, and the bank has already snapped the blinds shut.

"Excuse me!" I shout again. "I'm dying tomorrow!" I bang harder, my frustrated breath smoking the chilled air. My wool coat, missing four buttons and brandishing more than a few torn holes, warms me less than my irritation. Which grows with the incoming silence.

I'm *truly* dying tomorrow, but death is normative. I die. You die. We all die. The only difference between the bankers and me—I will die at seventeen.

I die young.

They die old.

And so it goes.

I spot a bulky camera positioned on the brick of the Bank Hall's outdoor window. *You see me, don't you?* They just refuse to answer. "I'm allowed my Final Deliverance check! Do you hear me?!" I yell up at the lens while simmering in place.

Behind me, men in sleek tailored suits and fur-lined wool coats amble along the alabaster-white sidewalk. Their hot, disparaging gazes heat my neck. They can act all miffed by me, but Fowler Street, Avenue Thirty-Four contains every shop for every type of person: hair salons, dentists, pubs, quaint overnight inns, and most importantly for *me*—the only bank.

And all the grand streets—all the ones with cigar parlors and high-end fabric shops that smell of rose petals and fig—hug the grimy ones. The streets with cheap apartments, crumbling brick, and foul, pungent odors with each step past. So in the end, the rich-clothed men have always seen as much of me as I've seen of them.

We just might not end up in the same place.

I watch some strut ahead, careful on slick cobblestone, scarves bundled up to their lips. They disappear past the warmth of a stone pub, nestled on the corner of Fowler. The opulent Catherina Hotel is only one block away, and by the men's attire alone, I imagine that's their true destination.

Really, they're not a priority to me. Not today.

Most definitely not tomorrow.

With numb fingertips, I dig in my pocket for my identification. I raise the card toward the camera lens. "I'm Franny Blue-castle," I declare, possibly speaking to no one. "Can you see my deathday?" I point at the print beneath my name. "I'm dying *tomorrow*."

A shadow passes behind the window, someone stirring. Blinds rattle and I press my nose against the chilled glass, scraping my fingers down. "Please! I'm on time!" Backbiting insults and curses nip my tongue, and I swallow them, going down bitter like blood.

The blinds suddenly spring upward, and I'm met with russet curls, thin lips of boredom, and stern, auburn eyes.

I speak before the fortysomething woman can. "I need to collect my FD check. In bills." I keep a watchful eye on the old mechanical drawer beside the window. She has to dispense my cash, and once the drawer opens, it'll *finally* be in my hand.

Most plan out their deathday to the finest detail.

At six years of age, I watched my mom die.

I traced her steps around her bed, a single-room apartment above a butcher shop. The scent of slaughtered pig clung more to our well-worn clothes than to the musty air.

She lit candle after candle and hummed to the gods, casting smiles back at me. Youth sparkled in her gaze.

And I'd known, like any stranger could see, that we did not match. It wasn't only my cool, beige skin and silky black hair— but the differences of our eyes, the heart shape of my face to her squared, and as I grew, I didn't develop curves or a chest like hers.

Even knowing she'd die by twenty-four, my mother found the will and courage to provide me a home when she was just eighteen. She adopted me as an infant, and I always knew that I'd say goodbye to my mother in only a handful of years. She prepared me for the day, so I'd be at peace with her.

And I was.

Moments after her smile, she blew out the tender flames and crawled onto the squeaky bed.

"Be careful of how you die, my little Franny," she told me. "You can set your terms but not the day."

Without question, I nodded in reply.

When we're born, we all know the day we'll die. It's been this way for over a *thousand* years.

Maybe someone solved a mathematical equation.

Maybe a scientist drummed up this revolutionary discovery.

I can't recall our history front to back like an Influential. I never attended school or read their books, and I didn't really care to listen.

I only have so much time to live, so why waste it on a history that won't be mine for long?

My mom snuffed the candles, avoiding Death By Fire as her ending. In my country of Altia, people about to experience their deathday must follow Injury Prevention Laws. Like me tomorrow.

Stay indoors.

Stay away from large groups of people.

Relax. Stay calm.

Be at peace.

Defying the first two could lead to mass accidents.

A boy of fourteen dumbly and selfishly took a joyride around Bartholo's packed and icy city streets on his deathday. The car spun out and collided with Mr. Rosencastle who was innocently locking up the butcher shop.

Since Mr. Rosencastle won't die until he's seventy-seven, all he lost was an arm. Not his life.

And ever since I witnessed my mom's death—the serenity in her upturned lips, the warm flush in her cheeks before her heart slowed to a stop—I've *dreamed* of my own deathday.

I might have planned it poorly, but I dreamed well.

I imagined using the last of my money for a one-night stay at the Catherina Hotel. Where harpists welcome guests through revolving doors, men in tuxes offer gold-foiled chocolates and sweet liqueur, where feathered pillows and satin sheets blanket beds made for five bodies.

At the orphanage, I sleep on a narrow bunk, coiled springs bruising my back. Only with my Final Deliverance check can I afford this single-night luxury. I've only heard stories, never seen it with my own eyes, but I still dream.

I want to lie against those sheets and gaze up at the hand-painted ceiling mural and smile as I drift off, as my heart slows or as my brain shuts down, as the gods take me.

The banker presses a button, and her monotone voice crackles through the speakers. "We've closed out today. No more transfers, deposits, or withdrawals until tomorrow at six o'morning." She reaches for the cord to the blinds.

"No wait!" This is not how I end. "You can't botch this for me! Listen to me. You have to listen to me." My desperation curdles my stomach, and I claw at the window, my hot breath fogging the glass. "I *need* this money now. I could die at midnight."

The banker scrutinizes my long hair: black roots growing in among vibrant blue and green knotted strands that contrast her natural hue. She homes in on my silver piercings: stuck along my black brow, a ring beneath my nose and another hooped around my lip.

It's possible that she ignored me because of the bright dye and piercings.

"All Fast-Trackers receive a Six-Week Decline payment," she says. "If you didn't waste your money on drugs and ale, like you all do, you wouldn't be in this situation."

I blister inside. My nails scratch the glass as I dig closer to the Influential banker. "I worked twelve hours every day since I was eight for Fast-Tracker benefits. Have you ever used Purple Coach? Have you been driven safely around the city?" My voice breathes fire, roiling with the last hours of my life. "I never once wrecked. Never once harmed a passenger. I spent *every day* driving people down these dangerous roads."

When I only had six weeks left to live, I had to retire from the job I loved.

That boy of fourteen who took a pointless joyride right into the butcher shop—I knew him. Purple Coach employed him too. We attended the same training courses, and at eight, we sat behind a wheel and began transporting people wherever they paid us to go.

Only Purple Coach employees know how to drive, especially in these harsh conditions. No one beyond us even has access to a vehicle, but some pity our jobs, thinking there are better ways to live and more valuable skills to learn.

I couldn't think of anything I would've rather been. Anything I would've rather done.

Maybe I shouldn't be rewarded for not being a complete wart and destroying a butcher shop and injuring a man. Maybe it's just expected of me, but at least I didn't steal a car as a means to die.

Her eyes flit to my nails that scratch at the window.

I shiver once, craving just a little warmth.

If I tilt my head and lift my chin, I won't meet the sky or the blazing sun. Purple smoke sputters from chimneys.

Like thick clouds, muddled sheets of lilac shield the apex of stone buildings.

All Influentials, Fast-Trackers, and little Babes know that burning a purple mineral called casia gives off the strongest kind of heat. I've heard that no matter how far you travel—to the other three countries, the iced seas, the barren mountainsides, or even the Free Lands—the lilac haze remains inescapable. Blocking the sky, the sun, the moon, and the stars.

People joke that one day the lilac clouds will kiss the white, white snow. Some days, I do believe the smoke has lowered, but no one wishes to live in this frigid climate without the comfort of heat.

Not even me.

"So," I breathe heavily, the cold burning my throat raw, "don't you tell me that I have enough already. The FD check is part of my compensation for *my* labor."

She settles her gaze on mine, hers softening a fraction. As though understanding what I contributed in order to be repaid later on. "What do you wish to do on your deathday? The Six-Week Decline payment is a hefty sum and should help fulfill your goal."

She's still harping on about my previous benefit. I open my mouth, but I struggle for a rebuttal. Like I mentioned, I planned this poorly. As soon as I retired from Purple Coach six weeks ago, I spent everything I earned on Juggernaut. I banked on the FD check for my deathday.

I'll have enough to die in luxury then. I'll have enough to die in luxury then. I'll have enough to die in luxury then.

I've spent my free time on my bunk, reaching for invisible lights and believing I was floating over a thawed ocean. I never heard of a warm ocean before, but a girl at the orphanage said that long ago, they once existed. Large bodies of water and no ice. *Make believe*, I countered with a sluggish laugh. Then I floated some more.

So I was high.

Really high.

Juggernaut, my drug of choice, always gives me a headache after it loses potency, practically willing me to swallow another pill, to float more often, to snatch up all the lustrous stars. To empty my pockets of bills in exchange for an out-of-body experience.

I like to indulge, but most Influentials choose not to—and we'd all like to believe we're not a bit jealous or sour by the other's perks of living fuller or longer. We are at times, but I wouldn't ask for another day. I wouldn't swap places with the banker.

I lived hard, fast, and full, like a Fast-Tracker.

She will live easy and long and slow. She's not better than me. We're just standing on two opposite ends of a cavernous hole, unable to ever reach the other side without dying first.

"What if the bills I have left won't help fulfill my last wish?" I ask her in all seriousness.

"Then maybe you should lower your goal to one that you can reach." At this, she tugs at the cord and the blinds tumble down.

I scream out and slam my knuckles against the Plexiglas, over and over, but only my spirits crack. After a minute or two, rage simmering, I press my forehead to the spot my breath warmed. I have nothing in my pockets for a Purple Coach ride back to the orphanage.

I never meant to return.

And I can't exactly reach out to any friends from my old job. They're all with the gods now. The rest of the employees at Purple Coach, I'd *barely* even consider shaking their turds for hands. I grimace at the thought of groveling for a ride to Oron or Gustel—with no bills to give.

I'd rather find my own way.

And where will that be, Franny?

"Mayday," I swear, still briny about the rejection, but I can't just slump here and wallow. I don't have much time left.

I straighten up.

Dressed in a tux, overcoat, and evening scarf tucked to his rich brown cheeks, a nearby young man lengthens his stride. Trying to pass me quickly.

And he's not alone.

He hugs a girl in a dazzling sapphire gown to his side. She twirls her blond hair over her glittery earrings, hiding them from my view. Then she fixes her white fur hat and pulls her fur coat tighter. I wouldn't steal from them.

I try to soften my scowl, but I've never been good at appearing as anything other than what I am. I look and breathe like a Fast-Tracker.

I'm not afraid to hold his gaze. A warning hardens his eyes, but I don't listen as much as he'd like. *I'm not afraid.*

He breaks contact first.

With a new impulsive plan, I follow their snowy footprints.

We turn the corner, skipping past the warm pub.

Then we cross the busy intersection. Each lavender-painted car, adorned with an Altian eight-pointed star, honks at one another to go when they should be stopped. The air nippy, I try to warm my hands in my wool coat.

We turn right to climb slippery steps, the Catherina Hotel in sight. Golden molding decorates the ornate building, doormen at the ready in top hats and tuxes.

Ahead of me, the girl bundled in fur must sense my lingering presence because she peeks over her shoulder. Ruby lips pursed. She murmurs in the man's ear.

I've never felt more like a wart.

As the young man rears to a halt, eyes plastered on me, I slow too.

I should start with good manners, like they tried to teach me in the orphanage. *Say* excuse me *and say* please *and don't forget your* thank-yous. I forgot enough that Miss Hopcastle would smack my wrist with a wooden spoon. Hard until a bruise formed.

I clear my throat, my voice still raspy. "Excuse me—"

"I don't know you," he cuts me off. "So please stop following us." He sets a protective hand on the woman's shoulder, tucking her to his chest.

They're Influentials.

Most surely.

I haven't met a Fast-Tracker that believed in coupling like this. It's a waste of time, most of us will tell you. Commitment takes decades longer than I have. I didn't need to find *the one*—just someone for the moment, people I can easily say goodbye to.

Before the young man whips around, I speak fast. "I'm out of bills and my deathday is tomorrow. I was hoping to stay at the Catherina for the night. Is there anyway you can—"

"No, no." He raises his hands at me. "We don't owe you anything. You knew you were going to die tomorrow. You should've made arrangements years ago. I'm sorry."

I lick my chapped lips, my gaze dropping almost at the point of agreement. The bank owed me something, not them.

As they forge onward, I hear the girl mutter the word *beggar*.

I'm not special because I'm dying. Everyone dies, and everyone knows when.

Yet, I still hoped for a different outcome. I've seen stubborn Fast-Trackers barred from entering the Catherina Hotel before, the spectacle loud with curses and disruption.

I don't want that on my last day.

I meander aimlessly along the cobblestone walk and into a dim, deserted alleyway, squeezed between a firehouse and a laundromat. Feet numb in my boots, arms quaking, tongue stuck dry to the roof of my mouth. I expect to meet another street, but instead I stare wearily at a brick wall.

Dead end.

If this is irony from the gods, I'm too nippy to laugh.

Something wet drips from my nose. With trembling fingers, I brush the liquid. *Red. Blood.* I've never had a nosebleed before.

Maybe this is the start of my death.

No fear in my bones, I dig in my pocket for the last of my Juggernaut and count them in my palm. Three blue pills. I look up, only to be met with churning purple smoke. Icy slush crunches beneath my boots.

So this is where I end?

This is where I'll die.

"At least let me go without pain," I whisper.

Stay indoors.

Stay away from large groups of people.
Relax. Stay calm.
Be at peace.

I take a seat beside a rusted bicycle and a dumpster. I might not be able to fulfill all of these laws, but I will die regardless.

I might as well do it on my terms.

I carefully inspect each round pill. Most Fast-Trackers will go out just like this, but usually forgoing some rules and surrounding themselves with friends. Not alone in an alleyway, with iced sludge soaking their bottom and seeping up the hem of their slacks.

It's not midnight yet, but maybe this will be enough Juggernaut to knock me out for much longer than that. If the drug won't kill me, the cold will.

I toss the pills back and swallow.

A weak smile inches my lips a bit higher. "Happy Deathday, Franny," I say, congratulating myself. It's not the celebration or finery I'd hoped for. I'm certainly not staring at a hand-painted mural, but this one day didn't define the rest of them.

And I lived hard and fast and full.

Now I can be at peace.

TWO

Court

One day later

Tonight, I wait for a man to die.

I share this in common with everyone inside the lavish ballroom.

It may be the only thing we share.

Crystal chandeliers in the Catherina Hotel gleam as bright as the jewels on women's necks. Champagne flutes pass between hands. I pluck one from a tray and glide farther along the red carpet. I elevate my carriage, my assured stride not slowing.

Curious eyes float to me. As though processing my existence.

I won't be a fleeting memory for those that gawk and this simple notion digs into my stomach.

Living in Bartholo for a good portion of two years, I've avoided stepping foot into the city's most prestigious hotel.

Now I force myself into the ballroom.

My shoulders and strong build are lined with tension that I hope to hide. The red carpet beneath my soles might as well be steel blades. Each wrenching foot farther I think, *I don't belong.*

But they can't see this. They can't see beyond my calculated exterior.

They see the dapper suit and the shined boots. Which, to be fair, aren't even mine.

They see my gait. Confidence encasing me like an outer shell.

My pulse slows to a better rhythm.

Make the bet. Make your money. And be done. No lingering. No backups or diversions. This is it.

I can't fail tonight.

The ballroom is divided into multiple high-top tables with bookies dressed in brass-buttoned red suits. All the scarlet hues are designed to perpetuate an air of warmth. When outside these very gold-glinted walls, it's nothing but gray, white, purple—and *cold*.

Bartholo News plays in a constant scroll across a hefty, bulbous television, hoisted near the gambling area. One of the nicest televisions I've ever seen. They're luxuries most can't afford.

Nearby, older men and women puff cigars and peruse newspapers for the city's daily gossip and weather reports.

I train my gaze on the television screen, barely audible over the chattering guests. A rosy-cheeked news anchor stands in front of a ruddy brick mansion. Gates closed. Her umbrella catches flurries and I strain my eyes to read the closed captioning: ... *award-winning actor, Pat Pincastle, resides in his home and awaits his death.*

I attended the cinema when I was a little boy and had the privilege of viewing Pat Pincastle's gritty performances in a heated auditorium and on a brightly lit screen.

I'd like to say that we've all gathered to celebrate Pat's life, but when famous people die, it's just another easy way to earn.

"It's already well past ten—will the bastard just die already?" an old man complains. He strokes his slender gray mustache as I approach his high-top table.

Sipping champagne, his brown eyes are casted angrily at the television.

"One more hour, Tal," a redheaded woman coos. "I have him down at nine o'night on the spot."

I slip up to the table. "Heya." I gesture to the bookie. He abandons small talk with a brunette as I say, "Five thousand on a hemorrhage."

Tal and the redhead's eyes shift probingly to me. I stay fixed on my purpose and slide my money to the bookie. While he meticulously examines the wad of bills, my mouth dries. Not all the bills have been mine for long. Some I just "acquired" on the street. Not that he can tell.

Bills are bills.

You're fine, I convince myself. *He won't notice.*

He won't notice.

An agonizing second stretches too long and I only force my shoulders to relax when the bookie nods, sans discourse.

I restrain from expelling a breath of relief, my face firm, body stiff. The bookie opens a bills drawer, flush beneath the high-top table.

Interesting. I didn't see that there, but I mute all idealistic thoughts about jumping the table and stealing the contents of the drawer. It'll never work. I know impossibilities when I see them.

My relief is short-lived when Tal, the older man, edges close. The redhead squeezes in on my other side, her cheek in her hand.

I roughly clear my throat as though to say, *Move away.* They don't shift, not even a toe. Frustration hardens my squared jaw.

"Hemorrhage?" Tal snorts at me. "Do you like losing your money? This man is sixty-two. He'll surely have a stroke."

Irritation creeps up my spine and I readjust my hold on the champagne flute. "Do you know Pat Pincastle's health records?"

"No." His eyes sweep me top to bottom in suspicion. "Do *you*?"

I couldn't leave this bet to chance. Bartholo's hospital has almost no security, so finding a nurses' station with patient records was easier than I even imagined. I learned enough to make a logical prediction.

High blood pressure, complaints of sensitivity to light, frequently imbibes alcohol and smokes cigars, and has a family history of hemorrhages.

However, *gambling* on deaths with insider knowledge has been illegal for many years. Which is why I force a dry smile. "Of course I don't know his records, but since you don't either, you shouldn't be so sure he'll die of a stroke." I take a small sip from my glass.

The redhead drums the tabletop, her gaze twinkling at me. "How many years do you have on you?"

Champagne barely passes the lump forming in my throat. I lick the sweet liquid off my lips. "I'm seventeen and still at university."

Tal scoffs. "You're seventeen?" He holds on to the one fact that is actually true. Most guess that I've lived twenty years so far, which I attribute to my height.

I think of Mykal.

He says I look older because of my assertive demeanor and gray, *grim* eyes. When he said that the first time, I stared at Mykal like he smoked something from a Fast-Tracker pipe. "Grim eyes?"

"You look like you've seen too much—let's put it that way," Mykal said, chewing on a dry root. "At least you don't have hard-hearted eyes."

Mykal has hard-hearted blue eyes. As cold as morning frost.

Tal squints at me, as though hoping I'll flash my identification for proof. He can believe I'm whatever age he'd like me to be— that's the least of my worries. The longer I have to wait for Pat Pincastle to die, the longer I risk Tal and the middle-aged redhead asking harder questions.

Like my name.

Just as his mouth opens, melodic bells chime throughout the packed ballroom. People fall into hushed whispers, the television heard clearly now. Gazes lift to the screen.

"Pat Pincastle has just died." The news anchor smiles. "I repeat, Pat Pincastle has died." She pauses, only for a brief second, before adding the colloquial, "Let his soul find peace."

Voices escalate with brash gossip. I crane my neck to read the closed captioning again: . . . *cause of death will be reported shortly.*

No one would've bet whether or not he'd die the next day or the next day after that. The gambling odds are *zero.* So was there ever a chance Pat could've survived beyond his deathday?

Little children would question. Most usually do.

Adults give the same rhetoric. "In time, you will watch everyone you know die on their deathday. No sooner, no later. Then you won't ask any longer."

It was true.

I did watch. I did see. I wondered if my brother Illian would live beyond his six years. He didn't, no matter how much he would've liked to. No matter how much I loved him.

He still died on the very day he was slated to die.

He just shut his eyes to sleep and never woke again.

I even wondered whether we could change the course of nature ourselves. Then I watched friends, all before their deathdays, place the barrel of a gun in their mouths. To test this theory.

I watched them pull the trigger.

I watched the gun jam.

I saw a boy of ten years replicate them, in jest, and blew off half his jaw. He didn't direct the gun to a fatal spot. He would live, albeit injured, but he would live nonetheless.

Eventually, we all do stop asking. We stop wondering. And we accept the number of years we'll come to live.

The redheaded woman slumps in defeat. "He couldn't hold out for forty minutes longer? Honestly." She gulps the last of her champagne.

"I still have ten thousand on a stroke, Margie," Tal says. "Don't sour the energy."

Margie snorts into a laugh. "Your energy." Then she mimes sharing a secret with me, her voice too loud for one. "Word of advice, sweetie, don't marry a historian. The dust from all the books does something to the brain." She chuckles again and waves for a server.

Focus on the screen. I only allow my eyes to flit away for less than a second or two. Out of all the distractions I'm embarrassed that it's this chatty couple that pulls my gaze.

"History is a fine subject," Tal argues. "You." He snaps his fingers near my jaw. I'm trying to will the cause of death to arrive on screen. *Don't talk to the old man. Let him be.*

He snaps again, persistent and most likely bored.

It takes a great deal of energy to meet Tal's eyes, but I do, lifting my brows in question.

He puffs out his chest, all proud that he caught my attention. "What are you studying at university?"

I'm not at university.

An incoming server interrupts my train of thought. He carries a tray of colorful fruit tarts: kiwi, strawberry, blueberry. My mouth waters at the sight of perfectly sliced bright vermillion apples atop a flaky pastry.

Since the Great Freeze and the dense lilac clouds, any crops that struggle to grow in artificial sunlight are scarce. For much longer than even my lifetime, fruit has been a luxury. I haven't seen an apple in years and I was six the last time I tasted one.

"Heya." Tal waves his hand in front of my face. "It's rude not to answer a man's question." He pokes my shoulder.

Hostility springs into my rigid arms, but I don't hold the faint feeling for long. "I just didn't realize the Catherina had apples."

"Just grown in their private greenhouses," Margie says before filling her mouth with a tart. She closes her eyes with a soft moan.

The server offers me one. Against my stomach's protest, I shake my head.

I'm not one of them.

I won't eat their apples and pretend that I didn't see a Fast-Tracker—high out of his mind—begging for scraps right outside these very doors.

I can do many things: wear their clothes, speak their words, walk their pace, lift my chin and steady my gait—but for some gods-forsaken reason, I decide that I can't do this. No matter how much I should.

I struggle and curse myself. *Just take the damned tart, Court.* I waver but never reach for one.

Their inquisitive eyes bore into me like serrated daggers.

I could have taken it. I should have.

What's another deceit? But somewhere deep inside, my soul is begging me to hold it. Just this once, at the very least.

"What did you say your name was?" Tal asks.

My pulse quickens. I don't speak.

Because I sense Mykal.

More strongly.

A chill stings my fingertips, so I slip my hands into leather gloves and shrug on my black overcoat. Almost everything is more difficult when I sense him. When I feel him. When he's outside. In blistering cold that contrasts the lush warmth of the ballroom.

Jarring wind smacks my face. I tighten my eyes closed and swing my head down. I sense him *running* through the bitter air. Through deep powdered snow.

My ankles are numb.

Urgency—whether mine or his, I can't distinguish fully—seeps into my veins. As my heartbeat rages forward like prey racing to survive—I turn my pocketed hands into fists. Attempting, rather pathetically, to focus on myself and not on him.

I'm warm. In a hotel.

Someone double-taps my shoulder and I force my eyes open. Margie rubs my arm. "You're shivering, sweetie." Her eyes dance around the room with worry. "If you're ill, you should see a physician."

Influentials dislike illness if it keeps them from their studies, but most find ways to thrive regardless. Some of the best visionaries have lost limbs. Injuries don't bar people from being extraordinary.

I shiver as raw cold snakes up my spine. I tremble more than I like.

I'm not ill. And I can't describe this feeling inside of me. You wouldn't believe me, even if I could.

I rest an elbow on the high-top table and motion to the server for a glass of water. I try not to draw more attention to myself, so I mutter an "I'm fine" to Margie and her husband.

I continue to sense him.

I can tell that he's stopped running.

He's still.

His body heat escalates, agitation brewing, but I'll take the warmth, even this kind. If I close my eyes, if I concentrate on him, I might be able to sense him speaking. I wouldn't be able to hear the words, but I could feel his lips move.

I don't zone in on him to that degree. Instead, I focus on my own issues. Margie collects the water from the server and pushes it at me. "Drink, drink."

I take the glass and slowly sip. "I felt a draft," I explain and then add to throw off suspicion, "Didn't you hear? Casia rations are decreasing this month. Government efforts to reduce the smoke." Complete and utter shit, but I say the words like I heard them from President Morcastle himself.

Margie balks. "They can't possibly do that. We're already freezing enough as it is." She tugs her fur coat closed to emphasize the fact. "I feel the awful draft too. Tal, touch my forehead. Am I cold?"

Tal grumbles before reaching across me and taking his wife's temperature. "Dare say, you're as cold as three hells and as shrill as it too."

Margie swats his hand away and scoffs.

I stare blankly ahead. My true sentiments pound and thrash to burst forth. I swallow bitterness, resentment—enough that my stomach churns.

No one, not a single soul, can talk to me about freezing unless they've crossed the Free Lands. Acres of barren ice and hundred-mile winds that slap exposed flesh. Bartholo, with its electricity and casia, is a sauna in comparison.

I set my water on the red velvet tabletop, my body flushed in much more comfortable warmth.

Mykal must be inside.

I turn, just seeing him crest the entrance. The doorman eyes my friend up and down as though he let in a stray, mangy creature.

I told my friend to wear a belt, black slacks, and shirt, plus a typical wool coat, hooded to combat the elements.

Mykal Kickfall did as I asked, but the dark green coat is not how I left it. Bark-colored muskox skins and fur are crudely sewn to create two sleeves, a hood, and a new neckline. With Mykal's bold stance and broad shoulders, you'd think he killed the giant animal with his rough hands and pieced the ugly garment himself.

Which he did.

I just about roll my eyes. No one in Altia wears the rugged muskox clothing worn by those in the Free Lands. I don't have to ask why Mykal altered the coat.

I remember what he told me. "Why should I bother with their clothes, Court? They'll see me and say *You, Mykal, are a part of no village. You have no country, no homeland. You're on your own. You're a part of nothin'—you're a Hinterlander.*"

I don't want it to be true. Because he needs to blend in as well as I can and we're running out of time. It'd be a lie to say that I had faith in Mykal's ability to pass as a citizen of Altia. I didn't.

I don't.

At least not as much as I sincerely wish to.

I talked to the doorman in advance, in fear that Mykal wouldn't be allowed inside. I told him that my brother would be joining me tonight. "Let in a Mykal Kickfall," I said. "No matter how he appears, he's my relation. I'll take responsibility for anything he may do that you find inappropriate."

The doorman agreed, but across the ballroom, I still spot displeasure curling his lip at the sight of my friend.

Mykal draws down his fur-lined hood and shakes snow from his blond hair, skin chalky white and cheeks rosy from the chill. Tough face, impervious to severe conditions, he rattles with fortitude. He's already been through eighteen years of life. Just a few months ahead of me.

Without searching the ballroom, he raises his head and instantly locks eyes with mine. His hard-hearted to my grim. It takes him just seconds to reach my high-top table.

"I heard he's dead." Mykal grins so wide his smile might as well fall off his face.

"We're waiting cause of death," I reply. Mykal splays his arm over my shoulders and hugs me tight to his side—to the point where I whisper lowly, "We're brothers."

Mykal drops his arm but makes a point of huffing loudly. Like my lie is as senseless as they come. We look nothing alike, but adoption is so frequent in the city that no one would question. It's not exactly why he's aggravated by this lie though.

"All right, *brother*," he says in distaste before eyeing the rich scenery.

Margie and Tal regard Mykal with as much decency as you would a wild boar. He smells a little of wood smoke and roasted meat, and the way he just crossed the room had more purpose than grace.

When I told him there was a proper way to walk, he looked me up and down and said, "Besides one foot in front of the other? Please, do show me, Court *Icecastle*, how does one walk?"

Strangers always see Mykal Kickfall as a brute, but he's as honest as they come and far more charming than first glance. Those same strangers seem to always embrace me first, but if they knew us at all, I'm the one they would truly fear.

I take no pride in that.

Mykal steals my champagne flute and scans the television screen. "We'll be flush in no time." In one gulp, he drains the glass of liquid.

His positivity only encourages more doubt. I'm not so sure we'll win.

"Who's your friend?" Margie asks me.

"Brothers." Mykal speaks first, his tone exceedingly dry but I doubt she notices. He pats my back once, almost twice, but his gaze drifts off. "Are those apples?" His blue eyes are astonished orbs. I think it may be the first time he's seen an apple.

"Ye—" I barely let out the word and he's already left my side. Not even a single hesitation.

I shake my head once and run my fingers through my dark brown hair. I mutter a *thank you* to the server who refills my champagne and then take a larger sip.

"Come on!" a girl yells at the television, two tables away from mine. Tattoos of colorful frogs peek from the short sleeves of her vibrant pink dress. *Fast-Tracker.*

If an Influential wears ink, they'd never choose a frog. Only Fast-Trackers sport cold-blooded animals on their skin.

"Give us a fykking cause of death already!" she yells again.

The ballroom explodes in a wave of disgruntled chatter.

"I don't know why they let Fast-Trackers in here," Margie spews.

"She's not hurting anyone," I defend. *Bite your tongue, Court.* It's too late and sweat beads up along my neck as Margie narrows her gaze like I've ripped off a mask.

I keep my eyes plastered to the screen, as though nothing went horribly awry, but beneath my stoic face and rigid stance, my heart thuds much faster. Worse even.

"I don't think we ever heard your name," Tal says.

Gods be damned.

Just as I rack my brain, the familiar bells chime again. Signaling new information. Heavier silence blankets the ballroom. Mykal slips back beside me, four small apple tarts in hand. He pops them in his mouth, one by one, before even swallowing.

The burst of sweet juice hits my tongue, and as soon as I think *Here's a benefit to sensing Mykal* his cheeks dimple at the sugary dessert and he cringes like it's all too much.

He gags but chokes it down.

Sensing his revulsion in my throat, I stifle a frustrated groan. I remember loving apples, but it's now sullied. Of course he'd rather eat a charred rabbit than a fruit tart. And he'd retort back, *I sense your disgust when I eat the brains, and guess what—I don't eat them anymore. Just for you.*

We ride down a two-way street of give-and-take. Push-and-pull. It's never really easy.

"We have confirmation from the coroner." The news anchor steals my attention, a piece of paper between her fingers. "Pat Pincastle has died by a brain aneurysm."

I inhale strongly and recall what I know to be true: *A brain aneurysm has to rupture and cause a hemorrhage for a man to die.*

People bemoan and cheer and holler all across the ballroom. My ears ring. Three women in floor-length silky gowns laugh in delight and collect from their bookie.

"What does this mean?!" Mykal shouts over the cacophony.

"We've won," I say, almost disbelieving. I face him and place a hand on his shoulder. Relief bursts in my chest. He can surely feel this. "We've won, Mykal!"

He laughs for the both of us, grips my other arm and rests a hand on my cheek. "Maybe the gods do exist after all!" It's not the first time I've heard Mykal speak positively of the gods.

But I'm not Mykal. "Let's not bring the gods into this."

He grunts but wears a constant, hopeful smile. "All right, *brother.*"

Tal suddenly squeezes into our huddle and breaks my hands apart from Mykal. Beady-eyed and overly suspicious, Tal asks, "You made a bet for a hemorrhage, did you not?"

"I did." I flag down the bookie. I understand how a hemorrhage could win out easily, but Tal's pause gives me a larger one.

"So you're studying medicine at university," Tal says, not asks, like he earned himself a prize in solving mysteries.

I don't have to reply. The bookie already sidles up to the velvet tabletop, hands cupped in formality.

"I want to collect," I say.

The bookie never glances at the bills drawer. "Pat Pincastle died by *brain aneurysm.* You lost."

Mykal's smile slowly fades. Fuming, he crosses his arms and his pinpointed blue eyes dart between the bookie and me.

I say the fact, "A brain aneurysm has to rupture and cause a hemorrhage for a man to die." I've seen too many in a hospital to count. More than anyone would care to know.

The bookie shrugs curtly, a clear dismissal of me and my facts and the truth.

Brows cinched, my voice laces with ire. "You're just going to shrug?"

"The reporter said nothing about a hemorrhage." The bookie raises his hand. "I'm sorry, sir."

I run my palm over my mouth, attempting to settle the blistering fury and annoyance I feel. "So . . ." I take a greater pause. *Don't lash out. Breathe.* In the back of my mind, I think: *I have nothing else to lose. This is it. I lost all of our bills here.* "You're going off what a reporter reads rather than logic?" Bite to my voice shrinks the bookie backward.

He eyes security: three men in gold uniforms. Gaze returning to me, he says, "I'm sorry, sir. Hotel rules."

Mykal plows forward. "Hotel rules?!" I clutch the muskox hood of his coat. "You want to be talking about hotel rules?!"

I yank him to my chest. My brawn may not match Mykal's, but I'm much taller. Effortlessly, I hook an arm around his shoulders. "Enough," I growl in the pit of his ear. We can't regain the bills we lost, but I can protect Mykal.

As I attempt to steer my hostile friend to the revolving door, he grinds his teeth and then spins out of my hold. He stomps back to our high-top table and hollers at the bookie. "*You.*"

I stiffen as his deep lilt fights to come out.

Mykal growls, "You can keep looking at me like a snot-nosed goat, but you won't be cheating us out of *our* earnings."

I clasp his wrist and drag him away, my grip so tight that I sense my fingertips digging painfully into his skin.

He roughly shakes out of my hold and sneers beneath his breath. "Don't treat me like a child, Court. I have enough sense about me to see what's wrong and what's right."

Lips sealed shut, I exhale a hot breath through my nose. "If that were true—you wouldn't be arguing with someone who refuses to move."

"Maybe I'm just not a quitter like you."

His cold words drip icily down my back and my eyes flash hot. "You can call it whatever you'd like," I whisper lowly. "But I won't slice myself at the neck, and I won't allow you to either."

Someone reaches for my hand—it's not Mykal.

Margie's fingertips glide down mine and I turn just as she says, "I don't think you ever told us your name." Smitten with either my fiery temper or my assertive demeanor, her cheeks are more flushed. She touches her face, almost shocked at the heat she expels.

It's the fire beneath my heart that prods me, that pushes me. I inhale something so bitter, so foul that I just stop and let it all out.

They want to know my name so badly. There's absolutely no reason to keep it a secret anymore. I lost the bills and I can't foresee a better plan than the one today. What does it matter?

They can hear my name.

So loudly, without disgrace, I say, "I'm Court." My shoulders lock, carriage raised. "Court *Icecastle*."

Margie retracts her hand faster than lightning, eyes widened and terrified. She mouths my last name, *Icecastle*. Fingers tremble to her lips.

Those that heard my declaration burst into audible whispers and gasps. They each mutter a word. I tune it out for a moment.

And I trek toward the exit with Mykal step for step behind me. My back straight, powerful legs unwavering. People create a wide path for me, for us, recoiling and inching backward. But they stare.

They stare like I carry seven blades and an ax. All meant to injure them.

They stare like I'm a figment of nightmares. A dark shadow they heard spoken but never believed to be real.

They stare like I do not belong.

And I don't. There was a time I did. There was a time I had all the wealth that they possess. But the moment I was sent to prison, I was stripped of so many things. Including my birth name. And then I was forced to take the surname that all prisoners share.

Icecastle.

Even when I reach the revolving door, I still hear one muttered word on their lips. It attaches to me, as permanent as the lilac smoke.

Criminal.

THREE

Mykal

Ankle deep in fresh snow, I circle Court behind the ramshackle brick flats. Our temporary home. Nothin' but a single dull torch to combat the night.

I mime a lunge.

Court doesn't flinch. Fists raised, he traces my circle but never closes the distance with an assault or barrage of emotion.

Hot breath expels from his nose. Smoking the air. And he sports a silly black overcoat and scarf. Prepared for fine dining in the heart of Bartholo. Not sparring a gnarled Hinterlander in the outskirts of the city at eleven o'night.

I chew on a shred of dry root and laugh, motioning to how he *waits* for me to spring first. "Court Icecastle, never *failing* at predictability."

The grayest, grimmest eyes stay fixed and humorless upon me. Never swerving left or right, never searching for a new direction—that's Court for you. Committed to his plans. His head is hoisted assuredly, shoulders taut but body agile.

He simply *waits* as though I'm prey.

I crack a crick in my neck and jump once or twice. Cold slicing through my lungs. I welcome it. As I have all my life.

Minutes pass and even with his chapped lips and flushed golden brown cheeks, I sense his consistent ease like still wind.

Impatient, I lunge.

My fist flies madly, but I catch air as Court ducks. Swifter than I. Then my arm jerks backward. He imprisons my limb across my shoulder blades.

His hard chest presses up along my back. Lips brushing my ear, he whispers deeply, "Mykal Kickfall, twice as predictable as me."

My mouth draws in a lopsided smile. "And twice as ruthless." I plow his abdomen with my elbow. So forceful that I feel the blow like it's my own.

My stomach caves, but I push past *his* sentiments, rattling inside. And I spin frenziedly out of the hold. Wind knocked from Court, he coughs into his fist.

My own throat vibrates like I hack too. Even if I'm not.

Rich, dark brown hair falls over his forehead. Just as Court regains focus—I crouch, scoop powdered snow, and toss the handful. The chilled debris explodes at his face in a white plume.

Jolting him, and me, like a harsh slap.

I swing my head.

More accustomed to severe winter, I shake out of the sensation faster than Court. Fighting dirty, I launch another handful of snow. Then I land a solid right hook into his jaw.

I might as well be battling myself. The *thud* pounds my face, but we've sparred enough to push past our strange link. I sense his emotions, his body, as equally as he senses mine.

No matter how much I *feel* him or how many starved wolves I've wrestled with only my hardened hands, I still fail at miming Court's lithe, sharp movements that carve through wind like knives.

Ones that always outdo mine.

As though he planned this all along, he uppercuts my jaw with firm knuckles. My teeth clank shrilly together. Then he sideswipes my legs from underneath me.

Breath escapes me as my back lands with a hard *thump*.

I lie on a mound of snow.

I prop myself to stand, but the frosted sole of his heavy boot meets my throat. Forcing my shoulders back down.

"Charming shoelaces," I pant. "Did your nanny help pick them out fer you?"

"*For*. Not *fer*," he reminds me.

I've spent two years trying to get rid of my thick accent and the least he could do is be happy that I rarely trip up nowadays. "Heya," I rebut, "you should at least be thankful I didn't say *yer*."

His face is void of amusement or *any* kind of merriment.

He taps the side of his sole to my cheek. So lightly that he might as well be patting me.

I laugh into a wry smile and look to his damned *shiny* boots again. "I forgot," I tease, "you stole your laces, you little crook."

"Will you ever shut up?" Court wonders, tapping his boot to my cheek once more.

I prod Court in hopes of seeing a smile that never appears, not in the two years I've known him, and because it passes the time. "Will you ever be uncrossing your brows?" I rebut. "You have this face, Court, like you need to go relieve yourself, you realize?" I shift to throw a punch.

He smacks his foot hard across my cheek. Blood pools in my mouth and I stifle a groan. His remorse comes and goes like an extra heartbeat. I spit. The snow stains red.

He extends his hand to help me up and end our sparring. I grab hold and with a strong tug, I bring him down atop me.

His hands find support on either side of my shoulders. Our faces a breath away.

With my callused palm, I tap his cheek twice. Expecting some sort of reaction.

Anything.

But his muscles flex and his worry mounts all over again. Not even sparring could blow off a bit of steam, or in the very least, take his mind off our failings.

While I have him so close, I say, "It'll be working itself out soon enough."

"Oh right." He tilts his head, his voice crisper than mine, every syllable pronounced with precision and refinement. "I *forgot* that bills just appear out of nowhere when you need them most, escorted by mystical creatures." He flashes the closest thing to a smile that he can muster: a bitter, sour face. "We aren't living in a fairy tale, Mykal, and only one of us can afford to keep our head in the clouds."

Court has spent the better part of a year stealing bills. Pocketing them here and there in small amounts. Enough to earn us five thousand.

Any more would have likely drawn suspicion of a thief in the city. We'd hoped to double the bills by gambling them. Now we're back to where we were a year ago. With sullen spirits and no money to our names.

His disposition threatens to break mine. He can ramble on about living in a fairy tale, but I can't live in Court's bleak world. No matter how all consuming it becomes.

I grit my teeth. He can surely feel that and my hot agitation. "Heya, I don't want your sass. I understand that we're ten thousand bills short—"

"And we couldn't attain that amount in an entire *year*, now we only have two months. Open enrollment for StarDust is in sixty days." *Sixty days.*

It's a looming date.

He goes to stand after mentioning the world's aerospace department, but I grip his arm. Keeping him above me for a second longer.

"*I'll* be finding a way to get the rest of the enrollment fee. Ye've done enough." I mumble a curse and then clearly say, "You've. *You've* done enough."

Court lets out a resigned breath. "You wait longer than a few days to find more money and it'll become my problem again." His sternness is nothing new.

"It won't be that long," I assure him. I have an inkling of what I'll be doing for bills, but if I tell Court, he'd slam the idea into the grave. My plan will be less kindly than anything he can conjure.

But I *need* to provide more than I am.

Before he rises, I tenderly press my lips to his cheek—or as tender as a Hinterlander can be. Warmth bathes him, then me. Like an ancient electric current sparking to life for the first time. I don't go beyond this.

We both know not to.

His gray gaze burns a fiery trail from my harsh blue eyes to my cheeks, then to my pink lips. Where he lingers for the shortest moment before pushing off to a stance.

In jest, I call after him, "I think you must prefer being miserable!"

He turns his head, just once, to give me a strict look that says most of the same: *Will you ever shut up, Mykal?*

With a stringent stride, he leaves me for the entrance to the brick flats. His shoulders are weighted with concerns and anxieties that only grown men should bear.

Not a boy of seventeen years.

Some days our linked senses feel like being shackled to six iron chairs and a bolted table.

Court struggles to fit a key into the fourth lock of our flat. Jammed. His *frustration* piles onto me.

Resting my arm on the wall, I put a cig between my lips. I only take one drag before he swiftly plucks the cigarette from my mouth. And stomps it beneath his boot. *That little . . .*

I blow smoke into his face.

He shuts his eyes tightly. *Burning.*

I end up pinching mine closed, the stinging worse than I predicted.

"Why?" he snaps like I've gone and put us in a bind.

Our eyes flit open together. "Why what?" I point at him. "You started it by being a real nasty crank. I might as well have strapped the world to my back. Sometimes I can't think right when I'm feeling what you feel."

Court glares at the ceiling. His eyes roll before he jiggles the key and unlocks our door. We enter a flat too small to escape each other.

I plop on a creaky cot and fight my wool coat off my arms. Cursing all the while. Then I bundle it in my hands.

Brick walls insulate the heat all right. But wet, heavy snow fosters mold, creeping from floorboards to ceiling. Too far away from city-center for reliable electricity, Court torches two lanterns for light and the fireplace for heat.

Fleece blankets. Two rickety cots. Sink and bath basin, water pail nearby. It's not our lack of necessities that drives me mad.

Two years in this gods-forsaken city and I still cringe at the enclosed, musty space and insufferable neighbors above us. *Jumping* like they're high-strung Babes. *Boom, boom, boom.*

Dust, dust, dust.

Pluming from our ceiling onto us.

Spending the first eight years of my life in remote, northern Grenpale villages couldn't prepare me for city living in Bartholo. Nor did the *next* eight years alone as a Hinterlander: wandering across the unforgiving Free Lands with barely anything but ice and snow in sight.

And while I see myself more as a Hinterlander, my time in Grenpale forged me. I still carry the Grenpalish accent. A deep lilt that I've been trying desperately to rid these past two years.

I wrench off my long-sleeved black shirt. Now bare-chested but warm.

On the nearby windowsill, I reach for a crumpled paper. My brows knot as I try to read the flyer, center-stamped with the triangular StarDust emblem. Black with three gold stars. No one in my Grenpale village could read. The one book my pa found, he threw in a fire for kindling.

I rub my temple, remembering what Court taught me. For months, he's fed my brain Influential knowledge: mathematics, language, histories. After I concentrate on vowels and letters, words begin to make more sense.

StarDust Wants You!
The worldwide association of aerospace research and travel is seeking skilled Influentials to make history. Become the first to voyage into space in over 300 years. Enrollment

begins on March 24, 3525, at Altia's Museum of Natural Histories & Figures, 892 North Rimerick Road, Yamafort, 9 o'morning. Enrollment fee is 5,000 nonrefundable bills upon arrival. Bring one bag with your belongings.

Only five will be hired for the prestigious Saga 5 Mission. Good luck.

The smallest print at the bottom reads: *The Saga 5 Mission will last beyond all deathdays. Expect no return home.*

One-way travel suits me. I haven't much to return to anyways. We have much greater problems.

StarDust only wants Influentials. And in Grenpale, none exist. My northern lilt is better than it was two years ago. I'm sure of it—but will it ever be erased completely?

I dunno.

We have to pass as Influentials. I'm far from one, and Court is a Fast-Tracker.

The thought gnaws at my brain. My sole talents were built from harsh climates. Right beyond the winter wood. In a country landscaped by snowcapped mountains, isolated from electricity and most everything else.

Grenpale depends on hunting and crafting durable shelter. Not the comforts of a market or a damned hotel.

I still don't fully understand Influentials. Maybe I never will.

When I met Court at sixteen to his fifteen, I was a Hinterlander, and I hadn't bathed in countless months. He asked me if I had any soap. I wasn't sure what he meant by that.

Without pause, he said that I had a stench about me. I'd been alone for so long that my smell went unnoticed.

And I wonder, every now and then, if I still have that stench. If it's something that won't ever be washing off. If these Influentials will be sniffing me out.

But to pretend to be Influentials and enroll in StarDust, I need to adapt as well as Court.

I crumple the paper in a tight fist and notice that Court

unbuttoned and shed his suit and waistcoat. Bare-chested among flickering flames. Eyes barbed and muted gray.

He steps closer to where I sit just to adjust a water pail on the fire.

I grimace at the old scars puffed along his muscular abdomen. Cutting crudely along his ribs. Slicing up his collar. Deep and light, they mar him and rip through black inked designs. Ones that I learned city Fast-Trackers often wear: the inked scorpion on his arm, spider on his side, crocodile across his back, snake threading a gnarled wound above his heart.

I asked him why the extinct animals. Court doesn't believe in the gods or a better world than the one that exists today and cold-blooded reptiles and arachnids represent a time before the Great Freeze.

All he said was, "I'd rather immortalize the creatures that basked in heat than the ones still living in frost and snow."

He despises the foundation of this world while I just loathe most people.

And I'm no stranger to scars. Claw marks from snow leopards became a right of passage for most Grenpalish children and I gained even more as I wandered on my own. But the ones that Court has—they aren't from the type of beasts you meet in the wild.

If anyone should leave this pitiless world and travel as *far* away from these people, it needs to be him. I unfurl the flyer again.

Kneeling on one knee, Court nudges a log with an iron poker. Windswept hair hangs over his brown lashes. Fire crackles, swarming the wood, and an ember sizzles on his cheek.

In effect, it tickles mine. I roughly itch my face—a damned reflex.

"Mykal?" Court breaks the quiet and cranes his neck over his shoulder. "I don't need your sympathy." Without even a glance beforehand, he felt me.

"And I won't be needing your foul attitude." Using my thumb, I flick my forefinger at him.

Court stares blankly. "You forget no one understands that vulgar gesture but you."

"I taught it to you—so you understand at the very least." I picked up the flick of the forefinger from my pa, a village Fast-Tracker who gesticulated and cursed at the gods during twelve-hour hunts. Then I shared the knowledge with a few other Grenpalish children my age.

Court tosses the iron poker aside and stands. "When we enter StarDust as Influentials, you can't act like you've been to Grenpale," he reminds me like I never understand this.

I *lived* in Grenpale.

Every time a lady gave birth, they'd swaddle the newborn in a blanket. Before they returned the baby to the ma, they pricked the tiny heel with a Death Reader. A small two-pronged, hand-held thing.

It looked like a strange gun with a flat screen. The only tech I'd ever seen growing up.

Minutes later, the Death Reader would reveal the newborn's deathday. Babes and Fast-Trackers would return to their ma. All Influential newborns were willingly sent to another country.

To Altia, Orricht, or Maranil. Where Influentials thrived.

The night a lady gave birth to an Influential, my village celebrated. *The child will be living fer forty years, did you hear?* Grins and hugs and toasts of ale.

I was surrounded by Babes: those who would die between infancy and twelve years.

I was surrounded by Fast-Trackers: those who would die between thirteen and twenty-nine.

Influentials were nowhere to be seen: those who'd live past thirty extraordinary years, some even reaching a hundred and fifty before they say goodbye.

"Influentials are meant fer somethin' greater than this harsh life, Mykal," my pa said, nudging my head with a rough, affectionate hand.

He never said it bluntly, but I heard the meaning. Influentials have enough years to improve our world. To learn. To progress. Fast-Trackers only have enough time for a laborious life. To work. To endure.

And Babes.

Babes have enough time to live however they like. In whatever way.

Really, they have no time at all.

I buried my pa when I was just eight. He lived to be twenty-six.

He'd even helped me dig his own grave.

I thought about those Influentials as I laid him to rest. They seem to live forever. While the remainder of us just do what we can in our time.

I scratch my jaw and smooth out the flyer. *That's just it, isn't it?* If I never grew up around them, I can't pass as one of them. Not well.

But Court can.

"We only need five thousand for one enrollment fee," I say, proposing a new plan that excludes me. "You might be able to steal as much again."

Gray eyes pierced upon me, Court freezes cold.

A shiver snakes down my neck.

Beneath his breath, he murmurs, "Don't."

I won't be holding my tongue. Not about this. "There are some things *deep* in my blood that can't dissolve. This'll never be working for me the way that it'll be working for you. As soon as I show up, they'll know I'm not one of them." I shake my head, gaze lifting uncertainly to the ceiling. "It's just as you said. Influentials aren't in Grenpale. You're the closest thing I've come to one, and you're not even an Influential. You're a damned *Fast-Tracker.*"

Court crosses his arms, muscles bulging. When he wears his silly suit, you'd never realize how his body reflects the long, backbreaking hours he's spent sparring me. Toning his torso and shoulders.

Vorkter Prison cut his muscles down. Broke him until there

was nothing but skin and bone. Every day, he fights to grow stronger than the day before.

I fight because it's what I'm good at. When I dress in those same silly suits, I'm unable to hide the definition in my arms and legs. Influential clothes wear me more than I wear them.

Court is the better liar. He's the better deceiver and I'm not gonna be the one to drag him down.

Before I add this, Court says, "This doesn't work without you."

I snort. He's become the illogical one between the two of us. "It'd work far better without me than with me. You have a chance on your own. You bring me along and we might as well check in for two cells at Vorkter—and don't act like you'd be okay with going back. After all you've told me, I'd never fucking believe you enjoyed that wasteland."

Vorkter's crimson fortress juts out of the blinding white landscape like a bloodred spear, visible only from the Free Lands. I never crept close enough to enter, but I heard the curdling echo of imprisoned men and ladies. They wailed like vicious predators and petrified prey all caged together.

Court motions to me with two fingers. "Stand up."

At his command, I glower but rise.

Before I open my mouth, he says, "You'll be fine."

"In no time I'll be *ruining you*, Court." My eyes pulse cold. "Can you see that?"

"*No.*" The strength in this single word shuts me up. "It's not what I see." In two assured steps, his legs touch my legs. His towering height surpasses mine. "And it's not what I feel."

Silence.

It speaks as loudly as the palpitating, aching sentiment that beats at me.

My chest collapses with each deep breath and his follows suit.

Court holds the back of my head. I feel the movement like my own. Like his hands are my hands. My hair is soft like winter wheat between his fingers.

I stand as rigid as him, but this strange force inside begs me to seek comfort in his presence. To draw closer, to be nearer.

Skin to skin.

Heart to heart.

Our eyes glide along one other, muscles flexed in taut strands, beads of sweat building across our chests. Heated more from these riled sentiments than the fire.

I lick my dry lips. "What are you getting on about—"

Court lifts my callused hand and places my tough palm on his bare shoulder. At the touch, he intakes a heavy breath. Or maybe I do. Not knowing the origin, him or me, sends a ripple of fear down my spine.

He's afraid too.

Another breath, his or mine, tickles my lungs. Our eyes meet. The longer we stand this close—the longer we touch—my nerves respond. Tingling and blazing like the bottom of a flame.

Dizzy, I blink a few times. Doubled emotions. Twice as strong. I'm here but I'm there.

In his narrowed eyes, Court so much as says, *You feel what I feel; I feel what you feel.* His thumb brushes my hand and my veins throb with his.

I keep a firm grip of his shoulder.

This connection was forged in an instant. Not over time. Not as we grew to learn about each other. Our attachment stems from a place that has no title or history. No one would believe us, and so after a while, we gave it a name.

Our emotions and some senses are *linked*, we say.

Court clenches my hair as though to plead, *Hear me.* "I have no chance without you, Mykal. If I leave you behind, I'm still here. We're still here. I'd feel you every day across these lands, and if that happens, we both might as well be in Vorkter." His palm falls to my neck. To show me. To remind me.

Why we can't split. Even if we wished to.

I almost rock forward, to place my hand on his cheek. On his head. To hold him closer.

I stay put, our hardened eyes digging into each other. Filled with pained, lonely times and emotions we've been sharing over the course of two brutal years.

I try to fight this link, a futile battle, but I try for his sake, at least. My nose flares. Bones grinding against the pull.

My abdomen and arms and legs coil taut. And I bear down hard on my teeth. Eyes welling and scorching. I dig my fingers into his shoulder.

His stoic face never reveals what his emotions do, but if my eyes well from my resistance, so will his. I watch the water brim.

He will always feel what I feel. We can't escape this.

"Mykal," he says through gritted teeth.

My head thumps. "Years or distance could break our link. Then you'd have no reason to care. Think about this." It's the last argument I have.

He processes my words quickly. Court always feels like he's running out of time. Urgency is an undercurrent to his emotions, no matter which one.

"And what if it never breaks?" he questions. "I'd never take the risk. I'd *never* leave you here, Mykal." We stare strongly at each other. Our hearts thud with the same beat. Same speed.

It frightens me first, then him. We don't move in farther, fearful of being too in sync.

I resist the pull that urges me to him. I grit my teeth again. I might as well bang my fists against brick, but I force my feet back. Our hands fall from each other.

Court used to say that I found him.

I used to say that he found me.

The truth is that we found each other, and while it never goes without irritations, I'm as afraid of losing this link as I am of strengthening it. I'd do anything for Court, but maybe he's right. We lose if I stay here and if he goes alone.

We have to work together. There's no other way.

I just nod in agreement and plop back onto the squeaky cot. *Together, then.*

I settle with this.

While Court grips the water pail with a mitt to remove it from the mounting flames, I toss the balled flyer at his cheek.

Without even flinching, it bounces off his jaw and falls to the floorboards. His ill-humored eyes land on me. "Everything with you is short-lived."

"At least I'm able to hold a smile." I kick my leg onto the cot and find a piece of dry root to chew on. It helps curb hunger and boredom and thankfully Court has grown used to the woody taste.

In jest, you'd think he'd flash a grin. Even a mocking one. But no. Seriousness fixes his features. I watch him pour warm water into the bath basin.

"Were you always this sullen, Court, or did Vorkter steal your smile?"

He eyes me over his shoulder. "I don't understand—what is a smile?" No lift of the lips or glimmer in his gaze. He tilts his head like he's over the banter before it's even begun.

I grin into a laugh. "Your attempt at a joke was mortifying. Please don't ever do that in front of me again."

Court straightens up, empty pail in hand. "You have the smallest room to talk about *mortifying*. Yesterday, you—" The pail slips from his fingers, metal clattering against the tub.

I gasp a lungful of air, suddenly jolted up. *What is* . . . My head heavies. Blinding cold dizzying me. I press the heels of my palms to my temples. My body quakes, my throat abruptly dry and raw.

"Mykal." Court grimaces.

"It's not . . . me," I grind out. Is this *his* agony? I try to reach him. Only a few paces away. He grips the sink basin for support. Shivering profusely. I feel his teeth clank together. Mine throb.

Then a crushing weight slams at my shoulders.

He rests his forehead on his hands. Knuckles white. I barely hear him breathe out, "It's not me either." We both grit down, head-splitting yells between our teeth.

Pain wrenches us to our knees.

Something icy wets my cheeks, my nose and ears.

We both look up, but flurries aren't falling through the ceiling of our flat. I pat the floorboards, but my fingers skim powdery snow. In reality, there is none. Cold blankets me in familiarity. Outside.

I'm outside.

Though I'm inside. Court is inside. Which means . . .

Court's eyes lift up to mine, filled with recognition of what this is and what's to come.

Our senses. Our emotions.

We're being linked to someone else.

FOUR

Franny

When I wake, I inhale sharp, brittle air with a panicked gasp. I tremble, teeth clanking and, with terrified spurts of breath, my gaze darts from side to side. Yellow stains wet my ankles and discolor the snow. Someone took a piss on me.

As I die here.

A rancid stench permeates from the nearby dumpster . . . and from me, lying stiffly beside sodden bags of waste. I fight to speak, but no sound escapes. I fight to lift my heavy head, but my frozen muscles ache. I lick my cracked lips, blood on my tongue.

Isn't the afterlife warmer?

It shouldn't resemble the same place where I sat down to die: the dank, dirtied alleyway between a firehouse and a laundromat. Tears gather and squeeze from the corners of my eyes, crystalizing on my cheeks. *Lift your head, Franny.*

I bite hard and stifle a moan as I raise my thumping head. I force my gaze upward. My jaw nearly unthaws and lowers.

No.

It can't be.

Morning light battles the lilac smoke, gathered like rumbling clouds.

I'm bathed in purple hues.

Silent tears glass my eyes and I shudder at the sight. Did the gods send me to the worst of three hells? What have I done wrong? Frightened, I wheeze out short, sporadic breaths and then roll onto my stomach. A bout of hope flutters inside—what if my death-day hasn't passed?

I could still die in an hour or two. I slow my panting and gather my muddled thoughts. *I'll soon die. Thank the gods. I'll soon die.* With haste, I wipe my frozen tears. At the entrance of the alley-way, a lavender car idles beside the curb.

If I'm meant for hell and hell is where I choose to die, I can't remain here.

I'm no car thief, but since Purple Coach did employ me to shut-tle people around Bartholo, maybe it's not a crime to borrow one of their vehicles. In hindsight, I should've made many more plans to save up bills and avoid *this*—how I wish I did.

I just never think that far ahead. I've never needed to.

Now, as I fixate on the car, I do make a better plan. *Die peace-fully.* Legs too buckled to stand, I dig my fingers into the snow. Cold steals my voice, but my mouth opens in a scream. I drag my body toward the entrance of the alley.

Soaked. Head pleading to split and burst, I scream. I scream violently and harshly, but all the noise is lost in my dry throat.

Just get there. Just get there.

I groan and dig and drag my body another foot. Another.

Once more.

I pause, but not to catch my breath. Voices emanate, chatter mounting, and footsteps crunch the snow. In seconds, figures round the corner with vibrant laughs still caught on their lips. The sound fades as they freeze. Seeing me clawing toward the car like a pitiful, wounded animal.

One fair-haired girl and two slim boys waver for a moment, eyeing one another, then me. No older than I am, they're dressed in Fast-Tracker rags. Torn pieces of cloth and ripped shirts, layers upon layers for protection from the cruel weather.

While they hesitate, my desperation climbs toward my lips. I mouth the only word that makes sense to me.

I mouth, *Help.* My voice squeaks.

I try again. *Help.* I see my breath cloud.

They nod to one another and then they approach my body. I stretch a quaking arm toward the taller boy, so he can help me to my feet.

No sooner do I reach out, does he swat my hand away. The sole of his boot crashes against my chest. My head and back thud to the icy pavement. Wind struck from my lungs, I heave for breath.

"I want her coat," the girl exclaims, jostling my arms through the holes of the wool sleeves. Her eager, beady eyes meet mine. She rotates my left arm until my bones shriek. *Stop.*

Stop.

As soon as I start to thrash against her, the taller boy whacks my cheek with the back of his hand.

He does so each time my lips part.

My head spins.

The girl unbuttons the last of my coat, ripping it off me completely. "You won't die without this." She knows this for a fact. The odds that today would be my deathday are slim.

But it is.

"Or without these," the shorter boy pipes in. He unties and yanks off my boots, his coarse laugh returning. "Unless it's your deathday, that is."

It is.

It is my deathday. I no longer fight to speak. The taller boy puts extra weight on my chest, his knee bearing down on my breastbone.

His smarmy grin better rot his teeth. I swallow an agonized, furious moan and struggle to move. He slaps me, my face numb to the pain.

"If it is your deathday," the taller, rougher one says, "then you won't be needing this kinda comfort." He winks at me.

I spit at him.

His kneecap rams into my chin. My teeth batter with piercing pain. I grimace, eyes tightened shut, and they hurriedly forage for more scraps of cloth, more clothes. Hands fumble with my zipper, my waistband, the sleeves of my shirt, ripping.

Disoriented, I raise my arms and mouth, *Stop, stop, stop!*

I use my last reserve of strength, kicking out my legs, battling their advances. The taller boy demands, "Let us have them! You don't need them!" He tries to yank off my slacks and underwear.

My next scream escapes, hostile and coarse and dry, but it bites like a wintery blaze. I elbow his jaw and he thuds on his bottom, gawking like I rose from the dead.

I unleash a gnarled, animalistic noise. *Get away. Get away!*

The girl collects the coat. The other boy, my boots. And the taller boy rises with torn shreds of my shirt. Without another word, they rush from the alley.

I cough hoarsely and plant my hand on the ground for support. My palm rests, not on snow, but sopping paper.

A flyer with planets and stars and wondrous colors. I brush it aside, a wet newspaper underneath. At first, too spent to see—I blink and blink and blink. I glaze over typed font and all the words, searching for numbers. Searching for the date. Only the date.

Just the date.

Please.

Up by the corner. I see it.

1-24-3525.

It's the day after my deathday.

I'm already in hell.

I choke back a sob at the thought of my friends who've passed. Did they meet this pain? Did they feel this unholy end? *It can't be.* I cry and flip through the paper, the date printed on each page. I throw it angrily aside and stubbornly return my course to the car.

"It's not over," I breathe, my voice raspy and raw. I don't end this way. I can't end this way. I will die better this time.

You're already dead.

I hush the horrid reality and I claw, barely clothed, to the idling lavender car. I gain a foot or two before I hear the patter and crunch of boots against snow and ice.

Fear spikes and I try to drag myself to a dark shadow. Figures round the corner, without hesitation, without stop, and I think the thieving Fast-Trackers tipped someone off to pilfer the last of my protection from the climate.

"Mayday," I mutter a curse and as two males near—I kick out my legs and raise my hands into solid fists. I scream out incoherent threats, cries scrambled with snot and wet tears. Fright tries to fog my brain and I blink for coherency to see the towering boy crouch in front of me.

Quickly, he shrugs off his long black coat and covers my shivering frame. I slow in confusion and scrutinize him. Not starved thin like the others, his lean build has brawn, muscle spindling up the stretch of his arms.

His alert gray eyes scour my body and snowflakes flutter into his dark messy hair.

Right behind him, a broad-shouldered boy sheds his green coat. I eye the sleeves and hood, roughly stitched with fur and skins of an animal. He places the coat on the other's bare shoulders.

I open my mouth to speak, but the gray-eyed one does before me. "We're going to help you."

Help? Hasn't it been proven? My face burns from the many slaps and my teeth ache painfully and shrilly.

No one helps anyone.

It's what the thieving FTs said: if it's not my deathday, I won't die out here—and if it is, then I'll be gone fast enough.

I'm in one of the three hells.

I say with scorched breath, "You're a hallucination."

I'm sure of this.

He tugs off his glove, about to press his bare palm to my cheek, but I recoil. His hand drops, and he peeks over his shoulder at the other boy.

Not a second or two later, the blond-haired one narrows his cold gaze onto me. He squats beside what seems to be his friend.

As the gray-eyed boy speaks, he draws my attention. In an assured, smooth voice, he says, "Will you let your hallucinations carry you out of the cold?"

Yes, I think upon instinct.

In my silence, he licks his lips and says, "Will you let your hallucinations help you?"

Yes. Tears slip from my eyes. *But why would you?*

Exhaustion drags my body down, the safety of his words soothing me like a drug. Before I slump into a heap, the one with harsh blue eyes lifts me in his strong arms. His touch carries familiarity, as though he's done this before. Held me.

Held someone.

In unforgiving conditions. In frost and snow.

As soon as my hallucination has me tucked to his chest, my cheek brushes his bare shoulder. Skin tingling along his skin. The sensation lights up my brain, dizzies me, like ingesting nippy air too fast, too quickly. My neck slackens and my head falls back.

The world darkens around me.

Hopefully into a better death.

FIVE

Franny

I wake to the sound of sirens. Distant, roaring noises that grow louder and louder. Eyes still closed, I can imagine the red and yellow flashing lights that accompany the high-pitched wails. Could the coroners be coming for my body?

Purple Coach drivers shuttle them in white sanitary vans. They scour the city for those who've died. My name is surely on their list. If they can't find my body, they'll scribble *Unconfirmed* next to *Franny Bluecastle* and continue on.

Unconfirmed.

Bodies either sinking at the bottom of the iced ocean or obliterated into too many pieces to count. Coroners used to tell me that most unconfirmeds were fishing accidents. Stepped on fissured ice. Down they went.

I keep my eyes shut for a moment longer. My sore muscles and limbs nearly forbid me from moving. The gums inside my mouth blister like I gnawed on them. *Gods.*

Maybe it's why I hesitate to look. To see. *This place can't be crueler than the alleyway.* I'm warm. Wherever I am, heat cloaks me and the cold has been shunned.

So I gather scattered pieces of courage and fight to open my heavy-lidded eyes.

They widen in awe, a shocked breath escaping my parted lips. I was last met with white, white snow and lilac smoke.

Now.

Now I'm met with *gold*.

Glimmering crown molding frames the vast ceiling and in the

center, a decorative oil painting contrasts with my last ugly view. Sapphire skies, streaked with a blend of blue pastels, paint puckered with stark white clouds. Rolling over a vibrant orange sun. No purple smears.

Just beauty that I've never seen until now.

Tears prick the corners of my eyes. I reach up, as though I can run my fingers through the ivory clouds and feel the heat of the sun soak my cheeks. The pounding in my temple almost subsides. The gods have sent me to an extraordinary place.

Thank you.

"Good, you're awake."

I startle at the masculine voice and shoot straight up, my limbs screaming to lie back down. I ignore their protest, but before I look at him, I notice the silky red sheets covering my legs and the humongous gold-framed bed beneath me. A robe fits perfectly around my frame, softer than anything that's ever touched my skin.

No longer frozen to the bone in wet, tattered clothes. I'm grateful to be rid of them.

I spot the boy.

He sits on a dignified kind of velvet chair that matches the ornate burgundy drapes, pulled closed over a full-length window. His demeanor is strict but commanding. Spine erect with purpose. Head hoisted like it never learned to lower. Hands on each armrest, he pushes himself to a stance.

Taller than I imagined.

Those gray, unflinching eyes, I recognize.

"You're my hallucination . . ." I sweep his features once more while my pulse tries to slow. He eyes me all the same. Up and down. Side to side. But he never steps nearer. Why would I hallucinate a boy? The opulence, yes, but a *boy* . . .

Your hallucination brought you here, Franny. To a place that resembles the Catherina Hotel. Where I've *longed* to be.

My mind reels and I remember my mother and all her stories about the three gods.

"Or . . . are you Caeli?" I ask. *He must be Caeli.*

I favored all the stories with them. How the gods would send protectors down to guide the dead to the skies. "The Caeli will clasp your hand like this." My mother clutched my hand firmly. I was so little that hers nearly sheathed mine. "And with them, you'll feel safe, no matter where you may be. Caeli will escort you."

The Caeli looks puzzled. "What?"

"Caeli." I massage my jaw, but then my weakened arm drops to my side. I try again, raising my arm to press my fingers to my tender cheekbone, skin stinging. It'd hurt less if I had a handful of snow.

Even with the room's warmth, the boy wears a black wool coat, the collar high, shielding his neck. He doesn't seem cold. I think he just hopes to leave soon. Somehow, I'm more certain about this fact than anything else. *You can't know for sure.*

I feel like I do.

It's not in the way he stands. It's not in the severity of his eyes. The answer is somewhere. Is it possible to know the core of someone without understanding the shell?

I watch him saunter toward a mahogany dresser with golden knobs shaped in Altian eight-pointed stars. Voice like varnished glass, he says, "I'm not familiar with Caeli."

Maybe it's called something different. I wish people talked about what happens after death in more detail, but most stories vaguely mention peace and not much else. I just have to believe he's Caeli. My mother learned about the gods from tales, not anything in fancy Influential books.

She could've botched the name—heard it wrong and then passed it wrong to me.

"It's what my mom called the protectors sent by the gods."

His eyes briefly flit to me as he collects a black handkerchief from a drawer. He keeps his mouth shut, popping a lid off a brass bucket. He shovels ice into the cloth and knots the fabric.

I remain completely still.

With a lengthy stride, he returns to the side of my bed. Closer than before. My pulse speeds, uncertain but certain. Curious but cautious. My warring emotions tell me to spout a million questions but then to contain each one.

It's why I stay mostly quiet.

He reaches out to press the covered ice to my cheek, but I flinch before he touches me. Then I stretch even farther back. We're silent, staring at each other. Overwhelmed.

He blinks once and then twice. "Put this on your cheek."

I take the covered ice. *He's here to help.* I'm just not used to helping hands. As much as I asked for them, I don't understand how they can exist without a catch. Maybe it's because I'm dead. He helps because I've died.

That's it.

I put the ice to my cheekbone and, on impulse, I extend my palm to the Caeli.

Please let this be the right way. "You can take me now."

His lips never upturn. They stay in an ill-humored line. He swings his head toward a wooden grandfather clock. Impatiently, it seems.

"Is that how this works?" I ask outright.

"No," he says with finality.

I frown. Of course. I botched my deathday, so why wouldn't I botch this too? I'm just the girl the banker shuts the blinds on. The girl people piss on in an alleyway. The girl most ignore while she drives them around the city.

I'm just Franny and all I've ever counted toward was *this*. I scan my surroundings, reminding myself that it's not close to terrible. My body may be furiously sore, but I'd take every weighted bone for this view.

My lips begin to rise at the painted ceiling, the embroidered drapes, and the intricately stitched rug, spooled with warm-colored thread.

I catch the boy studying my reaction, but I don't shield my emerging smile for him. It stays with my happiness.

"Death is beautiful," I whisper.

He tears his gaze from mine and eyes the clock again.

Then a bathroom door swings open, a second boy appears. Shorter than the one beside my bed, but bigger boned. Taut muscles ripple down his chest and carve his arms.

I remove the ice from my cheek, sitting more stiffly. *Another Caeli.*

He rubs his damp hair with a scarlet towel, buck-naked. Beads of water slip down his skin. Not noticing me, he says, "The hot water in the bath doesn't go cold here—damned miracle."

By his stature and blond hair alone, I remember. He was the one who carried me from the alleyway. I try to ease and hug my knees closer to my chest.

The first Caeli is about to speak, but the one drying his hair suddenly acknowledges me.

His cold gaze lightens like a ray of sun through fragmented clouds. "Well, aren't you just brimming with pleasure."

I touch my lips, but my smile has faded, leaving mostly the comfort I feel inside. Still, the corners of his mouth pull upward. Like he knows just how happy I am.

"Put some clothes on, Mykal," the first Caeli snaps.

"Why?" both Mykal and I say together.

Mykal nearly breaks into surprised laughter and a rumble tickles my throat—*strange*. I withhold a cough, and he scans me, toe to head, while rubbing the towel through his hair.

Then he ties the fabric at his waist, hiding his lower half. "Seems she's more like me and less like you, Court."

I catch the other Caeli's name. *Court.*

Court rolls his eyes. "No one is like you, Mykal."

I don't understand the opposition to being naked unless you're too cold. I didn't spend my days caring about whether someone saw me in baths. Not when I was lucky enough to take a lukewarm one. Most Fast-Trackers I know feel the same. I wouldn't be able to speak for Influentials, but they do have more time to be concerned about things.

Mykal combs back dangling strands of his hair, his smile expanding wide. "The same goes for you, *brother*."

Brothers?

Court withdraws from the bed to reach Mykal. "We're not brothers."

"You'll have to be reminding me what we are, Court. I forget every now and then. One day it's *brother*, the next it's friend, tomorrow it might be—"

"We have no time for this." Court gestures to the clock.

I ache to relax against the mound of feather pillows, but urgency binds my shoulders. I feel similar to how Court looks, ready to storm out and leave this place behind.

I don't want to go so soon.

"If you don't mind," I tell them both, "I'd like to stay here for one more moment."

Court turns, face deadly serious. "We do mind."

Mykal crosses his arms over his bare chest. "Let's let her pretend a second longer."

Pretend? A chill skates down my neck.

"We don't have *time* for that," Court rebuts.

I rise slowly to my knees, purplish bruises blemishing my calves and elbows. They've quieted, gazes latching directly on to me. I have no reason to war with them. If there's a window of time to see the gods, or take me where I need to be, then we should hurry.

I don't want to be late for what lies after death. I've botched too much already.

I clear my throat once and say plainly to Court, "You can take me, Caeli—or whatever the gods call you . . . or however this works." What else can I do but this?

Mykal tilts his head to Court. "What's she going on about?"

Court slips on a pair of black gloves, looking to me but answering Mykal, "She thinks we've been sent by the gods." As he yanks the last glove on, he raises his dark brows at me like *We're not.*

I swiftly scuttle backward, inhaling sharply. I press against the headboard and my muscles shriek to stop moving.

Mykal outstretches his hand. "It's all right. You're all right." His eyes freeze Court. "Gods bless, you couldn't let her believe what she wanted, even for a moment like she asked?"

Court glowers. "I don't exist to pacify you or her—I'm here to keep you alive."

Alive?

Mykal lets out a frustrated growl.

A tickle scratches my throat and I cough into my arm. I scoot farther backward, my shoulders digging into the wooden headboard.

"This isn't real," I mutter to myself, tears threatening to well. "I'm hallucinating."

That's it, isn't it?

I put my hand to my heart, the organ nearly beating out of my skin.

Maybe I really am in hell—

"You're not dead," Court declares.

I solidify and then my face contorts. "No . . ." I couldn't have botched *this*. Nobody dodges their deathday. *Nobody.* It's impossible.

Anxious heat cakes my skin and I lick my dry lips, checking over my shoulders and side to side for different news. For the truth.

I look to Mykal.

He rubs his neck, eyes gripped to the rug.

I look to Court.

He stands as sternly as before, gaze cemented to mine.

"Who are you?" I question loudly. "And don't say that I'm *not* dead. I have to be." I can't process a world where I'm alive.

How will I see my mother?

Where will I go?

When will my next deathday be?

No one lives with that much uncertainty.

"You are alive," Court says bluntly. "Whatever gods you believe in, they won't come for you."

"At least not today." Mykal softens the blow. "Court, here, isn't the spiritual type, but I am—maybe not as much as you. I never believed Court to be a boy sent from the gods." His shadow of a smile vanishes fast. "Though looking at him, I understand the mix-up all right."

Court rolls his eyes again, but they land back on me. I grip my knees to my chest, willing myself as far from them as possible, but something inside tries to soothe me and crawl toward them.

I don't listen.

Court continues, "You're at the Catherina Hotel, only three blocks from the alleyway where we found you."

I try to calm at one thought. *They helped me.*

When no one helped me, they were there. I still don't know who they are—and I still don't understand how I can be . . . *alive.*

I don't understand much of anything.

Maybe this is a test from the gods. Maybe my body is outside and my soul is here. Maybe—

"This is *real*," Court professes, his persistence and annoyance palpable.

It causes me to growl out, "How can you be so sure?" How can anyone be *this* certain of something so irrational?

"Because," Court tells me, "I dodged my deathday too."

"As did I," Mykal says.

I open my mouth to respond, but the words lodge in my throat, too stunned to speak. *No.* But they'd have no reason to lie. Who goes around saying *I dodged my deathday!* to strangers?

Madmen.

I cautiously eye Mykal who inspects a lamp. As though he's never seen one before. He peers beneath the shade and the burgundy fringe caresses his cheek—I swat in front of my face, thinking a fluttering feather tickled my skin.

With little grace, Mykal's bulky arm collides with the pole. He lets it clatter to the floor. Like a lamp's secondary purpose is to fall. He tilts his head and waits. I think he believes it'll spring to life and right itself.

Court must see me staring curiously at Mykal because he says, "Leave everything be."

Mykal stretches his arms out wide. "I did it no harm."

I repeat what they say is fact:

I'm not dead.

I'm not dead.

I'm not dead.

Confusion grows, shock coiling around my body, squeezing tight. "I can't . . . believe." I shake my head over and over. Part of me does. Belief knocks at my heart, asking to embrace every piece. I *feel* it growing inside of me.

"Dress," Court whispers to Mykal, hurriedly throwing slacks, a white shirt, and a green wool coat at him.

I shouldn't trust anything they say, but I was supposed to die. Yet, I'm at the Catherina Hotel. I believe in the gods, but I've never seen them. Can't I believe in this?

I dodged my deathday.

I still intake shallow, hurried breaths.

Mykal coughs into his fist while zipping up his slacks.

Court takes one step toward the bed. "Relax," he says in what I presume is his gentlest voice.

It's not gentle at all.

Court checks the clock for the umpteenth time. "We've been in this room for too long, so all introductions need to happen faster than they've been."

"Who are you?" I ask again.

"Court." He points to the other boy, who pulls his shirt over his head. "Mykal." Then to me. "You're Franny—"

"Wait." I stiffen. "How do you know my name?"

Mykal tucks his shirt in his slacks and looks to Court. Court looks to him. Then to me. A heartbeat later, he procures a small blue card from his pocket.

My identification.

"You stole my card." It hits me like a car slamming against a brick wall. These aren't good people. All my defenses catapult sky-high. They're not Caeli. They're not gods. They're not hallucinations.

If I'm not dead. If this is real. Then there's only one answer.

They're thieves.

SIX

Court

She lunges.

Brown eyes ablaze, Franny battles through her injuries and races across the bed to pummel me. I take a few controlled steps back, my calves and knees throbbing with hers.

Before I can explain myself, she lands on the rug and wrenches an iron poker from its rack. Crossing the room, she points the pierced metal tip at the hollow of my throat.

Purple soot stains my skin and I lift my chin higher.

Mykal charges forward, but I extend my arm—and he staggers to a stop beside me.

"He's of no threat to you!" Mykal shouts.

"I don't know *who* you are," she says, retightening her grip on the poker, her weak arm beginning to fall. "So if you like breathing and eating from your mouth, you'll give me my identification and my things." As she silently boils, my own blood swelters in kind.

Mykal growls coarsely and spouts off two vulgar curses.

She never yells back, but their hostility mounts together, trying to lasso me.

I clench my teeth and concentrate solely on *my* senses. I can't return her identification right away—because if she leaves this room and shouts about how she dodged her deathday, President Morcastle of Altia will likely ask for a countrywide retesting.

We can't be caught.

"We're not here to hurt you," I say, more curtly than I intend. "We *helped* you, Franny."

Her eyes burn. As do mine, but she's the source. Franny rubs at them with her biceps, still not retracting the weapon from my throat.

I'm running out of time—I'm *constantly* throwing myself against a clock and I'm afraid I'll break before I gain another minute, another second. We might be linked, but how much time can I afford to be compassionate?

I'd convinced a bellhop to sneak us in the back door of the Catherina by paying him off with bills I pickpocketed. We've had the room for five hours when we were only granted four. We need to leave, but she has to trust us first.

I eye the metal poker, the point still at the hollow of my throat. *Gods be damned.*

"But then you stole my things," Franny says.

"What things?" Mykal retorts.

She was barely even clothed when we found her in the alleyway. Franny had no possessions except her identification card. Our first meeting has engrained itself within me.

How we sensed someone pissing on her legs. How we sensed hands grabbing her body, ripping at her clothes—how her limbs felt like our limbs and her fright felt like our fright.

How we'd never run harder through the snow.

Just to reach her.

"So I don't ... have many things," Franny says, "but I'm no chump either, and I know how this works. You'll strip me of everything I have. If not my belongings then my dignity—and I won't let that happen."

Her malice drips into my veins. Who stole from her and what would they steal to ignite such hate? *It's of no importance.* I don't have time for more discourse. Or to connect with Franny that way.

Forcefully, Mykal says, "We'd never harm you."

The poker droops, but Franny raises it higher. "How can I believe anything you say? You could be banking on the fact that I'm some chump, ready to accept every word you give me."

Chump. My jaw twitches each time she uses Fast-Tracker slang.

I'm surprised she hasn't called me a *wart* yet, or even worse, yelled curses like *fyke* and *mayday*.

If she says *botch*, we might be in more trouble passing as Influentials than I realized.

Wasting not a second more, I clasp the iron poker. Her eyes enlarge, but she never releases her grip. I didn't expect or want her to.

"I don't believe you're a fool, Franny. And I doubt Mykal takes you for one either." I home in on her blue-and-green dyed hair, ratty and long at her shoulders, and the silver piercings stuck in her lip, brow, and nose. "I think you're a common Fast-Tracker. Hedonistic, pleasure-seeking—you spend most of your life's earnings on temporary experiences. Because you were supposed to die."

She frowns, her silver piercing pulling downward with her brow.

I purposefully step closer to the sharpened point and catch her off guard, the tip a breath from my flesh.

Franny inhales. "Don't—"

She doesn't want to hurt me, the thought flits out of my head. My skin rips, the metal digging until pressure wells with pain.

Her clutch slackens, dropping the poker just as I let go. Metal clatters to the rug. With her free hand, she reaches to her own throat. *She can feel this.*

She can feel me.

"What . . . what is this?"

I touch my throat, a dot of blood staining my fingers. I button my coat to the collar, hiding the small wound. Mykal rubs his neck, as though his flesh broke too. But it didn't.

Only mine bleeds.

"I'll explain it to you"—I fish the last button through the loop— "if you'd just be civilized." I collect Mykal's wool coat off the rug and shove it at his chest.

He growls a curse about my "foul mood" before slipping his arms through the sleeves.

We must leave.

Franny draws back her shoulders. "I am civilized." She pauses, rethinking. "For a Fast-Tracker, I'm *very* civil."

"As a Fast-Tracker myself," I retort, "I assure you, you're not." I edge closer as her lips part and brows arch.

I have little time to decide what I think of Franny Bluecastle. Bare bones: average stature, typical FT hair, freckles splashed across her cheeks, expressive brows that wiggle, scrunch, and arch. She should be no one to me.

I should be no one to her.

But our eyes glue together, shifting when I curve around her frame, my arm brushing her woolen robe.

Then her eyes glue on Mykal's and his to hers. Using his teeth, he pulls his leather glove to his wrist. The corner of his lip rises in a partial smile.

I sidle to the bed and try to remain alert, my joints rigid. Franny's abandoned ice begins to melt inside the handkerchief and soak the red sheets. I return to her with ice in my gloved hand.

My height far surpassing hers, I look down.

A dark welt purples her cheekbone. If I focus keenly, I taste blood from *her* stinging gums.

I'm sorry.

My nose flares, restraining the apology within me. "I was on the fast track to death," I tell her. "Just like you. Just like every gods-forsaken Fast-Tracker in this world. We're *all* meant to die young." I explain further, "I dodged my deathday when I was fifteen."

As gently as I can, I press the ice to her cheek. She lets me this time and the sudden cold bites all three of us.

I whisper, "I'm seventeen now."

Franny processes and tears surge, reddening her eyes. From the intensity, mine follow suit, filling to the brim.

Overwhelmed, pressure sits heavy, like someone began mortaring a house on my breastbone. Even linked, I have no idea why she's begun to cry.

Franny puts the heel of her hand to one eye, tears still gathering.

Her arm falls. "I don't cry . . . for no reason like this. I'm just . . ."

Overcome. By these new doubled—no *tripled* emotions: confusion, certainty, worry, and fear all collided and wrapped together as one.

Then she stares up at me and a tear rolls down her bruised cheek. "What is this?"

The door flies open.

I quickly swipe my cheek and then realize no tear escaped, thankfully. I spin around to confront—of course.

It's *him.*

The shaggy brown-haired bellhop props his body on the door frame. His satisfied grin causes Mykal's fists to clench. He wears the respectable red bellhop uniform: embroidered with gold and a cylindrical cap strapped beneath his angular jaw.

The young bellhop isn't the main problem.

The main problem struts farther into the room with a pompous, dignified air: a tuxedo-clad man of sixty or seventy years.

Crisply, the older man says, "My bellhop tells me you're at the Catherina Hotel illegally. I need identification and for the three of you to exit without complaint."

So the bellhop sold me out to one of the owners of the hotel. I expected to meet security, but maybe he ran into his boss instead.

I still need three things.

I need to provide Franny with warm clothes.

I need to keep her identification secret.

And I need to exit without any attention drawn to us.

Mykal always tells me, "You can lie better than the best of them, Court."

I'm not as assured, but we'll see. My confident stride propels me forward. I stop in front of the hotel owner. "Your bellhop lies."

The bellhop snorts, as though my attempt was pathetic.

Besides his entrance, I never acknowledge the bellhop face-to-face again.

THE RAGING ONES   63

I seize the owner's gaze. "I paid your bellhop extra to accommodate my injured wife and her brother in this very room. I used the back door because I had no time to reach the front. He guaranteed that the funds would see an owner—and now I see that he's kept the bills for himself and lied to you."

The owner's white mustache contrasts his rosy-red face, embarrassed.

I talk and dress the part of a wealthy Influential and I'm given respect and the benefit of the doubt. Whereas the bellhop is given none.

Bitterness runs in the back of my throat. I'm not better than anyone. I've ripped open enough bodies to see that we're all just made of flesh, blood, and bones.

"Zimmer," the owner scolds the bellhop but never allows him to speak. To me, the owner says quickly, "I'll see that our bellhop repays us for his mistake. I'm sorry for any—"

"You really believe this wart over me?" Zimmer straightens up, gawking in disbelief. I watch him out of the corner of my eye.

The flustered owner takes an affronted step backward. "What did you just say?"

Zimmer removes his red bellhop cap, unkempt brown hair covering his forehead and ears. "He's *lying*."

Franny and Mykal waver behind me, both silent, motionless, and unsure. Their uncertainty eats at me, but I push forward. Physically one step closer to the owner.

"He also promised my wife's fur coat would be dry-cleaned and delivered to our room *one hour* ago." I suck in a breath with distaste.

"We'll retrieve that for you, Mr.—?"

"Good because my medical staff left me a note about another amputation. We have to leave in fifteen minutes." I speak rapidly. "Try not to be late. I wouldn't want to explain to my staff that the service at the Catherina isn't up to par with Yamafort's Darla Hotel."

The owner adjusts his posture, clearing his throat at my talk of leading an entire medical team in Altia's second largest city. If you're employed young in more difficult Influential fields—like medicine—people assume you must be more knowledgeable.

And the more knowledgeable you are, the more prestigious.

"Of course. Of course." The owner rotates to the disgusted bellhop. "Tell the concierge to find his wife's fur coat and hail Purple Coach for the physician."

"No fykking way he's a doctor."

It's the only truth.

"*Zimmer,*" the owner sneers.

"If he's a doctor, why is his wife's face bruised? And when did Influentials start dyeing their hair colors of a fruit tart?"

I only react when the owner questions me and repeats Zimmer's accusations. I let him finish, angle my body, and gesture to Franny. Her cinched brows nearly offer her confusion to the owner on a gold platter.

Great.

"Lambkin," I say the highest-regarded endearment as sweetly as I can, but my trite tone catches the second syllable.

Franny approaches until my arm slips around her tense shoulders, only my wool coat touching her robe. I whisper against her hair, "Act as though you love me."

Her stomach flips, but she tentatively hugs onto my side and stiffly rests her cheek against my arm. Terrible acting. I'd think she never loved anyone in her life.

At least she chose to try.

I attempt to soften my agitated gaze onto Franny. "My wife is a Fast-Tracker. I know it's uncommon for an Influential and an FT to be married, but she'll live to see twenty-eight. We have eleven more years together." The Fast-Tracker cutoff is twenty-nine years.

I have trouble forcing a smile at the owner. So I don't.

Before he speaks, I add, "Now I have ten minutes."

Please believe me.

The owner glances between us. "I'll tell the concierge myself to find your fur coat. I apologize for the . . . disturbance." He spins on his heels and glares at the bellhop.

Zimmer gapes. "But—"

"Out, now." He snags Zimmer by the collar, dragging him through the door. It slams shut and the three of us exhale all together.

Franny immediately distances herself from me, her legs and arms shaking in shock and fright—she still has *no idea* that we're linked.

Mykal rakes his callused hands through his hair. If I shut my eyes, I can better feel the blond strands slip through mine.

He cuts the tension. "Why am I everyone's damned brother?"

I blow out a hot breath through my nose. *I didn't want to draw attention to you, Mykal.* I should have more belief in him. The same amount that he holds for me.

Franny dazedly wanders left, then right, then nowhere at all. "You have to tell me . . ."

Mykal and I exchange a look, knowing what must come next. He nods to me, handing me the wheel and the pedals and telling me to drive—when I've never driven at all.

This is a story we've never given to *anyone* else.

Quickly, without pause, without stop—I tell Franny that we're linked together. I'm worried. Truly worried. That she'll bolt outside, away from us, at any second. She stares haunted at the rug but listens intently.

I tell Franny how it first happened to me.

To us.

I was just fifteen. I'd been crossing the Free Lands and I knew, as my deathday approached, I'd die in the deserted landscape of snow. I believed that I'd fall beneath ice, but as I trekked forward, I never fell. Never plunged into subzero waters.

I went to sleep, expecting never to wake up again, and when I did—I thought, at first, I was suffocating. The cold became colder. The air more brittle. I gasped and clutched my throat, but I also thought I was *standing*—in deeper snow. I could feel it up to my knees.

I stood.

Snow stopped at my ankles.

As my pulse calmed, I paid closer attention to my senses. Warmth from a fire bathed my cheeks. I hadn't started one that morning or that night. I thought surely I'd die. So there was no need.

I believed, then, that I was going mad. It was the first day of many that I'd question my sanity. My limbs would quiver in cold when I'd crouch over my own fire. I'd think I sneezed when I didn't. I could feel water slipping through the back of my throat when I never drank.

I was angry for no reason at all.

Happy when I had many more causes to be sad.

I'd lost half my weight, more of my muscle. Ribs visible, even without inhaling.

The Free Lands are harsh and unforgiving. Only Hinterlanders willingly *choose* to roam the barren ice, so in the days that I hiked onward, my soles almost turned black with frostbite. A reddish rash puckered on my exposed skin and ice crystallized in the creases of my eyes. Until I could no longer close them.

Food was scarce.

Fishing would have served me well, but I leaned on the side of caution. I wasn't Maranilan with knowledge of fish and ice fissures. I feared plunging through a crack and perishing in the freezing depths. I had no more understanding of when I'd die, but I tried to remember that the next day would be one day *more* than I ever thought I'd live.

As I walked on, two winter vultures circled me. The rarest sight due to the lilac smoke clouding the sky. An omen of misery. Hunger should've been clawing me for weeks. Screaming at me to eat.

But fullness stuffed me throughout the day. Some moments, I savored the rich meat on my tongue. I thought I was chewing roasted hare.

In actuality, I was chewing nothing at all.

It was only when my body, physically, could no longer move

that I realized I was starving to death. Despite being satiated inside, despite licking grease off my lips—I was starving.

I'd learn later that Mykal was overeating, trying to compensate the insatiable hunger that I kept supplying.

I survived by killing the two vultures and eating them.

The next day, I'd find a single snowshoe hare.

As I saw the winter wood in the distance, as I stumbled toward the snow-canopied greenery, I collapsed to my knees.

In Yamafort, I was adopted into wealth and luxury.

In Vorkter, I met pain and suffering.

When I crossed the Free Lands, I hugged death, truly, for the first time. Whatever bristled inside of me—a soul, a life force—it slowly began to fade away.

My eyes cast ahead. To a sky I couldn't see. I watched a haze of purple smoke. I saw how it thickened toward the nearest city, Bartholo, like an arrow pointing to Altia's border. A direction I'd been following for weeks.

I was close.

Then I looked right. Pale, gray smoke plumed from the winter wood. Billowing above the trees.

Then I looked down. At the white snow beneath my withered frame. Where I could curl up and die.

Three choices.

Three paths.

Only one pulled me with such force and ferocity, granting me immeasurable strength. I rose. The gods have never been to my aid. Not once. I didn't believe they existed, not even then. Not even today, but deep in *my* core, something propelled me forward.

And I walked.

I staggered toward the gray smoke. I made it to the tree line. I held on to rough trunks for support. My legs shrieked in pain, but I moved. I made it halfway when someone rushed toward me. Sweeping through the winter wood like they knew where every tree rested. Where every rock was nestled beneath the snow.

Cloaked in animal furs. Mykal ran to me.

I picked up my pace. To meet him.

We found each other in the winter wood.

He threw his arms around me like I'd been his long-lost friend. I hugged him like I was meeting my soul again. There are some moments and some feelings that I can't even explain. I'm a young man of medicine and science and logic, but the sentiments I wield for Mykal transcend all three.

He let me recover in his ramshackle hut for the next few months. I thawed my frosted bones over a fire and we exchanged information about each other.

Understanding then that we'd been sensing each other for a long while. My life suddenly had clarity and blinding focus.

Mykal is a Babe. He was supposed to die at eight. When he dodged his deathday, he left Grenpale before anyone would notice that he still lived. And then he survived the next eight years alone.

The day I dodged my deathday, at fifteen, was the very day we became linked.

This explains why we suddenly feel Franny now. Why we have this inextricable connection that we can't shake. We've all experienced something unimaginable.

We're alive when we shouldn't be.

When I finish my story, I avoid all mentions of Vorkter. I still need her to trust me, and if she hates thieves, she'll most likely *despise* prisoners.

I wait.

And in this moment a single realization thrashes at me.

She can walk away from us. Franny can choose to leave us behind. It'll be hard for her to pass as an Influential. Yet, I want her to enroll in StarDust with us. I don't want to *feel* someone miles away and yearn for them to be at my side.

This choice, this road, this course for Franny—it never existed when I met Mykal in the Free Lands.

He was alone. I was near death.

Survival, together, felt right.

In the city, she has many more choices than we started with—ones that she can make. Ones that don't involve us.

I inhale a shallow breath. *I'm afraid.*

As I concentrate on Franny, all I feel is ambiguity. Vagueness like dense lilac smoke. Clouding our only sun. Our only sky.

SEVEN

Franny

My life is in my hands.

And for the first time, I don't know what to do with it. After exiting the Catherina Hotel and arriving at Mykal and Court's flat, they spent the rest of the day explaining *linking* and their future plans.

Mind spinning and body still aching, I had little to add or to say. I told them I needed to think.

At ten o'night, I fixed an abandoned Purple Coach that I spotted only a few blocks from their building of flats. The driver must've been eight or nine, forgetting how to jump-start the cold battery.

As the engine grows hot, I sit behind the wheel and instinctively reach for the heaters to warm my palms. I retract slowly, forgetting that the most lavish leather gloves protect my skin. I splay my fingers and examine the rich material.

My eyes well at a memory of my young mother—as she slipped the prettiest maroon shawl onto my arms, frill made of black feathers. The fabric smelled of Blur 32 perfume, and at six, I twirled and wrapped my body up in the garment.

She spent her Final Deliverance check on that tiny shawl. Just for me.

Her smile lit the room more than the waxy candles. As we cuddled for warmth on our creaky bed, I whispered into her ear, "When will I see you again?"

She would die in three days.

My mom stroked my black hair. Candlelight flickering against the walls, her eyes sparkled. "When you've grown to be a young woman. With arms as strong as your heart and legs that go wherever you choose to go." Her fingers brushed my cheek. "When you reach seventeen years, you'll die happily and peacefully. I'll wait for you with the gods."

I breathed out a short breath, confusion widening my brown eyes. "But what will I do until then?"

She smiled as bright and lovely as the smile she wore on her deathbed. "You will *live*, Franny. You will live hard . . ." She cupped my face. "Fast." She rested her forehead on mine. "And full."

My mom wouldn't want me to cry over her memory, but tears scald my cheeks. I cry more than I like and I aggressively rub at my snotty nose with my hand.

"I shouldn't be alive," I mutter to myself. *I should be with her and the gods.* I lick my cracked lips, a lump lodged like a hollow pit in my throat. Yet here I am. I think about what she'd tell me if she knew—if she knew we'd have to wait longer to see each other again.

Maybe she'd want me to try to meet her and the gods. To force my death if I can.

But I hear her words ring true in my head. *You will live, Franny.*

I nod tearfully. "I will live," I whisper. She'd want me to grab hold of the extra time I've been given.

I delicately rub my tear-streaked cheeks along the black fur of my new coat. *Soft.* The most expensive garment I've ever worn. I hug the coat the way I hugged that feathered maroon shawl, the fur snug around my frame.

Can they feel this and my tears?

I freeze and blink and then shake my unsettled thought away. Focusing solely on my new coat.

Court said that the hotel management wanted to please us, so when the concierge arrived, announcing they'd lost my dry cleaning, they offered this luxurious coat and gloves as an apology and replacement.

After traveling to the flat, Mykal lent me a pair of gray slacks, too baggy but I secured them with his belt, and I wear one of Court's long-sleeved black shirts too.

Dressed more warmly than usual, I need nothing else from them to survive on my own.

I squeeze the steering wheel. Torchlight illuminates the snowy street in glowing patches. I constantly glance to the right. At the building of flats where Mykal and Court remain. And then straight ahead, to the road.

I let out a tight breath. The car rumbles and sputters.

I can drive anywhere. I can take off alone.

"What now?" I whisper in the quiet of the night. Inside this tin can of a car, gray fabric torn on each seat, cigar butts and ash collected in the middle console.

Accept that you've dodged your deathday. I have. My gloved finger skims the hollow of my throat where Court bled. My skin burns because I feel Court's wound.

I believe we're linked like I believe we've all dodged our deathdays—because I can sense their lies.

Each one that Court spouted at the bellhop twisted my stomach in a vicious knot. Staying with them seems less irrational if I can weed out their falsehoods.

I frown deeply, lifting the fur coat to my lips. They laid out their plans for me.

The grand, delusional ones.

In less than two months, they'll attend the enrollment for Star-Dust. Where only five people will be hired for some mission. I'd heard mutterings about it in Bartholo for the past couple of years, but I never listened closely. It's always been an Influential matter.

Still is.

I have two choices.

To go with them to StarDust.

To go out on my own.

I inspect the fur, my leather gloves—then I sniff the coat lining, honeysuckle scented.

Blur 32 perfume.

I take a deeper whiff, the fragrance most popular among young Influential women. I haven't smelled this scent since I was six.

Another strong whiff.

And then a cough tickles my throat.

I cringe and hack hoarsely into my arm. *This must be the link.* One of them—either Mykal or Court—smelled the honeysuckle because I did.

They said I can heighten the link by *concentrating* on them. Mykal told me, *"At times, the link will be growing faint and other times, strong, but it won't ever be disappearing."* But I try not to focus on them now.

I don't want to heighten their sense of disgust toward a perfume I've loved. And when I make my decision, I want to be clear that it's my own. Not swayed by our link.

I shut my eyes, realities crashing against me. I remember Court's grave voice when he said, "You will *never* know the day you will die." I'll never be able to prepare for my death. It will just happen. Suddenly.

Tragically.

The air vent crackles—I flinch backward, heart lurching. Could the car blow up in a gust of flames?

I shrink.

Could the windows abruptly shatter and pierce me?

I go rigid.

Anything—anything in the whole world could kill me, at any second, any moment.

Don't think.

If I block it out, if I believe I'm to die at . . . a hundred and thirteen, then I'll never be frightened by anything. "A hundred thirteen, a hundred thirteen," I mutter beneath my breath, eyes wide open. "*Drive.*" I growl out the word. "Drive!"

I place my foot on the pedal, but I hesitate.

I have no true direction. I could head to another country, but

I can no longer work at the job I loved. I can't be a Fast-Tracker who shuttles people for Purple Coach. Not as I continue to grow older. They'll discover that I dodged my deathday.

And I asked Court and Mykal what would happen if someone found out.

"The worst," Mykal said.

They never specified what *the worst* could be, but I sensed their dread seeping into my veins like hot tar.

I wish I could drive toward villages of people who are just like us. "There could be others," I theorized. "What about finding answers about *why* we dodged our deathdays? Maybe these other people have all of them."

They reacted like I missed an entire lifetime of theirs. One that concluded without hope.

"There's just us." Court stopped my rant. "Mykal and me. Now you."

"We won't be finding some special person with all the answers, Franny," Mykal chimed in. "We have to rely on ourselves."

I didn't ask whether they were sure. Their emotions were like hardened cement.

Court explained, "If there were others, we'd sense them. We're linked because we dodged our deathdays." He said that he sensed Mykal a country away when they first linked, so proximity wasn't a factor.

There aren't any more of us, I realized.

We're it.

I suggested retesting ourselves. *The dates could be wrong.* They said they'd done just that with Death Readers in private and in secrecy. Their deathdays were the same ones that they dodged.

"We're not wandering aimlessly again to reach dead ends and more questions," Court told me. "That's not how I plan to spend my life."

It echoes inside of me.

That's not how I plan to spend my life.

You will live, *Franny.*

My life has always been dictated by how much time I have left. My career, my friends, my interests.

I stare out at the road, my eyes glassed. I inhale deeply—and I realize the street is silent and cold. It never beckons me. All my friends are dead. I can never return to the orphanage or Purple Coach. Everything I ever loved is gone, and if I head straight, I'll never be able to explain this life to another person.

I'll never be able to tell them about my mother or driving or the orphanage. I'll never be able to share the pains of believing I died when I lived.

I'll have to live a lie.

I glance at the building of flats. So maybe I'll pretend to be an Influential, but I won't always have to pretend with them.

When I reach the door of their flat, flames lick my cheeks and bathe my body in warmth. I almost expect to be beneath a burning torch, but cold whistles in the dank hallway.

I'm warm because of them, I realize. I better live to be a hundred and thirteen because I can't imagine being used to this link before then.

I slip inside.

Their heads swing toward me.

Both Mykal and Court sit casually on uneven floorboards next to a lit fireplace. They're dressed in long-sleeved shirts and soft woolen night slacks.

Their moldy flat is what I'd expect of any dwelling located on the fringe of Bartholo. I'm not briny about these accommodations. The orphanage had the same weathered appeal.

There's not much in this room besides two cots and a bath and sink basin.

I shut the door behind me, stiff, my battered muscles pleading with me to sit. On instinct, I remain standing, fighting the urge to plop down on the floor.

I'm not sure why I say it, but I feel the need to explain. "I'm here because I have nowhere else to go." At least, nowhere that I could be Franny Bluecastle, a Fast-Tracker who dodged her death-day. Here, in this room with them, I can be *me*.

The taller one, Court, opens his mouth to say something, but my nerves jostle and I quickly add, "But that doesn't mean I'm some chump you can walk all over. If you two treat me poorly, I'll choose *nowhere* over your company."

My chest rises and falls heavily, trying to catch my breath. It wasn't a very long speech, but every word came out a little louder than the next.

A moment of silence passes before Court says, "If you're going to stay with us, then you have to commit. Because I don't have the energy or time to spend on you, only for you to leave after a few weeks."

"Court," Mykal growls.

"What?" Court snaps at him. He waves his hand toward me. "She's a Fast-Tracker, Mykal. She can't read. Can't write. I had two years to teach you. She has less than two *months*. Not to mention we now have to find fifteen thousand bills. We can't afford for her to bail halfway through."

"I won't," I say, my voice rising.

They both turn to look at me and I see the worry . . . no, I *feel* their worry.

"I'm staying with you," I add, my legs aching from standing. Slowly, I cross the room toward one of the cots. It creaks when I sit down and my limbs relax in thanks. "Really staying."

Mykal shifts away from the fire. Closer to me, I notice the broadness of his shoulders. He's larger than most people my age—and somewhat tougher. His crooked nose casts an odd-looking shadow in the light.

I remember he grew up in Grenpale. I lean forward in intrigue. I only know fanciful tales about the Grenpalish. I once heard they're impervious to frostbite. *The cold is no match for the north-erners,* people will say in awe. Most revere them for their skills in the wild and ability to live without tech.

"For how long, little love?" Mykal asks. That last word crinkles my forehead. *Love.* Fast-Trackers don't believe in such things. I've never even heard an FT utter the word. At least none of my friends did.

I stumble over his question, stuck on *love* and the fact that I'm having a conversation with a Grenpalish boy who became a Hinterlander. "What?"

"How long will you be staying with us?" Mykal asks again.

"For . . ." I say, thinking of the right phrase. I don't have an end date, not like I used to. "For a long while, but I won't stay where I'm not wanted."

"We want you here." Mykal turns to his friend. "Isn't that right, Court?"

Court stares at me intently, his eyes narrowing into pinpoints. My pulse thumps. For some reason Court's approval means more to me. I think because it seems harder to come by. "I want you here," Court says.

Something in my stomach flutters. Can they feel that?

Mykal's lips curve into a smile.

Gods.

"But . . ." All flutters die with that *but* from Court. "I'm not kind. Whatever warmth existed in me died long ago. I'll treat you as well as I can because you're linked to me, but anything more than that and you're asking too much. If that bothers you, the door is open now. But it will close tonight."

He's trying to scare me off, not because he wants me to leave, but because he's worried I might leave down the road. But I meant what I said.

This is where I choose to be.

I adjust my posture on the cot, the iron moans and I kick my feet on the pillows, making myself at home—trying to prove my point. I'm about to comment on the woolen blankets, thicker than I'm used to, when my stomach lets out a low groan.

My eyes shift to the floor. There's a wooden plate with a hunk of grain bread in front of Court. Soft white cheese and three shreds of meat divide the other side.

An identical plate and portion rests in front of Mykal.

Between theirs, they set a third plate.

I sit up, fear pricking me. "Who else is coming here?" I ask. They never mentioned a third person.

"It's for you," Mykal tells me. He pats the floor next to him.

I frown. *They set a plate for me.* My stomach rumbles at the sight of the food. Growing up in the orphanage, we had stale bread that I'd drench with warm gravy.

I can't remember the last time anyone set a plate for me or even hoped I'd be their company for supper.

My friends at the orphanage would come and go, some working night shifts while others spent free time in bars or party flats— the location for twenty-four-hour raves. We rarely kept tabs on one another, so there was no need to worry if one of us had a meal or not.

I bend down tentatively and pick up the plate before shuffling back to the cot, my feet dragging heavily with the weight of the day. They keep on staring at me like I've grown three horns.

The first bite is less than graceful, my mouth filled to the brim.

I chew, open jawed, and stuff another piece into my mouth. I wince only a bit. My gums sting when food rubs against them. The insides of my mouth are still all scraped and scratched from being smacked in the alleyway. It's hard to believe that was just this morning.

Pushing through the pain, I shove another chunk of bread between my lips.

I have trouble letting my food sit for long. When I first entered the orphanage in Altia, other children used to steal leeks, cabbage, and onions off my dish—sometimes our only meal. They'd slip beside me, scoop up a handful of greens, and run off.

My eyes flit up after a minute and I catch Mykal smiling at me.

I choke on the next bite.

His smile vanishes and he coughs hoarsely into his fist. I bend, doubled over from the bread lodged in my throat.

Court rises from the floor like he means to help, but I quickly swallow the bread down with a cup of water. It takes me a few more seconds to inhale properly.

Thick tension layers the room. They really just felt me choke?

I'm about to mention how this link is pure madness when my gaze falls to their untouched food.

"You're not eating," I say and then shove my plate aside. "Is it moldy?" Not that I haven't eaten my fair share of spoiled food. I touch my throat, wide eyed. "Gods, did you put something in it?"

Court is the first to roll his eyes. "No."

"That's not exactly fair, Court," Mykal says, lifting up his plate to eyelevel. "I put a great deal of love into this meal. Caught, skinned, and cooked it myself."

I try to conceal my surprise, but I guess it's useless.

They can feel me.

At least I remember that no one bothers to hunt in Altia. Histories might make little sense to me, but for six years, I lived above a butchery. These shops sell packaged meat for consumption, livestock shipped from the farms in Orricht.

I have no idea why Mykal would choose to hunt in Altia, a country that prides itself on cultivating knowledge at the world's greatest universities and is home to some of the finest engineers of our time.

StarDust is in Altia, after all.

I sniff the cooked lamb. Fresh game should be similar to store-bought meat, I guess. It smells delicious, but it still doesn't explain why they haven't touched their portions.

My head swings from Court to Mykal, not sure what to make of them yet. Court and his no-nonsense attitude, his stiff rigid posture that makes my own back ache. Mykal and his lopsided smile that combats his angry blue eyes and muscular frame. They're so different.

We're all so different.

"If there's so much *love* in this meal," I counter. "Why haven't you taken a bite?"

"Because," Mykal says, "we like keeping food in our stomachs."

"You make no sense," I say plainly and turn on Court. "You. Explain."

He gives me another warty eye roll. "Linking isn't just emotional. It's about three senses: smell, taste, and touch . . ." He lets that word linger like it's more complex than I realize.

Touch.

I've just only grazed the surface of what it means to be linked. This, I know.

I'm the only one who tenses, it seems.

"If we eat food you dislike, you'd taste it and gag," Court says. "In turn, it'll cause us to gag and eventually, we may all vomit."

That sounds horrendous.

"Not our finer moments," Mykal says with a short laugh.

I stifle a wince, having trouble believing that my preferences will affect theirs and theirs will affect mine. I wouldn't want to sully anything they love.

"Why are you just telling me this now?" I question, staring at my half-eaten plate. They've been sitting over there hungry and letting me eat.

Mykal shrugs. "You looked like you were enjoying the meal and you've had a long day. No need to rush."

Court lets out an annoyed breath, one that causes tremors in my throat. He doesn't agree with Mykal. I wonder if he's counting each second until StarDust.

I'm in this odd group now and I vow to pull my weight. I won't be some lagging chump, bringing us down.

"All right then," I say, placing the plate on my lap. "I like most everything." My eyes dance around the food. "But this white stuff here."

"Cheese," Court corrects me as if I don't know.

I glower. "I know what cheese is . . . just not what type."

"Goat," Court counters in a matter-of-fact tone that grates on me.

"All right, *goat* cheese."

Mykal throws up a hand to his eyes and I feel his dread compound. "God of Wonders, she hates cheese," he lets out a heavy breath. "I'll never be able to eat it again."

Court shakes his head. "You promised never to speak of the gods in this room." He reaches for his own plate. "And don't be so dramatic, Mykal. It's just cheese."

"It's not what you think," I reply quickly.

Mykal's hands fall from his face and he straightens up, a burst of hope in his chest.

"When I was little, I learned I couldn't digest anything made of milk." I realize this may not make things better, so I wait for his displeasure to crash harder, but it . . . alleviates.

"But you like the taste all right?" Mykal asks eagerly.

"I mean, I guess . . ." I shrug. "I haven't tried it in so long, I wouldn't know." I sniff the cheese. It smells edible.

"Would you like to?" He scoops goat cheese on his finger and my hesitance diminishes, realizing exactly what he means.

I nod.

And he puts his finger in his own mouth. The long-forgotten taste instantly melts across my tongue like dessert. Creamy and richer than bread. Maybe not better, but it's wonderful in its own right.

They watch my reaction. The more the taste lingers, the more I stiffen and wait for my stomach to churn.

It remains peacefully at ease.

My eyes begin to widen. A door has opened. One to milk and butter. One to ice cream and pudding. A door to many foods that I never thought I'd taste again.

I nod over and over, rubbing my burning gaze with the back of my hand. I savor the flavor like I might not experience it in the future. *I will*, I remind myself. *The link.*

No one says anything more. They don't have to ask about my feelings, and in the next moments, we eat in quiet.

Wind beats at the sole windowpane, and while Court and I use a fork, Mykal tears at his meat with his hands and teeth, licking each finger. Maybe that's how they eat in Grenpale. I like it.

I remain on the cot, a good distance between us. My shoulders ache from Court's unbending posture and my fingers feel slimy from Mykal's handful of lamb.

I chew quickly, shoveling meat into my mouth, and I wipe my greasy lips on the back of my hand.

I sense Court eyeing me and I glare right back. Then I study him like he studies me.

He carries himself with refinement, but he's a Fast-Tracker, which means he was most likely raised in a house with Influentials. That doesn't explain his miserable personality, but I suppose that could come from just about anything.

I fit the last of my bread into my mouth, so large that I chew with all my might.

Disgust breaks across Court's face and he disrupts the quiet. "Is that how you always eat?"

I flash him a rude FT gesture, middle and pointer finger raised with my knuckles facing him, mostly because my mouth is too full to respond with rude FT words.

Court is shaking his head like he could earn medals in a head-shaking competition. "You can't eat like that. Not where we're going." *StarDust*.

I swallow down the chunk of bread with a gulp of water and rub my arm over my mouth. "Is it the way I eat?" I wonder, truthfully. What else will I have to fix?

"The way you eat," Mykal chimes in and lists off his fingers, "the way you talk, walk, dress, take a piss—"

"He's teasing," Court says flatly, but my stomach has already front-flipped. Becoming an Influential will prove to be more difficult than I realized.

"Only about the last one." Mykal keels back on his elbows,

plate completely clean. "I have firsthand experience in Court's *master Influential training.*"

I tense, eyes bouncing between them.

"Shut up, Mykal." Court is miffed about—well, everything. To me, he says, "You can't talk with food in your mouth or chew with it open."

I can't help but blister. "Whose rules are these?" They seem pointless. What does it matter if I chew with my mouth open or closed? I'm not disturbing anyone. If they don't like it, *look away.*

"It's not a rule as much as a custom," Court explains. "It's called etiquette."

Etiquette. I've heard of it. I didn't like the sound of it then and I don't like the sound of it now. "I think it's worthless."

"It's worth your life," Court says. "Is your life worth nothing to you?"

You will live, Franny. I'm still grappling with the concept of *living,* but even if I had a proper reply, I wouldn't let him hear it. His speech, while seemingly kind, rubs my skin coarse. He acts like I'm impossibly slow to catch on—like I'm dragging my heels when we all need to be running our fastest and hardest.

This is my fastest.

I promise.

Court continues, "If you're to pass as an Influential with us, you have to be more like—"

"You?" I interject.

"Like *them.*" His nose flares, his emotions too muddled to pick apart. He must not know what he feels either. "And yes, like me."

The air is more strained. I stare at my plate for a long moment. *Be an Influential.* They were forthcoming on their plans. I knew I'd have to pretend, but I just didn't consider all the requirements and all that I'd need to change.

"I . . ." I stammer, hands on my knees, palms sweating all of a sudden. "I don't know how to be an Influential."

Court's gray eyes soften just a fraction. "I'll teach you."

EIGHT

Mykal

With a hard thrust, I swing an ax down onto a log. Wood splits cleanly in two.

Wind whips through my hair. A midafternoon storm imminent. I'd rather be spending what time I can outside before I'm forced back into the suffocating flat.

These past few days have been challenging. Tripled senses and emotions are like walking through three-foot snow in a whiteout. Overwhelming. I only hope we'll be growing used to it soon.

Court has started his master Influential training with Franny. So far, it's gone sour fast.

Their frustration doubles, and during each lesson, our heads pound hard. Court says she's not as slow as I. And I hang on to that glimmer of good fortune.

After a bit of fussing, they both agreed to take an hour break from studying. While Franny bathes in our flat, Court joins me at a tiny thicket a few blocks away.

Skeletal trees sway and creak. I chop wood and Court sits on an overturned bucket, his back to a gaunt tree. He reads from a worn book. Quiet.

Mind wandering, I stare off at the snow. Steam blankets every inch of my body. Hot water encasing me. I quickly shrug off my coat. I'm about to stay in my loose shirt, but when Franny dunks her head beneath the bath water, my temperature rises tenfold.

I strip, bare-chested.

Using her hands, she scrubs her prickly legs and ankles. *Wood. Wood.* I chop another log.

Being linked, privacy is hard to come by. No matter how much we try. I can't control who I'm sensing that well. I try my best to focus elsewhere, but I sense her palms.

They drift higher and splay on her belly. And higher to her breasts. My jaw locks and I swing my ax harder.

Court looks up from his book, eyeing my bare chest, then back to his book. Eyes on the pages, he says, "It's not a failure if you can't acquire the bills, but I need to know now, so I'll have time to make plans."

Clutching the ax sturdier, my muscles strain. "I told you I'd be the one to fix it," I reply. "So I'll be fixing it."

I can feel that Court has no faith in me. Only worry mounts on more worry.

In the Free Lands, he never fretted over my abilities. He leaned on *me*, not the other way around. When he needed advice on edible herbs, on hunting techniques, and how to breathe longer in this climate, he turned to *me*.

Now it's all backward. I'm not going to be useful in his eyes until I prove that I am.

"It's fifteen thousand bills now," Court reminds me.

"I can count, Court." I slam the sharp ax blade into a tree stump, leaving the weapon there. "Or have you forgotten when you taught me mathematics?"

His voice lowers into a whisper. "I haven't forgotten." He frowns, eyes grimmer today, filled with a thousand doubts. "You're just dangerously optimistic." From his lips, it's not an insult, but I somehow feel like it is one.

I smile, a tighter smile than I'm used to. "And you're misery with two legs and brown hair."

Suddenly, I choke for breath. More powerful than before.

Franny submerges herself beneath the water for longer than a second. The odd sensation quiets us and we wait for her head to break surface.

When she does, I exhale gruffly and run a hand through my dry hair. A bit disoriented. I feel wet all over.

Before I met Court, it'd been eight years since I had a full conversation with another person. Over the next two years, we grew into our conversations. I enjoy his company. Even his moodiness.

Still, I really haven't conversed with anyone else. Not until Franny. She's the first lady I've talked to since I was eight.

"Do you like her?" I ask him.

"She's a common city Fast-Tracker," Court says, half of his attention on his book. "We would've been better off if she were raised by Influentials."

"That's not what I asked." I wedge the ax from the stump.

Court folds his book over his thumb, his attention now all mine. "I have no time to think of Franny in any way, *other* than how she'll affect our chances at StarDust. If your head was in the right place, you'd do the same."

"She's linked to us," I growl, my voice hollowing with anger. "She's not some stranger, Court."

Court thinks long and then blinks rapidly. As though he's trying to wake up. "Do you like her?" he asks me.

"She's not you. So I like her very much." My grin grows.

Light passes through his eyes before he grabs a hunk of snow and chucks the slush at me. I laugh, ducking and blocking the next snowball with my ax.

Bartholo News predicts an incoming blizzard will be shutting down the city for days.

We've abandoned our flat's makeshift table of hard-backed books for a real wooden table, lined with a champagne-colored cloth. Jeweled light fixtures swing above us, crystals clinking incessantly together.

The shrill sound of dying prey is more pleasant to my ears.

Twenty minutes at this fancy Influential restaurant and I'm about ready to push back the table and storm out the revolving doors. I've imagined the scenario a dozen times in my head.

I'm not the only one who knows we shouldn't be here. Influentials, dressed in their pristine tuxes and beaded floor-length gowns, ogle us with upturned noses.

Must be our clothes. We stand out in hard-worn formalwear. My collar is frayed and I stitched muskox skins in the lining of my blue suit. Though they're not visible to the eye this time.

Just this morning at a secondhand shop, we purchased Franny's emerald gown and a checkered, silk scarf that shrouds her colorful hair. She also took out her piercings.

Low on bills, we couldn't afford much else.

Franny lifts her goblet and her hand trembles. Her nervous energy spreads to my fingers. After one damned lesson on a makeshift table, she's not ready for fine dining. But Court refused to wait.

"There's no time," he said.

How I wish I could physically create seconds, minutes, hours out of thin air for him.

Franny shakily sets down the goblet, and I feel wine on her lips before I look up. Deep red droplets stain her mouth. I'd smile if we were at the flat.

In the presence of onlookers, I just huff.

Court touches the folded cloth on his lap. When the soft material grazes his fingers, it grazes mine too. Subtly, he tells her to use the napkin.

Air is caged in her lungs, eyes darting nervously every which way. With so many roaming gazes, I don't trust myself as much either. I haven't picked up my glass since we arrived.

"Napkin," Court ends up saying aloud. "Use the ends to dab at the corners of your lips."

Slowly, Franny mimics Court, both of them too tense. He said that we shouldn't leave until after our food arrives. It would be "impolite" to do so.

My throat is raw from not sipping anything. Maybe that's why Franny keeps drinking so heartily.

I reach for a glass, my movements more cumbersome than hers. Elbow inches from Court's goblet, he whisks away the crystal before I tip it.

I mutter a curse and take the longest swig. Hells, it may be my very last.

They watch me keenly, staying silent as our server skirts to our table. He meticulously places our barley soups, even wiping a dribble on the rim.

"And for your second course?" he asks Court, who ordered the soup.

"We have to be home early for a housewarming," Court says, seeming genuine. "So this will be all for us." In reality, we have no money to spend on a second or third or fourth course.

When the server leaves, I'm grateful for the momentary peace.

Franny stares hard at the liquid. Her heavy dread mounts in my stomach.

"You're teaching me how to be an"—her brown eyes dart around again, not wanting to say *Influential* aloud—"but what would you like in return?"

Court frowns. "Excuse me?"

I'm just as oblivious to where she's going.

"What do you want?" she states. "I owe you something."

"No you don't." Court shakes his head. "No, Franny. It's not that kind of relationship."

Her expressive brows bunch together, confused.

"We work together," he adds, motioning to me and then back to her. Trying to signify that we're all three equals.

"No one does anything *just because.*" Her voice softens, so I lean in closer to hear. "If anyone at Purple Coach lent me a spare tire, I'd need to give them something in return. Let me teach you something, please." Desperation clings to her brown eyes.

"You can't teach me anything that I don't already know," Court says.

I snort.

Wind roars outside and the brewing storm creaks the windows.

Sleet pelts the roof. *Ping, ping, ping.* Even city-center isn't invincible to the harsh weather. Men and ladies talk louder to combat the noise.

"I feel indebted to you," Franny says, "and it's not a great feeling, so if I could just teach you something . . ."

Now, I understand. I like being useful. To not burden others. She must feel the same. "What are city Fast-Trackers good at?" I wonder, keeping my voice low.

"I'm not scared of much."

"Neither is Court."

Court remains quiet. He chooses to share less whenever conversations diverge from StarDust or Franny's lessons. I'm used to his sulky disposition, but I worry that his unwillingness to open up will drive her away. If he wants all three of us to leave together, then we need to be doing this *together*.

His posture is agonizing. I knead my shoulder, but the action helps no one since his muscle is stiff, not mine.

"Fast-Trackers are good at working hard and then playing hard afterward," Franny adds.

"Not all of us have the luxury to play," Court says. His bones grind against one another, aching to be loosened. In the Free Lands, I'd massage his muscles for him, but he'd rather live in pain in the city. Court believes that our plans are too important to relax.

I ball my napkin in a fist. "Or you just don't know how to play," I tell him.

"I can teach you," Franny offers.

Court goes even more rigid. "No offense," he says tensely, and I know nothing good will come next. "I'm not looking to fall into a drunken, drugged stupor—and I'd bed any two legs in a luxury lounge before I'd bed you."

NINE

Franny

My throat closes tight.

No offense.

He meant no offense, but his words punch my gut.

My brows pinch, eyes in blazed points on instinct. Jeweled light fixtures clink together harshly as the weather becomes angrier outside. People start waving down servers, preparing to leave early to beat the storm.

Underneath the table, Mykal kicks his leg at Court but fails at seizing his attention. "Heya, she never talked of bedding you."

Court glowers at my glare. "Will you tell him or should I?"

"Is it a problem for you?" I nearly spit. He knows what Fast-Trackers think of *coupling*. Not the type to settle on one person, I've been to bed with my fair share of people.

Just because I liked the feeling.

"Because if it is a problem," I add, "I don't *care*."

Mykal falls further into confusion.

Court pauses, a pang of remorse beating in his veins, faint and then gone. "I had similar beliefs once, so no, it's not a problem."

"Good."

Mykal gestures to us. "Someone best be telling me what in three hells we're discussing." I'm not the only one who has to fight to keep up.

With the incoming storm, most every Influential peers out the window. No spotlight on me.

So I speak the whole truth. "Most Fast-Trackers do what we

enjoy in our short time, and most enjoy bedding many—not waiting around for the elusive *true love*."

Mykal digests the meaning slowly.

So I add, "It's fairy-tale nonsense. Stuff for Influentials to believe. They have the years for the fancy gowns and the beguiling princes and princesses in storybooks."

Why wait around for that when chances are, you'll die before it comes true?

His hard jaw constricts, cold eyes cast down at his soup. He slides his chair from the table to stand, but he doesn't lure attention. Others have already collected their coats and furs to leave.

Court chimes in, "It's just how it is, Mykal."

"Just how it is," he mumbles, hand firmly gripping the back of Court's chair, but then he lowers his head slightly toward me. His features hardening in the dim light. "You know how I'd see you in Grenpale?"

I shake my head once, my throat tight.

"You'd be a *princess*—and why shouldn't you believe you're one? You only ever live once, and by gods, why not be open to love?"

His conviction barrels into me before his words even do. I choke on my thoughts. I didn't need to search for love or hope for it. Because I didn't want to reach the end of my *life* thinking I didn't do enough or didn't achieve a goal I'd set. Who'd want that?

The banker called my sole goal to spend my deathday in the Catherina Hotel *too lofty*—and she'd been right. I keep my wishes to a minimum. I keep them soft and quiet like fantasies whispered breathlessly at night.

Before I can answer, the jeweled light fixtures flicker, and the owner tells everyone to return home. The weather is worsening and I already dread the walk to our flat. I wish I could drive a Purple Coach there.

Shrugging on my fur coat, I watch Court slip on his gloves. Mykal is already dressed, ready to sprint home. His words linger, all the ones about being a princess. Even sporting a gown tonight, I feel more and more like a fraud.

Right before we leave, I catch Mykal's gaze, and in jest, I ask, "If all the fairy tales come true in Grenpale, then why don't more people live there?"

He stares down at me, blue eyes carrying years I'll never know in a land I'll never see. "Because the whole lot of you have lost your minds."

The storm relents after a few weeks and it's the first time I don't yearn to be back at Purple Coach. Heavy blizzards bury tires, freeze over windshields, and batter engines. It's a downright pain to spend all your time tinkering on the car when you could be out driving and making bills.

Not that I've had a pleasant time here.

My brain is overflowing with information. A constant headache thumps my temple, worse than the morning after an all-night rave.

I never desired to learn and even now I struggle to retain all that Court has taught me. His angered huffs rattle my own throat and I don't blame him.

I know we're losing time.

We have just a month left until StarDust's enrollment.

If I can't pick up reading and writing and etiquette faster, then I might be the reason we fail. I've been reading through the nights, and every day I complete the number exercises Court writes for me in a notebook.

And apparently the letter *T* needs to be emphasized. I've been dropping that sound when I talk, so I practice speaking with all the *T* words I can think of.

Butter.

Mitten.

Temple.

Toad. Though Court chided me for that Fast-Tracker slang. He told me to practice with the word *tattering* and all its variations: *tatter, tattering, tatters, tattered*.

I like *toad* better.

Then I finish up with practicing walking back and forth across the room, spine straight, confidence emblazoned in my shoulders. Each step lighter than the next.

When exhaustion pulls at my eyes, I force them awake and I try harder.

Gods, I'm trying.

I lie on the cot, book in hand, and I'm glad that I'm not pretending to dine in a fancy restaurant today. The wooden chairs here cause my already strained muscles to ache. The inside of my mouth has healed, but my lips have cracked and scabbed over from the cold.

I raise the book over my head, concentrating on the sentences. "Morund?" I sound out the word and roll over onto my belly so that I can trace the word with my finger.

Court sits at the end of the cot beside my head. He leans against the brick wall, trying to roll out his own throbbing joints every so often. I wish he'd just lie down, but I don't think he's capable of relaxing.

His eyes flit to the book.

I try not to be demoralized by the fact that he can read *upside down* while I struggle reading words with my nose pressed to the pages.

"Marooned," he corrects. "It means—"

"I know what it means," I say, frustration bunching my brows. "I just didn't know it looked like that on paper." Silently, I repeat the word a few times in my head. My eyes are heavy lidded from staying up all night, strutting with Influential grace.

Mykal already complained about his sore feet, but I felt Court's appreciation and it was enough to know I'm doing right.

Every day, I stumble over words or throw books across the room, angry at myself for not learning faster. Court tells me, "It's hard, but it means your life."

He constantly stresses this.

It means my life. If I fail, I could die. Altia Law: people caught passing as Influentials will be sent to Vorkter Prison until their deathdays arrive.

Fast-Trackers talk of Vorkter like an idle danger.

"Nothing in sight but ice and snow," they say.

"Impossible to escape."

"Criminals left to starve. Too nippy. They'll freeze, you'll see."

"Eventually, they'll all rot and die."

Not how I'm going out, I always thought. *That won't be my end.*

I never heard of someone who was caught pretending to be an Influential, let alone tried to pass. Why would they want to? People can buy new identifications on the black market—like Court and Mykal, like they did for me yesterday; new name and all: *Wilafran Elcastle, dying at 104 years*—but no one really does what we've done.

A piece of paper won't change the day you die.

One of my old friends wished to be a full-time artist, but even passing as an Influential, she wouldn't have graduated from school in order to *be* an artist. They would've lowered her in a grave first.

Pretending seems pointless for most, but I bet some do try, just for kicks.

We sit in silence while I skim the next line with my finger. I subconsciously run my tongue over my lip, the absence of cold metal startling. No piercings.

Foils encase strands of my hair, which are caked with black dye that Court either stole or bought in the city.

I didn't ask.

No more blue and green.

My scalp itches madly, but I grip the hardback fiercer to keep from scratching. I glance at Court, knowingness etched across his stern lips and eyes. *Can't keep anything secret.* I asked if they sensed me trekking off to piss in the snow and they exchanged a look before Court said, "Lack of privacy has befallen us all."

As though linking is a curse.

"Take a break, Franny," Court tells me as my eyelids throb from the strain of keeping them open. Although he's been strict, this isn't uncommon for him. It's also usually followed by, *You're no use exhausted, if you can't retain what I'm teaching you.*

"I can read more," I counter. "I'm not too tired yet."

He hesitates for a second, before nodding. "Read to me then."

I hear the question at the end. *How well can you read now?* For someone who could only read a few Bartholo street signs, it's not as simple as it seems.

I focus. "I saw . . . the most . . . wonder . . . ful . . ." I pause on the next part. "Sea creatures?"

He nods—*boom, boom, boom.*

I recoil, dust fluttering on my shoulders. *Boom.* I flinch. The ceiling clatters. I protectively shield my head with my arms. This happens every other day, the tenants upstairs either jumping in joy or fighting one another. I like to pretend they're lovers. It seems happiest.

Boom. Still, I haven't grown used to the noise. The worst outcome: the ceiling is going to cave in. I'm going to die here.

"Franny, look at me."

I hesitantly force my gaze from the ceiling—*boom.* Back to the ceiling. "It'll crush us." I scan the small flat for an escape, for safety. Away from this death trap.

Boom.

I stand.

Court stands. He clutches my arm, gripping tufts of soft black fur from my coat. A stolen or bought pair of slacks, white blouse, and a bra beneath, discomfort everywhere I turn. "You must grow accustomed to formal and business attire," he'd said. One of the worst parts of being an Influential has to be this bra.

But it's not the most difficult part.

You must grow accustomed to living when you should be dead.

That is.

"Shhh," he coos, not as warmly as you'd think. He draws me closer and my raging pulse starts to slow in time with his.

My arms ache by my sides and his hand hovers beside my cheek, tempted to put his skin to my skin. Touch heightens the link, I remember. He fights the urge and stays put.

"One hundred and thirteen," I mutter to myself over and over.

"A hundred and thirteen what?" Court asks while I convince myself that I will live *so very long*.

"It's my deathday." I have to have one. So I won't be frightened to the bone by every gods-awful noise. All my life I'd made peace with dying. I wanted it more than anything and now the very thought of death terrifies me.

The infinite possibilities plague me like a sickness.

Court stares straight through me as though he understands this feeling. Like he's met it a long time ago. Then he says, "You die at a hundred and four years. It's written on your identification. You can't tell people differently."

"I know," I say tiredly, "but I can tell you, can't I?" I blister at his stern features that say *no*. "Court—"

"You'll slip up. It's easier if you pretend you'll die at a hundred and four at all times."

I huff, encumbered by so many restrictions and customs I need to remember. I just thought . . . with them I could be more myself. Like a Fast-Tracker. Why does he have to snuff out the only fragment of light?

I try to be calm, my shoulders dropping, and I expel a breath. "Will you tell me I'm safe?" I shouldn't even ask.

Court is a fortress of miseries and cold realities that now belong to me. He towers above my frame, forehead lowered toward mine, staring down. "I won't tell you you're safe because none of us are. It's why you must study."

And why he refuses to waste time talking about himself. And why he's asked little about my life unless it pertains to StarDust. I'm not sure why I even care to know more about him, when he doesn't seem to care to know about me. Maybe it's the fact that I can feel his emotions, his senses, and I'd like the full story, not just the bits and pieces he's offered me.

But I respect his reasons enough to plop back down on the cot without arguing.

Court remains standing, putting distance between us and I feel more like a chump for panicking in the first place. Over a ceiling.

If I start believing the sink basin will kill me, I've gone absolutely mad.

From the towering stack of books, I reach for the heaviest text. My head still pounds from trying to read *World History: From Ancient Civilizations to the Thirty-Sixth Century*. A hefty book that Court apparently stole years ago to teach Mykal about our world.

I remember the part about Influentials spending most of their time and funds studying agriculture, and since the Great Freeze of 2501, StarDust has done nothing more than collect data and pretend to have the resources to do more than it can. Last Court heard, the Saga 5 Mission was supposed to dust the cobwebs off the aerospace department.

I already asked what the mission entails and why now, after all this time, they're focused on space travel—and what the aerospace directors at StarDust are searching for in a candidate.

It appears as if Court knows everything—he *is* a know-it-all through and through—but he knows next to nothing about this. He shook his head and said, "I'm uncertain."

The mission is cloaked in as much secrecy as StarDust itself.

I'm not confident about our odds and Court keeps talking about how we don't even have the bills for enrollment yet. It stresses him more than my poor reading.

Too exhausted to dive into the dense history text, I focus on my other novel. I spot the end of the sentence. More confidently, I read, ". . . that swam . . . deep in the . . . okean."

"Ocean," he corrects.

I frown and inspect the word. His certainty binds me.

I wish he'd mention his childhood in Yamafort, but he acts as though that life died with his deathday—and he was reborn again.

At least Mykal tells me about his "pa" and Grenpale and the Free Lands. I once asked how Court knows how to read.

Trying to cross the cavernous hole between us.

Just once.

He said, "It's not important." Even if it is to me, he still considers it *inconsequential*.

I stifle my hurt and move on.

"Heaviness," I read, ". . . weighed deep—" *Boom.*

I jump.

Someone cracks a smile in amusement. I feel their lips upturn at me, but Court's remain pin straight. I turn my head, half expecting to find Mykal, but he left early this morning. *He felt me from far away.* As I concentrate on Mykal a little harder, a chill whips along my cheeks.

I shiver, not searching for a draft. Mykal is outside in the snow, dedicated to catching game for us to eat. Just this morning, I asked them why Court couldn't just buy meat or thieve it from a market.

Neither spoke a single word. I sensed Mykal's disgruntlement coiling uncomfortably around his ribs. Then the pang of pity from Court.

It caused Mykal to slam the door on his way out.

The link granted me a deeper perspective of their feelings. So I realized then that Court *can* steal all the essentials to survive. He could thieve a loaf of bread, cheese, and even the meat.

But what makes Mykal happy cannot be stolen.

Boom.

"Mayday," I breathe.

"Franny." Court sinks onto the cot, the open space beside my head. I stare up, lying on my back as he stares down. I thought he'd chastise me for using a Fast-Tracker curse, but he doesn't scold.

His shoulders bow toward me, leaning down so close our noses almost kiss, and he whispers, "A hundred and thirteen."

My lips part. He's letting me pretend with him, even if it could cause me to "slip up" and fail? Even though it also grants me security. And comfort. "Are you sure?"

Court nods. "Just with me."

"And Mykal?"

"And Mykal."

So I whisper, "A hundred and thirteen." *Don't be afraid.* I trace the flaking gold-foiled title on the blue hardback. *A Tale of Two Pirates.* My pulse slows. "Later, it's my turn."

He stiffens. "Your turn for what?"

I begin to smile.

TEN

Court

After her reading lessons, Franny leads me outside. A lilac tint shadows the snow, overcast at two o'noon. I seize a blazing torch beside the creaking door and swiftly peruse the deserted area, only rickety brick buildings lining snow-blanketed curbs.

No watchful eyes.

No one who'd take interest in us.

The outskirts of Bartholo contain far more noise indoors. People prefer to leave the cold, not enter it. We may be the only bodies along this very stretch of road.

"This way." Franny gestures me forward while tucking her chin and lips beneath her fur collar.

My black wool coat braces against the wind. I easily maintain her brisk pace, unaware of our destination, but I trust Franny to the same unspoken degree that she's trusted me. This link isn't easy to maneuver, but in the past month with her, I've found footing. I no longer fear she'll leave us if I voice an opinion contrary to hers.

Our boots sink into the snow, her stockings beneath pleated slacks providing warmth. She reaches up to her chest and grabs at the underwire of her bra. Her angered breath smokes in the air.

"Stop fidgeting," I snap. I don't like nagging her or Mykal, but as the days end and the nights begin, as our time slips through our fingers, we lose the ability to make mistakes. A month from now, I don't want to look back on *this* day and regret not doing more. Not saying something. Not helping in my own aggravating way.

"Says the boy who doesn't have to wear one of these things," she spits back and then abruptly stops. I halt and watch her combat the undergarment, shifting it up and down, right and left.

I wait, trying my hand at patience. It's not easy.

"Fykkin—"

"Franny," I say, my voice rising.

Her eyes pin to mine. "This contraption is ridiculous. Ungodly. Who would want to cage their breasts?" She reaches to her back where the clasp is located.

"What are you doing? You can't take it off," I say hurriedly, looking around. The street is emptied, but that's not what concerns me. Franny has been excelling at studying—picking up words and equations much faster than Mykal. But it's her impulsive behavior that causes me to panic about our future.

"Why not?" She struggles with the hooks, grunting in effort. "It's an undergarment. No one will know if I'm wearing one or not."

"Influentials will. It's for . . . support."

Her fingers pause over the clasp before she drops her hand and her eyes. "You can tell?"

I pinch the bridge of my nose. An unabashed, common Fast-Tracker would be fine in any other circumstance, but where we're going people would pause at her question. *You can tell?* They would stick their noses up at her bluntness.

Part of me wants to stand by her side and spit at those people, the other part—the stronger part—needs her to be someone she's not.

"They look more . . ." I cringe, stopping myself. "They look supported. And I know it won't make a difference, but I can feel how uncomfortable it is, and I agree . . . it's ridiculous."

She lifts her head slightly, hair hanging over her eyes. "You're wrong," she tells me.

"What?" I frown, confused.

"It does make a difference." She tilts her chin up in the air. "If I have to wear this *thing*, then I'm glad you're uncomfortable too."

Of course. "We agree on something then." I reach into my coat, my gold-plated watch warm from being in my pocket. As silly as Mykal sees my attire, I hate wearing the dress suits and formal coats. Every extra button suffocates and *binds* me. I only do it when it's necessary to fit in.

Today, outside of city-center, it's not as dire.

Franny situates her bra and then picks up her pace. We head for the street and pass a skeletal shrub in an ankle-deep snowy trek.

She endures the raw air as well as a Fast-Tracker would, more resilient than some Influentials. I should be pleased by her strengths, by Mykal's, but for some gods-forsaken reason, I choose to fixate on their failings.

When I possibly have even more.

"As soon as my lesson starts," Franny says with a measured breath, "you're to put that away for good." She nods to the watch, brown eyes ablaze, but the foils in her hair dull her authority.

The gold casing lies in my gloved hand. Uneasy, I clasp my fingers around the watch, hiding it from view.

Her brows curl, as animated as her eyes. "All the way *away*," she instructs, trudging one step ahead of me as though to say, *I'm your teacher.*

She is, but I still have no idea *what* she plans on teaching me. As I reach her side again, I don't tuck my watch in my pocket.

Franny shakes her head once and then stares straight ahead. "Aren't there papers in schooling telling you how awful you've been?"

"Report cards," I say. We walk carefully onto the iced street, salt only spread on city-center roads.

"And what do teachers write on report cards?" she asks.

I eye her, but she purposefully observes the street. Even without the Fast-Tracker hair, the piercings, the clothes—she's *proud*. I carry her sentiment like its my own, so foreign and unusual.

If I'd ever been proud of myself, I buried the feeling. Long, long ago.

"They give letter grades."

She contemplates this. "Then if you don't listen to me, you may receive your very first P."

My brows rise. "P?"

"For *poor*."

I roll my eyes. "That letter isn't used in academia, and you can feel elated by calling me *poor*, but you certainly wouldn't be the first to award me a bad grade in school." I used to back-talk if I thought the teachers were wrong.

They didn't appreciate my tongue.

Franny suddenly falters, just slightly, at the knowledge of me attending school. Fast-Trackers aren't allowed to go, but we're not barred from learning on our own time. She might've assumed I taught myself all that I know.

Which would be a lie.

I went to school. To university. I'm educated beyond recognition, beyond perception.

My gait is nothing short of rigid. I wait for her to pry, and I'd struggle to explain a life I've hidden and tried desperately to forget. My muscles constrict, my skin colder than the glassy ice beneath my boots.

Don't ask. Please don't ask.

And she asks, "What is the *proper* letter then?"

I swing my head to Franny, surprised. It pains her to not question me; I *feel* every morsel building between us like a jagged mountainside. But I'm thankful. I would rather crash against stone—I would rather crash against *her* than regurgitate my past. And I hear Mykal in my head, pleading with me to let her in, to not treat her like a stranger. My stories aren't wild tales like Mykal's, beautiful on the tongue. I can't so easily speak them.

So I accept the mountain between us.

Quietly, I say, "The worst letter grade is an F."

"You're close to an F," she says before marching ahead. "Keep up!"

I inhale strongly and lengthen my stride to match hers. Halfway down the road, our eyes meet constantly, but we stay silent. Then she abruptly stops beside a lavender car, the Altian insignia painted on the door.

Franny spreads out an arm, showcasing the abandoned Purple Coach. She plans to teach me to drive.

"No," I say instantly, fist tightening around my watch. "If someone—"

"Sees us?" She simmers, already prepared to combat me. *Am I that predictable?* "What if someone saw you stealing hair dye in the city? Or bills? Driving is a useful skill. I'm not trying to start a stew with you over it."

I cringe. "Don't say that."

"What?"

"*Stew.* Use *fight* or *quarrel*. Stew is something you eat."

Franny fumes, lips tightened. "Now's my turn, Court. *Please.*" She's right. Driving can be useful and I have no knowledge of cars. Not even the slightest.

I nod tensely and then I drop my head to peer through the car window, my dark brown hair sweeping my forehead and neck. The gray seats are ripped and a rodent built a nest on the back windshield's dashboard.

"Before you enter the car, you have to inspect its current state." Franny bends to the tires and angles toward me. She tugs on the spiked chains, secured. "If these come loose, you'll spin out."

I listen more intently, especially as she wanders around the vehicle and pops the hood. I realize I'm clueless about machinery and the new terms even surprise me. I ask a few questions and find myself pocketing my watch.

Torch in my hand, the flames illuminate the car's mechanisms.

Franny gestures to a metal cylinder, eyes lit bright. "The power steering enables the car to turn sharply." Her finger drifts as she lists off, "Pump, fluid, belt, hoses, and steering gear, which includes the rack and pinion."

I watch her more than I do the car and she notices.

"What are you doing?" Franny slams the hood closed and then forcefully tugs open the car door. I think she's prepared for me to piss all over her profession.

I grip the frame of the car. "Remembering how smart common Fast-Trackers are."

She tries to hide a smile, one beginning to form. Then it vanishes entirely. "What—you thought I was dumb? Really?"

Yes. "You thought I was a *god*," I say with an edge.

Franny rips my hand off the door. "You're driving—and I only thought you were a *protector* of the gods because I thought I died, not because you look like one."

I roll my eyes again. "Fine."

"*Fine*," she mimics me since I told her not to say *all right* if she can help it. I digest the first portion of her rant.

"Wait. I can't drive."

Franny already opens the passenger door.

"Franny!" I hiss.

She slips inside, leaving me no choice but to follow suit. I stake the torch in the snow and climb into the driver's seat.

Anxiety mounts, the wheel right in front of my chest. Pedals beneath my feet, the odd gearshift in the middle—I have no idea what to do. Franny stretches over my body and shuts my door, locking the cold weather outside.

"Ignition." She rattles a heavy string of master keys; I missed her motion toward the ignition. "Key. Each model car has a different one, so we use . . ." She clicks open the empty glove compartment, a code scrawled on red tape. "*45B3.*"

My hands hover over the wheel, afraid to touch *everything.* "We should switch seats."

"You'll never learn if you don't experience it yourself." She unhooks the correct key that corresponds to the code. I expect her to lean forward and fit it in, but she passes the key to me.

"No."

"*Yes*," she refutes. "Stop being so stubborn. You won't wreck. If anything happens, I'll grab the wheel and take over." Then she prattles on so quickly about shifting gears, the gas and brake pedals, the rearview and side mirrors, directions tumbling in and out of my brain.

Then she says, "You can start the car."

"Wait, wait." I ask at least ten questions, ensuring that I can sufficiently succeed at this and not kill us both.

She answers patiently enough, but when I begin inquiring all over again, she interjects, "How about we just start? You'll learn as you drive."

She's mad. "This is a *vehicle*. That I've *never* driven before, and you want me to just . . . try and see what happens?"

"Exactly," she states with the arch of a brow. "Begin here." Key between my fingers, she clutches my wrist and guides my hand toward the ignition.

I stop. "Wait." I let out a tight breath.

"Court, it's not that difficult. I promise, you can do this."

She's more encouraging with me than I am with her. I realize I'm equally a terrible teacher as I am a student.

My eyes flit once to her, my facial features always taut and grave. She nods to me. I decide to shed a layer of clothing, too confined. After removing my wool coat, left in a black buttoned shirt, I gingerly fit the key into the ignition.

"Turn right," she instructs.

I turn and the car rumbles to life.

"Now shift, press gently on the gas pedal, and pull further onto the street."

I slowly—very, *very* slowly—follow her directions. The car crawls unhurriedly, spiked tires grinding against ice. I grip the steering wheel so firmly that my knuckles ache.

"You can blink," Franny says.

I force my eyes wide open, concentrated on the street. "I'm fine."

Almost unnoticeably, Franny writhes in her seat, uncomfortable because I sit painfully straight. "Press your foot harder on the gas."

"That will make the car go faster."

"Yes," she says like I'm *slow* to catch on.

I lick my lips, tasting blood—*her lips*. Split down the center, she rarely puts ointment on them. It bothers me, but I try to focus on driving. "We're not going faster," I snap. "We'll spin out."

"No one drives this slow, Court. We'd move faster by walking." She slumps forward and fiddles with the heaters.

"Sit still." I readjust my clutch on the steering wheel and she places her palm on the top of my hand. I almost begin to ease, her confidence pooling inside of me. Like descending into a warm bath. Glove to glove. The link would grow stronger if we were skin to skin, but I wouldn't push it there.

"What are you afraid of?" she asks.

Everything. "Wrecking."

"You won't. I never wrecked a *single* car. Never even shuttled a person in the wrong direction."

"You're not the one I don't trust behind a wheel." It's *me*.

We fall into silence and I let her emotions fill me more, apprehension waning. I press harder on the pedal, not fast, but enough that we accelerate from a crawl to a jog.

Exhaust plumes behind the car and I slowly pass building after building. *I'm driving.*

I'm driving.

I could laugh, but the noise refuses to leave my throat. "Illian would be jealous."

My little brother often played with toy cars on our father's desk. *Vroom. Vroom,* he'd sputter between his lips, pushing our father's physics papers and pens to the floor. When our father appeared, he cast an earnest smile, dark eyes effervescent and magnified with joy.

Illian could be as mischievous and as ill-tempered as he'd like.

He was a Babe. He knew he'd die as a child, and even so, Illian was sweet. He smiled and laughed more than I did.

"Illian?" Franny frowns. "Was he a friend?"

You said his name aloud. Of course I did. I swallow a lump and stiffly, I give her what I've given Mykal. "Little brother. Babe. Dead."

Franny stays quiet and then says, "Turn left up ahead. We'll drive around the block."

Instead of hesitating, I force myself to finish the task in one maneuver, only breathing after I've succeeded. The car grinds to a stop and I practically see her mind reeling. To shift her thoughts off my brother, I speak.

"Your lip is cracked."

Franny runs her tongue over her bottom lip. "It's not a bother to me."

I procure a little bottle of ointment from my pocket. "Well it's a bother to me." I pass the bottle to her. "Keep it. Use it. It'll heal faster."

She peels off her gloves and unscrews the lid, then dips her finger in the cream. "You hate tasting blood that much?"

I dislike the bitter iron taste on my tongue, but it's much more than that. Franny has a greater reason to take care of herself now. She can live much, *much* longer than she ever fully dreamed.

I'm quiet before saying, "It's not the blood I hate."

She applies a second coat of ointment. I spin the red knobs, letting the heat die down, and I roll my sleeves to my biceps.

I freeze midway, alarm stabbing my chest.

Mykal.

I turn my head—no. It's *Franny.* She fixates on the beginning of a tattoo that peeks beneath my sleeve, the stinger to a scorpion. She opens her mouth, but loses her voice, too flummoxed at the sight.

I inhale sharply, not intending to show her these tattoos . . . not yet, at least.

I've talked about her being *common*, but I wear the most common markings among Fast-Trackers.

Suddenly enraged, her palms thud against my chest.

I don't shove back. However, I begin unbuttoning my shirt, fingers tensed, jaw hardened. *She deserves to see.* She has a spider tattoo on her hip, lizard across her shoulder blade—and she asked what she should do about them.

"We'll have them tattooed into different designs," I told her. Influentials don't usually have tattoos, but we'd pass if they were warm-blooded creatures. I left out the fact that I too need mine tattooed over.

Franny boils. "You constantly act like I'm *beneath* you, but here you are . . ." She trails off, confusion scrunching her soft face.

I fiddle with the middle button. I'm careful not to touch the steering wheel, angling sideways toward her body. "I've never believed you're beneath me," I say. "You're beside me." Last button. "We're just different and each tattoo reminded me of a world I'd rather live in. That's it."

I remove my shirt, sitting bare-chested. Vulnerable. Inked snake above my heart, my puckered scars are in plain sight, as well as the old ones that slice my ribs.

Franny tentatively scoots forward, elbow on the middle console. My head far above hers, but she inspects my ribs, her fingers hovering over the white scar that cuts the inked spider in half.

She whispers, "I've seen boys lose arms, girls pull themselves from the wreckage of a four-car pileup, and I never batted an eye."

"They'd live," I say.

She grazes my scars, only with her eyes. "Now I care." She takes a breath, collarbones jutting out. "Why should I care?"

"Because we can die at any moment." The grave thought passes toxically between us.

"A scar is not just a scar," she says beneath her breath.

It overwhelms me, the *empathy*. I hold on to the steering wheel, trying to detach from my darkened memories, but I need to warn Franny.

"I'm not overly calculated and vigilant because I want to be," I tell her. "I *have* to be this way."

"Why?"

"Some people will do *unimaginable* things if they knew you dodged your deathday—if they believed, even for a moment, they could too."

Franny sits up. As straight as me. "Who'd want to dodge their deathday?"

I bet she counted down to hers in celebration. Everyone usually does. "People are satisfied with their deathday because they've accepted the fact that it can't be altered. They've never seen hope or been given any. The minute you tell a person there *is* a way to live longer, their outlook will change. They will fight for a chance to see tomorrow when they thought they had none. No matter the consequences."

Blood rushes out of her face. "You're telling me that people *hurt you* knowing that you could die?" Fear blankets her, chokes me, and I shake my head—but it's true.

Something sinister lies in each old wound. They were formed from malice, darkness that festers inside of me, clawing at all that I am.

I desperately try to drown the image of four people who learned the truth.

Who escaped Vorkter with me.

Who awoke with me and saw that I still lived beyond my deathday. They brandished their blades and . . .

My throat bobs, sickness rising.

I engrained their deathdays in my mind, so I know that two are dead. The other two still live—and they could be coming for me. At any time.

"Franny . . ." I stiffly put on my shirt. She'll sense any lie, but I can't tell her that people could hunt me down, hunt *us* at any moment. "We're leaving for StarDust," is what I say first. "It's important."

She stares out the windshield, haunted. "If anyone finds out that we dodged our deathdays, we won't be sent to Vorkter. They'll just try to kill us."

Yes. It's not what I wanted her to conclude, but she's not co-matose with fright. *That's a start.*

"It's important," I say again, other words feeling marginal compared to these. The world is shaded in unusual colors when you can die at any time, without any knowledge of when. All we can do is find a piece of it that isn't as cruel to us as what I've met.

I should paint the whole picture for her, tell her that the people who caused these scars escaped from Vorkter, but it would be admitting that I too am a criminal. Her loyalties lie with me because we're a part of each other—whether we like it or not. But it'd make her ill knowing she shares a soul with someone like me. For now, I can spare her that tragedy.

Suddenly, a feeling scrapes at me—I swing my head to the left, then to her. "Is that you?"

She freezes, concentrating.

There it is again. I grimace and clench my teeth, an emotion barreling into my stomach. Roiling. I wrench open the door at the same time as Franny, heaving for air. *Something's wrong.*

I grab my coat, then stand, and hang on to the frame of the car. *Mykal.* "It's Mykal." I focus intently, trying to find a name for this feeling. Before alarm and concern gut me.

Halfway through pulling on my coat, I have to tug at my collar, my skin crawling. *Mykal, what's wrong?* I nearly scream the words.

Franny scratches at her skin. "What is this?"

My nose flares.

Disgust.

With myself.

It runs rapidly through my veins, the sentiment eating at my flesh. My eyes are cast downward and I concentrate harder on my friend. *Where are you, Mykal?*

I won't be able to picture him—but I abruptly *feel* him. My knees aching. Digging into a wooden floor. Someone . . .

Someone tugs at the back of my hair. Gently, not rough.

Something presses to my lips. *Gods dammit.* I whip my head toward Franny and she stares keenly at the snow. I run to her.

"Franny!" I shake her shoulders, tearing her out of a daze. "Don't focus on him."

She skims her finger across her lips. "Is he . . . is he kissing someone? I could've sworn . . ." She touches beneath her eye, tears building.

Mine mimic.

Franny looks to me in horror. "Why am I crying?"

I brush the tear beneath her eye, then I wipe my own. "Because he's crying." I can barely distinguish the origin. That these are *his* tears first, ours second. "I have to find him."

Delicate lips breathlessly press to mine—*What are you doing?*

"Court . . ." Franny knows, fingers still to her mouth.

"He's doing something foolish." I force myself off the car. I have to hike toward city-center.

"Why would he?" She steps away from the car, about to follow me, but I stop dead in my tracks.

"For *bills*," I nearly spit.

Realization sweeps her face, tears pricking the corners of our eyes.

"Stay," I tell Franny.

"I have to go with you," she says like her whole body begs to be at Mykal's side, to change his disgust into bliss. She feels as called to help him as me, but she can't come.

"Your hair needs to be washed." I've lost the feeling of her burning scalp, focused only on Mykal.

She has as well, her hand lingering by the foils. "I'm having trouble feeling my own senses and emotions."

Mykal fears that all the time. "Go to our flat," I say quickly. "Wash your hair, keep us out of your thoughts. You'll be at ease again."

She nods and then whispers a common farewell, "May the gods be in your spirit."

I have no belief in the gods, but the second verse rings inside of me. Pausing, only long enough to murmur it. "And I in your heart."

I don't waste one more second. I walk urgently. And then my walk shifts to a sprint.

And I run.

ELEVEN

Mykal

Each year, Grenpale hosts a Winter Warrior contest among every village. As a show of valor to the God of Victory.

Babes and Fast-Trackers hunt for five days by ascending the indomitable glacial mountains. Where roaring winds battle against every harsh step. Where air dries your lungs to brittle sticks and heart to heavy stone. Where you stalk the wild as often as the wild stalks you.

Our president, a solitary young lady in the mountains, would descend to the villages only one day per year. She awarded the title Winter Warrior to the one returning with the most game. And then she vanished in the mountain's dense fog.

Whoever won, their village leader would anoint them with hallowed water and crown them with dried river reeds and ivy strands.

For they were mighty enough to reach the gods.

I couldn't rank the villages from gods-awful to most valiant, even if I thought hard. Huts were scattered and people minded themselves. It was too tough to see what one possessed over the other.

Though my pa always told me, "Yer ma used to say this village has more fierce heart than brawn."

My ma might've been right. I was five the first time I ever saw someone awarded Winter Warrior in my village. Pa would claim they crowned many before, just not in my lifetime.

I remember that Winter Warrior well.

Reed and ivy wreath upon his gnarly brown locks, he spread his stocky arms and legs at a log table in our village's sanctuary that was used mostly for rituals and worship to the gods. There, he sliced freshly cooked ram with a knife. Ladies and men salivated across from him.

I salivated.

Chalky mouth, knotted stomach. I desired grease and fat more than anything.

The Winter Warrior ate and chewed, a grin at the corner of his lip. Rare, to see a man or lady *share* with their village. I should've expected his greed.

No one starves to death unless it's their deathday, but the discomfort is real. Many kill enough fresh game to feed themselves for months, and they'd still leave their families and their village to fend for themselves.

My pa stopped offering me food that same year. He shoved a bow and arrow in my chest. "Ye're hungry, then *go*. Ye're big enough now."

I was ravenous and I thought the damned Winter Warrior would be different and hand me, a boy of five years, a bit of meat.

Because he was mighty enough to reach the gods.

He packaged up the remaining ram and left the grease splatter. No one licked it clean, afraid of being mocked.

After the famished villagers shuffled out, I lingered. Hesitating, aching, *starving*. Wondering about the measure of my own pride.

I left without a lick.

After that, I was determined—blood, heart, and bones—to *never* be that boy again. I relied only on myself. The next year, I entered my very first Winter Warrior contest. Standing shoulder-to-shoulder with teens and men and ladies of twenty years.

I was just six but I believed I could beat them.

They stared down at me and all they saw was a little Babe trying to fill his days.

Wind beat at our raw faces. Splitting my lip. I never quit. By the second day of the hunt, most Babes staggered to the villages empty-handed. Some injured from lynx attacks. Others just frostbitten and cold.

I outlasted them all.

With steady bronze hands, my village leader lowered the wreath on my wheat-blond hair. And the next year, he crowned me again. At eight—the year of my deathday—I would win for the final time.

I was the only Babe in history of Grenpale who ever became Winter Warrior.

They often asked how I did it. How I slayed white bears twice my size. How I heaved them back to the village. How I managed to not slip and twist an ankle on the grueling mountainside. How I hiked and killed and lugged it all alone.

I'd flash a lopsided smile and say, "Ye're just not better than I."

The secret warmed me and I only ever handed the truth to my pa. The day before his deathday, a month before I believed I'd meet mine, I told him the real story.

Accent thick, I said, "I wore yer snow fers." My pa had pelts as stark white as the snow. They engulfed my small frame and camouflaged me into the scenery. I resembled the beast that I was hunting. "Couldn't see me on the mountainside and they paid me no notice. Barely even realized I was on top until it was too late." Neck snapped.

Spear plunged into their torso.

Sometimes, I'd even put an arrow through their heart. Just to quicken their end.

His weather-beaten eyes bore confusion. "But how'd ya lug 'em back? They'd be three times yer size, Mykal."

I quieted, unable to find a suitable answer. One that I could put in real words. I just shook my head and shrugged. "I dunno."

Years later, while traveling through the Free Lands, maddening thoughts my only good company, I found the source of my youthful grit. Never once did I crave the damned accolades. Never did I aspire to be just like the Winter Warrior who shoveled ram between gluttonous lips.

I heaved meat and pelts on my back. I descended rock and ice. I did it all.

And I shared every bit of what I caught.

With my pa. With my village.

I imagined their full bellies and their comfort of being filled to the brim. Even the ungrateful snot-nosed goats in my village, I *even* fed them.

I—Mykal Kickfall, the little no-good Babe—provided for a village. I had purpose when I was told I had none. Babes, we take up space. We eat your food. We drink your drink. And then we die.

Not me.

I had reason to live.

That pride, I thought maybe, just maybe, it'd fill me up again today. Just this once.

How wrong I'd been.

Bills stuffed in my pockets, I exit a ritzy seven-story building, windows shrouded by red velvet fabrics. I refuse to glance back at the painted orange sign bolted to the brick. Spelling out *luxury* and *lounge*. I barely even register a silky voice as the door slams behind me.

One that says "Good day."

Dazedly, my boots begin crunching the snow along the cobblestone. I pass every fancy shop and the bundled and finely clothed bodies of ladies and men. They pay more attention to me than I do of them, sidestepping around my broad frame, wary of bumping my shoulder.

I rarely travel this far into the city.

The taxing journey would dissuade most everyone, as it takes two hours to hike from the outskirts of Bartholo to city-center. It also calls for breaks at warming outposts every so often where casia burns. Compared to where I've lived, this is only a bit of ice and a bit of snow.

So I never break.

I hardly trek this far because I start longing for home.

I prefer the torches that light the night to the wires strung across each narrow road, brightening apartments and shops and streetlamps. I prefer traipsing in ankle-deep snow to the exhaust that gurgles from car to car.

The city is made of cobblestone and gold, but if asked, I'd give up nearly anything for a sole tree from the winter wood. And I wouldn't be begging to return to Grenpale. I wouldn't be dropping to my knees and pleading for the Free Lands.

I'll be planting that tree in city-center where Court would want to be. And it's all I need.

Just one lonesome tree.

I distance myself from the city buildings that tear into lilac clouds. Farther and farther away, perfume still scalds my eyes and I taste the sugary, nauseating scent on my tongue.

I roughly wipe my mouth on my arm, licking my muskox skins. My vision only blurs more. I try to blink away whatever burns, but I can't rid this sense.

I just walk. *Faster.*

Wind kicks up with my pace and bites my exposed cheeks. I lift my fur hood and find myself taking the long route to my flat. I go 'round busy streets. I go 'round the honking cars. I go 'round all the noise.

And I wonder if I'll ever be feeling even a bit of what I did in Grenpale. When I became Winter Warrior.

What if I never do?

I only slow at the sight of an abandoned bridge. Iron lattice frames the giant relic. Covered poorly—it was meant for a train to ride on top and cars on bottom. Snow slips through the wooden pallets of the ceiling. And the brick foundation lies unevenly.

Court said the bridge meant to connect Bartholo to Yamafort and Yamafort to Bartholo. Over the years, no one maintained the damned structure. With focus on agriculture after the freeze, it slowly and surely began to crumble.

I walk onto the bridge. Wind screeching as it whizzes between the lattice. I scuff up debris and snow with my boot and stare off, clusters of brick buildings in the horizon.

I tug at my collar. Choked. By this city. By these people. By this damned world. I stop beneath an arched beam and I overturn enough snow to spot the faint yellow line on concrete.

I sense him.

Behind me.

Truth being, I spent the past hour or so concentrating solely on me. Just to desert Court and Franny's emotions. Whatever they may be.

His footsteps pound the snow forcefully. I nearly feel the impact beneath my own soles. Not far from me, his boots come to a halt.

Don't go sensing him now, Mykal.

It takes me a long moment. A long, *quiet* second. To do anything but stand motionless. Then I finally peek over my shoulder. To see him. Instead of just feeling.

Gusts of wind unsettle his dark brown hair, coat collar high to block it. But he pays no mind to the chill. He just stares firmly. And long. Not wavering. I can't recall the last time Court ever did.

"What'd you do, Mykal?" His voice shakes with ire. Pumping into me with each heavy heartbeat.

I turn fully. To face him.

The tension condenses too much to push forward.

"I fixed our problem." I slip my gloved hand into my pocket and then flash my thick clipped set of bills. Worth more than anything I've ever held. I force some kind of smile and say, "Got us a bit extra too."

Court grinds his teeth. He steps forward, closing the gap to an arm's length away. His chin tries to tremble; his gray eyes try to well. He fights it all—I see him screaming at his emotions to just *cease.*

I sense it because it's inside of me.

"At what cost?" he nearly yells.

I rigidly return the bills to my pocket. "Nothin' I can't live with." His anger lances me. Ripples through my chest. I let out a slow breath.

"You didn't need to do this!" He expels hot air from his nose. "We could have found another way. *Any way.* Anything but *this.*"

I laugh into a pained choke. "Be happy for me, would you? I've done something good here." I need him to be proud of what I've done. If I can't feel it for myself . . . *Please feel it for me.*

He stares off, shaking his head. "Happy?" His features twist in hurt. "Before now, you've only been kissed once."

By him.

In my hut within the winter wood. Our lips met for a short moment. Practically smiling against his mouth. But the kiss, our closeness, heightened the link.

As we parted, I felt the faintest breath leave my lips. *His breath.* But I wasn't sure. Maybe, possibly, it was mine.

I couldn't make sense of who swallowed—was that me or him? Was my stomach churning or was that really his?

I was afraid. Of the confusion, of not knowing if my hunger belonged to him or me. Of our linked senses that overpowered everything. We predicted that if we kept kissing, the link wouldn't ever be faint. It'd forever stay at a heightened peak.

And so we agreed to never kiss again.

Court gestures to me. "And you want me to feel *happy* for selling your second kiss and whatever firsts that went along with it? How can I be *happy* knowing you hated every second?"

"I didn't—"

"I felt you!" he screams, blood rushing to his face. "I *felt* you, Mykal!" I stare up at the snowfall through the wooden slats while his eyes puncture me cold. "It was one girl. Rich, by the jewelry on her neck, and she wanted you—"

"Yeah, she wanted *me*," I spit back. "For a lot more than you ever thought I'd be worth." His wrath stings, but I keep going. "Seventeen thousand bills, Court. I did it. *Me.*" I wipe an angry tear before it falls. "They pay high for first-timers. So go ahead. Keep yammering on about my firsts."

If I were crueler, I'd mention how I only thought of the luxury lounge because of *him*. When he mentioned the place during our fancy Influential dinner with Franny.

Court silently fumes.

I point at him. "Don't act like I'm the boy here, Court. I'm *older* than you. I'm *tougher* than you. While you were reading your damned books, I wore the skull of a wolf and speared beasts fiercer and moodier than *you*."

His hurt knots his brows. "You truly believe that I think your virginity makes you *naïve* and *weak*? I couldn't care less!!" He breathes heavily before asking, "Is that why you did this?"

"No," I growl through my teeth.

Meeting Court two years ago, the solitary life I built changed in an instant—and I thought less about returning to loneliness and I started thinking more about who I'd love and kiss and go to bed with.

For me, *love* always came first.

Still he slings it at my face when I did him a favor, and his glare rips through me. The words behind his eyes are clear: *How could you do this?*

Just to spite him, I sneer, "It's not like you can wait for me. So what do *you* care?"

Something stirs in Court. Something he stomps down and my stomach coils—but beneath the intensity, I sense the grind of his teeth. The scrunch of his dark brows.

The prick of jealousy.

"I'm not barring you from kissing . . ." His voice staggers. "Or bedding other people. If that's what pleases you, then do it." His throat is nearly swollen closed. Tears brim and he curses, raking the heel of his palm across his eyes to rid them. And he says slowly, as though to convince himself, "I'm upset because you weren't pleased."

"Ignore it then."

"I can't!" he screams.

His animosity surges into my bones and I growl coarsely until my throat sears. I tug at my hair, claw at my clothes, frustration like a beast on my back.

"Be gone, will you?!" I yell, spite dripping from my words. "No part of me needs you!"

I hate this link.

"Leave me!" I scream.

His reddened eyes burn hot. And he nears . . . his fingers on my coat, he brings my chest to his chest.

Court holds me tight. His hand to the back of my head. "I need you," he whispers. His rare compassion pours through my veins.

I go still with him. His hurt is my hurt and my hurt is his hurt. There's no way around that, and in this silent moment, we both concede.

Water slips out of my eye, freezing my lashes. I feel the same happening to him, and in our embrace, I'm not sure who's the true source. Him or me. It could scare me. Usually it does, but for now, I sink into everything but fear.

"I'm sorry," he breathes against my cheek. Snow flutters onto his hair and mine. "I'm sorry you had to do that and I will never forget that it was for us. That you made it possible for us to leave."

Another tear crystallizes beneath my eye.

He ends with a very soft "Thank you."

His words mean more to me than anyone else's.

TWELVE

Mykal

Never been much of a liar, so I'll be saying it straight. If someone tells me flatly to "wait outside"—with no instruction to stalk prey, not even to snare a feeble hare; just *wait* for them—I struggle to listen.

After a long while, I stop pacing. I just stand outside an ugly, brass-hinged door in the ugliest part of Bartholo's city-center. It's all right—I'm used to ugly.

Grimy canvas tents canopy the wide street called Graywater Crossing. Whoever thought to construct a black market in plain sight had some pluck. But no Altia Patrol bothers the buyers and sellers here.

They let them be. Even when the outdoor booths carry strange objects: pelts I've never seen, vials of bubbling fluid in every hue, and weapons of all kinds.

People chatter earsplittingly loud. Animals squeal violently. And noises funnel in the street and echo off crumbling brick shops.

Not to mention, it stinks.

I put a cigarette between my lips. Next to me, Franny waits more patiently. Bundled in her black furs. My green wool coat with muskox sleeves warms me, and with both of our hoods drawn, I eye that ugly door.

Hurry up, Court.

Cupping a hand around my mouth, I light the cigarette and suck deeply. Embers eat the paper. I half expect Franny to hack up a lung at the sensation. Since she's been linked to us, I've smoked only twice, but not while she stood this close.

She never balks or flinches or shoots me an indignant look.

I blow gray smoke upward and then I study her heart-shaped face and toughly set jaw. Like she'd bare her fists if you neared her wrong.

Franny has some spirit about her. Blazing. Constant faint smiles peeking in the corner of her scowls. While I know only bits and pieces about city Fast-Trackers, she's more uncommon to me than she is "common" to Court.

Reaching out, I pass her my lit cigarette, certain now that she's smoked before. Franny accepts my offer and takes a short drag. Smoke slips down her throat as casually as it glides along mine.

When she hands the cigarette back, I ask, "So Court taught you about telephones and hologrammies—or whatever the three hells they're called." Yesterday, I lugged in wood and overheard her history lessons.

Since the luxury lounge a week ago, I've tried to keep busy by hunting alone, but in doing so, I've had no time to speak to Franny without Court in earshot.

Out of respect, it seems, she's kept quiet. Lately I've missed our talks about sewer rats and mountain goats and how life is as amusing as it is cruel.

"Telephones," Franny muses, that little smile emerging from her perpetual scowl. She rolls her head toward me. "I asked Court if telephones were sorcery. He said people could talk from *countries* away without the use of paper and pen. What else should I've thought?"

"He rolled his eyes at you," I assume, my lips rising.

She nods. "He rolled his eyes at me." Deepening her voice, she mimics Court, " 'Sorcery has *never* been real, Franny.' "

I choke on my laughter, cigarette hanging from my mouth. "Heya, I once told him that Grenpalish call lifelong devotees of the gods *sorcerers*—I thought his eyes would permanently stick to the back of his head."

Franny pulls her hood closer to her reddened cheeks. "We call them mystics here." Her little smile vanishes and she stares off with a heavier frown. "My mother said most old rituals have been lost in time. Mystics would sacrifice cattle at dawn and shake bones for foresight."

My mouth stays shut, not wanting to deepen her longing, but Grenpalish haven't abandoned those practices. Before every hunt, I visited my village sanctuary as a boy. Knelt by a sorcerer, he or she streaked goat's blood beneath my eyes, chanted incoherently and smacked my forehead with fervor.

Boldness invigorated my spirit, as though the God of Victory kissed my cold skin.

"All lost in time . . . ," Franny ponders further. "Just like telephones, I guess."

"Telephones," I mumble, glad they don't exist anymore. I remember what Court once said. After the Great Freeze of 2501, Influentials halted studies of technology to pursue agriculture. Food was scarce. Telephones were forgotten and now what's left—bulky televisions and cameras—exist only in major cities where electricity prospers.

I think about StarDust. The most technologically advanced place, supposedly. And then *space* travel, which seems downright impossible to me. I realize wherever we go, it'll be more suited for Court and Franny than it'll ever be suited for me.

Sucking the cigarette deeper, my throat tickles.

Dammit.

I cough into my arm the same time a hoarse one leaves Franny's lips. Beyond that door, Court must be dry heaving, the smoke finally irritating his lungs. I can't quit everything that ruffles him or her. I've already given up enough.

Facing me, Franny straightens off the brick siding. "About the bills—"

"I don't wanna talk about how I got them." The luxury lounge is behind me and I'll never be selling my body for bills again. Next time I bed someone, I'll be enjoying every bit of it.

Franny says, "But I plan to pay you back for my share—"

"What?" My cigarette falls out of my limp fingers.

"I owe you—"

"*Nothing*," I interject again and edge near. My thick-soled boots knock into her high-laced ones. She raises her chin, and even though I tower above, her sweltering spirit equalizes us. "You owe me *nothing*, Franny Bluecastle. What I did was for all three of us and you needn't repay me one bit."

Franny opens her mouth to protest.

Whack.

We flinch at the sound of a cleaver, two booths away. A shrill scream rings afterward. *Wild boar*, I distinguish easily enough.

A drunkard stumbles down the snowy road and bumps into a basket of mittens. The seller hollers and wastes no time clasping a nearby bucket. She dumps its contents, and yellow liquid sloshes onto him. Drenching his dark hair and lanky body.

The rancid stench floods my nostrils and Franny's.

Not recoiling, we simply watch the man stagger toward a dumpster and collapse ass-down.

In our brief, shared silence, the door creaks open.

Our stances straighten, but as soon as Court slips outside, he stands taller and graver, his dark mood storming overhead. If the news were good, he'd still carry the same weight on his shoulders.

The three of us huddle close, no one able to overhear us.

"And?" Franny asks him.

Court lowers his voice. "And to tattoo over our designs"—he gestures between his chest and hers—"he wanted a toe. From us both."

I growl a curse between gritted teeth and go to charge into the back-alley tattoo shop, but Court clamps a forceful hand on my shoulder. I swing back around. "You're not giving him your damned *toe*," I snarl.

Franny's brows scrunch. "What does he want with a toe?"

"Who in the three hells cares, no one is giving him a toe!" Veins protrude in my neck. "*Court.*"

Court raises his hand for me to quiet, cautiously glancing

around. But I'm making no more noise than the squealing hogs.

"*Court*," I growl his name again. "I'll be drawing on you myself; don't tempt me." Give me a damned needle piece and some ink. I can fix this before they each lose a toe.

He raises his black collar higher up his neck. "Calm down, the both of you."

Bitter, Franny says, "I am calm, thank you for noticing."

"I'm *not*." I run my tongue over my teeth, distaste eating me up. "You can't ask me to be calm when—"

"I have a plan," Court interjects.

I shift my weight. "So you convinced him to take something else then?"

"No." Court stares grimly at me. "I couldn't convince him of anything less than two toes."

Head raised, I swear crudely at the gods.

Franny glares. "That'll bring us worse luck."

"What can be worse?" I extend my arms, ready for the gods to smite me. No Influentials have cold-blooded creatures tattooed on their bodies. Court has said so every day for the past *month*.

"*Dying*," Franny hisses under her breath. "Dying is worse and I'm out of my mind for even thinking it."

"We're not dying today," Court snaps.

Franny marches over his curt tone. Though both often bite at each other. Harmless, like little pups fighting to leap ahead in deep snow. "Then what's your plan, Court?"

"Yeh—*Yeah*," I correct quickly. "What's this plan, Court?"

Court is quiet, his haunted gaze upon ours. "I need you two. *Badly*. It can't work without you, Franny, and you, Mykal. I can't do everything by myself—I just can't." At first glance, most people mistake Court's poise and dominance for arrogance.

But he'll be the first to tell you he's not good enough.

And I'll be the first to remind him that he is.

Franny asks, "What do you need from me?"

"How much is Juggernaut?" Court whispers.

"Jugger-what?" I swing my head between them.

"It depends how much you want to buy," she says, both of them tuning out my bewilderment. *Juggernaut.* Sounds like a strange sort of animal.

"Enough to knock out a boy the size of Mykal."

My jaw tenses. "What's this about?" *No one is knocking me out.*

"Four pills, maybe." Franny skims the length of my sturdy build. "Five could be better."

Gods bless. "Heya." I point between them. "Someone best be telling me what the hells this Jugger-business is."

"Drugs," Court says flatly, his gaze boring into Franny's.

Hers just as daggered on his. "Remember how Court called me *common*?"

Pleasure-seekers, I recall one of the attributes. Common Fast-Trackers do drugs, then. I don't understand these kinds of recreational pills, but if it's of use now, I'm glad for her knowledge.

"You are common," Court says without breaking hold of her pierced gaze. "If you find the truth insulting, that's your problem."

Franny boils. "I only find it insulting because *you* see it as something to be ashamed of."

He groans shortly. "I never said that."

"It irritates you," she points out. "I *feel* it."

As do I, but this back-and-forth is no use to us. "All right you two—"

"I'm irritated," Court cuts me off, "because I'd rather be linked to an Influential than to you. It'd be easier. Just as it'd be easier if we were all *never* linked."

"*Fine,*" she forces out the word. "I'll buy us the Juggernaut because I'm common." She flattens her palm to me. "Just thirty bills."

I fish out bills from my pocket and do a poor job of counting. Franny helps, more used to handling money. "So you mean to drug him?" I ask Court before Franny leaves our sides.

"Not me." Court pauses. "You have to do it, Mykal. Just before he's finished with our tattoos, put the smashed pills into his ale. And don't let him see you."

Inside the nearly empty, damp room, I grunt at the sight of the Fast-Tracker tattooist. His thick fingers rummage through a tin box.

Franny squats beside him, sterilizing the needle pieces with my makeshift lighter.

As soon as Franny bought Juggernaut, we slipped through the ugly door and the tattooist said, "You want the needles clean, you do the work."

Court argued with the boy, but Franny went ahead and started disinfecting the metal. "It's easier to just do it ourselves than complain about it," Franny told Court, which shut him up.

A boy the size of Mykal, I remember Court's description of the Fast-Tracker, and so I examine him up and down.

A boy the size of Mykal.

He's no older than nineteen years, his unnatural vibrant red hair hangs ratty around his surly face. Sideburns extend oddly to his wide jawline.

To Court, I mumble lowly, "We're nothing alike, him and me."

Standing close, my friend unbuckles his belt, his coat and shirt already shed and tucked beneath my arm. "You're the same height," Court rebuts, our talk quiet enough for only us to hear, "and you have his brawn."

I grunt again. "He has *my* brawn."

Court's lip twitches, wishing to rise, but he still hasn't smiled in a long while.

Facing him, I point at his bare chest. "I'm more chiseled. Tell the story right or not at all."

Court whips his belt off and meticulously coils the leather. "Then I'll leave the storytelling to you."

"And what will you be doing?" I question as he passes me the belt. "Standing there and looking pretty?" Anyone with eyes can see that Court is the kind of refined handsome made for paintings and portraits. Too striking to be forgotten. Too stunning to be anything but immortalized.

Leaning strictly toward me, he breathes, "In what world is this *pretty*?" I follow his stern eyes that graze the gnarled scars above his heart and down his abdomen.

"My world," I say easily. "In my world, you're still rightfully beautiful, but don't let it swell your head." He rolls his eyes. *Predictable.* I continue, "You're already sullen enough, can't have you cocky too." I tap his cheek twice.

Where Franny would smack my hand away, Court stays unmoving. Like nothing transpired. Then he unbuttons his slacks and tugs them to his ankles. "You and your naïve fantasies."

"You and your wretched realities," I combat with a crooked smile.

He shoves his slacks to my chest—and pauses for a strained moment, not letting go of the fabric. I hold on too, our gloved fingers tangled, and the heavy beat of his heart drums inside of mine.

The same instant as him, I flinch—my forefinger burning for no reason. Metal clatters to the floorboards.

Our heads swing to that tin box. Needle piece and lighter dropped, Franny winces and sucks her scalding finger. She stays crouched, narrowed eyes flitting once to us, and then spouts "*Mayday*" at the lighter.

Court grimaces.

"Let her be. We're in a black market, no one gives two shits what we say here," I tell him, watching as she determinedly picks up the needle piece again. She must've taken off her gloves to protect the pricey garment over her own skin.

Court's stringent body tenses my shoulders. Left in black underwear, he folds the fabric higher, revealing an array of abstract tattoos with dragonflies inked on each thigh.

"I sensed her before, Mykal," he suddenly says beneath his breath.

I cock my head. "Is that supposed to surprise me?" We can't shut off our link.

"Before the lighter." He swallows hard, his irritations gripping his muscles and neck. Taller than I, he drops his head a fraction. "Outside, she bought seven pills but only gave you five. Then she kept two in her coat pocket."

I remember that exchange and feeling the extra pills in her soft palm. I didn't think much of it, but maybe I should've. "And you're worried about what exactly?"

"She was excited by the drug. Her heart flipped with *glee*."

"So?"

He stands sternly. "She's impulsive."

"She's spirited," I counter. "Look, Court, she may react hastily but she's *here* with us. If you want to know whether she's the sort of person who *needs* these pills like I need to hunt, then ask."

"It's not like when you hunt," he whispers. "If she takes Juggernaut, we'll feel the effects like we've taken the drug."

"Then remind her of that. But in a semi-decent way. Don't go about it like an ass."

His nose flares, restraining deeper feelings. "I am an ass. So *you* should be the one to ask Franny." He's about to step around me, but I catch his shoulder.

He doesn't turn. So I edge closer to his back, my lips behind his ear.

"Be afraid of people all you like, Court, but you have no reason to fear her." The more he shuts down on Franny, the more he drives a glacier between us all.

Court rotates his head, enough that our cheeks brush. "I'm not scared." He's frozen stone. "You can add 'understanding my emotions' to the never-ending list of things you're horrific at."

My jaw tics, my gaze growing coarse. So he wishes to push me away now? That's his mighty fine plan? "Insult me again, Court. You don't care what anyone thinks about you, so go ahead, do it again."

He can't even look me in the eyes as he says, "You're just a brute."

I growl in his ear, "And for someone so smart, you act so *dumb*." I throw his neatly folded clothes at his boots and leave his side.

His stomach twists while mine inflames.

Franny rises as I approach her, needles cleaned. "Should I even ask?" Her gaze darts between us, our bodies taut and enraged.

"I have a short temper." I eye the Fast-Tracker who finishes sorting through his ink. "Court knows how to set me off." *This is what he wished.* I'd like to stop feeding into his hand, but I'd also like to stay mad.

Air thin, Court stands in the middle of the room alone. I feel badly not being by his side, but not badly enough to douse my anger. Ribs constricted, *he* contains hot breath in his lungs.

Usually I try to sigh away his discomfort. Even if my sighing just agitates him further. But instead of sighing, I find myself growling.

Franny rubs her collarbone, not sparing her glares toward us. "I hate when you two fight."

I don't recall the origin of our last feud, but with StarDust enrollment looming, our fuses have been cut plenty short.

"As do I," I mutter. While the tattooist nears Court, I concentrate on the one person here I don't trust.

The tattooist inspects my friend's height. His little chuckle at Court's inked thighs hoists my loathing.

Observant beside me, Franny crosses her arms, scowl returned.

I reach into my wool coat for my serrated hunting knife, a mountain peak discreetly etched in the rosy hilt. Grenpale's emblem.

"Maaaydaaay," the Fast-Tracker whistles. "Someone did you bad." He waves to Court's scars, the ones snarled with the inked snake. Right over his heart.

We all go rigid. I don't bother trying to discern whose joints locked first.

"Heya." I aim the tip of my blade at the Fast-Tracker's thick neck, my threat clear. "You be careful with him."

He smirks at my knife. Then at me. As though no fatal harm can reach him.

Right. We're the only ones afraid of death. In the entire damned world.

"Why do you care if I hurt him?" the tattooist asks, casually strolling around my friend.

"No questions," Court interjects, voice crisp. "That was the deal."

After the Fast-Tracker finishes assessing Court's tattoos, he picks up the clean needle and black ink. "I can make the crocodile on your back into a botched-looking snow leopard."

Court nods. "Fine."

"You said you wanted all warm-blooded creatures?"

"Yes." Court is firm.

I tilt my head at the silver needle piece in that tattooist's hand. *Odd thing.*

"Why do you want our toes?" Franny asks bluntly, reminding me that she's been surrounded by Fast-Trackers like him all her life.

"I collect them." He kneels and braces his hand on Court's thigh. "I plan to reach a thousand before my deathday. Yours will be eight hundred forty-three." He nods to her foot.

I step forward, my strong build partially blocking hers. The tattooist catches sight of my advance and smirks again. *Go ahead and smirk, you little bastard.*

"Gods." Franny bristles. "Of all the hobbies in the world, you've chosen toe-collecting. Really?"

"No one needs every fykking toe," he rebuts, the needle buzzing. As he concentrates on Court's tattoos, we quiet.

Court shuts his eyes.

The needle nears the golden-brown flesh of his thigh. The sharp tip presses light, tickling. Then much, *much* deeper. Court grinds his teeth. Pain shoots up my knee and I recoil, more so than either Court or Franny.

Never did I dream of ink on my body. Nor experiencing the process through someone else.

Court opens one eye, scrutinizing me while I curse and shake my head repeatedly. We've just begun and the stabbing radiates to my hip and ribs—no, *his* hip and ribs.

I can't thwart his senses that easily. Distance wouldn't solve a thing. So I try focusing on the leaky ceiling, the rotting floorboards, on Franny's measured breaths. But my bludgeoned mind circles to Court.

Like I need to check up on him. Almost hoping to sense *relief* instead.

Franny rubs her eyes, mostly. Knowing she can't reach the itch that needs scratching.

I find myself squatting and breathing heavily. *I hate feeling his torment.*

I hate it all.

Agonizing hours tick by. Sweat caking our skin. Warm, Franny discards her fur coat and shirt, and is in nothing but slacks.

Whether out of spite or indifference, the tattooist is anything but careful. He scratches harsh jagged lines into Court's arm and tender ribs. Blood bubbling to the surface. After a while, I stop watching, but I never stop *feeling*.

Franny tells me that his scorpion is now a snowy owl. "Not as botched as you would think," she whispers. The spider along his ribs is a wolf, and the twisted snake has become an off-kilter Altian star: eight crossed lines.

Toward the end, I no longer sense his pain. I think it's over and I look up. But the Fast-Tracker still digs the needle along Court's shoulders.

I no longer sense pain because Court has cemented himself in a trance. His pinpointed, unblinking eyes burn holes into the floor. Though I can't read his mind, I understand why he chose this— not because he can't stomach the pain.

Because he can.

Because *I* can't stomach feeling him this way.

Franny experiences all that I do. All that *we* do. I touch my brows, thinking they've knotted, but they're in a scruffy line. Hers are bunched together.

I nudge her arm.

Her gaze lifts to mine. "He's more complicated than he lets on," she whispers. "I wish I could ask, but I'm just waiting." I hear the unspoken finish: *for Court to explain himself.*

"You're not the only one," I murmur lowly.

Surprise jumps her cinched brows. "I thought you knew everything about each other."

I shake my head. "We don't."

Truth being, Court has never spoken his full history to me. I know bits and pieces, somewhat more than Franny. Like how he spent five years in Vorkter Prison. But Court rarely speaks about his life there. He prefers sharing the flesh of his story, never the bones or the heart.

"I don't pry for the same reason you keep quiet," I whisper, "the same reason you keep *waiting.*"

Our heads slowly turn toward Court.

Unblinking. Unwavering. His eyes like knives impaling the floor.

Stoic exterior aside and disregard the authority and whatever dominance he wears as armor, we sense fragility. Fragility encased delicately around his heart. To jab profusely at Court, to ask questions that may touch the glass casing, could shatter him completely.

"So we wait," Franny says softly.

We wait.

The tattooist takes a step back and admires his abrasive handiwork. Surprising no one, he *smirks.*

"You ready for your turn?" I ask Franny.

She takes a deep breath that fills *my* lungs. Or at least, it feels that way. She nods. "Ready."

I follow her wandering gaze to the mug of ale and I remember what has to be done.

Soon, I must be ready too.

THIRTEEN

Franny

Ourt can call me *common* as often as he wants, but not all Fast-Trackers are the same. Just like not all Influentials and Babes are. We can box one another up and stamp labels on our foreheads.

Reckless Fast-Trackers.

Snooty Influentials.

Useless Babes.

Some will fit, but the differences between us matter just as much as the likenesses.

Every now and then, I revert back to Court's perceptions of people while the tattooist *rips* at my sensitive flesh. The needle burrows deep into the blade of my shoulder, scratching at nerves that wail for this to end.

I stifle a wince and my whole body twitches.

The tattooist snickers behind me. Like I'm not tough enough to be inked. Why should I have to act tough for him? Or for anyone, for that matter.

My scowl sours.

Court called the tattooist a common Fast-Tracker too, but we are *not* the same. If I inked a person, I'd practice a small measure of kindness. I'm not asking to be fanned or given a break. Just don't etch my skin to the bone and gloat about it.

As though you take pleasure in my pain.

I have trouble staring at the freshly covered tattoo on my hip. No more little eight-legged spider. The new design is nothing I'd choose for myself. He carved a furry hare with a warped ear and bent tail.

For life. I wear this ugly, mangled hare *for life*, and even worse I'm not sure how long my life will be. Getting to know Court in these past weeks, I can guess his rebuttal to my peeved thoughts.

"You can't be a Fast-Tracker anymore, Franny, so you need a tattoo that you'd never choose. That's the point."

It's why I don't argue, but I'm allowed to be sad about the hare— and whatever else the Fast-Tracker inks on my shoulder. Even being linked to two boys, this is still *my* body. *My* skin.

I'm trying to hang on to who I am. And to remember that how I lived and saw the world made me a Fast-Tracker, not just the tattoos I wear. *I'm trying.*

Court currently rests on the floorboards, his forearms propped on each bent knee. Blood shrouds most of his newly inked designs. If I saw him on the street, I'd think he lost a knife fight.

I wince.

The tattooist snickers.

I glare. Besides the sharp pinch of the needle trudging along my shoulder, my chest and ribs sting like mad from Court's raw skin.

Sweat gathers uncomfortably on my breasts, neck, and forehead. I wipe the stickiness with the back of my hand, but I still burn inside out.

The needle hums, silence stretching, and out of the corner of my eye, Mykal crouches and fixates on the laces of his boots. Pretending to retie them.

The mug of ale is only an arm's length away. If I stay hopeful that he'll succeed, he may sense my belief in him.

I try to concentrate on encouraging Mykal through our link, but so much tugs at my mind: the tattooist, the needle, the pain, *Court.*

I scratch at my arms. His itch, not mine. I ball my fingers into fists, our linked senses a disaster. It's not the doubled pain or an aching, empathetic heart that disturbs me.

Just yesterday at the flat, Court bathed in lukewarm water, his long limbs scrunched in the bath basin. I hate that no matter how hard I tried, his hands felt like my hands—*my hands* gliding over the grooves and divots of his battered skin, his calluses and knotted scars.

My hands traveling up and down the ridges of his abdomen and planes of his arms.

My hands.

His hands.

A pit is wedged in my gut. I hate that I stand many feet away from Court now, and without my body meeting his body, I can recall the crevices of his build.

Easily, he could've already sensed me the same way. Maybe my hands have been his hands. Maybe his hands slipped along my breasts and journeyed down my narrow hips.

Maybe they fell even farther.

Yet it wouldn't change how terrible *I* feel.

Court has been clear about not wanting me metaphorically or even physically close to him.

I'd rather just be linked to Mykal, who makes me feel less like a worm invading someone's body. Kindness exists in Mykal where coldness festers in Court.

From across the tiny room, a pair of eyes roasts my face. My cheeks heat, and like he willed it to be, Court captures my hot gaze. I sweep his features, only to find *knowingness* cut in every stern line.

He can't read my thoughts.

Just feelings.

Court may be one of the most bookishly intellectual Fast-Trackers I've ever known, but he's far below average at interpreting the meaning behind Mykal's emotions. So I doubt he'd be able to untangle mine.

I flinch. The needle pricks another nerve. With gloved fingers, I rub the sweat beneath my eye and then suddenly pause. Court slowly, *very* slowly, brings the canteen to his lips. All the while, his gaze remains cemented on me.

He chugs and a trickle of water slides pleasurably down my throat. My lips part, coolness rushing through my boiling veins.

I drink while he drinks. Emotionally quenched.

Could he have known this would soothe me? I wonder if this is Court's way of saying, *"What happened is fine, Franny. We're okay."* Probably wishful thinking on my part, but I wish anyway.

His attention reroutes to Mykal. Who has yet to dump the crushed Juggernaut into the ale. He fumbles with his laces, acting more harebrained than suspicious.

I crane my head behind me, and the tattooist flashes a halfhearted smirk my way. His left ink-stained hand clutches my shoulder while his right squeezes the needle device that drives into my flesh.

"What do you do for Fast-Tracker benefits?" I ask, my voice as wooden as my body. Altia provides deathday benefits to FTs for laborious jobs.

To be a professional artist, actor, musician, you'd need to attend school. To attend school, you'd need more time to live.

Influentials only.

Lack of deathday benefits rarely stops Fast-Trackers from pursuing their passions, and if they need more bills, they'll work a second job. Mostly for that Final Deliverance check.

His needle buzzes beside my ear, not replying. Red-dyed tips of his hair stick to his crusted lips, and he spits out the gristly strands. No smirk or glance up from my shoulder.

I guess, maybe, he prefers privacy. It'd account for why he hasn't shared his name. I'm not dying for him to answer me anyway, but I thought I'd distract him from Mykal for a minute or two.

Using the fabric of my shirt, balled in my hands, I pat the sweat from my armpits. "You seem like the type," I say vaguely.

"The type for what?" His breath reeks of spoiled goat's milk.

My throat bobs—*not* my *throat*. I touch the hollow of my neck, motionless. Court is the one who forces down a gag.

I tense. "The type who'd plan to die surrounded by a thousand toes and nothing more." I muster the strength to raise my brows at him. "I'd call that a *lurk*."

He pushes his ratty hair with his elbow and laughs once. "Sure, you say I'm the lurk when people sell soiled undergarments just outside the door." I must cringe because he sniggers, "I don't seem that unnerving now, huh."

He's still not anyone I'd try to befriend.

Off my silence, he adds, "I work electrical maintenance in city-center." *For FT benefits.*

"What's your plan for your deathday then?" I can't think of a less invasive question than this one, so routine that most people have a response at hand. In the back of my head, I remember Mykal. *Concentrate.*

Concentrate.

Head turned forward, I shut my eyes for a brief second. *Velvet.* Velvet skims my fingers. *His fingers. The pill pouch.* In fear of drawing attention to Mykal, I don't dare sneak a look.

His pulse races, soon alongside Court's. Then mine. *Tripled.* Like three cars revving, three cars peeling off at varying paces, all pulsing frenziedly in my veins.

"My deathday plans," the tattooist says in thought, "I plan to go the *best* way out. Party at my apartment with my friends."

I stuff my shirt beneath my armpit. "You have friends?" I joke.

"Prettier than you." He tries to be cruel.

Mykal grinds his teeth and my jaw contracts from the pressure.

To the tattooist, I say firmly, "I'd much rather be ugly in your eyes than pretty."

Right as the last word escapes, he punctures my skin *beyond* the standard practice. A wounded noise scratches my throat. *Mayday.* Out of all that could've offended him, this is really it?

Someone suddenly stands. Without peering around, I'm con-

fident that legs bend and rise. Less so about whether that someone is Mykal or if it's Court.

I careen away from the tattooist on instinct, but he clasps my
arm, then the base of my neck.

Mouth to my ear, lips curving in an oily smile, he says, "Don't
move."

"Then don't stab me," I growl, suppressing the urge to stomp
on his foot.

Court sidles near—*he's the one who stood up.* My head whips,
doing a double take of his stance. Almost disbelieving.

Court stood up for *me*? Maybe surprise shouldn't flood me.
At the Catherina Hotel, Court passed me ice for my bruises. When
I taught him to drive, he gave me ointment for my lips. He just
rarely lets me see whether or not he cares. On the other hand,
Court could just be creating a diversion for Mykal.

The tattooist gradually retracts the needle from my back. I bite
my tongue to keep from wincing again, and the needle device begins slowly buzzing. Not finished.

Court rounds me with a decisive stride, shirtless but otherwise
clothed. His authority rains down on me and lifts my sore shoulders. I have *never* felt this stern or arched my limbs this high.

Mykal and Court have told me many things since we've met.
They said that they were a part of me. They said that I was a part
of them. These are just words—weightless, nothingness *words*. Yet,
Court saunters forward, and his presence grants more than just a
touch of security.

I have more than Court's towering frame and grim gaze. I have
his power. His austerity. His unflagging heart.

I'm as afraid as I am content. How can I be more than just me?
Why do I feel this way? They said it'd drive me mad to wonder, but
I will. Every day, I'll continue to wonder why we're linked. Why
we dodged our deathdays. *Why us?*

Why me?

I watch Court silently. In one moment, he can be the most dom-
ineering person in the room, and in the very next, the most fragile.

It makes it harder to loathe him, and even harder to under-stand him.

Court shifts behind me, scrutinizing the handiwork along my shoulder blade. Before he even speaks, his stormy grays roar and rumble. His lip starts to curl and disgust dredges the bottom of his stomach, then churns mine.

Straining my neck once more, I pull the skin of my shoulder to see, but the tattoo isn't visible to my eyes.

Court blocks the tattooist from me. "You're done."

I shuffle backward until my heels hit the edge of the moldy wall. Melted snow drips from ceiling rafters to my cheeks. I don't bother wiping the liquid away. I just urgently try to peer at the tattoo. Jumping. Hopping, twisting left to right. Probably looking like a chump—*fool*. Like a fool.

I wish I had a mirror.

The tattooist chews on his crusted lip, laugh deep in his throat. He spins the needle device between his fingers. "It's a winter crea-ture. Isn't that what you wanted?"

Court fumes in place, heavy breath pumping his chest. Heat gathers in my lungs, but I won't boil for nothing. I need to *see* first and then I can react. Otherwise, I'm relying solely on Court's feel-ings, not my own. *Don't let go of who you are.*

I try not to blister too soon. Breathing just as heavy, I glue my-self to the filthy wall.

Mykal stretches up from his crouched position. I didn't see whether Mykal slipped Juggernaut into the ale and his muscles are too bound to sense any sort of relief.

"What's this about?" Mykal asks.

Court bears hard on his teeth, jaw protruding.

The tattooist twinkles in amusement. "At a loss for words?"

"I've met handfuls of people more clever than you," Court says through his teeth. "All you've done is made a mess and if that's your talent—*making messes*—then I pity you."

"Mayday," he laughs. "You pity me? Aw." His jeering face

hardens. "Like I care." He bends to the tin box and clasps his mug of ale. He packs away his ink, not drinking yet.

Simmering down, Court returns to my side. Mykal lingers much closer to the Fast-Tracker and obstructs his path to our toes.

Quickly, Court slips his belt through the loops and begins to dress. He gestures me to follow suit, but I stand cold and uncertain.

I open my mouth to ask about the tattoo. I bundle my shirt in my fists.

Court swiftly collects my coat and hangs the garment over his arm. He uses his free hand to yank his shirt over his head. "Dress, Franny." Dotted blood seeps through the gray fabric along his ribs.

I fight to find the armholes of my shirt. "How bad is it?" I question, my nose flaring. *No—wait.* His nose flares, not mine. "That bad?"

The lump in his throat ascends and he jerks on his tight leather gloves. "I wouldn't mind the design, but you will." Court may be vague about his past, but for all else, he's been unfailingly honest toward me. "I'm sorry."

"Why are you apologizing? It's not your doing." Frustrated and upset, I chaotically yank the shirt over my head, toppling toward Court. He steadies me with a hand to my hip. I growl out and just notice the tattooist searching noisily in his tin box.

Metal clatters together, Mykal swings his head from us to him, cautious.

"Tell me quick," I whisper to Court, slipping on my gloves, then lush fur.

Dressed, he lifts the collar of his black wool coat. "The tiniest fox."

I frown, about to shake my head. I can live peacefully with a fox.

"And Mal's tree."

Color drains from my face. "Mal's tree," I mutter, wide-eyed and horrified. To worship Mal means to smite the three gods: of

Death, of Victory, of Wonders. Where Caeli brings you to the gods—meant to dine in a great hall together—Mal guides you to a decaying tree and sends you to one of the three hells for eternal damnation.

No gods.

No mother.

"Could it pass as any old tree?" I ask in the smallest, weakest voice I've ever owned.

"He drew three withered roots and Mal's trident crest cut in the trunk. It's unmistakable."

Well then. I blink back fiery tears. This is life. Wretched, cursed *life.* I wipe at my eyes rapidly, sniff, and tilt my head up. We have more to worry about than my ugly tattoos.

His are ugly too.

I smile a sad, tired smile.

Court watches me more than I like, but I refuse to meet his eyes and gush forth my *feelings* when he rarely shares the meaning of his.

The tattooist finishes groping in his tin box and he rises . . . with a meat cleaver in his left hand. Ale in his right. "I pity *anyone* who thinks I'm stupid enough to fall for a trick." He overturns the mug and amber liquid splashes the floorboards.

Mykal clutches his knife harder.

The Fast-Tracker chucks the mug aside. "Someone put Misty in my drink a few months back. It didn't work then, and it won't work now." He displays the cleaver, blade rusted and bent.

"You." Mykal points the tip of his knife at him. "I'll be slicing off your toes before you lay a finger on either of them."

Someone breathes shallow breaths. I'm standing near Court, his gloved hand on my hip. I struggle to discern whether it's him or me. *I think him.*

My temples pound and instinct overwhelms me. I turn to Court and whisper rapidly, "I'm running. Are you?" I'd never believe my fists could defeat a meat cleaver. Mykal may be armed, but I'm not.

"Just wait." He tucks his arm more fully around my frame, as though to say, *With me. Wait with me.*

Wait?

Panic erupts in my eyes. Am I waiting for Mykal's death? Am I waiting for our own? I shake my head over and over. And he thinks *I'm* reckless?

The Fast-Tracker boy sidesteps to avoid Mykal.

Mykal stalks every movement. Plainly obvious that he is *not* prey to be snared. He does the trapping. "You've forgotten something."

The tattooist adjusts his grip. "What?"

"*Me.*" Mykal elbows him, cracking his nose. Blood gushes profusely. Quickly, he twists the tattooist's wrist, cleaver clattering to the floor, and he kicks the weapon away. This is where we should all run. We have the advantage. We have the time and space.

"Let's go," I say aloud.

Court remains absolutely stationary beside me. Not in a trance. I could snap my fingers in his eyes and he'd just as easily swat my hand away. Purposefully, he stays here.

Mykal stays here.

What more is there to do?

The Fast-Tracker shrieks, face drenched in crimson red, spilling from his nostrils to his mouth and chin.

Mykal wrenches his foe's arm to his back and wraps his own biceps around the tattooist's throat, airway imprisoned. His strength is *my* strength, unprecedented force and vigor. Vibrating my muscles. Searing my lungs.

My arms are his arms. Tiny bones in the FT's neck break. One. Two. They snap against my forearm. I never let up. I crush harder.

The Fast-Tracker kicks out, cheeks purpling. Mykal grits his teeth, veins bulging in his arms, spit spewing. He holds tighter, stronger—longer.

He chokes him.

I choke him.

I shut my eyes, rattling. Shaking. I open them and impulsively step forward.

Court pinches my coat, tugging me to his chest. Again, his arms curve around my frame. So I won't interrupt Mykal.

My beliefs may seem silly, but they're all I have. The Fast-Tracker tattooed us, even poorly and grossly, he did. In return, we made an agreement. We owed him something and I settled with the idea of drugging him. Not harming him.

Not this.

"We can run," I say. *We can run and then no harm will come to anyone.*

Lips against my ear, Court murmurs, "He'll chase us."

"We'll outrun him."

"He'll find us."

"We'll disappear." *Somewhere.*

"I'm not taking that risk." His voice frosts.

I shouldn't care about someone who tattooed Mal's tree on my shoulder and wanted my toe in exchange. No matter how much life Mykal tries to squeeze out of him, he'll live tomorrow. But never have I thought or wanted or dreamed of hurting someone for doing me a favor.

I watch the Fast-Tracker's hurried, alarmed feet go sluggish, and his arms slacken. Eyes close. Mykal drops the bulky body, weight crashing down onto the tin box. He's unconscious.

Court lets go of me. "Now we leave."

I stand frozen, the only one in a daze, and I only wake when Mykal pats my cheek. I'd slap his hand aside, but I shake my head instead, more and more stunned.

Mykal extends his arm over my shoulder and directs me to the door. On my own, I doubt I'd be able to move anywhere but a confused circle.

"You didn't realize, did you?" he asks, and as he stares down at me, I finally understand why he calls them hard-hearted eyes. They fissure through me like saw-toothed ice.

"Realize what?"

"That we'd be a bad influence on you." He pauses. "That we'd do just about anything to survive."

I'm frightened to look behind me and see what we've left in our wake. I feel a little bit of my soul hardening and I'm so afraid to change.

Gods.

I'm so afraid.

FOURTEEN

Franny

Night has fallen, the last one before StarDust's enrollment tomorrow. Journal open, pen between my dry fingers, I sit cross-legged on the cot next to a dying fire. Mykal made a firm bed out of woolen blankets for himself, right on the flat's uneven floorboards. Long ago, he graciously offered his cot to me and refused to take turns.

"It's yours," he said the first night. And the second. And every night thereafter.

I scribble *59th night on a cot—owed to Mykal.* Thinking, I bite the end of the pen and add, *Roasted fox—owed to Mykal.*

Court gave me the journal to improve my writing skills and I guess he thought I'd document my tedious daily routines or curse him on each page.

I haven't done either.

Every day, I tally all the debts I owe them. All that they deserve. I may not be able to capture a fox for Mykal, but I'll find something of equivalent value.

Altia presidential history knowledge—owed to . . . I spell Court's name wrong, so I cross it out and—the journal is torn from my hands.

"Mykal," I hiss, keeping my voice a whisper. Court just now falls asleep. Truthfully, I'm not always attentive of his slumber.

Mykal shows no interest in the contents of my journal and throws the leather-bound notebook on our cleaned supper plates.

"Heya." I spring to my feet.

He clasps my hand, his palms already gloved, I realize. Dressed warmly in his green wool coat, thick boots—he has yet to peel off his heavier clothes for bed. "Come outside with me?" he asks.

All right.

After bundling in furs, knotting my high-laced boots, I trek outside the building of flats. Snow kisses my cheeks and I block the light flurries with my hood. Mykal pries the torch off the brick siding, leading us only twenty paces away.

Using our link, I try to make sense of *why* he wants me out here, but there are no smoke signals or answers laid at my feet. All that happens? I *warm* to his temperature, the weather not nipping at him like it nips at me.

Mykal stakes the torch in ankle-deep snow, illuminating the vast white space surrounding us. I look up. At night, darkness blankets sheets of lilac smoke. No one on this planet has ever seen a star.

Maybe we will. I nearly smile. I'd never thought much about stars before.

"You know how to spar?" Mykal catches my attention.

"Spar? Like start a stew?" I crinkle my nose. "I mean, a *fight*." *I won't slip up tomorrow.*

"That." Mykal nods and stands a few lengthy strides away.

"Not really, no."

"Then I'll be teaching you."

My face falls.

He wants to teach me in the middle of the hollow night, the *day* before enrollment?

I march forward. "You've had *two* months to teach me and you choose right now?"

If he thought it'd be important, he should've taught me ages ago. I showed him the inside of a Purple Coach *long* before today. Mykal enjoyed driving even less than Court—grumbling about how hiking made sense and the "noise machine" made none.

Mykal flattens the long pieces of his blond hair. "Well, I always thought you'd never flinch in a fight, but after the tattooist, I wasn't so sure. So here I am, trying to prepare you a bit more. Is that all right?"

"All right," I say, "but if I learn to spar, it'll help us how?"

"We'll be fighting our way out of trouble." He raises his fists to his jawline. "Like this."

With less reluctance, I mirror Mykal. "Now what?"

He stalks close, build and height outsizing mine, boots crunching the snow. Mykal halts an arm's length away and then makes a *come hither* gesture with two fingers.

"Hit me," he says.

I hesitate. "I can't hit you just because. Give me a reason. Even a pretend one."

He lifts his muskox hood over his ruffled hair. "You're defending yourself."

I stand straighter, fists rising. "Against what?"

"Me." One step closer. "I did you wrong."

My lips tic upward. "And how did you wrong me?"

"I stole from you, little love." He tries to boost his knotted brows like mine, but they move far less.

My jaw drops in jest. "You *stole* from me?" I work myself up, trying to simmer. I rock on my feet, shoulders bowed.

He smiles a crooked smile. "I stole *every* pair of socks you own—"

I fake a right hook to his jaw, distracting him, and then I knee his gut—*Mayday*. I double over in unison with him. Thanks to our link, I just kneed *myself*.

Mykal coughs hoarsely. Then I cough. We clutch our stomachs and I shoot a glare in his direction.

Catching my breath, I snap, "And you and Court do this to each other? For practice?"

He swallows another cough. "You'll be getting used to it in time."

Gods. My slackened limbs jolt as soon as Mykal swings his fist. I duck and slip between his legs. I kick the backs of his calves and he staggers forward but braces himself from falling. He faces me and we circle each other.

"You're not as bad at fighting as I thought you'd be," Mykal pants a little. "But still not as good as I."

I charge with all my might. Fists bared, I roar in the pit of my throat. *He stole my socks!* I come at Mykal like someone running headfirst into a brick wall. I slam into him, fist to his chest that throbs my knuckles, not his body.

Tear at his clothes.

Scratch his cheek.

Kick his shins.

Poke his eyes.

My options rattle in my head; some I couldn't bear doing to Mykal. Not even while pretending he thieved my socks.

He shoves me. I fall on my bottom and quickly pick myself up.

We tussle awhile longer, my scrappy maneuvers very different from Mykal's natural strength and dirty tricks. He chucks snow at my eyes. I elbow his ribs.

Minutes later, he wrenches my body upright and imprisons my wrists behind my back, his chest against my shoulders. Breathing heavily, we go very still.

I sense what lies beneath his cold, harsh exterior. Mykal is like the South Sea. Crack the ice and just below, there is water. And warmth.

"Have you held Court like this?" I ask.

"Closer," he whispers against my ear.

Stifling a smile, I squirm out of his hold, rotate, and kick, my hefty boot banging into his abdomen. He sways. I wince, instinctively touching my stomach. He's acquired the actual beating.

I take longer to recover and he pushes my shoulders until I trip over my feet. Falling, I catch his wrist and bring him down. We wrestle in the snow, our hot breath cocooning us. Sweat prickling our skin.

Biting his biceps, I roll on top of Mykal and straddle his waist, but he seizes my forearms. He lifts his shoulders off the snow, his muskox hood falling down.

My lungs expand and contract harshly. Sensing each other has put us on equal footing. We could spar for a century—if we lived that long—and for every little bit of ground I'd gain, he'd advance just the same.

I taste blood from a blow that split my lip. "There can be no winner between us."

Mykal releases my arms. "Then it's a good thing we're not at war with each other."

We're together. A team. The three of us. I slide off his body and thud to the snow beside him. On our backs, we stare up and our pulses start to decelerate.

And then a strange thing happens.

I toss. I turn. Yet, my limbs are stationary. Sheets entangle my legs, my fingers clawing at the thin mattress of a cot. I reach out and pat snow. *Court is inside. Sleeping terribly.* I sensed his horrible sleep one other time and he woke to my pity. After that, he made sure to never fall asleep before me.

Tonight has been different. I almost imagine the dank ceiling and mold crusted on torn wallpaper and chipped paint.

I'm two places at once. *Sort of.*

Court lets out a ragged groan. I touch my neck, my lips—the noise is muffled in his pillow. *Inside.* I scoop a handful of snow. *I'm outside.*

I prop myself on my elbow toward Mykal. He stares empathetically at the building of flats, the rotting roof caked with ice.

Court's torment snakes through my body like unearthly vines. I'd like to scissor each one. I'd like to help him somehow.

My face contorts. "Court is never at peace, is he?" Not even when he shuts his eyes.

Again Mykal considers the darkness above. "For as long as I've known him, he's wrestled invisible enemies, and after Graywater, he has more to add to the list."

The Fast-Tracker tattooist. I didn't think he'd follow us, but I guess if he enjoys the hunt, he'd pursue us. For revenge or something simpler.

Our toes.

I drop off my elbows, lying back down. "Are you worried about the Fast-Tracker?"

"No." His husky voice is as deep and heavy as the night. "I worry about Court, and I worry about you. That's it."

My thoughts tumble fast. "You worry about us. Court worries about everything else. There's nothing left for me to worry over."

He tilts his head to me, cheek cold to the snow. "Be glad, Franny Bluecastle. One of us needs to be weightless. Maybe then we'll be running faster." His pink lips begin to curve upward, his smile contagious.

"You mean Wilafran Elcastle." My new name. New identification. New life.

He dips his head to whisper, "You'll be staying Franny to me."

I nod once and twice, blinking back a surge of emotion. "I'm glad."

His cheek numbs and he rolls his head up. Court must be awake, no more thrashing, no more agonized moans. I think he sits, forearms on his knees, slightly bent over in exhaustion.

We talk about ways to help Court for a while, but we mostly conclude that linking is not beneficial on that front. Mykal said he's tried holding Court at night, but he still lashes out, his nightmares enduring and prevailing over Mykal's senses.

"StarDust is the only way he'll be finding peace," Mykal says.

A chill slips down and I shiver.

"What is it?" Mykal asks, stretching as he sits up.

I follow suit, confusion eating at me. Easily, I can discern whose knees ache, *Court*, whose ribs throb, *Mykal*, whose throat dries out, *me*—but what if one day it's not as easy? This fear has crashed into me before, but I mentioned it to Court, not to Mykal.

"Have you had trouble knowing which emotions were yours and which were Court's?" I lick my bloodied lip.

Mykal nods and scratches his tough jaw, stubble grown. "Court and I—we kissed once and it heightened the link. Made it more confusing than it already is. If touch strengthens the link, then bedding would most likely do the same."

"*Bedding*," I repeat. "When Court said he would bed anything with two legs over me . . ."

"He was referring to our linked senses," Mykal explains. "He didn't mean it to be cruel. For Court, it's just *fact*. None of us can cross that boundary, not unless we're ready to accept the consequences."

In the past two months, my priorities have been so focused on readying myself for StarDust that I haven't thought much about kissing or bedding anyone. Let alone Court or Mykal. So as this news falls on me, I feel nothing less or more than strange.

"Sparring?" The accusation echoes from the darkened porch steps.

The tall, exceedingly stiff figure emerges into the torchlight. Court stuffs his fists in his long black-buttoned coat, the hem sweeping the snow as he nears. Pieces of his dark brown hair fall over his lashes, more disheveled than usual, and purple circles shadow his grave eyes.

I rise and dust wet sludge off my slacks. "Mykal stole my socks, so I kneed him."

Mykal stands slowly. "And she bit my arm like a damned tiger." He hoped to cheer up his friend, but Court's stoic features never change.

Mykal scratches the back of his head.

I end up itching my scalp, the tickle too aggravating to leave alone. A yawn also grinds at Court's jaw, but he bites down, refusing what his body demands. *Yawn*.

Fyke.

I yawn. Right out in the open. My yawn then triggers Mykal, who mumbles a curse while he does so.

"Your lip is bleeding." Court studies me, his tone less scolding than most days. He licks his bottom lip, blinking a few times, checking over his shoulder. Hanging his head. Lifting his head.

Restless.

"If you're worried, I can easily lie and tell people I slipped on ice tomorrow," I say quickly. "I've seen plenty of Influentials fall as they step out of Purple Coaches. Everyone will believe it." *Stop talking, Franny.*

I shut my lips, not intending to worsen his anxiety.

Court takes a long moment to respond, but he nods more than once. "It's fine." Then he trains his gaze onto us, more precision, less flighty. "Tomorrow or the next day, whoever we meet will be Influentials and they *cannot* die in any situation, but we may, so if we need to fight, we fight smart."

My face scrunches. "What is fighting smart? Do you mean running away?"

Mykal grunts, not a fan.

Court shakes his head. "The body is as fragile as it is resilient." His deep, smooth voice is like satin in the night. Court unbuttons his coat, careful and tentative, as though he's shedding a protective layer of his soul. "You just have to know which places respond negatively to pressure."

He folds his coat and sets the garment aside, and then raises a single knuckle from his fist. "Strike the sternum."

"Sternum?" I mumble.

Court motions to the middle of his chest. "Don't try this on each other, but if you break someone's sternum, you could puncture their lung."

Mykal soaks up the instructions with me.

"Same single knuckle to the temple," Court says, pushing his knuckle to the tender side of his head. "The outcome will be a concussion or hemorrhaging. If done to us, it might be fatal."

My eyes widen. Hemor-what-ing? How in three hells has *Court* learned about bodies and limbs and organs?

Court displays other maneuvers: jabbing fingers behind the collarbone to force someone to the ground; striking a forehead with the heel of a palm, which jostles the brain in the skull; applying pressure to the highest point of the jawline to cause pain and loss of speech; and chopping someone's neck with a flat palm to choke them.

I listen and digest all that I can, but it'd be disingenuous to not mention how much I wonder about Court. My mind fogs with each passed second.

When he finishes, I unconsciously slip my hand in my coat and finger the pocketed Juggernaut. Court stiffens. Mykal swings his head between us.

I freeze.

Maybe I should release the pills, smash them beneath my boot, but carrying them, keeping them, has reminded me a little bit of the *me* before I dodged my deathday.

"What?" I ask Court, a pill hidden in my pocket between my fingers. They can *feel* every crevice of the chalky blue Juggernaut. "I heard what you said about brains and sternums and knocking the wind out of our enemies. It's all up here." With my free hand, I tap my temple.

His gaze drills into mine.

Mine punctures his right back.

"Franny," he breathes, wind whipping strands of his hair.

"Court."

"I was a physician," he suddenly says. "A very, very young physician . . . or what you may call a doctor."

My lips part but only surprise escapes. And I remove my hand from my pocket, no longer touching the Juggernaut.

"I worked at a hospital in Yamafort with advanced equipment like surgical tables"—Court blinks rapidly, pushing through memories fast—"fluorescent lights, anesthetic machines, heart monitors . . . the list goes on, and since I've been gone, I'm sure it's grown."

A doctor.

I swallow, choked up. Not because a *doctor* has been in my presence—a profession more than one Influential bragged about in the back of my Purple Coach—but because he finally gave me something more about himself than just *It's unimportant.*

I wipe hastily at my watery eyes. "You're a doctor."

His gaze glasses. "Was." He nods to Mykal. "I told him about a year ago."

Mykal rests his hands leisurely on his head. "Then I asked *how* you came to fill that sort of role."

"And you were met with silence." Court acknowledges a fact that I never knew existed. Mykal has been in the dark about Court's source of wisdom, histories, and apparently, his profession—a profession meant for Influentials.

People who'll die much older than just fifteen years.

Court licks his lips, maybe since mine are dry and split. "I . . ." He's shaking, his fingers quaking to his mouth, and I ache all over for him.

"It's all right," I say quietly. "You don't have to explain."

"Court." Mykal steps near—he ceases. Court has raised his hand toward him.

"I'm a Wonder." In one breath, he frees the stunning answer.

Court is a Wonder.

Mykal's eyes grow to my inflated size. Wind crashes against my lungs and I crouch to gather more air while Mykal staggers. Then he pauses.

And he drops to his knees in front of a glassy-eyed Court. Before he bows forward in adoration, Court clasps Mykal's arms, prying him to his feet.

"Get up, *get up.*" Court supports most of Mykal's weight. "You're being foolish."

His hands hover beside Court's jaw, afraid to touch someone so holy. "You're a Wonder."

I scour Court's frame, his body—*his mind.* I should've known he was a Wonder based on his intellect, but he denounced the gods so much that it seemed wrong for him to be one.

Court takes Mykal's face in his hands. "I'm the exact same as I always was, Mykal."

"You're blessed by the God of Wonders," he rebuts, hypnotized by Court.

I rise, in a lesser trance. Only because Court has not changed, has he?

My mother told the tale, but she'd shorten it to the good parts. "Once upon an era, the God of Wonders was stuffed full of awe. It hurt his belly. He knew something must be done, so he watched all the newborn children and took interest in the ones who were meant to die young. Readily, he unbound the extra wonder inside and each piece descended. Some rare children swallow the awe until it fills their souls. They are not just kissed by the god. They are Wonder."

Only Fast-Trackers and Babes can be chosen as Wonders. And very few are.

"I'm not *blessed*," Court forces again, gripping Mykal tighter. Their hands are my hands: his fingers threading through Mykal's wheat-blond hair, his neck stringent, and Mykal's pulse, thudding fast and hard.

"You just said—"

"It's a title, Mykal," Court says with such raw conviction. "It's a title they give children who show quickness to learn and high aptitude. It does not mean that I'm blessed by the God of Wonders. It means that I took a test, and they knew I'd be more use flying through academics than . . ." He slowly looks to me.

Than living a laborious life. Like me.

I shrug at him. I loved my job and I'm definitely glad that I never passed any test that said I should be in school. He doesn't look any happier for it.

Mykal rubs at his eyes with a rough hand. "I won't be worshipping you if that's what you want."

"It's what I want," Court says firmly, arms falling to his sides. "And I want you *standing* next to me."

Mykal nods over and over. "I'll always be next to you."

Court's silent, hot tears scald his cheeks. I feel each one slip down his jaw, like they could easily be my own. Then he swipes them away and takes a few rigid steps back toward the building. "We all need sleep before tomorrow, so don't stay up too late."

Before he turns his back to us completely, I shout, "Wait!"

Court hesitates, staring off at the snowy road beyond us, and then slightly rotates his head to me.

I haven't said anything to him yet and only one word bites at me. One word that I remember to use now and again.

I smile a tearful smile and say, "Thank you." What he shared was no small feat. I see that.

I *feel* that.

His nose flares, stifling emotion. Then his gray eyes ping between Mykal and me, and in the hollow of the night, he whispers, "May the gods be in your spirit."

Mykal and I both smile and together, we say, "And I in your heart."

PART
Two

Rage, rage against the dying of the light.
—DYLAN THOMAS

FIFTEEN

Court

"Give it to me." Franny wags her fingers heatedly at my pocket. Her scowl could kill someone on their deathday.

The three of us just spent four unbearably silent hours squeezed in the backseat of a Purple Coach, the car bumping along an icy stretch of road to Yamafort. As we rode into Bartholo's large neighboring city, our silence drew my gaze to the window.

And there it was.

An affluent, ice-covered city made of blanched stone and elaborate crown molding. One that contains my forgotten name and a childhood that I touch sparsely and sporadically.

Welcome home, I thought and then hung my head.

I prefer the muted blue and gray cobblestone of Bartholo and its rust-colored brick buildings. In Yamafort, the stark white skyscraping opulence is almost painful to the eye, and when the sun radiates behind layers of lilac smoke, the whole city is swathed in purple.

After the driver dropped us off a few blocks from Altia's Museum of Natural Histories & Figures, I convinced myself of a miserable idea. That an enraged Franny Bluecastle would remain in that car and ride far, *far* away from me.

I was wrong.

The Purple Coach peels down the road, joining a jagged line of vehicles—and Franny is right beside us. Fuming in place.

Still waving her hand at my coat pocket. Anger crosses her black brows and pinches her lips, and I don't have to be a Wonder to know that I'm the cause.

"Give. It. To. Me." Franny snaps her fingers at my coat. "Or I'll take it myself."

I raise my brows. "You don't steal." Which is why I dig in my wool pocket.

"There's a first for everything," she refutes beneath her breath.

"Not that," Mykal interjects. Cramped from the car ride, he stretches his muscular arms a few feet from us. He said he'd let me smooth this out with Franny on my own, but he can't hold his tongue for long.

I open my russet wallet.

And I crave to just *hurry*. To the museum. To the end where we all survive . . . or where we all die.

The sole of Franny's boot taps the cement sidewalk repeatedly. Waiting. *An hour to spare. We have time.* My shoulders tense, no pressure releasing.

While I flip through my wallet, men and women dressed in typical Altia fashion—dark wools that kiss the snow, many jewels, leather handbags, fur mittens and shawls—saunter up and down the sidewalk and tend to their own business as though wearing blinders, not seeing us.

Purple Coaches idle against the left curb, and to the right, winter-clad bodies slip into a Bank Hall and Mortimack's Sandwiches. Lilac smoke billows out of each chimney stack.

I swing my head away from the shops. My older brother and I would often bring Illian to Mortimack's. The storeowner knew his order by heart: lamb on wheat with goat cheese and chives.

Don't think about them.

I extract my blue card. "I would've given my identification to you in the car."

"I couldn't stand to speak to you, let alone touch something of yours." She tries to pluck the card from my fingers, but I retract.

"But now you can?" I ask, bite to my voice.

"I don't want to, but I need to." Franny huffs. "I can't believe you decided to tell me *right before* we climbed in the fyk . . .

car . . ." She trails off, glances over her shoulder, and lowers her voice. "Just give me your card so I can see the truth for myself."

I hold the card out. "You can sense when I lie."

She seizes my identification. "I want proof of your truths." Eyes narrowing, she searches the card for my name.

For weeks, I constructed her reaction in my head to *"I'm an Icecastle, Franny."* I said those exact words before we left Bartholo.

Yesterday she thanked me for opening up about my past profession, but with this news, I prepared for her to grow ill. To curse me. To shove me.

I've tried to keep Franny at a distance. *She's just common. That's all she is.* Maybe not knowing Franny will be less painful when she rejects me. As her lungs expand and contract indignantly, I restrain the urge to touch my abdomen. I sense the heat of her anger.

I sense her hurt.

And I can stand here and say that I kept Franny Bluecastle at a distance, but I didn't. Not entirely. Because I know her.

I know that riled girl. Her radiant and unfailing morality burns eternally bright inside of me. When she boils at the sight of cruelty and unkindness, I boil. Part of me has grown callous toward indecencies, so to *feel* my heart ignite again—I am more and more alive.

But then, I take a breath, and I remember.

I am what she despises.

My soul is at war and I would rather not care what she thinks. *She's just common.*

That's all she is.

"Say something," I breathe, her glare scorching holes in my card.

"At least you aren't a thief." She must recall my other explanation. I told them the truth of how I landed in Vorkter.

I can't touch the memory again, but I was glad to finally share the story with Mykal. He said that it made no difference to him, but his shock coiled through me for two hours straight.

"I'm still a thief." I push my dark brown hair out of my eyes.

"Not grand theft though." She tries to justify my immorality to herself. "Which is a capital punishment."

Capital punishment is just the polite way of saying "sent to Vorkter" where most will live until their deathday arrives. Those freed before their deathday are rare and few.

I dip my head and say quietly, "I'm a criminal, Franny. Accept it or move on." I gesture to the long street, my jaw locking.

Mykal shakes his head at me and mouths, *Stop it*.

I'd rather her like the ass that I am than love the god that I am not.

She flips the card between her fingers. "I accept that you're the most complicated, *cold* boy I've ever known." Quickly, she adds, "But do you really think StarDust will accept you? You couldn't find anyone to change your identification?"

I stiffen, surprised at what she homes in on. "It's um . . ." I rub my lips. "Removing an *Icecastle* surname from a card is a capital punishment. No one was willing."

Whipping away from us, Franny marches to an empty Purple Coach—and then crouches by the chained tire.

Without pause, she scrapes my identification across the sharp iron spikes. Scratching my last name. As the wind howls and sky darkens, a storm gathering overhead, I can excuse the damage by citing a *blizzard* as the cause.

"Looks like she's more resourceful than you," Mykal says with a crooked smile and we both sidle near Franny with leather travel satchels in hand. Towering above, we block her frame from anyone's sight.

I have no response to Mykal. Since his words are true.

Dense snow begins to pour down and settle on the collar of my black coat, on Franny's sleek, center-parted hair, and on Mykal's refined green wool. No crude patchwork of animal skins. My friend has even donned a suit beneath his proper coat. Polished and clean.

It's harder on the eyes than I imagined it'd be.

Mykal lifts his hood and studies the dimmed lilac clouds, sky rumbling. "Sounds like a nasty blizzard."

I tighten my gloves and stare off at the stark white stone. When I was just a boy, my older brother would wait outside of an extravagant apartment building with me. Eight-pointed stars and winter hares were etched finely in stone window frames. We lived on the twelfth floor and each morning we would exit those revolving glass doors, reach the shoveled sidewalk, and stand beneath an overhang. A pristine scarlet mat beneath our buffed boots.

We would wait for a Purple Coach to drive us to school. My older brother, Kinden, always hugged his arms and repeated the same exact phrase.

Every morning.

Every time.

"Cold is a monster."

In the Free Lands, I often thought that Kinden was right. Cold is a monster. It clawed down my spine; it gutted and knifed me, slashed through my body little by little.

Today, covered with rich fabrics and expensive leather, it can't reach me. I try to take comfort in this fact, but other miseries cling too hard.

"Hurry," I tell Franny, my tone sharper than I intend.

She shoots a darker scowl, then rises and returns my identification to me.

While I lead them to the museum, I examine the card, my first name perfectly intact and legible. She could've easily carved *Court* away, but she let me keep that part of me.

I have three names. Three lives: before, during, and after Vorkter. I have shed myself too many times to count and put on new clothes, new layers. I am a jumbled mess of who I should be and who I want to be and who I am.

The Museum of Natural Histories & Figures hasn't changed since I last visited for a school field trip. We enter the rotunda where vaulted ivory ceilings broaden the spotless area. Our boots, along with many others, clank the glossy marble floors.

Throughout many, *many* years, the museum has kept the same glass display in the middle: a taxidermy crocodile with bared teeth, set on fake flora and a murky river. Mykal scrutinizes the display, then me, clarity in his blue eyes.

The tattoo that I had covered across my back—it was a replica of that *exact* crocodile.

I walk farther inside and unconsciously canvass the walls, most decorated with pieces of old fighter jets, black helmets from wars I've never seen, and classic art salvaged from eras with no names.

I don't want to travel down these memories where I'll trip and fall flat on my face. We're here for one reason only.

While Franny and Mykal peruse the lobby, I watch a cluster of Influentials in fur-lined coats meander down one of five hallways, flyers in hand. Their voices rebound.

"Maybe it's this way."

"What if the location was misprinted?"

"The date could be wrong."

I crack my knuckles to trounce my nerves. Since the hallways lead to exhibits of extinct creatures—*Reptiles & Amphibians*, *Arachnids & Domestic Pets*, *The Great Deserts*, *Tropical Specimens*, and *Warm Oceans*—I doubt that's the right direction.

Every so often, two or three more young and old Influentials push through the revolving doors, carrying travel satchels and inquiries that no one answers.

Two fashionable fiftysomething women strut ahead of us, hand in hand. The couple takes a seat at a wooden bench. Right next to an empty podium for collecting tickets.

"Are we supposed to be standing around doing nothing?" Mykal removes his green coat and carefully folds the fabric over his arm. Just how I showed him. His tailor-made black three-piece suit fits the muscular contours of his broad build, but his harsh features and hard-hearted eyes contrast with the finery.

"We're waiting," I say. "Some more patiently than others."

"Heya, I'm patient." He fiddles with his cuff links and rambles about how patience came naturally to him, and I just haven't opened my eyes enough to see it. Shorter than me, his shoulder rests slightly lower, but he still props his arm on mine.

I nearly smile, too fleeting, and then I lean my head down to him, whispering, "Will you ever shut up?"

"Will you ever be growing a better sense of humor?" He searches his pocket—*I search his pocket.* My hand might as well be fumbling around in his empty slacks. No dry root. No cigarette. His heavy sigh fills my lungs.

A few feet ahead of us, Franny ogles the ceiling's intricate oil painting, a visual dedication to the God of Wonders. "Maybe the welcome station is on the second or third floor?"

"No, this is the main entrance," I say. Last I remember, the second and third floor change annually, most likely showcasing the history of deathday marks.

In 2420, every citizen had to ink their deathday below their right ear, which led to a divide in classes. Subsequently, the terms *Influentials*, *Fast-Trackers*, and *Babes* were formed. The Law of Deathday Marks caused uprisings and rebellions that threatened the established presidencies, but with the Great Freeze of 2501, the need for peace and unity became necessary. So a little over a *thousand* years ago, the four presidents abolished the law, helping mend bridges between those who'd die old and those who'd die young.

"Just remember, times could be worse," my father used to say. *Times could be worse.* I believed it, and then I dodged my deathday—and I wasn't sure of anything that I'd been told.

Elevator doors suddenly ping open. I stand at rigid attention.

A short, lively female is inside the leaf-wallpapered compartment; her strawberry-printed sundress and golden jacket contrasts with her smooth brown complexion.

"So many of you!" she exclaims, causing people to assess one another. There are about forty of us lingering in the rotunda. "I apologize dearly for being held up. I was assisting a much smaller group before you."

Shuffling out of the elevator, she secures her brunette hair with two pencils, clipboard tucked beneath her arm. "If you'll form a line, please."

Everyone rushes toward the podium, squeezing and bumping to be first. We don't have to be first—in fact, I don't want to draw that much attention. So I clutch Mykal's shoulder to keep him from shoving his way to the front.

Somehow Franny has been pushed far ahead in line and she hugs her leather satchel protectively to her chest, as though someone will steal it. Glancing back and forth, she locks eyes with me.

Before I can mouth a word, she makes up her own mind and snakes her way back to us.

"Everyone's talking over one another!" Franny shouts over the chatter and slips behind our builds. "I can't even hear the woman—"

I smother a wince.

Franny truly winces.

Someone just elbowed her in the lower back and she staggers forward. Mykal catches her waist before she barrels into him.

"You cut in front of me!" A little rosy-cheeked girl in pigtails and a fur hat perches her hands on her hips. She's unattended by a parent since she's probably ten years of age.

Franny glowers. "So you thought you'd punch me?"

"I tapped you. Don't be a baby."

Franny's mouth drops and her accusatory gaze drills into me like, *You said Influentials are proper, not insulting.*

They can be both.

I wedge myself between a vexed Franny and the little girl. "She didn't cut you," I say bitterly. "She was far ahead of you, so you're not waiting any longer than you were."

She tilts her nose up and averts her eyes.

I roll mine. *I hate this city.*

"Can you all hear me in the back?!" Behind the podium, the woman cranes her neck and Influentials begin to hush and nod repeatedly. At the very head of the line, the fashionable couple stands perfectly straight.

"Good, well then"—she clears her throat and adjusts her clipboard—"I'm Amelda Hobblecastle as said so by my . . ." She flashes the pinned nametag on her sundress. "I assume you're here for the StarDust enrollment. When you reach my podium, I'll need five thousand bills apiece and then your identification. The majority of you *will* be turned away, our spots are limited, and you're to leave at once."

I watch how quickly that becomes true. Amelda snatches ten thousand bills from both of the women, hardly examines their identification, and then says, "I apologize, but you're not qualified."

Qualified?

What other qualifications are there?

As the line continues to shorten and we move forward, no one truly speaks except those at the podium. Only two young girls have been enrolled, maybe twelve or thirteen years of age. They're given directions to wait on a bench in the rotunda.

Mykal continuously *grinds* his teeth, so much so that my head pounds. A second later, Franny nudges his arm so he'll stop. He nudges back and they nearly start pushing and shoving in jest.

When he ruffles her hair, I pinch my eyes and then whisper, "*Stop.*"

Their arms fall to their sides and the bottom of their stomachs drop.

I have to be this way, I remind myself.

"I'm sorry, sir, you're not qualified," Amelda tells a man of thirtysomething years, trimmed stubble along his fair-skinned face.

"And why not?" He refuses to budge and yanks at the sleeves of his trench coat.

Amelda recites, "To preserve the integrity and confidentiality of StarDust, you would have to be enrolled to know why. I apologize, Mr. Frycastle—"

"I gave you *five thousand* bills to be here." He repeatedly jabs at the podium's sleek surface.

"And we thank you greatly for your contribution to the world's aerospace department. We promise it'll go to good use." Amelda forces a bright smile that shakes a little as the man starts yelling about refunds. "I implore you to write a letter stating your grievances. It's more helpful than shouting at me, hmm?" She waves the boy behind him forward. "Come here, little lamb."

In one minute, he's enrolled.

I start to think that they're only taking children, but then two men in their twenties smile wide, hug each other, and wait by the benches.

We watch a redheaded mother and her freckled son split up, the mother trying to pull a smile from the boy, but he stares morosely at the floor.

She whispers, "If this is the last I see of you, look up at me."

He looks up.

"You will go down in history, Seifried, and I will be with you, right where the gods lie." She puts her hand to his heart. Securing his travel satchel on his shoulder, she says gently, "May the gods be in your spirit, my Seifried."

He apprehensively holds the strap of his satchel. "And I in your heart."

I should have no emotion toward this scene, but my eyes feel like they've sprung an irrational leak. A chord struck that deep makes no sense. I glance at Franny.

She rubs aggressively at her watery gaze as the mother lingers and then exits the museum. If I ask the *why* to her emotions, I'm afraid of growing more sentimental.

I don't want to cry.

I don't want to be angry.

Or paranoid, worried, maddened—I don't want to be anything at all.

Franny sniffs loudly and a few heads turn. When she wipes at her dripping nose with the back of her hand, I reach into my waist-coat for a handkerchief.

Just as I offer, she grabs the red cloth and the longest pause passes before she remembers to say, "Thanks."

I see how hard she tries to remember etiquette. I'm just not sure if Franny's best will be enough.

Almost there.

We're next in line.

Mykal rests a consoling hand on her head and, with a smile, she smacks it away. He glances at me—*Focus.*

Assertive. Straightened. Readied.

No distractions.

"I apologize, you haven't qualified," Amelda says to a girl no older than eight.

She begins to cry. "But my father said I can't go home until I'm hired for the Saga 5 Mission!"

"Then tell your father you were *over*qualified. He'll still be proud." Amelda smiles warmly at me; the little girl slumps and drifts away.

I approach the podium and procure a stuffed envelope from inside my suit. "For all three of us." I motion to Mykal and Franny who flank my sides.

"Set your identifications on top while I count." She licks her finger and flips through the bills, mouthing numbers to herself.

I think I'm holding my breath because Mykal clears his throat roughly, hating when I cage in air.

Swallowing hard, I try to inhale fully. Franny massages her throat, adding to the layers of senses that crash at me like a brash orchestra. Out of tune, wildly annoying. I'd like to shut it off.

Just once.

Just right *now.*

Identifications on the podium, I close my eyes for a long moment, then open as Amelda exclaims, "The bills are all here. Now let's see . . ." She gathers our cards. "Wilafran Elcastle of Altia?"

Clucking her tongue before smiling. "You've qualified for enrollment. Let me just . . ." Amelda uncaps a marker and bows forward, scribbling.

None of us can relax.

"Here you go." Amelda stretches to hand Franny a rectangular name badge with a purple Altia emblem.

"Thank you," Franny says, voice stilted.

"You're quite welcome. Now for you and you." She lifts another blue card. "Mykal Kickfall—Ah a *fall*. Not a single *fall* has been turned away, isn't that something? Though there haven't been many of you." She gives him an extra smile, which is common for *fall*s to receive.

Mykal's mother died giving birth to him. Therefore he became Mykal Kick*fall* instead of Kick*castle*. Many cradle superstitions like treasures, and mothers who choose to conceive nine months before their deathday are bringing life at the moment of death.

For most, it's a holy ending. And many say the God of Death has touched the newborn. A symbol of great fortune. And so they shall *fall* into luck throughout their lives.

I've told Mykal plenty of times that no god kissed him. He's one of the most unluckiest individuals I've ever met. His reply, *"Then my luck will be coming in due time."*

The rest of us are just *castles*. Sturdy fortresses, together, in this world.

"Great," Mykal says to Amelda. "So have I qualified?"

"Yes you have." After she makes his name badge, she inspects my battered identification with confusion. I explain that I dropped the card and a Purple Coach ran it over during the blizzard.

"Oh bad luck. Maybe your friend can give you more." She laughs at the joke.

I try to force a semblance of a smile, but Franny wrinkles her nose at me. I'm cringing, I realize.

"Court . . . Iv . . . I apologize, sir, what is your surname?" she asks.

"Idlecastle of Altia."

She squints at the card for another full minute.

I rub my lips like any second I may scream.

Amelda passes the card to me. "I think this will do. You might look into applying for a new one through Altia mail."

"I will." *I won't.*

I pocket the identification, tensed, and then she hands me a name badge. We wait by the benches in complete silence, the line dwindling quickly.

Only one other Influential enrolls after us. The little girl who elbowed Franny arches her shoulders and ensures her pigtails never cover her nametag: *Odell Petalcastle*, Altia emblem.

Not everyone wears the Altian eight-pointed star. Seifried wears Maranil's silvergill, a fish that no one mocks since it's said to be favored by the God of Victory.

"Ten total." Amelda hurries to us "Six born in Altia, three in Orricht, one Maranil. That's quite a decent size out of fifty-eight." She pushes the elevator button, doors springing open. "Go, go, go—before more come. I'm doing a batch of candidates at a time."

We're ushered inside the spacious elevator. Mykal scrutinizes his surroundings. With added weight, the elevator wobbles. He grabs hold of the railing, eyes hardened and alert.

Mykal hates riding elevators and almost refused the last time we were at the Catherina Hotel. He calls them the "silliest contraptions he's ever seen," and his eyes speak those same opinions.

I only convinced him to abandon the stairs when I said, "You've slain bears in Grenpale. You've survived backbreaking winds in the Free Lands. Do you truly plan to waste your energy and fear on this?"

I'm frightened of much more than Mykal. That is the truth.

And very rarely do I need to instill the same confidence in him that he instills in me. I believe that I'm terrible at that, but he stayed in that elevator.

Just as he stays in this one now.

Franny hugs her satchel and stares upward. I can practically hear *one hundred and thirteen* repeated in her head.

"You're all very lucky." Amelda shrugs off her golden jacket, *Museum of Natural Histories & Figures* embroidered on the breast pocket. "So many people want to enroll and they never will."

"How did we?" I ask first.

Amelda swiftly turns the jacket inside out with two tugs of the arms. As though she's done this many times before, she easily fits the jacket back on.

It's black now.

This time, a golden triangle with three stars is stitched over the heart. The StarDust logo is unmistakable.

"It's simple, truthfully." Amelda lights up the only button, no labels or floor numbers. "StarDust is only looking for Influentials with the *most* possible years ahead of them. We only let in people who'll die after a hundred and who are currently younger than twenty-five."

I try not to glare at the ceiling, so I end up rolling my eyes. They could've clearly written age and deathday requirements on the flyers, but they chose not to. For that extra five thousand bills.

If that'd been us, I would've . . . I don't know what I would've done. Cried. Screamed. Wished for a sooner ending than a later one.

The elevator descends.

Lowering far beneath the ground.

More of us inquire about being hired for the mission, but Amelda evades the extra questions. "I can only explain so much at a time," she says. "All candidates will learn more later."

Ping.

Slowly, the doors slide open to a quiet, warm common room: dark purple sofas and velvet chaises, rich-threaded rugs on hardwood, an oak staircase, casia crackling in a fireplace, gold-leafed walls with wooden panels. If not for the ornate paintings of a galaxy and planet, I'd believe we walked into an Influential's home.

"Dessa will mark your bags."

As though summoned, a wrinkled woman with a gray pixie cut and cross face walks down the staircase. She is dressed in slacks and a buttoned blouse. "Let it be known, this is not my primary job. I will *not* clean up after you or unpack your things. The porters are busy with the welcome dinner and I drew the short straw." Nearing us, she yanks the satchel out of Franny's hands.

Welcome dinner. Beyond a wooden door, voices pitch and seem to echo . . .

"This way," Amelda says, guiding us to that very door after we've dropped off our possessions. "Four hallways will connect you to the schoolroom, the common room, the dining room, and the training facility, which includes a medical wing. Above the common room are your dormitories and baths." Turning the knob, she pauses. And smiles. "Are you ready?"

"Yes!" the younger children exclaim first.

Amelda pushes into a wide marble hallway that stretches to another door.

Odell gasps and races toward the left-side wall. Which is not so much a wall as they are windows, looking out toward a cavernous room. The children press their noses to the glass while we all near. They ooh and ahh.

My eyes too, start to grow. My chest swells and I stare at my only hope: the sleek, saucer-shaped starcraft, three tubular engines and *Saga* painted in gold across the onyx shell. High above is a dome window, lilac smoke clouding the panes. Since we're under the museum, the dome must be the only window to the outdoors.

"The launch area is the center of everything."

This is why we're here.

"Pardon the tools and machinery beside the starcraft; the technicians don't always clean up if they're working late. This way to the dining room." Amelda spins on her heels and directs us forward.

Halfway there, the door cracks and a figure looms behind it, shielded by the wood.

Amelda walks so urgently that the pencils slip from her brown tendrils. She ignores them and then clutches the edge of the door, speaking in a hushed voice to the hidden figure.

I find myself increasing my pace. Swift, uncertain. I have a strange feeling all of a sudden and I turn to Mykal, to Franny, and they shake their heads.

Is that feeling mine?

Forward.

I walk forward, and as the deep voice on the other side escalates, I know for certain.

The strangeness belongs to me.

I've never met anyone from StarDust, but that voice carries eerie familiarity.

Forward.

Closer.

Nearer.

Amelda unconsciously cracks the door farther open.

At the sight of the man, I skid to a stop. I stand like a crimson fortress to the west. Like Vorkter. Unmovable, impenetrable—stuck rigidly in ice. *"Never touch the iron bars,"* my cellmate said when I first entered. Without casia to warm Vorkter, flesh would stick to the freezing metal. And rip right off.

I do know that man.

Unbridled mirth with no counterpart, no comparison, shines through dark twinkling eyes, his strong jaw and high-set cheekbones. He wears a tux effortlessly, like he was born in one. Head smoothly shaven, only a grayed prickled goatee is rough against his dark brown skin. His poised stature welcomes Amelda. *Friendly.*

My father.

He has always been friendly.

He's older than I remember. In his late fifties now.

The last time I saw him, he gripped my arms, shaking me with heart-wrenching sorrow. Hot tears poured down his cheeks. His broken voice bled into my ears for *seven* long years after. "Why did you do it?!" he screamed. "Why did you do it?!"

There were no answers that'd appease him, nothing I could bear to say. Eyes burning, I stood unblinkingly. His legs buckled at my tearful silence and my mother's sobs wrung the frigid air.

I was ten years of age.

He only let go of my shoulders when the Altia Patrol ripped me from him, and they pushed my head down into their black car, Purple Coach driver at the wheel. Ready to bring me to Vorkter.

"Why did you do it?!"

Everyone smiled when we buried Illian. Everyone smiled but me. And my father—he cried when he last set his eyes on mine. He lost me before he ever thought he would.

"Why did you do it?!"

The memory slices my eardrums.

My father glances absentmindedly to the hall, his benevolent eyes catching mine, but I turn to the side—*he can't know me.* I look much older now, but more than that, he believed his son died.

My face heats and I listen to his voice trail off before he says a flustered goodbye to Amelda. The door shuts.

I buried so much of my life with my family. I never planned to excavate it.

Not to this degree.

But I believed that I truly knew my father. As a boy, he'd lift me on his knee and let me peruse his physics books, pointing out surface plasmon resonance and polariton, sometimes thermo-dynamics and casia. He hoped I'd follow in his profession, but he never chastised or swayed me when I chose medicine.

At our oak dining table—cream doily cloths beneath plates and robust chairs occupied by my mother and father, little brother Illian and older brother Kinden—no one ever talked about aerospace or astrophysics.

So I ask Amelda, "Who was that man?"

She reaches for the door again. "Tauris Valcastle, Director of StarDust. He ultimately decides everything."

SIXTEEN

Mykal

Amelda swings open the dining room door to extravagance that befits kings and queens in fairy tales. Suited for polished men and ladies with grace learned from birth.

Hundreds of tufted chairs line endless rows of mahogany tables. Brass chandeliers hang low. Dark green and maroon tassels dangle off lamp shades. Tables are stuffed to the brim: red rose centerpieces, sugar and salt boats, crystal goblets, five-tiered plates, and forks, spoons, knives galore—who needs that much silverware?

Blood drains from my head. Realizations pound at me. I'm supposed to fit in here?

"Take a seat wherever you can find one." I hardly hear Amelda, my focus brewing elsewhere. "Dinner will be served once I've enrolled the final batch of candidates." She pads away.

I take a step forward and glare at my feet. *Carpet.* I loathe carpet. Floor should be hard beneath every boot.

I thought Franny would match my discomfort, but she's nothing short of awed, eyes glittering at the nauseating décor.

Many ladies here wear a similar style blouse to Franny's sapphire silk: big bow over the chest and thimble-sized buttons cascading down the spine.

Her senseless bra pokes at me, the underwire bothersome. I'd scratch my chest, but I know better now.

Three rows of tables and Court chooses the one closest to the kitchen. Doors thrash open as porters rush feverishly in and out to fill wine goblets.

More than a few empty chairs here, I settle next to Franny. Court faces us.

We're quiet. Influentials seated right beside us. Ranging from twenty-five to as young as seven, they prattle among themselves.

Court drums his knee incessantly. Until he catches the tic and closes his fingers into a fist.

I haven't ever been able to read his mind, but I know the name Tauris Valcastle rattled his core. In the hallway, Franny and I were able to ask what was wrong, and he whispered three words, "He's my father."

His father. Court had talked of him somewhat, but not often enough to paint a vivid picture. I gathered that he wasn't nasty or malicious to where I'd arch my back and bear my knuckles. When Court mentioned his father, it was with sorrow. And guilt.

I try not to be concerned about all the complications that'll be arriving with his father here.

"We should be given more instructions by now," a boy sitting closest to me says crisply. "The dining room is practically full." Name badge: *Symons Ravelcastle.* Emblem: a horned ram. Orricht born, a country known for farming wheat, shearing wool, and raising livestock.

Symons pinches a cigar between jeweled fingers. His suit chokes the hollow of his throat, dapper and clean-cut with slicked black hair and warm beige skin. To his left, a thin brown-haired boy fiddles with a lighter, flame dying. Bronze glow to his cheeks, he huffs in frustration, but Symons doesn't hassle the boy to go faster.

Court kicks me, not hard, but I shift anyways.

I'm peering *close* to Symons, so near that if he turns, our noses would whack, I see. So I ease back.

In the past ten years, I can count on two hands the number of people I've spoken to. I don't always know how to react around others so they won't label me as strange.

"StarDust is secret for a reason," the boy tells him. *Click.* From the corner of my eye, I see a flame from his lighter.

Symons puffs the cigar. "So secret they'd allow any Influential to join," he rebuts. "Did you see Patrik on our way in, Sel? What does he plan to do, play the flute in space? At least be sensible enough to have a background in the sciences before you pay *five thousand* bills."

Franny frowns darkly at the dish and then she takes a breath and traces the golden lip of her five plates. Court has his fingers to his jaw, more alert than every Influential combined.

I'd like to believe our chances are as good as theirs, even if we have no real knowledge of science.

"Patrik is enrolled," Sel says, "so your point is moot."

"He applied zero skills to be enrolled, so my point isn't moot. It's applicable."

"It won't be if he's hired for the mission." He adjusts his silver-framed glasses. Name badge: *Sel Ravelcastle.* Of Orricht too. Same last name as Symons, but dissimilar features.

Could be a couple or could be siblings. Since more Influentials are adopted than Babes and Fast-Trackers, I've learned it's hard to tell.

Symons taps ash into a leaf-shaped dish. "I love how you never take my side."

"I just don't make predictions based off personal bias," he says matter-of-factly.

"Personal bias?" He blows smoke away from Sel, turning his head—subsequently toward *me*. We almost brush noses and he catches me gazing right at him.

Gods bless.

Smoke slithers from his nostrils, his thin lips in an accusatory line.

Not noticing, Sel continues, "You hate the arts. Therefore, you've disregarded the professional flutist. *That* is personal bias."

"Can I help you?" Symons snaps to me, ignoring Sel. His lips twitch as he inspects my name badge. "Mykal."

I won't be turning away and cowering like nothing transpired. I did spy, and we are sitting side by side with nowhere else to go.

I open my mouth, but Court is faster. Acting wholly relaxed, he says, "He's fond of cigars."

I wish I'd thought of the excuse first. I clear my throat and rid my accent. "I am. Would you mind sparing one?" I gesture to the timber box between Sel and Symons.

Symons assesses me with a blank look.

Do I smell?

I sniff roughly, unable to decipher my stench. I smell what Franny smells: the quiet girl next to her, doused with sickly sweet perfume. A scent much worse than mine.

"Do you have a preference?" Symons asks.

I blink hard. "A preference for what?"

"*Cigars,*" he enunciates like I'm dense.

I grow hot, but I'm trying not to play into my own short temper. For Court and Franny's sake.

Truth being, I never paid much attention to types of store-bought cigars. Tobacco seeds grow a lot easier indoors than most, so I'd fashion my own.

What would Court do? I think quickly. "I like them all."

Symons sighs like talking with me is painful. But he plucks a stubby cigar from the box. "And I was under the impression that Altians are the foremost thinkers of our generation. With stalwart opinions and wit." He hands me the cigar and a lighter. Warm in my coarse palm. "Thank you, Mykal," he says evenly.

I nod tensely, unsure of what he means.

"Thank you for proving that Altians are more useless than the rest of us."

Useless.

A rock lodges in my throat and I grip my knee to keep from clenching my fists. Franny boils and Court gives her a look not to chime in.

We just arrived. We can't cause a scene. I know that. *Useless.*

If I speak, I'll surely be yelling. So I shut up.

Symons sucks on his cigar.

Don't ruin Court and Franny. Don't ruin them.

If I repeat it enough, maybe it'll be coming true.

"I apologize for my husband," Sel says mechanically, nudging his glasses up. "He has a bias against *Altians* as well as the arts."

Symons puffs smoke upward. "Find me an Altian who believes Orrish are better for more than milking goats." He scrutinizes me. "Before returning home, I spent five years in Altia university for biochemistry, and they *still* undervalued and underestimated me. Just because I was from Orricht." To Sel, he says, "We're all full of biases, lambkin. So is the way of the world."

My mind spins, not used to this quick talk. I hardly digest it and his insult starts feeling justified. I busy myself. Cigar between my lips, I light the end.

"May I have one?" a lady asks Symons firmly. No meekness in her voice or bold features. Her black eyes lance the couple directly across her seat.

She's nearly shoulder to shoulder with Court. I hadn't noticed her before, but somehow she blended seamlessly into the background. Until she decided otherwise.

Symons raps the box while studying her outspread hand. "You haven't spoken in five hours, Padgett, and now all of a sudden, you talk?"

Court's stomach flips, but I don't understand the cause.

Padgett raises her chin, hair tied in a fuchsia ribbon, and where her brown bony arms and stature could be awkward and gangly, she wears her thin size like sheer muscle. Teeming with confidence in a magenta velvet dress, the collar made of taupe fur.

"What did you want me to talk about?" Padgett says smoothly. "Did you want me to say how spectacular I am at science and that I will beat you in every round that comes to pass? Oh no, wait." She mocks surprise, fingers to her lips. "I'm confusing myself with *you*. The difference between you and me, Symons"—she leans forward, feigning a whisper—"I don't have to tell everyone I'm smart for it to be true."

I laugh. Delighted that someone finally twisted his arm.

Symons scoffs at me and passes Padgett a slender cigar anyways.

My laughter dies. I don't understand any of these people.

Court gestures between Sel, Symons, and Padgett. "How have you all been here for five hours already?" This question didn't cross my mind, but enrollment began less than an hour ago, didn't it?

Symons slides the cigar box between a sugar boat and rose centerpiece. "Orricht and Maranil had earlier entry times on their flyers. You didn't really believe this dining room filled this quickly in just . . . what, fifteen minutes?"

Court falls into silence. His gaze drifts to the head of the dining room. Where StarDust tapestries hang motionless and an oak podium waits for someone.

"You keep touching your wrist, why?" Padgett's question steals my focus. Lit cigar between her lips, she dissects Sel's mannerisms.

I thought he'd just been fidgety, nudging his glasses and such.

"I lost my bracelet before arriving. It must've slipped off when I stepped out of a Purple Coach—"

"It was *stolen*," Symons interjects. "Right off his wrist."

Sel shakes his head, gaze dropped. "You don't know that."

Symons adds, "Then how do you explain the four other Orrish who've lost necklaces and watches?"

"Thieves are everywhere," Franny says, somewhat loudly and sourly.

Symons stretches forward to see who spoke. "Great, another eavesdropper. We should be charging for everyone who listens in."

"Your words aren't worth a single bill," Padgett says like she announced the weather, tapping ash into the same leaf-shaped dish.

Symons swipes up his goblet of wine like a sword—*And people say I'm strange.* "I generously gave you a cigar," he says, "and I can generously take it away."

"I'd like to see you try." She seems unworried and that's when I finally read her name badge: *Padgett Soarcastle* of Maranil.

"Heya, old *friends*." In a single instant, that familiar voice wrecks the moment. Heat perishes in all three of us. Replaced with icy dread.

A shaggy-haired boy slips into the free chair next to Court, facing Franny. I'll never be forgetting the day Franny awoke in the Catherina Hotel and how we confronted this very bellhop. How management dragged him out by the ear.

Only Zimmer isn't in a red bellhop uniform anymore. His dark blue suit, three sizes too big, swallows his scrawny frame. His clothes may've changed, but he's still a Fast-Tracker.

Pretending to be an Influential. Just like us.

SEVENTEEN

Franny

Why?

Why would Zimmer use a fake identification? Why would a Fast-Tracker want to join StarDust when they'll die much sooner than everyone else?

He followed us. Tracked us down. My paranoia pricks my neck. After we left the Catherina Hotel, we lost sight of Zimmer. He could've thought about us. More than we ever thought about him.

Fast-Trackers are taught to create short-term, achievable goals, and it's more likely he's here to ensure we fail than a lofty desire to join the Saga 5 Mission.

Zimmer plants a sly, self-satisfied grin on me.

Gripping the table, I press my chest against the edge. "What are you doing here?"

He extends his arm over Court's chair, the ruse obvious to me, but it may fool the other Influentials. "Why is anyone here?" Zimmer swings his head to the length of the table, not afraid of stealing every gaze. "Glory . . . Prestige . . . *History.*"

I don't believe a fykking word he says. Even if they all do. "Unlikely," I growl.

Court pinches his own thigh hard—*Ow.* I swallow my briny feelings. He's telling me to cease the argument for appearances' sake.

Zimmer puts his finger to his cheek, gaze dipping to my name badge. "I like that shade of blouse, Wilafran. I bet that would make a lovely *hair* color. Don't you think?"

I go cold. *Gods.*

At the Catherina, I was introduced to Zimmer as a Fast-Tracker with piercings and dyed hair. Not as Wilafran. Not as an Influential.

"Enough," Court says with finality, his glare puncturing threats into Zimmer.

He feigns hurt. "I thought you would've liked your wife's hair the color of ripe fruit." Looking to Mykal, he adds, "What does her brother have to say about this?"

Our last names don't fit the ploy we built in the Catherina. Where Court is my husband, and Mykal is my brother. I feel snow and dirt being shoveled on top of us. Suffocating. I'm unsure of how to claw our way out.

I burn inside and I peek at my armpit, a large stain seeping through the silk.

Mykal tries to subtly waft his waistcoat.

Court lackadaisically unbuttons his suit. "Last I recall, *you* were using a variety of words that wouldn't sit well with anyone here." He shrugs off the fabric and pops the buttons of his waistcoat, cooling us. "And let's not mention your profession—"

"Funny." Zimmer drops his arm from Court's chair and clears his throat. "You're funny. We all *joke*. You don't have to take everything I say to heart."

My lips part, baffled. Zimmer really intends to keep his disguise intact. If he's not here to solely botch our chances, then *why*?

Zimmer even goes a step further, flashing a lighthearted smile at the Orrish couple and Padgett. "We were all in early education together. Childhood rivals, you know how it is."

Symons sets his cigar aside, letting it burn out. "I married mine."

I try to relax, but Court is always on edge. And Mykal has been pushed to a scorching point. His closed fists hurt my palms, fingernails digging deep.

Padgett blows perfect smoke rings. "If Court and Wilafran are married, and Wilafran and Mykal are related, then why are all your surnames different?" She speaks casually, but I trust no one.

Court once said, *"Some Influentials can be duplicitous when pursuing competitive, long-term goals, especially if the reward is attractive.*"

"We used to date." Court's quick lie twists my gut and he motions from his chest to mine. "Zimmer likes to mock our short romance by calling us *husband* and *wife*, even if we haven't been together in years, and Wilafran has a close friendship with Mykal. They're brother and sister in spirit, not in real relation."

If my stomach didn't flop because of the link, I'd believe all of his words. I hope they do too. Beneath the table, Court rubs his sweaty palms on his thighs.

"How amusing," Padgett says, unenthusiastic. Cigar hangs from her pink-stained lips. Her delicate pearl earrings dangle like water droplets and painted nails shimmer the shade of a raspberry.

I engrain her in my mind. She screams *intelligent* and *observant* and I bet my life that she'll be a threat.

Padgett notices me staring and studies me just as hard before saying, "You should be more focused on Zimmer, Wilafran. He's the one who mocked you."

"He knows what he is," I say without much thought.

Zimmer raises his white wine. "I am a wiseass."

He's a wart and I can't believe he used an Influential phrase: *wiseass*. How is he so good at pretending? My face must be scrunched because he adds, "You have something right there," and he gestures to his own upper lip and brows.

"Looks like annoyance," Padgett says with a flickering smile.

"Better yet, *hatred*," I say coldly at Zimmer, though I find myself not feeling *hate* as strongly as I express. In my heart of hearts, I know what we did to Zimmer at the Catherina was worse than anything he's yet to do to us.

I owe him. I make a mental note to jot down *Damaging his bellhop reputation* in my journal.

"I guarantee you, Wilafran Elcastle"—Zimmer lowers the goblet to his lips—"my hatred exceeds yours."

Hiding a shiver, I rotate toward the podium and cup my goblet in two hands. *Etiquette.*

I take dainty sips, not swigging the wine. My arched shoulders ache as much as Mykal's and I wish he could spread his legs wide and slouch until his back cracks. Alleviating our combined discomfort.

Boom.

I flinch as doors slam closed, chatter subduing to muffled muttering. My lungs engorge full of air thanks to Mykal, who inhales deeply while Court imprisons his breath.

I wait for their shared agitation, which comes next. Biting me. So routine that we could schedule it in with eating and sleeping.

Eight commanding figures enter. Both short and tall, big and small, men and women. They walk in a single line through the aisle between the tables. All wearing onyx cloaks with a golden StarDust brooch: three stars within a triangle. In their dignified presence, I find myself sitting more upright.

Whispers escalate, candidates gleaming bright in their seats.

Court said that he'd only heard rumors about StarDust. "It's not militant," he told me after I finished reading *The Hunter in the Snow* out loud. "In my lifetime, StarDust has always been regarded as sophisticated. Like someone speaks about an elite university or exclusive academic society."

I didn't understand then, but I do now. Each figure in StarDust has earnest eyes, demeanors more regal and ceremonial than authoritarian. They don't march.

They glide.

I like the beauty and grandeur of it all. In Bartholo, I never had enough bills to spend on fancy movie theaters or heated orchestra houses.

My mouth curves up as these gorgeous figures in gorgeous clothes slide to a stop by the podium.

The truth crashes against my lungs. That here I am, Franny Bluecastle, a part of a world I was never supposed to see. What would my mother think?

Live, my little Franny.

My eyes widen and well.

Amelda stands among the StarDust personnel, but Tauris is the one who breaks from the line and nestles behind the podium. Fingers go to my lips—*That's not me.* I hug my arms around my waist.

Without looking, I feel Court touch his mouth, his senses overpowering some of mine. His face set severely, muscles taut. Chest on fire.

His father is the cause. Tauris surveys the crowd with a radiant smile, so unlike Court whose lips never upturn. His father's infectious joy causes hundreds of Influentials to return a dazzling grin.

"Welcome." He speaks into a microphone, his silky voice rebounding through speakers. Mykal swings his head backward, confused about how his voice traveled so far and so loud.

Everyone within the dining room suddenly claps their hands together.

Why we're applauding already, I'm not sure, but I clap with the other candidates.

Mykal joins in as the applause weakens and his cheeks roast a little. He scratches his neck.

"Firstly," Tauris says, "thank you for showing your commitment to the future of our world by being here." More applause.

Mykal catches the tail end again. Symons gives him a snooty look. I blister and try not to kick his chair. *Be kind.*

Be proper.

"I'm Tauris Valcastle, Director of StarDust, but trust me, the aerospace department would be nothing without these seven Influentials next to me." He waves toward the line of cloaked personnel. "StarDust's directors, all of whom will help in deciding who's hired for the Saga 5 Mission."

Heartier clapping, some whistles.

Mykal is on time and I feel his lips tic up. I smile much wider than that. In turn, his smile stretches.

Tauris introduces the line of directors, some for engineering the starcraft, others for flight, and when Amelda curtsies, we learn she's the Director of Enrollment for StarDust.

"Besides myself," Tauris says, "Amelda Hobblecastle will be in direct contact with you. Your questions should be posed to her first." He pauses with more severity. "And I'm certain that *many* of you have questions, but to protect the integrity and confidentiality of StarDust, we cannot answer all of them yet. You've all been enrolled in a rigorous training course and those who fall behind will be expelled. The thirty most qualified candidates will be hired full time and hear StarDust's closest kept secrets. And the top five will make the Saga 5 Mission. You may be here for weeks. You may be here for months. If you're lucky, you'll be on the Saga starcraft for an entire lifetime."

Court blows out his first measured breath. No one claps, too apprehensive.

"Your training . . . well, you'll discover the details soon enough."

The dining room groans.

Tauris sports a humored smile. "Patience. In the common room, we've posted your dorm assignments, and daily schedules are on the main bulletin. There are one thousand and twenty-four of you. And only five will see the stars."

EIGHTEEN

Franny

Up the common room staircase, we walk. On the hardwood floor, we stop. Doors curve around a circular hallway, brass plates numbered: *1A, 2A, 3A, 1B . . .*

"So . . ." I face Mykal and Court's tired gazes while Influentials push past us, hurrying to their assigned dorms. Ours couldn't be farther away from one another: 3A for Mykal, 2G for me, 1P for Court.

I gather myself for a short goodbye, the weight of the competition compounding on my shoulders as fiercely as it does on Court. On Mykal. We huddle near one another, their heads dipped toward me.

I hesitate to separate.

They hesitate.

Since I dodged my deathday, I haven't spent a single night away from Mykal or Court. I didn't imagine it'd be this difficult. Leaving them has always seemed easier than staying.

"So," Mykal repeats before taking a step backward.

I force myself the other direction. Court watches Mykal and me turn our backs, the three of us splitting apart without another word. Our emotions speak louder.

I meander slowly along the hardwood, careful not to bump into fast-paced candidates. Emptiness festers, as though I'm missing something.

Someone.

Two of them.

Go back.

I halt and glance over my shoulder, the curved hallway shadowing my view. I've always been on my own. Relied on myself. But this call . . . this *longing* for someone else pounds at my body like a second and third heartbeat, electrifying the blood in my veins. Rushing to my head. Dizzying.

Go back.

I fight the call. Adding more and more distance. My stomach grumbles, then gurgles—empty but overly full. Which sounds mad in itself.

Rather than shoveling food in my mouth at supper, I tried to consume the five-course meal slowly. But before I even bit into leafy greens, porters carried out sweet pea soup and swept my salad dish away. It happened again and again.

To satiate me, Mykal and Court overate, filling themselves beyond full of lamb, garlic potatoes, gravy, and squash. Court also tried to eat a strawberry and Mykal nearly vomited. We're a true wobbling mess when it comes to our link.

3F . . . 1G . . .

I wonder how many bunk beds will be in each dorm. At the orphanage, I used to clamor for a bottom bunk, colliding hips and arms for the chance to be low to the ground.

I have no problem rooming with other people—I've done so all my life—but what if they're briny by what I do or say and it lasts for ages? I never had the chance to really befriend an Influential and I could easily botch that before it begins.

Passing 2G by accident, I shuffle back, the wooden door partially ajar. Instead of peeking inside, I just walk straight in—*gods.* There are no bunks.

Golden canopies drape over five humongous beds. All fitting snugly against paneled walls and consuming the small room.

Court briefly mentioned how his childhood bed in Yamafort had had a canopy. All to insulate him from the night's chill. I imagined canopies would look like the tarps from Bartholo's black market, not luxury that could exist within the Catherina Hotel.

My leather satchel waits on the furthermost left bed.

And I'm not alone here.

As I reach my possessions, an argument brews in front of the five beds and an armoire, hangers spilling out and luggage zipped open.

"I have more clothes that need to be hung than you do," a boy says matter-of-factly. "It's only fair that I take more room in the armoire." He unclasps an expensive watch that lies flat over his dark brown skin. Tall, with lean muscles, and dressed in stylish champagne-colored slacks and a wide-collared coat, he looks like he could pose for a fashion ad in Yamafort's newspaper.

A much shorter girl squares off with him, her fashion choice different than most here: black leather skirt-overalls, frilly shirt beneath. Her honey-blond hair cascades in messy, crinkled waves, molding her pale face. "You think you're being fair?"

He shuts his watch in a black case and assesses the clothes rack. "You're right. I should just take the entire armoire."

Barely anyone likes to share, I swear to the gods. I try to spy their names, but they've both removed their badges.

"Holy Wonders, you're actually being serious." She gapes. "I thought to myself, *Oh Gem, try to like him. Do not jump to conclusions based on his parentage. He may have a decent-sized head on his shoulders.* Instead, you're *exactly* how you appear. Big-headed. Conceited. *Snobbish.* What's more unfair is *you* being here at all. StarDust shouldn't play favorites."

The boy casually refolds a pair of slacks from his three-piece luggage set. "StarDust obviously doesn't play favorites."

She rests a hand on her hip. "And why's that?"

"Because if they did, I wouldn't be in a room with someone who talks to themselves. *Oh Gem,*" he mimics her high-pitched, youthful voice, "*that boy is so horribly mean to me.*" He mimes wiping his tears. "Little girl, why don't you go weep on your mother's shoulder?"

What a chump.

I breathe out an aggravated breath, crossing my arms. Forcing myself to lean on my bedpost. Even if I dislike him, I don't intend to draw attention to myself or join their stew. Anyway, I'd rather sleep with my satchel than mix my belongings with theirs.

He stares down at her with pompous hazel eyes.

She stares up at him with wild greens. "I'm not a little girl. I'm *fifteen.*"

"And I'm twenty-one." He tucks his folded slacks under his arm. "No matter what you say or do, I'll always defeat you."

Gem crouches and hurriedly gathers all the hangers on the floor. "Do you need these?"

"Yes." He extends a hand.

"Well now they're *mine.*"

My smile widens while Gem marches to her bed and chucks the hangers on the mattress.

The boy shoves his luggage in the armoire, procuring a toothbrush and paste. "None of you will last long enough to become comfortable, so take as many hangers as you want. They'll be mine in a week's time. Maybe less." He shuts the doors and then acknowledges me with a quick once-over before rolling his eyes.

I prickle. "You can't be so sure about that."

He twirls the toothbrush between his fingers. "I'm Kinden Valcastle. I'm more certain of how this'll play out than you'll ever be." He winks and saunters to a narrow door inside our room.

Kinden Valcastle.

I'm in a room with Court's older brother.

And the son of the Director of StarDust. I go cold and my mind races while Kinden fiddles with a broken brass knob. The door swings off its hinges, a sink, tub, and toilet on the other side.

Instead of using the bath without a door, he makes a concerted effort to slide over a mahogany privacy screen, commonly used by Influentials for dressing. Now it's a makeshift door that he hides behind.

I stay completely still. In frozen shock.

Sometimes I believe the memories Court gave me, all the ones with his little brother Illian, were accidents. He was equally surprised when they surfaced. As if his past lingers in the darkest, most painful crevices of his brain, and I grazed the depths. Out arose Illian.

Not Kinden.

"He's unequivocally insufferable," Gem mutters beneath her breath. "And I just met him." If Kinden hears this from behind the privacy screen, he ignores every word.

As I sit stiffly on my maroon quilt, I catch eyes with Gem.

"Thank the gods, another girl," she exhales, relieved, and then glides to her bed beside mine. Brushing the hangers off to take a seat.

"Is this all mine?" I ask, pointing to my bed that could fit three bodies comfortably. More people must be rooming here. Not just one per bed. Right?

"Of course it's all yours. They'd never make us sleep in the same bed with perfect strangers. Speaking of"—Gem stretches her hand—"I'm Gem." Beds so close, we easily clasp palms and shake, her grip sturdy but friendly, causing me to smile. "Gem Soarcastle."

Soarcastle. My lips drop. "You're—"

"Padgett Soarcastle's younger and more confrontational and chatty sister, yes." At the talk of Padgett, her smile illuminates her whole face. While mine vanishes completely.

For the shortest second, I thought I might find an ally in Gem, but if she's Padgett's sister, then she could be more calculating than what meets the eye.

I'm afraid I'll be so eager to discover someone like me, I'll forget that we're all different. We all have our motives and mine don't align with anyone but Court and Mykal's.

Remember that.

Defenses raised, I greet her: "Wilafran Elcastle. You're Maranilan, right?" I rarely drove to Maranil, the southernmost country landscaped by iced-over ocean, temps a little bit warmer, but not by much.

Maranilans always had less bills to pay Purple Coach drivers than Orrish and Altians. Last time I drove to the south, I was nine.

Wet sludge froze on my tires once I returned to Bartholo and I spent two days chipping it away.

"Maranilan through and through." Legs locked, she drums her kneecaps. "Though please tell me you're not the type to make fish jokes. If one more person wafts their nose at me like I smell of trout, I may scream."

My brows scrunch. "People do that?"

"To Maranilan girls and boys. All the time."

I guess I've been in the heart of Altia too long to notice the other three countries. "I wouldn't make fun of you," I assure Gem, hoping with every word I chose the most Influential-like phrasing.

"So you're Altian then." Gem nods to my name badge. "Let me guess." She squints. "You just graduated from university for . . . mechanical engineering."

I lick my lips, thankfully not chapped, and recall the backstory I created with Court. "I'm seventeen years, so still at university. I've been studying a little of everything, actually." "Keep it vague," Court had said. My back sweats even thinking about being challenged on the world's history, engineering, or aerospace.

"A little of everything," Gem ponders. "I should've done that at university. I was so bored with horticulture that I dropped out at thirteen. Padgett and I study on our own now. Most parents would throw a fit, but Mother had been the one to suggest becoming self-taught." She stares off sadly. "I'll miss her most. Are you leaving anyone behind?"

"Not really . . ." I think of all those who've died and all those who're still alive: Oron and Gustel, Purple Coach drivers who'd spit on me each morning. I'd walk by to choose a car for the day, and wet saliva would splat in my hair. "It's what we do here, chump," they'd laugh. I'd launch a thick wad back at their turds for faces.

They never stopped spitting.

And so neither did I.

"No one that I particularly *like* at least," I say more honestly.

"Understandable." She pulls off her polished boots. "There are many faces I'm happy to forget."

"Like who?" I pry more out of curiosity than strategy.

"All of my professors who said I'd amount to nothing in life." She takes a breath. " 'There goes that dropout, Gem Soarcastle,' they said. 'She'll never impact the world the way she dreams. If anything, she'll be no one. And nothing.' "

"Your professors sound like toads."

She laughs, full-bodied, shoulders jostling. "*Toads*. Holy Wonders, that's perfect. Extinct *toads*."

My brows arch. "Big warty ones."

Her laugh dies a little.

Mayday. I said *wart*. I stand and rummage through my satchel. I'm being obvious. Should I just sit down then . . . ?

I end up freezing in place while she examines the length of my body, my blouse tucked nicely into my slacks. Hair combed straight. Outwardly, I appear like an Influential. *You know this to be true, Franny.* I breathe in a stronger breath.

Gem asks, "Do you have a Fast-Tracker in your family?"

"A sister," I lie quickly. "She's dead."

"Did she have fun while she lived?"

I think about my orphanage friends and my lips curve, fond and happy. "So much."

The floorboards squeak and we turn together to see a freckled-faced boy trudging awkwardly into the room. I recognize him from the museum. Seifried. He clutches his arms timidly as he approaches a bed on the far right. Remembering his mother's farewell wedges a pit in my hollow stomach.

"Maranilan," Gem calls out in pride, noticing his name badge.

He hangs his head. "Father . . . he . . . he told me not to make friends." Seifried encloses himself within his canopy bed.

Don't make friends.

Gem and I exchange a wary look and we both mutually drift apart. She slips off her bed and unpacks her clothes into the armoire's drawers.

Kinden is still shrouded by the privacy screen, the faucet running.

No more public bathhouses.

No more poor plumbing.

It's hard to believe this is my new life. Not every aspect is an upgrade though. I have to consciously change my clothes in private. Just to dress in night slacks and a long-sleeved shirt, I use the canopy to shield me since Kinden has taken the sole screen. I stand on the mattress that oscillates as I shift my weight.

Do better, Franny.

Slacks off, I struggle with the buttons on the back of my blouse and huff. *Last one.* I free myself—not completely. Just when I think I've succeeded, there's a bra contraption.

I hear the *clap, clap* of boots. Nearing my bed. I pause, listening, and then the thick fabric of the canopy flings open.

Zimmer.

I startle at his presence. "You?"

"You." He startles just as strongly, recoiling a step.

"She was dressing in there!" Gem shouts. Abandoning the armoire, she charges Zimmer. With the heels of her palms, she thumps his chest until he backs up into the wall.

Zimmer raises his hands high, shoulders taller than Gem. "I didn't know anyone was in there, I swear on the gods. I thought it was my bed."

My face falls. "This is your room?"

"Yes," he says as smooth as any Influential. I wouldn't trust him, but we both seem horror-struck at the idea of sleeping so close, our intentions for entering StarDust a mystery to each other.

"Wilafran . . ." Gem blushes, embarrassed for me.

I look down at my body. Standing off-kilter on a mattress in nothing more than underwear and an itchy bra, I've been in much less in the view of many more eyes. While I cover myself with a pillow, Gem politely lowers her gaze.

Zimmer captures mine, his two soulful eyes burrowing through my core. As though knowing who I am. His lip hikes in a tense smile, *conflicted*. Pained.

Because I think he understands not caring about undressing or privacy. And that makes me more like him and him more like me.

Or maybe I'm hoping again. Hoping that someone out there is experiencing exactly what I am.

There is someone.

Court.

Mykal.

I miss them, I realize. Is it possible to miss someone after only an hour or two?

Zimmer tears himself away to find his bed beside Seifried's and Gem offers more privacy by returning to the armoire. I finish dressing and then tie my canopy back with the tassels. All the while stealing glances at Zimmer.

He steals even more.

I work myself up to approaching him without causing a stew. My neck swelters. Two tugs and I shrug off my fur coat.

Impulse kicks the back of my knees and I just *go*. I confront Zimmer by his bed, his satchel half open, floral-printed button-downs strewn over the quilt.

Clothes that I've seen older Influentials wear during leisure activities. Like indoor bowling. His few slacks are wrinkled . . . some stained. He could've stolen them, but by their poor state, I bet that he found them in a dumpster. I imagine Zimmer diving into the trash and my temper lowers to a dull simmer.

"What do you want?" he snaps.

There's so much I'd like to know, but I say what flies to my head first. "I wanted to know why someone of sixteen—"

"Nineteen."

I flinch. "What?"

"I can't help that I look younger. It's because of my build." Gangly. Bony. His scruffy ash-brown hair frames his angular jaw, youthful and bright-eyed.

"Then nineteen . . ."

Zimmer peeks over his shoulder like he'd rather be chatting with the wall than to me. That's fair.

Softly, I say, "I just wanted to know why you're here. At Star-Dust."

His eyes fall to me. "What makes you think I'd tell you a thing?"

"I know, all too well, that I deserve nothing from you." I drop my voice. "But for someone who made me a target at supper, I thought you'd want to explain yourself."

"I. Hate." He pushes his finger at my collarbone. "*You.*"

I grit my teeth, anger swelling faster than usual. *Mykal*—it's his hostility. He felt Zimmer's finger jab me.

I eye his name badge, pinned to an oversized suit jacket. "Zimmer *Creecastle.*" After I dodged my deathday, all I've done is try to cope with my surroundings. I turn. I wobble. I turn again and I'm maddened. I'm confused.

There are more questions than answers in this world and I'm so *tired* of not asking anything. So here I am, in front of Zimmer, asking something. And hoping.

Hoping. That I'm struck with the smallest, tiniest clarity.

Don't give up, Franny.

"Tell me why you're here," I say. "Anything. *Please.*"

His face twists. "You'd beg?"

I nod. I'll beg. I'll do almost anything for just one answer. Just one. "Please," I say again. I feel like the Franny Bluecastle who clawed at a Plexiglas bank window. Zimmer is behind the glass. Watching me, gripping the cord to the blinds. Prepared to snap them shut.

Please.

Please.

"Please," I say with all my heart.

Zimmer clasps my elbow and draws me toward his headboard, farther from Gem. We're both aware of Seifried, who's concealed by his canopy.

Tilting his head to me, Zimmer whispers, "That day at the Catherina Hotel . . ." He pauses, eyes reddening with much more than just hatred. "That day . . . I was *fired* for what you did."

My nose flares.

He drops his hand like he can't stand to touch me. "Is that not what you wanted to hear? You and your husband—or whoever he is—had me *fired* for losing a coat you never had and calling you out for overtime in a hotel room that *I* snuck you into."

My throat closes.

"I had that job since I was eight—I *loved* that job." He points passionately at his chest, tears welling in his bloodshot eyes. "I fykking loved it and you took it from me in one second."

My body shakes. "I'm sorry."

"You're sorry," he repeats, feverishly studying me to see if I'm lying.

"That's what I said," I say, heated, voice trembling. "I'm *sorry*." I jab my finger to his chest. "I'm sorry."

He inhales a pained breath, confusion warping his face. "Just . . . leave." I doubt he expected me to carry even a fragment of remorse, but I shouldn't have been alive that day. I shouldn't have been alive to destroy his passion. Or to ruin the little time he has.

I was on the fast track to death.

I wish—I wish more than he would—that I had just died when I was meant to. Now I just wonder what's out there for me. What am I supposed to do in the extra time I have? What is my real purpose in this world?

I'm nothing.

And then I'm something. I'm whole enough to amble back to bed, untie my canopy, crawl beneath the covers, and tuck my satchel next to me. Like another person sleeps close.

Lights shut off, the room bathed in darkness. Head on my feather-light pillow, hands folded on my belly, I shut my eyes and feel Mykal in a sweat, rolled on his side. Facing me. His muscled legs are tangled in his comforter, palms beneath his jaw.

He wants to smile, but his heavy lips turn down.

Court is upright, his forearms on his knees. Breath shallow, he murmurs softly. Lips moving like they're my lips. I distinguish the word. *Sleep*, he mouths.

Sleep.

Through our senses, he speaks to us.

Sleep.

I mouth, *All right.*

Mykal closes his eyes, his deep breath flooding me with comfort. Right before I doze off, my roommates speak.

"Night, little children," Kinden calls, his mattress squeaking as he climbs into bed.

Gem calls back, "May your dreams be nightmares, Kinden Valcastle."

"And may your dreams be my dreams," he replies, bed quieting. "Because none of you would last in my nightmares."

NINETEEN

Court

J ust ask me already," Mykal says to me, the three of us settled on velveteen seats inside StarDust's classroom auditorium, attendance mandatory as noted on the main bulletin. More and more candidates arrive, but the oak stage is empty, and a projector screen is blank.

"Why are your cheeks burning?" I finally ask Mykal after staring for well over a minute.

Franny sighs heavily between us, trying to alleviate the foreign pressure on her chest. I may be anxious, but not as much as she is right now. She worries that we're about to take a series of written exams. And the threat of expulsion looms over everyone.

Mykal bows forward, eyes fixed on mine. "I said one damned thing to all my goat-brained roommates at breakfast and you know what they did? They *laughed* for a good fifteen minutes."

That's why he lost his appetite? I thought my stomach—*his* stomach roiled from the sip of orange juice I drank. "What did you say to them?" I ask more curtly than I intend.

Mykal grinds his teeth, thinking that I care more about appearances than his feelings.

My ribs tighten. "I didn't mean it that way."

"Yeah," he mutters.

I care about your feelings, Mykal. More than you'll ever know. Why can't I just say it? Instead I stare at his roasted cheeks, my concern flaring, my fingers to my lips. Hating that he's upset. And hurt.

"I said to pass the griskin," Mykal says suddenly and quietly, "and they snickered like I spoke a dirty word." My heart falls.

"Griskin?" Franny frowns.

"Pork loin," I define the word that only Grenpalish use. A word that I learned from him. "Think worse of them, not yourself, Mykal." I try to cheer him, my voice low as more candidates enter. "They laughed because they had no knowledge of a word that *you* did. You know twice as much as they do."

"I dunno about that," he says deep beneath his breath.

I stretch my arm over Franny to squeeze his shoulder. He eases only a fraction, but it'll have to be enough for now.

Franny fiddles with the bow of her blouse, distant and anxious again. Unless we talk about Mykal, she's been avoiding me. *I don't care.*

I do care.

I care more than I can quantify. It's why I ask, "What's wrong?"

Now she picks at her nails, downcast and slumping.

I rub my lips. "Is it about . . . ?" *Vorkter.* Our last argument.

"No." Franny straightens, especially as the auditorium floods with watchful eyes. "Kinden Valcastle is in my dorm."

I stare unblinkingly ahead. *Kinden Valcastle is here.*

"Who?" Mykal whispers and Franny murmurs, "His older brother."

Outwardly I am stone. Inwardly my past crushes my lungs; I rock back, then forward. Face in my hands, screaming. Crying.

I'm stone. I can't blink. Can't move. Memories scrape my brain. Flying past like unburied razor blades.

Mykal always tells me that I carry a thousand miseries, but not all my memories are bad. Most are good—*so good*—but they're shaded and clouded in dull gray. They belong to someone else. Someone worthy of holding them. Touching them.

I'm not that boy anymore.

But I return there. For this single moment, I'm eight.

I arrived home from my training at the hospital past dinnertime, exhausted and spent. As a Wonder, I was expected to *be* so much more. Where Influentials were lightly pushed toward an education at three years of age, Wonders were shoved full-force. In-fluential children could play outside, take breaks and naps, but I was required to open another book. Read a little more. Study a little more. *Fill your Wonder brain a little bit more.*

Open your eyes.

Ignore the pounding in your head.

Stay awake. Stay alert.

Be the very damn best.

I sped through the core curriculum in two years, pushed through science courses in three, and jumped into medicine when I was eight.

Mentally, I clawed to catch up with every older Influential. Mentally, I scraped my way to the top. And yet, I loved medicine. I could never complain because I *loved* every book I read. Every fact I learned. Every single time I walked the hallways of a hospital.

I chose medicine. I was not forced to, but I had to sacrifice a childhood for that future. Because I was supposed to die at fifteen.

I was so drained most nights, but *one night* surfaces again. All these years later, this *one night* speeds toward me.

On the kitchen counter, my foil-wrapped plate sat cold. Right next to a small antiquated television that played reruns of a corny game show. The host cackled too loudly and the contestants won romantic dates instead of bills.

We kept our only television in the kitchen. Our father liked watching Altia News while he cooked and no one argued with that logic.

While my mother and father had gone to bed, Kinden waited up for me, lounging at the table. Four years older, his hazel eyes lifted from the television and sank into my features.

"You look tired," he said.

Exhaustion was my constant companion. Always pulling at me. Talking took too much effort, so I fell onto a tufted chair and chewed on cold lamb.

Kinden leaned back, watching. He was twelve, but I'd already surpassed him in studies. Some would say that I even flew past him in life.

His chair squeaked, so he bent forward and nodded to me. "You know how Father always says 'Wonders are blessed by the gods'?"

I nodded back, sipping a glass of goat's milk. *Wonders are blessed by the gods* had been one of my father's favorite phrases. I can almost feel the weight of his hand on my shoulder, gripping affectionately. A proud smile overcoming him. Tauris Valcastle adopted me because I was a Wonder.

Because I was blessed by the gods.

My belief in the gods ended there. I never thought of myself as holy, so I decided that the gods did not exist. I was just an ordinary boy who'd never become an old man.

Kinden shook his head a few times, his halfhearted smile more pained than awed, and I listened to him. I looked up to him.

And he told me, "I wish Father would stay up late enough to see you come home. Maybe then he wouldn't think so highly of you." Forearms on the table, he leaned forward, sincerity bursting in his eyes. "Your value has an expiration date. *You* have an expiration date. They will break you, little brother. Your spirit will die before you even do. I see it waning every night." He laughed a weakened laugh of disbelief at how this world worked. At how much divided him from me. "And yet, you will be lauded and praised."

Kinden took a sip from my milk and then casually changed the subject to the newest opera opening on the weekend.

"They will break you, little brother."

I loved him. Kinden's unfailing honesty reaffirmed what I always believed. I am not greater than anyone. I am not *better*. Kinden saw me as fragile before I even cracked and I loved that I wasn't a blessed Wonder or a physician in his presence.

I was just his little brother.

Before we headed to bed, he said to me, "Wake me before you leave. I did not appreciate you letting me sleep in, you little—"

"Fine." I nearly smiled. "Will you wait with me for a Purple Coach?"

"I always do." Kinden wanted to squeeze in as much time with me as he could. He thought I'd die in seven years. Really, I gave him just two more.

Truthfully, I never believed I'd see him again.

I wake from this stupor that burns my eyes. The StarDust auditorium is louder than before, almost every seat occupied. Searching for him, I swing my head right and left, and I freeze.

Diagonally across and seven rows down, Kinden laughs, his polished boot perched on the back of a seat, riling the person who avoids his rubber sole. He's so much older, but he has the same brash confidence that sits uneasily with many.

"What if he recognizes Court?" Mykal whispers to Franny.

I acknowledge them and they both jump in surprise. I was drifting for a while. "It's the same as my father," I say beneath my breath. "Even if they recognize my features, they won't believe it's me. I have a different name and I'm supposed to be dead."

No one dodges a deathday. It would be irrational for Tauris or Kinden to believe that I did. More likely, they'll think I coincidentally *look* like a son or brother they once had.

Mykal cracks a crick in his neck. "So what're you planning? Becoming his friend—"

"No," I cut him off because I can't fathom speaking to Kinden in any capacity. "I act like he's nothing to me. I'll evade him at all costs."

Franny nods, head hanging with a pang of hurt that I don't understand. Then she massages her neck, but Mykal has the sore muscle, so he tries kneading his shoulder.

Elbowing Franny, he whispers, "I'll be the one visiting your room, you realize. I need familiar company." Mykal reads her emotions far better than I can, and only now, the realizations suddenly well my throat. By avoiding Kinden, I avoid Franny's room altogether.

I just mortared another wall between us.

Franny elbows back. "You would love the lighting in my room, I bet. Great bulbs."

His humor lifts his lips and heart. "How big?" he teases. "And what's the wiring like? I don't do well with cords."

I rub my tense jaw. Somewhere in the past couple of months, I missed out on their jokes. I have no idea why lightbulbs and cords cause both to sport pleased smiles.

Abruptly, I interject into their conversation, "You don't want me visiting your room anyway."

Franny bears every sliver of emotion in her face. Each one kisses her lips, her nose, her chin, her cheeks. Pulling and cinching and frowning. I see it all.

I feel it all.

"That's not true," she says hotly. "I'd want you to visit me if you could." Maybe part of her believes I wouldn't, even if I could, and that's why she's hurt.

Franny stares ahead and adjusts her posture. "We should focus," she says, using my usual phrase seriously.

Focus. I try, but I glance curiously at Franny a few more times. While she's unconcerned, our stagnant friendship, or lack thereof, plagues me. She deserves so much more empathy than the coldness I've given her—and yet, I find myself leaving the wall intact.

Amelda strolls onto the stage, a bounce in her energetic step. One thousand and twenty-four candidates quiet down.

Amelda taps her bulbous microphone. "Is this working? Can you all hear me?"

"Yes," the crowd responds in waves.

"Good." Amelda paces the length of the stage. "I begin with this: Be your best because StarDust is looking for the *very* best of our world."

The best in what: science, medicine, mathematics, athletics, art, or something else? She doesn't clarify.

"We're looking for the thirty best candidates for StarDust. If you underperform, we won't hesitate to expel you at any time. That includes today." Amelda halts in the center of the stage and takes a robust breath. "We begin with a written exam."

Franny sinks in her chair, gripping her armrests tightly.

I place my palm on the top of her hand. An instinct.

Her head turns, but I don't meet the question in her gaze. The *why?* I can't answer. I don't know *why*.

I just let my hand cloak hers.

She eases a little.

"The exam covers a fundamental understanding of our universe that you all should know." Amelda clears her throat. "After the exam, you will be given class schedules where your performances will be monitored by the StarDust directors. Think of this as university where the courses are more demanding and your chances for expulsion are much greater."

Mykal blows out a heavy breath, his stomach caving in.

He'll be fine, I want to believe.

Amelda tucks her microphone beneath her arm and unzips a purse snapped around her waist. She procures a stack of indigo cards and then adjusts, microphone in hand again.

"If you're lucky enough, if you've lasted weeks and months on end, these will be your final exam." She fans the cards and raises them. "Later today, you'll be given one card. Each card has a corresponding word—and that word belongs to you and you alone. Show your card to others and there are great *disadvantages* in the final exam. Keep your card a secret and there are immense *advantages*. But learn the cards of your peers and you just may succeed."

She stops there, not explaining what the final exam entails. Only that we must find a way to discover the other candidates' cards. Even though it'd be a "great disadvantage" for them to share theirs.

"And so it begins," Amelda singsongs and trots down the few stairs. As she passes out exam packets, the wrinkled woman named Dessa replaces Amelda on stage.

Everyone begins to flip their desk trays and then Dessa clicks a tiny remote. Behind her frame, blackness and little glittering orbs project on the screen. *Space. Stars.*

Dessa puts the microphone against her lips. "Do not open the packet until instructed—you, in the far left corner. Red shirt. I see you." Heads whip, bodies shift, and we all settle uncomfortably.

I'm not worried about my skill set. I think of Franny. And Mykal. *They'll be fine.* I wish I could feel something stronger than doubt.

Packets on our desks, turned upside down, and pens between fingers, we wait.

Franny exhales, "Gods be with me."

"Flip," Dessa commands.

Papers rustle and I quickly read the directions: *Look at the screen. Answer each question in the time allotted.* The packet is just numbers and blank spaces for our answers. Franny and Mykal will have no time to skip around and process the questions.

"Question one," Dessa calls out, lifting my attention to the screen.

Blanketed by outer space, the projector zooms in on five spherical planets and a sun. Simple outlines, no topographic distinctions or characteristics in the image.

"In order of nearest to farthest from the sun, list our four sister planets and our planet. Please draw a star next to the planet everyone here resides on."

This should be one of the easiest questions. All the planets are called Saltare, but they carry a reference number that correlates to the sphere's size. Saltare-1 is the largest planet, twice the breadth of the sun, whereas Saltare-5 is a dot on the diagram.

Unsure of how much time we're allowed, I hurriedly list them in the correct order, my pen flying across the paper.

Saltare-5
Saltare-1
Saltare-2

Saltare-4
Saltare-3

I draw a tiny star next to Saltare-3: average in size but farthest from the sun—and therefore the coldest.

That is our planet.

Looking up, people continue scrawling. While Franny treads slowly, seemingly certain about her answer, Mykal second-guesses himself, hesitating to write a single word.

Sweat beads across his hairline and he uses his biceps to wipe his forehead.

My pulse pounds and I think, *I sense him.*

He senses me; why can't we use that to our advantage? I've concentrated more on the difficulties than the values of linking, but being connected to Mykal and Franny has significant worth. More than we even realize.

I tap my desk a few times to gain their attention. Drawing their senses toward mine. When their focus trains on me, I begin to trace my answers with my fingertip.

Franny's lips part and she scratches out one of her answers.

Mykal concentrates for a long second before writing.

"Question two." Dessa clicks her remote. Outer space whizzes away from the Saltare planets to somewhere farther in the universe. Homing in on one giant sphere, she says, "Name the planet that was taken from us. And what year did we flee to the five planets?"

Quickly, I write, *Andola, 2450.* I outline my answer for them, but Dessa soars through questions much faster than before. By the time we reach the fifteenth question, Mykal stalls about five behind me. Franny is nearly caught up.

"Question sixteen," Dessa announces. "Name the person who invented the device used to read deathdays." *Rosanna Rolcastle.* Possibly the most influential woman in the world. A biomedical engineer who took thousands of pages of theoretical hypotheses over deathdays and made it into a reality. Now we have Death Readers.

I can't remember if I explained this to Franny, but I'm sure I mentioned deathday histories to Mykal once or twice. Still, he lags behind.

I run my fingers over my page, trying to identify each question for Mykal by touch alone. His frustration grinds inside. I can't make this any simpler. I don't know how.

Franny tries to whisper answers under her breath, but she stops when a little boy whirls his head backward and casts a glare.

In an hour, the exam ends.

Mykal sweats through his shirt, and no matter how much Franny and I say that he did well, he just shakes his head vigorously and leaves us with, "It's what I expected of myself."

My heart breaks into three.

TWENTY

Mykal

As my pa would say, "Got through that by the skin of yer teeth, Mykal." That initial exam ranked me as part of the bottom eight hundred candidates. Out of a thousand. Luckily, they expelled only the first hundred or so. Even cheating, I just scraped by, tail between my legs.

Franny did about average, but Court—he made a perfect score out of two hundred questions. I was proud of her and him.

But as weeks fly by and I shuffle from jet propulsion classes to fluid mechanics to flight dynamics, I'm more and more ashamed of myself.

Nothing makes much sense. Three-hour-long lectures throb my head, spewing words that I can hardly pronounce. Chalk scratches blackboards and all the candidates exit rooms, light on their feet. Like they ingested nursery rhymes.

My stomach lurches, sick as I believe, *This is it for me. I'll be expelled right here. At this very moment.*

I don't celebrate or breathe easy when I realize that I'm still here. Tomorrow is another class that I can't comprehend with people that find me brainless and dull.

Outside of the classrooms and simulations, it's not better. In three weeks, I gained two enemies in my dorm for spilling bathwater and forgetting to mop up. I overheard them whispering last night. Theorizing why I haven't been sent home yet.

"He's friends with the top of the class. What's his name? Court Idlecastle?"

"StarDust needs some muscle, obviously. That's all he's good for."

"That has to be it."

Their wretched guesses are as good as mine.

Midafternoon, I'm on time for my mandatory physical with the Director of Health, but he's not here yet.

Paintings of bones hang on the clinic's periwinkle walls and strange metal devices line the sleek countertops. I squat to inspect a jar of flat wooden sticks. "What is that?" I mumble to myself and peer into a container of white . . . puffballs?

Food, maybe?

I pluck one out, squeeze the woolly substance, and then lick—*not* food. Grimacing, I return the puffball.

Someone smacks their lips. *Franny.* Confused about what I'm doing, she must think I'm losing my damned mind. Licking strange things.

An odd-looking lounge chair is bolted in the middle, lined with thin paper. What in all of three hells . . . ?

I choose the most sensible seat: the stool on four wheels.

It goes without saying, but Grenpale has no physicians or hospitals or any of these strange instruments.

Court has taught me a whole lot about the world beyond my homeland, but he rarely spoke of medicine and everything he once loved. He skipped these details as if they disturbed his mind, and there's nothing more I desire for him than *peace.*

Now that I see what a clinic looks like, I wonder if Court used to touch those puffballs and wield these instruments with great, wise understanding. He was just a little boy alongside grown ladies and men.

The door swings open. I watch the Director of Health examine a clipboard with great interest. Out of all the directors' introductions from the first dinner, I remember Dr. Raf Duncastle the most. For no other reason than he's old—older than anyone I've ever laid eyes on.

Wrinkles sag heavily beneath his sunken eyes, little ridges

stretching his thin lips. Bronze skin folds in lines across his fore-head and right below sit bushy gray brows. Bones pucker from his frail fingers. Hands splotched with dark marks like large freck-les. And I think, *Age did all of that?*

The oldest in Grenpale is twenty-nine years and most every-one appears weather-beaten. I'd no idea that age could change a person as much as the cold wind.

"Mykal Kickfall." He raises his head with a fading smile, gaze dropping to the stool under my ass. "You may take a seat on the bed."

My face heats. And I jump off.

This is the strangest bed in the whole damned world. I hope he knows that. Climbing on top, the paper crinkles, and I go still as can be. A grunt sticking in my throat.

The stool creaks as he sits carefully. Too old to go any faster, I suppose. Dr. Duncastle rolls closer. "You're the first *fall* I've seen so far. I believe only two or three of you are still here."

I take long pauses to think about my words. "I'm not surprised there aren't more." So few of us even exist, and unless someone points out the fact that I'm a *fall*, I forget that my name is differ-ent than most.

Every crease of his face shifts with his smile. "It'd be good luck for the department to have a *fall* among them." He dips his hand in his white coat pocket. "My colleagues and I believe at least one of you will be a part of the final thirty. Just between you and me, we have a little bet going to see which."

"Save your bills and don't choose me." I eye the spool of yellow tape in his hand.

"Stretch your arms." He stands and I cautiously extend each arm. He whips out the yellow tape, numbers ticked in black ink, and he starts measuring my wingspan. "Too late."

I shake my head once. "Too late for what?"

Dr. Duncastle jots numbers on the clipboard. "Too late, I've already placed my bet on you." As if I need more pressure and *more* people expecting *more* of me.

As he measures my biceps, legs, and width of my neck, I say, "You must like losing bills."

Setting the tape aside, he smiles. "I like underdogs."

Underdogs? I dunno if I should be offended or appreciative. I'll be asking Court later.

When the doctor checks my hearing and eyesight, I try not to jerk away or flinch, and then he sinks onto his stool with a robust sigh, out of breath from standing for a short while.

"Excellent vision," he notes, scribbling. "Hearing is adequate." Dr. Duncastle snaps on disposable gloves and wheels near again. I stiffen as he clutches my jaw and inspects my face. "Did you have a previous injury to your nose?"

"I cracked my nose at thirteen . . ." I trail off, not about to describe the scuffle I had with an ornery muskox.

"It healed quite poorly."

I laugh. "You can call me ugly. That's fine."

He blushes, but truth being, I didn't mean to shame him. I don't mind being harsh in anyone's eyes.

He says, "I only meant with proper care, the bone could have been set straight."

Maybe I shouldn't speak.

"Do you smoke?"

I shrug. "Sometimes . . ." I grow hot as his pen zips across his papers. "Is that a problem?"

"Not unless it hinders your performance." Next, he instructs me to lower my jaw and he peers at my crooked teeth with a puzzled look. Then he writes without a word.

"What?" I have to ask.

"Your molars are abnormally sharp."

I try to seem surprised. "That's"—*What's the right word?*—"peculiar." It's not. I filed my back teeth into points when I was seven so I could better chew the bristled fat off animals.

"It is," he agrees. "Were you an athlete at university? You outsize many of the other men and women here."

"I played some"—*Think of an Altian sport fast, Mykal*—"iceling."

"Difficult sport."

"It is." I use his words.

"Almost finished." He rises, places the clipboard aside. "I'll draw some blood and then we'll be done. Sounds good?"

Like most everything, I have no idea what *drawing blood* means. I nod with a forced smile. "Good."

I leave shell-shocked and woozy. Wandering dazedly back to my dorm. Only waking when I notice Court, arm propped against the wall, outside my door.

Glued there, his eyes cast on the floorboards as if willing himself not to pace.

"Heya." I kick his boot with mine.

Instantly, he straightens off the wall and clasps my hand. "I should've told you the doctor would most likely take blood samples."

I expel a knotted breath. "It's all right." I check over my shoulder, seemingly no one in the circular hallway, but I lower my voice anyway. "Is that what you did at a hospital?"

He glances over my shoulder for passersby. Two young boys giggle, hardback books held to their breastbones, and they slip into their dorm opposite mine.

"Most of the time, yes. I mostly worked in the trauma unit." He pauses like he wants to say more, but he's not sure if he's able. "For someone who has no concept of physicians and healthcare, I can understand how—"

"I'm all right," I say again, but I almost smile at his concern. "For a second there, I thought I'd punch him."

"Me too."

I laugh. I did flinch as the needle neared my arm. A gut reaction, but Dr. Duncastle said lots of people are scared of them.

We slip inside my dorm room. Roommates gone.

Court reaches into his black slacks and turns out the pockets.

I plop onto the edge of my bed, quilt not as finely tucked as all the others. Gold-stitched pillows sit off-kilter too.

"What're you doing?" I ask and eye the clock. "Don't we have a gravity simulation soon?"

"In ten minutes." Court knows the time without looking. And then he reveals . . .

"What the . . . ?" I spring off the bed and step toward the splayed indigo cards in his hands. At least *forty* of them.

My smile spreads and I jump in pleasure, hugging Court roughly to my chest. "You know how much I like you, you little crook?" I kiss his cheek and hold his face with two callused hands. More than anything, I needed this right here.

Hope.

Tall above me, his gaze dips to my lips, his stern jaw beneath my palms. *Closer. Closer.* The link tugs at us.

We stay put, but I fear nothing at this moment. Nothing at all.

"I stole them this morning," he says in his smooth but biting voice. "We can meet in the library later tonight and memorize them with Franny."

Nodding, I let go of Court and inspect a few cards. The front is plain, but vibrant paint splashes the back, this one crimson red. The drawing is unmistakable, but even so, tiny script below reads: *Heart.*

A heart.

Easily, I recall my own card, given to me weeks ago. I saw the painted image, pinkish-red hues bleeding into green, and I wanted to chuck the silly card out the window. My card, my word, is *strawberry*. A nauseating, overly sweet *strawberry*.

Even with a vague warning about disadvantages, we shared our cards with each other. Too trusting not to.

Franny had a good laugh at my strawberry until she flipped over her card.

Bear.

She expected something fancier. Like *crown* or *earrings*. "Let's trade," she joked, wafting her card at my cheek. I pushed her face. Then she pushed mine right back.

Court couldn't care less about his own card. *Torch.* Flames painted on a wooden club. All that time, he must've been pondering ways to see everyone else's cards.

Now that he stole them, we should have an advantage for the final exam down the line.

The training room is righteously ugly. Metallic walls and concrete floors, gray and more gray. Monstrous, silver apparatuses and mechanical boxes landscape the long stretch of sterile space.

Most everyone is dressed in collared shirts or blouses and slacks. A hundred or so candidates linger in the open center. Careful not to touch any equipment.

Court theorized that our schedules are random and candidates are rotated to certain lectures and tasks at different times. All three of us haven't been assigned a single class together.

Until now.

We join the group the same time Franny weaves through bodies to reach us, and then we stand together by a chair contraption that I've heard spins candidates rapidly upside down. That better not be a part of today's gravity simulation.

Franny's eyes sweep my frame. "Earlier—"

"I'm fine." I use the proper sounding word. I rest my arm on her shoulder. "Where were you when I was at the clinic?"

Franny acknowledges Court with a weak, tense smile.

He nods in greeting.

Then to me, she says, "Seminar on emergency landing protocols. I tried to pay attention, but I knew something was wrong." Fire in her brown eyes, she rakes her short nails through her flat black hair. "Should I go talk to someone for you?"

I wear a crooked smile. "And what will you be saying?"

"*Don't poke my friend with a needle and make him fainty.* And I may stomp a few times."

Court side-eyes her at the word *fainty*.

"Oh you'll be stomping?" I shuffle to the side. "Let's see how."

Franny tries not to smile and plasters on a sizzling scowl. "I'm serious." *I know.* I'm just not used to being the one that needs so much comforting.

"He's fine," Court assures her and then asks if anyone was expelled at her seminar.

"Five candidates. They quizzed me at the end and luckily, I"—she mouths, *cheated*—"off of Symons. I bet he'd burst a blood vessel if he found out." Her eyes ping to a cluster of Orrish candidates by a water fountain. Symons and Sel among them.

"Probably," Court agrees. "You did well though."

She fixes her skewed blouse. "I did, didn't I?"

Court tilts his head. "That was where you say *thank you*." Since he rarely seeks gratitude, he reminds Franny only due to etiquette and appearances.

Franny smiles a bit more. "My roommate said that I should be proud of my successes." Must be Gem. She's grown close to the young Soarcastle sister, but we sense Franny's caution at times, so I don't concern myself over their fledgling friendship.

"*Be careful,*" Court emphasizes.

"I *am,*" she emphasizes right back.

Wrapping my arm around their shoulders, I hug them to my sides and nod to what the Orrish candidates point toward. A yellow door labeled *G-Accelerator (Do Not Enter)*.

What lies through that door could be my undoing.

TWENTY-ONE

Mykal

n the event that Saga's anti-grav shields fail, you must be able to handle high levels of gravitational acceleration called a *g*." I try my best to listen, but Tauris Valcastle's voice booms out of an intercom system within the g-accelerator. The glaringly white circular room is lined with fifty bolted chairs, harnesses attached.

We were split into two groups. And told to dress in an emergency g-suit and to strap ourselves in a metal seat.

Zipped from crotch to neck, my black g-suit fits me too snugly. Made for someone with less muscle. To worsen my wretched luck, a familiar lady nimbly sits beside me.

Dark hair tied with a pink ribbon, Padgett Soarcastle stares intently at me. Waiting to capture my hard gaze.

Ten times I've fallen for this ruse. I could bang against the headrest. Frustrated. Since the first day, our schedules have been matching, and every day thereafter, she's chosen to be right next to me.

Not out of fondness. Padgett has picked me out as the slowest goat, the one scraping helplessly behind others to reach a mountain peak. I'm falling.

And she's ready below with an ax and an arrow.

Earlier, I prayed for a familiar face like Court or Franny. But both were placed in the second group. The gods enjoy toying with me.

"We'll proceed after everyone settles in," Tauris says. I whip my head left and right. Searching for his voice. Acting a fool again.

My face contorts at the hellish intercom and bulky cameras screwed into the ceiling. How no one else finds those disturbing, I dunno.

I dunno anything.

"Six hundred and eighty-three," Padgett says to me.

Don't eat her bait.

I grind my teeth and then spit out, "Six hundred what?" Court is right. I can't shut my mouth.

"Candidates remaining." Padgett buckles her safety harness, tightened to her thin frame.

"Why tell me that?" I ask in an incensed growl.

"I've said this before," she says smoothly, "and I'll repeat the same words until you believe them. I want to share information with you."

I trust nothing that escapes her lips. Leaning toward her, I say lowly, "Why me?"

Padgett skims my features with rapid haste. "You're peculiar. I think you recognize that you're peculiar, and your peculiarity intrigues me."

I scratch at my head. "Are you sure you don't just want my card?" For the better of three weeks, Padgett has implied that she'd like to "swap indigo cards" and examine mine.

Padgett crosses her ankles. "I want to share information."

"Which includes cards?"

"Yes," she says bluntly.

Court's warnings are engrained too deep. I decline her offer and mention that I need to concentrate.

She's about to press further, but the director's voice grows.

". . . loss of vision may occur, and some of you will experience loss of consciousness."

I start securing my harness. Pulling at the straps and buckles over my bulky chest. *Gods bless.* They don't reach.

I need slack. Yanking for more. The two metal ends won't meet. My brows knot. Do I ask for help or will they just be expelling me on the spot?

Hurriedly, I try to wrench tighter. To suck in a breath. *Be smaller, thinner.* It's not working. I grit my teeth. I shift and dig my shoulders into the seat.

". . . don't be afraid if you lose consciousness . . ."

While I tug at the straps, my head whirls. For Franny and Court's sake, I can't be passing out during this simulation. When we found Franny in the Bartholo alleyway, she was limp and unconscious, which caused wooziness in Court and me.

Candidates start looking my way. Chuckling.

Snickering.

Padgett stays silent and watches my distress.

I dip my head, nose flaring. This isn't working. Thinking quickly, I wrap both straps around the armrests and my wrists. Binding me to this damned chair.

Please, gods, I like my arms. Don't let them rip off.

"As we expose you to more g's, blood will flow out of your brain. We will begin at one g, and then we'll increase you to nine g. If you lose consciousness before seven g, you'll be expelled." Tauris orders us to practice a quick g-straining maneuver before we start.

I flinch as the chairs mechanically recline. My stomach twists. The g-accelerator room lets out a groan, like air gurgling through a tunnel.

Godsblessgodsbless. At first, I breathe heavily through my nose. Other candidates no longer jeer at me. Their eyes dart unsurely around the room.

With a high-pitched screech, the whole room rotates in a slowly accelerating circle.

What in three hells!

"Oh gods," a little lady cries. A few more candidates complain about sickness.

Heaviness pushes painfully on my ribs. Violent pressure like several bears collapsing on my body. Suffocating. Straps cut into my wrists. I wince, jaw clenched.

"Three g," Tauris calls.

We whirl faster. More and more pressure mounts. Pushing my body backward. Shoulders slam against the chair.

"Breathe," he instructs. "Remember g-straining!"

I breathe rapid, short spurts. Exhaling less often than I inhale. Flexing my muscles, contracting my abdomen and legs in taut, burning bands.

I'm not ready to die.

"Five g."

Breathe. Breathe. Breathe! I'm crushed by an invisible force, and in my concentration to remain alert, I lose sense of the director's voice. Vision fogging, I fight for air in my compacted lungs. Veins protruding in my neck, heart on fire—I *breathe*.

And then my world darkens.

"I'll give you all a second to collect yourselves," Tauris says through the intercom. "You may unbuckle but do not leave the seats."

Blinking awake, I massage my wrists. Deep red indents on my skin. That'll be bruising in no time. *Franny. Court.*

I fainted and that surely affected them. I aggressively shove off my seat. Padgett unclips her harness, and I have no heart to inspect the other candidates.

Failure weighs on my chest more than any damned g could. Gripping my kneecaps, hunched, I listen keenly.

"Kinden Valcastle," Tauris says loudly.

My head jerks to Kinden who stands across from me. Stretching his arms, he feigns a yawn and smiles pompously.

I asked Court if I'd like his older brother, and he said, "No one likes Kinden at first sight."

In that regard, I thought we'd be similar, but I've come to discover the most I share with Kinden Valcastle is the place we stand. We're cabbage and onion, two different vegetables growing in the same garden.

I'm afraid that I'm the one rotting.

". . . he's the only one to stay conscious at nine g," Tauris declares, much to Kinden's pleasure. He dusts his shoulders like we're the dirt. "Eighteen of you failed to reach seven g. When I call your name, you're to pack your belongings and leave through the museum's entrance."

Court's father starts listing out names, and I wait and wait and wait for *Mykal Kickfall*. Boys burst into tears, ladies yell in displeasure, and hands cover faces. Hearts are breaking. Dreams crushed.

I wait and wait and wait.

"Sel Ravelcastle."

My neck creaks at that familiar name. The thin boy gapes despondently at the floor in shock. So am I. He's articulate and tough-skinned. I would've rather seen Symons leave before Sel.

I raise my head to the intercom, but no other candidates are called.

"Congratulations to the rest of you. You lasted beyond seven g."

Got through that by the skin of yer teeth, Mykal. Next time, I may not be so lucky.

TWENTY-TWO

Franny

Late that night I sit cross-legged on my bed and scribble in my notebook. The door swings open and a downtrodden Gem trudges into the dorm, shoulders bent and head hanging.

Knowing she had the late-night grav session, my face falls. "You failed?" *You should be glad, Franny.* One less candidate can only strengthen my standing, but I like Gem. I tried to add distance and speak to her less, but she didn't care if I talked little or not at all.

When she notices that I miss breakfast, she brings me muffins. She offers to study with me when I do poorly in class, and I like listening to her wild tales about crafting electronics from scratch with her older sister.

She's as strong-willed as she is kind. During a talk about archaic telephones, Symons had told Gem, *"No one can build a telephone."* Pieces of wiring and metal are scattered on Gem's quilt, determined to prove that she *can.*

She eats daintily, blushes at most nudity, and combs her honey-blond hair a thousand strokes before bed. I detect no sinister qualities, no bad intentions.

I can be upset if she leaves, can't I? Setting my journal aside, warmth leaks out of my face.

Gem stops in the middle of our dorm and animates all at once, throwing her arms jubilantly. "I passed! Just barely, but I passed." She puts a hand to her heart. "Your face . . ."

I'm too emotive, too caring. Hopping off my bed, I say, "You tricked me well."

Gem perches her hands on her wide hips. "My first successful trick. We have more to celebrate then."

I hesitate, hanging on to the wooden bedpost. *How do Influentials celebrate?* "What kind of celebration do you have in mind?"

Gem drums her lips with two fingers. "We could toast, but I'm not fond of liqueur, and my mother says toasting with water brings bad fortune. Any suggestions?"

Mayday. I look upward at the gods for a brilliant idea because all that runs through my mind: *Juggernaut, bedding, more drugs, and definitely ale.* "Dancing?" I say impulsively, my gut lurching.

Gem gasps. "I love dancing!"

Thank the gods.

Keeping a foot of space between us, she suddenly splays a hand on my shoulder and one on my waist. "Padgett always leads . . . do you know how?"

"No." This is not the "dancing" I had in mind. "I actually never learned to dance like this." At her alarmed surprise, I quickly lie, "My Fast-Tracker sister taught me how to dance."

"Oh." Gem drops her hands and steps back. "Well, how did she dance?"

At first I waver, unsure if I should show Gem, but what's the harm if she believes my imaginary sister is the Fast-Tracker and I'm the Influential?

So I let go completely. Impulsively. With reckless desire. I thump my head every which way, shuffling side to side, pumping my arms up and down. I shake my straight hair, laughter in my chest.

Gem, enjoying a challenge, begins mimicking my frenzied movements. A joyful smile enveloping her round face.

Until we're two girls. Dancing to the rhythm of our success.

Two knocks freeze our limbs and our boots thud to a standstill.

Our heads swerve to Zimmer, his knuckles to the door frame, a knowing brow quirked at me. I'd be more threatened if deep dark circles didn't shadow his eyes. He yawns into his arm, his floral-printed shirt hanging loose over khaki slacks.

Sleep has not been kind to Zimmer, but I don't know what's been keeping him awake.

"We were dancing like Wilafran's sister." Gem pats down her tousled hair. "Wasn't it wild?"

"Wilafran's sister," he says with faint disbelief and shuts the door behind him. Zimmer props his body against the armoire. "Right, *that* sister. The one with blue and green hair." He waves at his nose. "Piercings . . . *three*, to be exact. A tiny brow one, a lip . . ." He bites the corner of his mouth.

I glare. "You look ridiculous."

Zimmer snorts into a laugh, which morphs into a yawn. Followed by an annoyed groan.

"You should go to bed early," Gem suggests.

"Sure. I'll try that," he says flatly. "While you two were dancing like two left-footed FTs"—I shoot him a mightier scowl, he nearly smiles—"someone we all know just left StarDust."

Dismay strikes my eyes. I think of Mykal and Court. *Concentrate.* I try, but my mind is a blur. Senses chaotic. I feel—one of them brushing their teeth? Fingers to my mouth, I taste mint . . . and a tongue running along sharpened molars.

Mykal.

If Mykal is still here, Court should be too.

Gem places her palms together. "Please say Kinden has left."

"Symons."

"What?" Gem and I say in unison.

It makes no sense. "I saw him pass the simulation today."

"He left of his own accord," Zimmer clarifies. "Something about not willing to spend 'eternity' without his husband. I told him that he's not immortal, and he snapped at me for interrupting his 'departure monologue.'"

"That's all happening right now?" I ask.

"It's over. Sel and Symons just disappeared in the elevator."

Gem sinks on her bed. "At least they're together forever."

Zimmer yawns again. "Eighty-plus years is not forever."

I hide my journal beneath my pillow. "What do you care if people see themselves as undying?"

"It's obnoxious." His brows hike, surprised I don't share his sentiments. "Some people . . . Fast-Trackers, *Babes* have deathdays smashed against their eyeballs. Staring them down every fy—" Zimmer nearly spits out an FT curse.

We both look at Gem.

Gem looks between us. "Am I missing something?"

"No," we say together, and I nod him on, my body unbending. Sweltering hot. Gem definitely sizes us up, but I pretend like nothing happened.

Zimmer combs an anxious hand at his mop of hair. "I understand that *we*," he emphasizes to conceal the lie, "will die much later in life, but we'll still die. We're not better than Fast-Trackers and Babes just because we have extra time. We're *not*."

I try hard to smother my smile, my entire chest swelling. When my friends died, I didn't think to make new ones. *I only have three months left,* I thought, and since then, I'd somehow forgotten about the infectious passion of die-hard Fast-Trackers.

"I disagree," Gem says cheerfully, and my lips fall. "We will be the ones to change our world in historic, unparalleled ways. Fast-Trackers and Babes *cannot* do that based solely on the fact that they will die sooner than all of us."

I cringe. Is that really the measurement of our worth? How greatly we impact this world? I drove people safely around Bartholo. That matters.

I still matter. Blinking repeatedly, I try to sort out my thoughts.

Zimmer lets out a weak, tired laugh. "Sure."

Beyond our dorm, stampedes of feet rumble the floor, the commotion jolting us. The last time anyone yelled this brashly, fifty candidates were expelled at once. Without a word, we all bound into the hallway and follow the onrush down the stairs.

Bodies skid to a halt in the common room, stone fireplace hissing with lilac casia. Someone increases the volume to a television nestled between sturdy bookshelves.

Candidates in nightgowns and wool slacks cluster on the purple velvet furniture. Others standing in silence.

All watching Altia News.

On the fuzzy screen, an old woman buttoned in furs puts a bulbous microphone to her full lips, wind thwacking her reddish-brown cheeks and tossing her lush brown hair. Static crackles her voice and the image, snow dumping hard. The camera pans up to a stone building, white against the dark night.

I recognize the architecture as Yamafort, not Bartholo. Weaving between candidates, I stop by an end table and frilly lamp. My mind drifts for one second and then . . . *I'm racing. Running.*

Turning my head, Mykal storms down the stairs, more alarmed candidates in tow. I jump as a hand rests on my shoulder. Court sneaks up on me, so swift. He carries his padlocked expression to the television, his palm falling off my arm.

Only a few feet away, Kinden sits at the edge of a chaise, fixated on Altia News.

The camera descends to revolving doors, the scarlet overhang emblazoned with *The Rose Glades*. A high-end apartment building, I guess. The reporter's voice breaks in and out.

"Someone fix it!" a candidate yells.

Gem slides through bodies with "excuse me, excuse me," and slips behind the bulky television, fiddling with cords. Just as the static disappears, Kinden shoves himself in the situation. Much to Gem's displeasure.

"I have it," she insists.

"It's not working." Kinden pulls out a cord and the whole screen flickers black.

Everyone hollers, and I crane my neck to see Mykal beside Court. "What do you think?" I whisper to them.

"Overreacting, the whole lot of them are." Mykal chews on his toothbrush like its dry root. "They'd piss their slacks by the sight of a mountain lion. It's most likely nothing."

He believes what he says, but my arms shake, my own dread filling the hollow places that belong to Court. Who remains eerily silent.

I wish I'd worn my coat. I'd hide my face in the furs and sniff the lingering honeysuckle perfume. I'd hug it tightly and remind myself that everything isn't so wrong.

Gem crouches, but Kinden follows suit. She tucks a hair behind her ear. "I can do it myself."

"*Oh Gem, you can do it,*" Kinden mocks, pestering her constantly. "Hand that to me."

"Never." And then they topple into the back of the television. The screen flickers. Picture returning.

"It's on!" several people call out.

". . . Altia Patrol has begun an extensive investigation." The reporter raises her voice over the wailing wind. "Today at eleven o'night marks the twenty-eighth recently reported theft in the country. Nineteen of those are in Yamafort alone, and three are now being cited as *grand theft*, the stolen property worth one point five million bills—"

Collective gasps tune out the reporter.

I stagger numbly back between Mykal and Court. As though to distance myself from this proposed thief. Hatred slowly and surely grinds at my insides, my face twisting painfully.

The reporter lists off items the thief has stolen so far: porcelain figurines, music boxes, jewelry, feather hats, fur rugs, and on and on and *on*.

Mykal and Court's hands immediately drop to mine, and they tenderly open my closed fists, my nails burrowing too deep in my palms. They lace their fingers with mine, their sentiments not as sweltered. Not as hot, but I still bristle.

I still brew.

"I hate someone without a face."

Court says, "You're not alone." I think he means himself, but I skim the room, half the candidates enraged, the other half frightened to the bone.

". . . the most recent theft occurred right here at The Rose Glades with famous residents like Everly Storycastle—"

"I adore her films!" a little girl exclaims, quickly shushed by Odell.

"—Altia Patrol will not tell us what has been stolen from The Rose Glades. As the investigation continues, the list of suspects remains confidential. More to come with updates. Until then, we'll replay President Morcastle's good luck message to the candidates of StarDust."

Someone lowers the volume, the message aired so often that no one reacts. StarDust refuses to name the candidates and our location for television, so the only information Altia News has are handfuls of wet flyers and Morcastle's stale "good luck" to us.

Chatter escalates but dies quickly as lightbulbs flicker. The howling wind echoes, and heads turn cautiously.

"It's a storm." Kinden stands by the television, hand in his pocket. "If you fear the wind, you shouldn't be here."

"Maybe they fear the Two Thieves of Yamafort," says a girl by the stairs, her tamed curls casting shadows on the wall.

"Maga and Cissy Icecastle are dead!" several people shout.

"Quick-Hands Jakker," Zimmer predicts, grabbing everyone's attention. "His deathday is in five years, and he likes shiny toys."

"Vorkter." Kinden shuts down the theory.

I blocked out the famous thieves in Bartholo. I'd rather scrub my nail beds with Mykal's dry root than spotlight a thief. Some probably like the accolades and seeing their images on Altia News where Influentials gasp and recoil.

"What about Bastell Icecastle?" Seifried murmurs so softly that the whole room hushes, his words so rare that we all listen closely. "My . . . my father and mother said he was the greatest thief in the past century. I was . . . a baby when he crept into my nursery . . ."

The temperature plummets, coldness draping the room like rolling fog.

"They said he stole my teddy . . . and crept out."

My nose flares just as Gem whispers, "Talk of Bastell reached Maranil. We heard that he stole what people value most."

"He was an affluent Influential," the curly-haired girl interjects. "He never needed the bills." *An Influential thief.*

My cheeks burn.

Seifried murmurs, "They say he stole for sport."

For sport. My pulse races ahead. Court wouldn't even steal for sport.

Candidates nod at Seifried's declaration. I shiver from toe to head and then Kinden barks, "You're forgetting he's in *Vorkter.* No one ever escapes."

Court's hand tightens around mine.

No one ever escapes.

I clutch proof of someone who has.

Thief theories persist until bedtime, my canopy drawn shut and legs restless beneath the covers. Darkness cloaks my silent dorm room. Hands on my stomach, I stare up and sense Mykal hugging a pillow, breathing heavy in a deep slumber.

Court is awake. Sitting against his headboard, he flips through a textbook, dim light causing him to squint his dry eyes. He rubs them repeatedly with the heel of his palm and sometimes he glances to his left side. As though picturing me, and my head turns.

Picturing him.

He mouths, *Sleep.*

I'm trying, but my satchel, tucked in bed with me, contains a *stolen* fur coat that no longer feels right to wear or hold. And my fanciful imagination refuses to quit picturing Quick-Hands Jakker. I cover my face with my palms, about to groan, but floorboards creak.

I stiffen.

Creaaaak.

I prop myself on my elbows just as someone draws back a sliver of my canopy, the figure shadowed before he clicks a handheld reading light.

"Zimmer?" I hiss.

A warm glow bathes his tired, sunken eyes, as he slouches in plain blue slacks and a sleeveless shirt. My guards lowering only a smidge, I straighten up and press my spine to the headboard.

Very softly, he says, "I'm not asking you to like me." He rests a single knee on my bed. Caught between staying and leaving. "I'm not saying that I like you either . . . but I can't sleep—I haven't been able to since we've been here. And I just . . . I thought you'd understand."

As he stares intently, exhaustion welling, it dawns on me.

Zimmer Creecastle has never slept alone. Most Fast-Trackers would rather cram in one bed and spend their bills other ways. At the orphanage, I had a narrow bunk to myself, so I'm more used to our current situation than him.

Mattress undulating, I move closer to Zimmer. Arms crossed, I whisper, "Ask me."

"Will you let me in your bed?"

"No." I reject him briskly. I'd never offer my bunk to someone I mistrusted. No amount of exhaustion would sway me then, and I won't let it sway me now.

Zimmer grips my canopy, not shying away. "Why?"

"Why would I? Especially knowing you dislike me."

He cocks his head. "Then maybe I like you."

I hate that I can't sense whether he's lying like I can with Court and Mykal. Part of me wants to chuck his handheld light toward the armoire and tell him to *"go chase after"* but the other part would rather hear him out.

I lift my chin. "You just want to use me."

"If that's how you see it, then maybe a little." He leans nearer to breathe softly, "But you used me too."

I owe him. Not *this* in particular, but I owe him something. Sharing a bed may be the easiest exchange, and I've never minded lying next to another person. It may be nice.

Like old times.

I won't be some chump either. "Only if you tell me what your sleeping arrangements used to be in Bartholo." I make these terms to gauge his desperation. For weeks, we've played a distant, coy game with each other, skimming the surface of our Fast-Tracker pasts but never treading deep.

"Scoot over first." Spotting my glower in the orange light, he adds, "I trust you about as much as you trust me, Wilafran." He hisses lowly, "If that's even your fykking name."

"All right, all right." I thud to my bottom and slide, granting him half the bed. He climbs in, enclosing us in the canopy, and then sits on my satchel.

"What the . . . ?" Zimmer unburies the leather luggage and gives me a look. "Because you're lonely or you're afraid it'll be stolen?"

"The latter."

He throws my satchel onto the floor.

"Heya," I snap under my breath and then stretch across his waist to fish for my bag.

He reclines on his elbows, rooting himself to the bed, not helping. Just watching me struggle for my possessions. "They're Influentials," he whispers to me. "No one cares about your socks and sweaters but you."

Retrieving my satchel, clutched to my breasts, I ensure my elbow drives into his ribs as I return to my side of the bed. He grunts and then flashes a "wiseass" smile.

My heart hammers at three different speeds.

Court slams his book closed and is motionless, and Mykal has woken, sitting up in bed. His arms hang on his scarred kneecaps. Both concentrating solely on me. *Worried.* Otherwise, they wouldn't pry so intently. We've never invited anyone else to our beds before now.

Zimmer crawls under the quilt and sheet.

I situate my satchel on my left, pushing me a bit closer to Zimmer, but I'd rather protect my belongings from any thieving hands. Cheek on my pillow, I whisper, "You better tell me now."

Rolling on his side to me, he whips the quilt and sheet over our heads. Light still lit in his palm. Cocooned in a warm fort. I relax more than I should, and as he breathes easier, I wonder if he feels the exact same.

In fear of our roommates overhearing, Zimmer speaks in an even more hushed tone. "Have you ever been to Putter's place off of Fowler Street, Avenue Thirty-Four?"

"Putter Vosscastle?" He's not a particularly popular Fast-Tracker, but he often threw parties in his run-down flat. More so, I digest the fact that I have mutual acquaintances with Zimmer. Bartholo feels less like a giant, cold city and more like home.

"Yeah." Zimmer sets the little light by our shoulders, illuminating our faces. "I lived across from Putter's, shared a space with eleven . . . no, *twelve* others. We all worked in hotel hospitality."

"Hmm." I ponder what that means while our eyes dance along each other.

"*Hmm?*" He scrutinizes me harder. "*Hmm* what?"

Tempted to ask more, I open my lips. Then shut them. I wish to paint a picture of his life before StarDust. Even if I shouldn't know or care. Impulse overtakes me. "How many beds did you have?"

"Two, but half of us worked nights." Growing comfortable, he slips his hand beneath his pillow, his long fingers unintentionally skimming mine.

Mykal's back arches, no longer slouched, and even farther away, Court bears hard on his teeth. Bottling emotions before they plunge hot to his cheeks.

Gods. They have no visual of the person in my bed, so they're left to assume. I doubt the truth would calm their fretting hearts, but as I lie serenely, they should understand that I'm in no danger. Hopefully they'll stop forcing themselves awake and try to sleep.

Zimmer supports his head up. "You all right?"

I blink twice, focusing on him. "Why wouldn't I be?"

"It looked like . . . I think you must've zoned out for a second."

My brows spike. "You're worried about me?"

"About *you*? No. I'm worried you may knife me in the night . . . a little bit." He pinches his fingers together, lying back on his side.

"I wouldn't *knife* you." I pause, serious. "I may kick you if you aggravate me."

Zimmer yawns. "You're a horrible bedmate."

"I lived in an orphanage. So it's not like I shared a bed unless . . ." *I bedded the other person.* His sudden understanding passes between us. I miss hands roaming my skin, nerves blistering, and head lolling backward.

Zimmer's gaze softens. "Hmm."

My face roasts. "*Hmm* what?" My sharp tone prickles my ears.

His lip quirks. "Hmm, you make more sense. I had a decent friend from the orphanage, used to complain about his boots being stolen in the middle of the night. He got so miffed that he began stealing from other orphans." Gesturing to my satchel, he smacks the quilt above us. "Makes sense you're protecting your socks."

"Were you raised by your parents?"

"Not for long." Zimmer fights grogginess by blinking. "They were Fast-Trackers: had me at sixteen, died when I was ten. I'd already been working at the Catherina for a couple of years, so I wasn't required to live in an orphanage."

I was. My mother died when I turned six, so Altia paid for my living expenses at Bartholo's orphanage. To avoid overcrowding, they release FTs once they turn eighteen, but thinking I'd die before then, I never considered alternative housing.

My jaw aches from Court biting down. I hug my feather pillow firmer beneath my cheek. "I was a Purple Coach driver," I admit so unexpectedly that my lungs collapse.

Nostrils flare—*Mykal*. I try to mutter a *don't worry* but my lips barely move.

Zimmer lets out a long breath, his gaze dripping down my body like he unmasks Wilafran to discover a stunned and bare Franny.

I wrap my arms around my belly. "Say something."

"You've been yelled and cursed at, had bills thrown at your face, cleaned their puke off car seats, and now you're pretending to be one of them. *That*," he says with conviction, "makes *no* sense." We've subconsciously scooted nearer, his breath warming my face.

"You were a bellhop," I combat.

He gawks. "I was *fired*."

"Maybe I was fired too."

"When's the last time Purple Coach fired one of you?" Forcefully, he swallows another yawn. "They need drivers so badly, you'd have to injure the whole fykking city to be tossed."

It's true. No one likes learning to drive. *Time consuming. Risk of personal injury. Little pay for dealing with high-strung personalities.*

"I can't tell you why I'm here," I whisper heatedly. "It's not like you're awfully forthcoming on these facts either." Sitting up, my legs entangle with his.

Mykal groans into a growl. This link is difficult when they only know my senses and emotions, not my intentions.

I untangle from Zimmer and ease back.

He hoists his head again to better look at me.

My voice is a hurried breath. "You think I haven't wondered how you blend in so well and speak so formally? At the Catherina, I *heard* you."

"What did you hear?" If my voice is urgent, his is gentle but scorched. As though to say, *I am still a die-hard FT.*

I tuck my legs loosely to my chest. "You spewed Fast-Tracker slang like bullets, and here, you've been more like silk than a slingshot."

Zimmer rolls onto his back, his bent knees tenting the quilt along with my head. Staring up for a long moment before saying, "Truth? It starts in the core." He jabs a finger at his chest. "I'm going to die one day soon, and because of that, I'm at a disadvantage. And they'll lie to themselves and say, *They're the best opportunities for your life span.* Pig shit. It's not the lack of wealth that gases me. I don't want their amassed familial fortunes or decades-long careers. It's not that they're 'properly' educated. It's not that when I wake up, I'm on a stained mattress, intertwined with five other arms and legs—it's not that the ceiling is rotted and the walls are chipped. It's that every morning—every *gods-forsaken* morning that I strap on my cap, carry their bags, prop open doors—I know the only way to gain respect is to act like them. I earn better tips by my shift's end, and then I go home and lie on that stained mattress and stare up at that rotted ceiling and curse with my friends."

Turning his head to me, he finishes, "Choke back Fast-Tracker slang long enough, it becomes easy to do it on command."

I lie back on my side, quiet while his fatigue heavies his eyelids. "If you could've saved your job that day at the Catherina, why'd you use slang in front of management?"

He blinks and blinks, eyes reddening. "I was stunned and furious that Court lied—and that my wart of a boss—who'd known me since I was *eight*, sided with him. At the time, that was as much restraint as I could give but I botched it."

My throat is swollen, brain full with knowledge about how he's pretending to be an Influential. Who he is. I think he'll fall asleep now, his lids drooping and drooping. His drowsiness contagious, I yawn into my pillow.

"I didn't know you'd be here," he says in the quietest whisper of all. "I saw you in the dining room and that day at the Catherina just flooded back. All my anger. For a split second, I wanted to hurt you and your friends as horribly as you hurt me." He shuts his eyes, exhausted tears slipping from the corners.

Turned toward each other, I breathe, "I think I deserved it."

Eyes still closed, he murmurs, "No."

No?

"You've been kind."

As silent seconds pass, my own eyes sag closed, sheltered by a quilt. Warmed by dim light, we breathe fully, softly—freely. Unburdened from the weight of our hatred.

TWENTY-THREE

Court

"We need to address what we've been avoiding." I break an hour's long silence between the three of us; Star-Dust's library is relatively empty during breakfast.

Most candidates study in the nonfiction sections on the ground floor. On the second, where fantasy novels are shelved, we've spread aerospace textbooks over our circular table. And with the nearby balcony, we overlook everyone below. The view and seclusion allow us to speak more candidly than anywhere else in StarDust.

Mykal shoves his books aside, leans back, and smacks on mint gum. I only offered the gum when he longed for dry root and complained about "teeth being used for chewing"—I forgot how irritating this could be.

Massaging my sore jaw, I wait for Franny to shut her journal. "Any day."

She shoots me a glare and then continues writing meticulously. "I haven't been avoiding. It just hasn't been important."

I drop my voice. "I woke next to a boy for the *second* night. This morning, my face was buried against his chest, and his arm was draped over my waist." Her cheeks burn, and mine heat in kind.

"A *bony* boy," Mykal says huskily.

I roll my eyes. "That makes absolutely *no* difference."

She frowns. "I didn't realize that you felt like you were me in bed, Court," she whispers. "Or else I would've had this talk much sooner."

Maybe I was concentrating too hard on her, but I don't trust Zimmer.

Franny didn't bed or kiss him, nor did she imply that she desired to.

I rake a hand through my thick hair. "I don't trust Zimmer," I finally announce.

Franny reroutes her glare to me.

I add, "We still don't know his intentions for being at StarDust."

"We know they have *nothing* to do with us."

We still don't know his intentions with you, I think but struggle to admit it aloud. Not knowing my place.

Mykal rocks forward, chair thudding. "He sleeps in your damned bed."

Incensed, Franny presses her chest to the table. "*Sleep.* That's all it is." Eyes narrowed, she says, "If you both think this is more important than StarDust right now, then let's acknowledge the *real* issue."

My abdomen tightens. "Which is?"

"The link," she whispers. "Are we expected to never touch anyone or never let anyone touch us?"

Mykal chews rougher on his gum and growls, "Yeah," just as I say, "I don't know." His head whips to me so angrily that he strains a muscle.

I rest my hand on my neck. Our talk is so new—I don't have the right answers, but if we think logically, maybe we can find them. "Can you really ask that of her?"

"No, I'm asking that of *you* too."

"What are you saying?" My arm falls to the table, fingers on a worn hardback. He's made it vitally clear that he's too afraid to heighten the link. So we'll never kiss again.

Mykal extends his arms. "I'm saying that we're not cozy with *anyone*. We're losing nothing that way, you realize."

Franny and I exchange a knowing, apprehensive look. He's been alone more than he's been with people, and I haven't been entirely blunt where my past is concerned.

"We are losing something," Franny says, brows raised. "Because I have needs that haven't been met, and as far as I can tell . . . especially during baths, you both do too."

The closer we've become, the less we actively try to focus elsewhere. Our minds wander, we feel one another; it's not a secret. So none of us balk, but the more Mykal processes, the harsher he grinds his chewing gum.

He white-knuckles the table. "I'm not bedding anyone unless I love them."

"That's fine. That's what you choose, but I don't have to be that way," Franny says hurriedly. "Court doesn't have to be that way either."

I say what's been silently known, but they deserve the words. "In Vorkter," I whisper, tension gripping our muscles, "I bedded people for the first time and I can't say that I loved any of them."

Mykal rocks back, his jaw hard as stone. "So you'd do it now? You'd do it again?"

I don't know. I shake my head. "I don't know. It's not what's important right now."

His biceps flex, and he pushes his chair away from the table. His hurt punctures my heart.

"Mykal—"

"You're both fools." He lets out a daggered breath. "Just stretch your itty-bitty minds for a moment. Imagine sensing one another with someone else, and tell me, how do you *really* feel?"

Franny inhales shallowly, head hung.

I fight the truth, but the second I imagine Mykal and Franny with someone else, my chest concaves, my heart sinks. Her features twist, the realizations crashing against us.

Tensely, I say, "Not well." I lean back, loosening my tie. Needing air.

"Me too," Franny whispers and stares off, haunted. "What does this mean?"

I don't know. We may be three people in three different

bodies, but our senses erase the lines that tell us what we are to one another. I truly believed I was in bed with another boy this morning. I had to blink five times, pat my quilt, and focus intently to realize that I sensed Franny.

At times when the link is truly heightened, I am so much a part of Mykal and Franny that it feels like we share bodies.

Tie loose on my neck, I take a breath and say, "We're not intimate with other people, and if any of us ever has a change of heart, we'll open this up for discussion again. Agreed?"

They voice their approval the same time the library doors burst open. The after-breakfast crowds file boisterously inside.

I peer down, watching as they choose tables on the ground floor, clamoring for the one closest to the aerospace shelf.

I'm not surprised. At five o'morning, my father said only 433 candidates remain, and he keeps hinting about a starcraft components exam that'll most likely expel half the candidates.

"Has anyone seen my engine notes?!" someone yells to the library.

"Maybe Quick-Hands Jakker stole them!"

Candidates laugh and whisper among friends. I freeze, my pulse frantic. I lick my lips and try to move, but dread snakes down my spine.

Mykal scoots his chair closer to mine. "Kinden isn't coming up here," he assures me, but he misreads the source of my panic.

My whole body is numb. I shake my head, dazed.

Franny watches me with furrowed brows, her pen between her fingers.

Mykal frowns. "Court?"

I turn my head. I look down, and I spy my older brother perusing a bookshelf. He rotates his head and our eyes lock. A weighted heartbeat passes before I tear my gaze away.

I know his expression. *Incredulous. Suspicious.*

Uncertain. Questioning who I am. Why I look so much like his "dead" brother.

It's not the first time he's noticed me. Every day his interest escalates. He followed me out of a flight seminar last week, and he only gave up because I acted like he was unhinged. So I muster a fragment of courage, and I throw another look his way that says, *You're delusional.*

Kinden drags his suspicions to the ground and then trains his attention to the bookshelf.

A hardback book crashes to the floor.

I jolt, more strongly than I should. I check behind me again, and Mykal clasps my neck protectively. "Heya," he breathes. "What's going on?"

"It's not Kinden, then?" Franny asks just as quietly.

I rub my sweaty palms on my thighs and then clutch my knees. "It's not my intent to frighten either of you—"

"Forget about us," Franny says, shutting her journal.

"I can't forget about you both right now." I breathe heavily. I've hesitated to tell them the truth because if I say it aloud, then it becomes more real. Then I know they're thinking the same as me, feeling the same as me. That's *three* times the emotion and the energy than I ever want to spend on a person I loathe.

But I stare at them. Mykal's hands fall to my chair, eyes like battleaxes. Ready to injure anyone who may cross our path.

Franny blisters, heart full of fire.

I feel them. For the first time, I realize they've been my strength, my hope, and they can be my peace. I just have to let them help me. And to do that, I need to grow the courage to speak.

I'm ready.

I shift my chair, my back to the balcony, and I explain my time at Vorkter in a quiet but tight voice.

"One of the people who scarred me"—I feel beneath my shirt, the callused scar puffed over my heart—"was not just a prisoner who escaped. He was my cellmate."

My words carry weight but die off my tongue, like they mean nothing, but inside, I'm screaming a thousand terrors and nightmares—and they *feel* the anguish against their ribs like rocks piled in both lungs.

"As Seifried said," I continue, "he was the greatest thief in the past century."

Franny glares at the bookshelves. "Bastell Icecastle."

Mykal digs his bitten nails in the table.

The invisible monster is no longer invisible. Mykal remembers the day I was attacked. He knows every wound, felt each blade rip open my skin, but I never let him paint a full portrait of the memory. I never gave him a single name or a single face.

Now that's changed.

"I lived with Bastell for five years in Vorkter," I breathe. "He taught me how to steal."

I'd slip through the iron bars at night and practice on neighboring prisoners. Stealing their blankets and socks and whatever else I could find, and then I'd return the items next morning before they woke, not wanting to get my skull bashed in just to learn a new skill.

Our individual cells were never as heavily guarded as the entrance, or else we would have tried escaping much earlier.

Franny is horrified, crushed, sympathetic—so many hot and cold emotions at once. All written on her brows. "You're afraid he's the one who's in Yamafort."

"Yes." I pause. "But there's no proof, other than . . ."

"What?" Mykal scoots his chair even closer, arm stretched over the back of mine. And then Franny edges her seat near. I think I would smile if I could.

"The Rose Glades," I explain. "Before I was sent to Vorkter, that's where I lived. With Kinden and my father, my mother and Illian—Bastell knew this. I told him." *I told him too much.*

How was I to know that I'd dodge my deathday? Or that my cellmate would try to cut out my heart with two daggers and a dull pickax?

"It could be coincidence," Franny says.

I doubt.

"He'll never be finding this place," Mykal adds.

I doubt.

They reassure and reassure, and I doubt and doubt. Then Mykal clamps his hand on my shoulder, and Franny seizes my frozen fingers from the top of a hardback. They both squeeze, and my muscles try to unbind.

I try to be at ease. It takes many moments in their company, in shared silence, but I gain a sense of security. Whether false or fleeting, I don't care. Right now, I breathe.

TWENTY-FOUR

Court

On Holy Wonders Day, and during the feast at eight o'night, my father clinks his glass and readies himself for a speech. "Set down your wine and silverware. Tonight, out of the two hundred candidates here, only one hundred of you will remain. Make your way to the launchpad and please wait in a single-file line."

Great.

On the launchpad, the enormous, sleek body of the Saga starcraft lies in the center circle, engineering motor-machines and tools packed neatly away.

StarDust displays the vessel like a work of art, spotlights directed on the onyx shell. The cement shines beneath eight sets of retractable wheels.

From my eyes, I see beauty. My chest swells with new possibilities and freedoms that I'm closer and closer to grasping. Every time I view the starcraft, our plan to leave this world seems more feasible. And real.

I don't gaze long.

Panicked candidates ascend the metal on-ramp to the Saga starcraft's locked entrance. In everyone's haste, Franny and Mykal lose their spots directly behind me. The line forms after the pushing ceases, and I stand at the base of the on-ramp while they wait farther back.

At least I'm ahead of them. I calm myself.

I can't imagine what would happen if Mykal had to take this exam before me. After he failed a communications simulator, I asked Amelda why he wasn't expelled, and she said honestly, "Star-Dust wants a *fall* in the final thirty for good luck. There are only two left."

Raina Nearfall is his true sole competitor, but she's a girl who assisted her father in designing this very starcraft's engines, and she's scored higher than me in most simulations.

Only eleven, Raina is treated like an engineering virtuoso.

"Excuse me. Pardon me." Amelda jogs up the ramp with a towering stack of clipboards.

The line bends, allowing her space before she stops at the entrance.

She hands a clipboard to the first candidate and adjusts a stopwatch around her neck. "The timer starts from the first moment you enter," she explains. "Read the packet for directions, and when you're finished, leave through the starboard exit." Amelda unlocks the entrance with a keycard.

After the first candidate disappears inside, the doors slide closed.

I wait and wait, the line shortening as candidates vanish into the starcraft. When I reach the middle of the ramp, someone disrupts the straight line. Murmurs echo. I lean sideways for a better view.

And I go rigid.

Kinden descends the ramp, briefly asking candidates if he can move toward the back of the line. I doubt he'd listen if they told him *no*. His boots clank against the metal grate.

Closer and closer to where I stand.

"I'm going to cut in behind you," Kinden tells a boy, who's eager to move ahead. My older brother then wedges his tall frame right in front of me. For many weeks, I've ignored his curiosities, dodged his advances—and now here we are.

"*Those Valcastle boys,*" my father's colleagues would say, not always out of kindness, "*will not stop until they follow their minds' desires to the very end.*"

I've been on my brother's mind for too long.

Don't acknowledge him. I'm stiff and unblinking. Even as Kinden turns to face me.

"You know who I am," he states.

Yes. My honest brother.

I blink once, eyes on him. "Yes." I abandon the light inside my body. "You're the pathetic candidate who's been obsessed with me."

Kinden shifts his weight, jaw muscle twitching, but he's steadfast in his pursuit. Scrutinizing me with pierced eyes. I stand taller. Glaring down at him with malice that I don't wish to feel.

"I'm obsessed," he repeats like he can battle the world till the end. He gives me a once-over, trying to place me in his memories.

I want to scream shrilly, fully. Until my heart bleeds. *"It's me! It's me! I'm your brother! I'm right here. See me. Love me."*

There is no solace. If he found out the truth—that I dodged my deathday—he may tell our father, who'd report me to Altia Patrol. Who'd do worse than send me to Vorkter. They may physically prod me to find answers that have no origin.

"You've been following me," I add. "You stare at me for extended periods of time. What else would you call it?"

"Intrigued."

I scan his fashionable attire: high-collared coat, champagne-colored slacks and white, buttoned shirt. "I'm flattered, but I'm already promised to—"

"I'm *not* romancing you," he snaps. "Tell me why no one has heard of you before?"

"I lived beneath a rock," I say dryly. "It was cold and dark, and you wouldn't have liked it there. No armoires."

Kinden isn't easily deterred by insults. "I like clothes, but I like honesty more. You're not very honest, are you?"

If I could be honest, I would tell him, *"I'm sorry I forgot to wake you that morning."* The day I was driven to Vorkter, I never saw or heard from Kinden.

He'd been asleep.

Before I answer, the line shuffles forward, and Kinden walks backward, his attention still cemented to me. With a pained, bitter smile, I say, "I value privacy above honesty, and if that irks you, then so be it. I never asked to be your friend."

Kinden laughs scornfully. "And I never asked to be yours. Yet, I left my spot, second in the row, to speak to an enigmatic boy with no history, no background, no *family* or known wealth."

I'm numb. My voice is dead. "I have a history."

His widened eyes blaze with raw memories. "Where is it?"

Dying. Dead. Gone. "In my hands." I step forward, taking command even if it knots my stomach. In this second, I appear older, better, wiser—but I am not. "You will *never* be privy to my history," I sneer, my lips near his cheek. "I will laugh as you crawl toward me, thinking you can be me. Wake up to your own pathetic sensibilities." I breathe lowly, "Wake. Up."

As our chests bump, he shoves me back, not forcefully. His interrogative gaze bores straight through me, and I wail inside, *Wake up! Wake up!*

Wake up, Kinden.

See me.

In a thick stupor, Kinden dazedly faces the starcraft. Ignoring me without a final word.

Systems test directions:

   Find Saga starcraft's bridge.

   Give this packet to a StarDust director waiting for you.

   Exit through the starboard side.

   (You are being timed.)

My boots clap loudly on the steel starcraft flooring. I run through the wide metallic corridor, a cascade of lights illuminating the curved path. Hatches and archways lead to several other corridors and bays, but I need to find the command station, commonly referred to as the bridge.

While I run, I shelve all my concerns regarding my brother. *Focus.*

Franny and Mykal depend on my precise movements, so they can copy me during their turn. When I see a square violet button, I skid to a stop and push. The door swooshes open vertically and reveals the circular bridge.

The first time I'd stepped foot inside, the sheer beauty stole my breath: glossy control panels, multicolored blinking screens, a humongous overhead light shaped like a steering wheel from a fictional boating vessel, and five stately chairs for five candidates.

Technology this advanced exists nowhere else on Saltare-3, but right here. And StarDust keeps it a secret from everyone on this planet.

"Clipboard." A StarDust director emerges in a dignified gold and black suit, and I pass him my clipboard as he says, "You're to correctly identify the pieces of equipment and systems that I point to."

All business, he moves swiftly around the bridge. First to a sole leather chair propped high in the exact middle. Overseeing all the other command stations.

"Captain's chair," I identify, hoping Franny and Mykal feel my lips. Purposefully and inconspicuously, my fingers glide over the armrest.

To the right, I pinpoint the maintenance-engineering unit, better known as MEU. A silver chair is bolted in front of blue panels and lit screens, percentages and numbers detailing the craft's data. As my father has said, "The MEU is like a physician to the starcraft. If the craft can't fly, they must fix it."

To the left, I label the communications station. Another silver chair faces a headset and spread of dials, buttons, and four tiers of screens. Aloud, I identify the function of each knob and switch. Most of us had never even seen a radio until a seminar about comms.

"Down." The man passes the captain's chair and steps down three little stairs to reach the cockpit. I follow. Two full-bodied leather seats with attached chest-belts sit side by side, joysticks positioned between each pilot's legs. Multicolored keys to the left and right.

"Pilot A and Pilot B," I say aloud.

He scribbles on the clipboard. "Differences?" he asks.

"Pilot A controls the speed. Pilot B the direction." Their seats face the vast windshield that begins at the steel floor and extends as far as my peripheral. *The eyes of the starcraft.* From the outside, it looks like a curved visor on a saucer plate.

After he asks a few questions about the joysticks, I'm finished. Clipboard back in hand, I sprint through the starboard exit. Rushing down a ramp on the opposite side of the starcraft. Hidden from Amelda and the other candidates.

My father waits below.

I slow as I near him. Without much expression, he clicks a stopwatch and collects my clipboard.

We've spoken little, if at all, but I've heard from Amelda and the other directors that Tauris is fascinated by my aptitude for knowledge and simulations. Whether or not he's also intrigued by my resemblance to his criminal son, I don't know.

When I see him, I try to imagine he's not the father I once knew. That he's as different as I've become.

Then he offers a genuine smile and the past barrels into me.

"Why did you do it?!" He's crying.

Screaming painfully.

"Court." Tauris waves a hand over my eyes—I nearly flinch. "Did you hear what I said?"

"No, I apologize." I stand straighter, combing stiff fingers through my hair. It's strange hearing *Court* from his mouth. A name I gave myself.

"You're to wait with the other candidates." He motions to the candidates who've completed the test, all dressed in their very best for the Holy Wonders Day feast: suits and ties, glittering blouses and furs.

No longer merry, they wait in nervous clusters.

No one is allowed to leave until the exam ends and the expulsions are made.

Time ticks slowly. The starcraft is stationary nearby, and most candidates sit on the concrete. When Mykal joins me, he nearly coughs on his gum, surprised that they all risk dirtying their "silly" slacks.

"Everyone cares more about the results than their clothes," I tell him.

A grunt in his throat, he plops down and props an elbow on a bent knee. *He did fine,* I try to convince myself, but I sensed him tripping over his words when describing the comms panels.

I focus on Franny while Mykal chews his stale, flavorless gum. *She's fine.* Franny speeds through the command station much faster than Mykal, and in a few minutes, she drops down beside us with a huff.

"I hate exams," she says beneath her breath. "You know what I'd like?"

Mykal blows a bubble. "A greasy hare with the skin still attached."

"To run over every exam packet that ever existed," Franny says, stretching out her legs and massaging her knees to compensate for my rigid body. "And the hare, for you."

Mykal wears a lopsided smile, and then Franny pushes his arm lightly with a closed fist. Responding fast, he drapes his arm around her shoulder and tugs her frame close. He rests his chin on her head and then mouths proudly to me, *She likes me more than you.*

I didn't realize we're competing for her affection, but in a place where not very many understand Mykal—and most flock toward me at first impression—I can see why he'd relish Franny's fondness for him.

Still, I roll my eyes. Jealousy bites me.

I've had him all to myself for years. And there's still a mountain wedged between me and Franny. It's my own fault. Whenever they joke and banter, I separate myself.

I try to loosen my shoulders by rotating them. "What about me?" I ask Franny.

Her brows spring.

Mykal rocks back a little.

"You?" Franny shuts her mouth. After the shock wears off, she thinks and says, "For you, I'd like a . . ." She trails off. "What do you like to do besides study for StarDust?"

I don't know. I used to like medicine, but I don't *yearn* for it. I don't want it.

They must feel my uncertainty because they both start listing ideas.

"A mirror," Mykal says with a crooked smile. "So you know exactly how beautiful you are."

"Books," Franny says. "All kinds. So you're never bored."

My lips want to rise, but I just listen and nod. They list a wristwatch, stars, a perfect planet, and good people. At that, we fall silent.

As the launchpad fills, many more candidates are in earshot, so we stay quiet.

Zimmer tells an animated story about extinct pigeons to a girl and boy of eight years. I don't want to trust him. I don't want to even like him, but as Franny's hatred fades, mine begins decreasing in kind.

I don't trust him, I have to remind myself. *I don't like him.*

Nearby a young man in fur complains to his little sister, "Heral vandalized my world planet textbook for no reason."

"He scratched out *Saltare-1*; I would've done the exact same if you gave me a marker."

I tune them out. Everyone's apathy toward Saltare-1 confused

Franny for a while. Candidates will even mockingly gag at the name, and I had to explain that Influentials don't personally know our sister planet.

Their dislike stems from Saltare-1 being the largest planet in our solar system and the perfect distance from the sun.

Saltare-3 prides itself on overcoming a horrific natural disaster— whereas Saltare-1 appears like the more privileged, unchallenged sibling. Resentment naturally built over the years.

Almost all two hundred candidates are on the launchpad as Odell struts into the seated crowd. The little blond girl fixes her ivory fur hat and says to her friend, "I found out why they're really making us wait here."

Whispers die all around us, heads whipping toward Odell who remains standing, upturned nose pointed at the floor.

I didn't think there was an ulterior motive to my father's directions.

I couldn't have known.

Odell says, "They're *finally* searching the rooms for the stolen indigo cards." I chill and Mykal has to cover his face to hide his emotion. Franny is frozen with me.

"Thank the gods," someone says.

Others voice their approval. "The culprit should be expelled today."

"Without a doubt."

I shouldn't be this upset or uneasy. I've already burned the cards I stole and memorized the words, so they won't find any evidence in my dorm.

"Court." Padgett Soarcastle calls me out from many feet away, across a hundred suspicious eyes. "You look dismayed."

Mykal grinds his teeth. Franny scowls darkly, and while I try to layer on deception, their heat boils like my own. My smile is not a smile, really—it's coarse like Mykal's and blistered like Franny's.

Raising my voice to be heard, I say, "I'm concerned that resources are being used toward catching a thief and not on StarDust."

Gem has her cheek on Padgett's shoulder, and she lifts her head suddenly like a thought bursts in her brain. "What if the indigo card thief is Quick-Hands Jakker?"

"No," a few say, followed by a few more candidates exclaiming, "Yes."

Padgett started this giant group discussion and now she sits upright and observes, her arm protectively around her little sister's waist.

"It's not him." Everyone turns to Kinden, who checks his gold-plated watch for the hundredth time. "As I've said before, no imprisoned thief can escape Vorkter, let alone find a way into StarDust."

Padgett says, "And you would know all about criminals."

Some candidates hold their breaths, their shock homed in on Kinden. He drills a malicious glare into Padgett, and she reacts as though nothing transpires.

My stomach twists and flips and dives.

"You think Kinden stole the indigo cards?" someone asks.

"No," another candidate clarifies, "his own brother was sent to Vorkter."

"Maybe it runs in his family."

"Shut up," Kinden interjects, "all of you." He picks himself off the cement and grazes the crowd with two scorching eyes. "My little brother wasn't a *thief*. None of you can speak like you knew him because you didn't."

Odell, the only other person standing, refutes, "I've heard the facts. The story. He was a criminal."

"He was so much more than a criminal," Kinden sneers.

I ice over, a *memory* slamming forward. When our father told Kinden, "Tone down your arrogance." My brother would turn to me and ask, "Is my arrogance bothering you, little brother?"

"No," I would say.

"Why not? It seems to bother everyone else." He'd sport a pompous smile, sometimes eating vanilla ice cream from a pint.

"You're more than your arrogance," I'd say at eight years, at nine years, at ten years. And he would slide his ice cream across the table. Always offering me a bite.

"I realize you loved Illian the most," Kinden once said to me, "but outside of myself, you're my favorite in this small world."

I suppressed that memory for ages.

Kinden believes that I loved Illian most because I grieved for our little brother in ways no one else did. In Vorkter, after my deathday—my past with Illian surfaced more often, but I could never reach Kinden. I buried him so deep. As though knowing the piercing agony that would outpour with each thought of him.

My immeasurable love for Kinden bangs at my heart like two iron fists. Weeping and howling to let him back in.

I can't.

I can't trust him. I can't trust anyone but Mykal and Franny.

Kinden towers above the crowd, chest rising and falling heavily. "I hate him for what he did, but you don't have the right to hate my brother. That is *my* right alone."

"Maybe he had a reason," I say aloud as Kinden spins on his heels toward me and every pair of eyes zeroes in on me—I feel the enormity of my mistake.

Keep quiet.

It's too late.

Kinden scans me up and down, probably wondering why I'd defend his little brother. And he tells me, "Etian never gave a reason."

My birth name sounds foreign to me. *Etian Valcastle.* I flinch—*no.* Franny is the one who flinches. Mykal has his fingers to his jaw, both trying to suppress their shock at my birth name.

"What'd he do?" someone asks, yanking Kinden's attention away from me.

"You don't know?" Odell says like he's uneducated.

A young boy adds, "People have been whispering about it all month."

"None of you have anything better to do?" Kinden snaps. "I'll laugh as you're all expelled today."

Padgett says coolly, "So it's the Saga *1* Mission now, consist-ing of just you."

Kinden points at the starcraft. "If I could operate the Saga by myself, I'd be the only one chosen, so *yes*, Padgett. I am this mission."

Gem snorts. "Gods, tell me you're joking."

"*Gods, tell me you're joking,*" he mimics Gem, knowing how to irritate her last nerve.

"You're awful."

"What you mean to say is that I'm the best." He sweeps us all again, but then lands on me. "Court. Why don't you tell the un-informed candidates *why* Etian Valcastle was sent to Vorkter Prison?"

I don't falter this time. "Because I'm uncertain as to why," I lie. "I don't pay attention to hallway mutterings."

"Then I'll tell you." Kinden speaks solely to me, even as every-one else listens with bated breath.

I already shared these answers with both Franny and Mykal, but I never was able to see Kinden's reaction after he learned I went to prison.

So I watch him as intently as he watches me.

"Etian was a Wonder and a physician," he says like he reads from a history book, unemotional facts bleeding from his lips. "A little Babe was wheeled into the trauma center on her deathday. Etian tried resuscitating the girl." *I did.* "He hovered over her body and gave her compressions." *Yes.* "Other nurses and physicians screamed and fought Etian, but he just kept pounding on her chest. Two hours passed and then security pried my brother off the dead Babe."

I inhale, my eyes almost glassing.

Physicians are sworn by oath to treat injuries to our greatest ability. There is one exception. If a person needs aid on their death-day, we're to do nothing. They will die no matter how hard we fight, how skilled we seem, how enraged we become.

Lives are not something to be saved.

Not when we know the day everyone dies.

My medical professor wrote that on the chalkboard the first day of class. It has always stuck with me.

I leave my memory as Kinden says, "Altia Patrol gave Etian a warning after the first time. They reminded him of Altia Law—"

"*No physician will use resources on the dying or dead*," I recite, my voice hollow. "Everyone knows that capital punishment."

Even Fast-Trackers. Even Babes.

Kinden nods once. "Three days later, he tried resuscitating a dead Fast-Tracker. While giving him compressions, his fellow physicians told him that he knowingly broke oath *twice*, and he'd be convicted. They ripped Etian off the body, and the next morning, Altia Patrol arrested him outside of the Rose Glades."

As Kinden's story hangs heavy, someone asks, "Did he know the Babe and the Fast-Tracker he was trying to . . . ?" There is no word for what I was trying to do.

Lives are not something to be saved.

"They were strangers." Kinden says the truth. I never knew them. Not even their first names.

"Your brother sounds like he lost his mind," someone says from the back. Almost everyone nods in agreement.

Zimmer chimes in, "Or maybe he just wanted a vacation at Vorkter."

I actually laugh—a strange laugh, but I laugh. All eyes dart to me again.

Kinden glares at me. "It's not amusing."

I know. Before I add anything else, my father's footsteps resound, clanking on the concrete, and we all clamor to our feet. Bodies rising from the ground.

Tauris sighs. "I'm deeply disappointed."

Mykal glances worriedly at me. I glance back and shake my head, uncertain of the outcome. Franny crosses her arms and tries to breathe out a tight breath.

"Your performances today were adequate," he explains, "and one hundred of you will be leaving tonight as promised, but we were hoping to find the person who believed *stealing* was a solution. In Altia and StarDust, theft is not only frowned upon, but it's illegal."

Some candidates clear their throats but no one whispers.

My father slips his hands in his pockets. "Since we were unable to find the stolen cards, anyone who uses those words will be immediately expelled *and* turned over to Altia Patrol. The candidates whose cards were stolen will be given replacements tonight."

Mykal lowers his head to shield his horror from view. His fear grips his lungs so fiercely that I have to unbutton my shirt and then extend my arm over his shoulders.

"Mykal," I whisper in the pit of his ear, trying not to draw attention.

He's unmoving. Those stolen cards had granted him more hope than *anything* thus far. I know that.

"We'll find another way," I breathe lowly.

Unresponsive. Franny elbows his side, but he's in no mood for her either. He looks like he'd rather walk out of StarDust and never return.

"Please exit when I call your name."

It happens quickly, and out of a hundred eliminated, we're all safe—but I believe with every last breath that Mykal wishes my father had spoken his name.

TWENTY-FIVE

Mykal

I'm failing.

I've been failing. Those stolen cards were my last shred of hope for StarDust.

Now it's just . . . gone. My surname has been propelling me ahead this far, but I can't see them accepting me if I keep stumbling behind. *Fall* or not, I'm ranked in the bottom of the class.

I charge into my dorm, slam the door behind me, and viciously pace.

My remaining two roommates are celebrating downstairs with most everyone else. Rejoicing in their accomplishments while I wallow in my wretched failures.

Alone here, I rip off my silly suit. Tearing the rich, ugly fabric. Popping buttons off the shirt. These slacks—I wrestle with every bit of clothing.

An angry growl rumbles deep in my throat. Breathing desperately, heavily, I stand in gray underwear.

"Court," I say his name aloud and shake out my arms, frenzied from what Court calls *adrenaline*. I once told him not to nickname my senses with strange-sounding words.

"Court."

I feel him pause for a second, lying on his bed, reading some book. Though he chooses not to move.

"Court," I growl louder. "*Court.*"

He shuts his hardback, worry cresting his face. Quickly, his feet locate the floor. There aren't many places I'd be, since I'd rather gnaw on my own foot than celebrate in the common room. So he'll be finding me easily enough.

I focus on Franny and sense her packing a box in her dorm, eyes glassing. As though she's recalling the past. I suppose she's finally mailing her fur coat back to the Catherina Hotel. A plan she's considered for a few weeks now.

I pace and pace. Then I head to the armoire, ripping my clothes off the hangers. Too many suits. I pluck off casual slacks and a forest-green shirt, Altian emblem on the breast.

I fight with the leg of my slacks, and the door flies open.

Slowly, Court closes it, all the while watching my struggle. I grunt, trying to tug the fabric above my muscular thighs.

He raises a brow. "If you needed help dressing, could you— maybe, next time—not say my name like it's dying on your tongue."

"I didn't call you in here for *this*." I button my slacks at my waist. Then I run a coarse hand through my hair.

"Then what?" Court stands stiffly by the armoire.

I search for the armholes to my shirt. *Damned thing.* I throw the garment on the bed, done wrestling it. Done wrestling with most everything.

I look up. His fear already weighs as heavy and cold as piles of dense snow. I practically see the words *Don't quit, please don't quit* etched over his frightened eyes.

Once upon an era, I had those same words etched over my tough gaze. When we first found each other in the winter wood. *Don't you quit, Court. Please don't you quit on me.*

But I'm not the kind of boy who kneels down that easily. Like three hells, I'd take a knee now. Not after I've come this far.

I called him in here for another reason. Something else. I near him in two lengthy steps. I nudge his foot with mine.

He hardly stirs. Just stares morbidly. Fearfully. I nudge again— and the faintest bit of light flutters in his stomach. His carriage *aches* to raise.

Come on, Court.

"Heya." I tap his cheek twice.

He sweeps me from toe to head. "Is that a Grenpalish sign of affection?"

I smile a crooked smile. "Took you over two years to figure out."

He rolls his eyes. "I had a feeling."

I rest a hand on the armoire by his shoulder. "Yeh," I say in a heavy lilt, not bothering correcting myself. "I like a lot of your feelings, you realize. The grave ones, even the sullen and sad—I don't mind feeling them all."

He shifts his weight, and his gaze hits the floor. "Funny."

"That's no jest, Court," I say, and I lick my dry lips. "You keep saying that you make my life dismal and bleak. But my world never felt as bright, as worthwhile and full, until I met you."

His defenses start dropping. Shoulders lowering, no longer squared. "Are you teasing—"

"I'm *not* teasing," I say strongly and nudge his foot again. "I'm done being afraid. There's so many other things that rightfully deserve that emotion. Fear of being expelled, fear of Bastell, fear of being caught. But you . . . *us*. This link. I won't be wasting my energy fearing that. If I'm expelled tomorrow, I want to know that I had the courage to choose a future where I could kiss you." I edge nearer. Till our chests nearly touch. "That's all."

"That's all," Court repeats my words. An emotion battles its way through his body. Fighting tooth and nail to emerge. Our eyes dance across each other's features.

Our chests rise together. A powerful breath filling our lungs.

"I'll be kissing you," I say more bluntly. "More than once."

And then slowly, a breathtaking smile overwhelms his face. A smile unlike anything he's ever worn. Bright and vast. Enough to crest tears in the corners of his eyes that look more happy than grim.

He's smiling.

His smile stretches his cheeks like they're my cheeks. I can't stop feeling. Can't stop staring. *Gods bless that's beautiful.*

And he says, "You called me in here so we could kiss?"

I laugh. "I did." Something flutters in my stomach—and his stomach. We eye each other tentatively. A good kind of nervous. And excitement.

No more restraint in my bones. In his bones.

I lightly push his arm, then his cheek. My rough, coarse, and playful movements all I know. All I've seen in my youth.

Court stays unbending, but his hands *glide* around my waist, up to my shoulder blades.

I cup his jaw, and then my callused palm travels to the back of his neck.

His heartbeat thuds fast in my chest, and with one look, Court consumes me whole. "Name this feeling," he whispers, our lips a breath apart.

A feeling that overpowers me, that wraps me up warmly in the coldest hours. Through ice, through snow. A feeling that has never let go.

"*Love,*" I breathe deeply.

Court lowers his head just enough. His soft lips meet my cracked ones. Light bursts inside our lungs. He urges my lips apart, his hands sliding gracefully up my neck. I hunger forward, and I grip the thick strands of his hair. Tugging.

We both smile beneath an eager kiss. Tongues tangling, our bodies grind. Needing, aching to be even closer. I swelter hot, and by now, most Grenpalish would be on the ground. Rolling around together, but I let him take the lead.

Kissing a bit longer—and then our lips abruptly break.

Franny. The same thought, the same name widens our eyes. She can feel us.

I breathe raggedly. Trying to return air to our lungs. I focus my energy on Franny.

Court flattens his hair, lips reddened, and then glances at the door, then me. His concern felt, but no regret. No guilt.

Good.

The more I focus on Franny, the more my brows knot. "I can't sense what she's feeling." Right now, I only feel Court and myself. *The link heightened then.*

"We'll talk to Franny later," Court says stiffly, smoothing back his hair more. We stay a couple of feet apart, a bit more tentative.

My lip quirks. I rub my mouth, a silly grin not leaving.

Court tucks in his untucked shirt. His hair falling over his lashes. But I spot lightness in his eyes.

"I've been meaning to ask you something."

He lifts his head.

"What's an underdog?"

His brows rise. "A person expected to lose."

I frown. "Why would someone be rooting for a damned underdog?"

"People want underdogs to win because they fight harder for less, but they deserve more."

I nod to myself a few times. I think, *All right.* Then I waft my hand, finger suddenly stinging. I put it to my mouth and suck.

"That's me, from a paper cut this morning," Court explains and raises his finger.

I near and grab his hand. Squinting at the tiniest slice.

Gods bless . . . I felt that?

Our bodies tense. This heightened link will be new territory for us to cross.

TWENTY-SIX

Franny

After packing my fur coat into a cardboard box, I leave my dorm and jiggle a knob to room D1.

I peer over my shoulder. *No one will catch you, Franny.* Everyone has been celebrating in the common room downstairs with brisk word games. Well, *nearly* everyone.

My lips are swollen from a passionate kiss. At least, they feel this way.

As soon as Mykal and Court's lips touched, I concentrated on *everything* that I could think of to pull my mind far, far away.

Furs.

Blur 32 perfume. The most luxurious garments in Bartholo storefronts. My old friends, my mother—the list really goes on and on.

And while it worked all right, I wish I could've just turned off the link this once. What I felt was so pure and belonged to them.

But there's no off switch.

Luckily, my mind will be preoccupied for the next while.

Entering the dorm takes a hair clip, a narrowed eye, and a memory of an old friend breaking a lock to the bathhouse, but the knob finally rotates.

I slip inside an identical dorm to my own, but four of five beds are stripped bare. Only one candidate still here.

I begin racing around Raina Nearfall's room. Searching through the armoire, whipping through the hangers of blouses, I find clothes and more clothes. I unzip her satchel.

Empty.

"If I were an indigo card, where would I be hidden?" I mutter to myself. Pausing only a second, I run to her bed and peer in each pillowcase. Nothing.

After Tauris said every stolen card would be replaced, I had a brilliant idea: *Find Raina's card.* Not steal, just discover her word and tiptoe out of sight.

We know little about the final exam involving the indigo cards. What we do know: showing your card will put you at a greater disadvantage.

I want to see Raina's card.

If I can't locate it, then I deserve to be called the poorest sleuth in all of Altia. Just as I kneel before her bed, I fear that Raina secures her card in her pocket like Court. Never leaving it unattended.

"Mayday," I breathe, but I keep scouring. Today may be the only time so many candidates are occupied. I scan beneath the bed frame. Dust and a few hardbacks. I stretch and grab the books.

Sitting, I flip through the pages hurriedly

Peppy footsteps resound in the hallway. My pulse races. I open a book titled *As You Wish It* and something falls out of the folds. The doubtful part of my spirit hardly believes the fortune at my knees.

I quickly pry the indigo card off the polished floor, and I inspect the drawing: muddy brown strokes combined with dark forest green splashes.

Tree.

As soon as I engrain the word in my mind, I return the card and books to their spots and then rush out of the room. *Act normally.*

The footsteps have already drifted beyond Raina's door, the circular hallway barren.

My lips rise again.

I could cheer and dance and twirl with reckless desire. In Bartholo, I would've swallowed Juggernaut and sprawled on my bunk. Here, I won't. I've even made peace with the fact that some old pleasures of mine have no place in my life anymore.

The hallway is quiet enough that I take one small risk. I'm an Influential here, but my Fast-Tracker heart sings songs of *victory*. With a running start and a smile on the brink, I slide across the slick floor in knee-high socks.

Flying on my feet.

A body suddenly rounds the corner. Unable to slow, I crash against a hard, muscular chest that knocks me backward.

I stagger and lose my balance, but Mykal catches my waist and tucks me to his build.

His hands are my hands, coarse and large and caring. Those palms rise to the spot between my shoulder blades. The link disorients me with our touch. Just for a second. I blink, my heart skipping further and faster than his.

Mykal's crooked smile brightens the hallway. "I told Court, 'I'll be looking for a Wilafran Elcastle'—and never did I think she'd smack right into me."

"That's not how I saw it. You clearly ran toward me."

Mykal knocks on my forehead to check if my head is "cracked." I never understood this gesture, but Court explained it's a Grenpalish quirk. I slap his hand aside and then knock on his forehead for good measure.

I may as well rap my own forehead. Again, feeling his body like it's my body.

Mykal pushes my hand, then cheek, and whispers in my ear before I respond, "In seriousness, I need to have a few words with you." Worry dims the light in his blue eyes.

"I've been thinkin' . . ." Mykal plops on the edge of my bed, hunched.

Standing near, I lean my hip on my bedpost. "You've been thinking about . . . ?" Unusual tension strains the air.

Mykal briefly explains why he and Court kissed and heightened the link, and when he finishes, he says, "I'll just be asking you straight. How much of the kiss did you feel?"

My neck heats. "I didn't mean to."

"Heya." He holds up his hands. "I'm linked too. I know how hard it is to control it. No need to blush, now, little love."

My face is still on fire. "It was a good kiss."

Mykal laughs. "Thank you."

"The three of us—we're an odd sort, aren't we?"

"In all the world," Mykal agrees. Because no one else has this link complicating everything. "Are you all right?" He rubs his sweaty palms on his thighs. His nerves surprise me.

I fiddle with my fingers. "I don't want you and Court to ignore your affections because of me."

"Then what about you?" he questions.

My cheeks burn more. "What about me?"

"Who will—" He stops himself and rephrases, "Is there . . . ?" He frowns. "So you're to be alone then?" He looks pained. Someone who preferred loneliness in the Free Lands. Now he can't see that for me?

But even without a kiss or bedding someone, I still have Mykal Kickfall as a friend.

Loneliness is my furthest feeling.

TWENTY-SEVEN

Court

No one has been expelled in two weeks.

Seated stiffly at the end of a dining table, I ignore the platters of breakfast sausage, rare raspberries, toast, goat cheese, fig jams, and much more. One hundred candidates still remain. That fact plagues me each morning, but no more so than Franny.

Three tables out of earshot, she chats with two Altian brothers known as Gef and Evers. Franny has constructed a dangerous ruse for the *tenth* time in fourteen days.

I can easily imagine their conversation because I've heard it with nine other groups.

Franny: *"I'd do anything in the world for chocolate. I miss the taste, and the kitchen refuses to supply me more."*

Gef: *"We're too busy with studies to help you."*

Franny: *"I have a brilliant idea! I'll tell you my indigo card. I don't have it with me, but I promise it's right. Please, please. I beg you. You're here already and near the kitchen."*

Gef and Evers silently debate her offer, and the prolonged anticipation locks my joints.

"Heya." Mykal snaps his fingers, stealing part of my attention. "There's no reason to fuss, you realize. She's been doing *fine*—and would you stop holding your breath?"

I breathe out as I whisper, "She's lucky no one has caught her yet." If her plan is foiled, she'll make enemies out of the other candidates.

"I think you just like fretting over nothing," Mykal says, his chair squeaking beside mine as he peers over my place setting. Then he points at a platter to my left. "Pass me the flat bread."

My lips ache to lift, but I concern myself, nearing obsession, with our reality. Which is not as content as I'd like. Seventy candidates still have to be expelled, and not to mention, being in the final thirty means nothing when our goal is to leave the planet. We have to be hired for the Saga 5 Mission.

"Court." Mykal jostles my shoulder.

I wake from my thoughts and grab the warm platter. I hold the dish out to Mykal. "It's not called flat bread." I worry less about anyone overhearing, our table empty except for us. The dining room is far less crowded than the first night here.

"Round bread then?"

"Pancake," I say as he stabs the golden stack with a fork.

"Why have I not seen pan cakes before?" Mykal piles three more on his plate before I return the platter. Light-as-air emotions flutter inside my stomach.

We kissed. It still feels like a dream. One that I have trouble believing belongs to me.

"Look at my lips," I tell him.

Mykal extends his arm over my rigid shoulders. "I'm looking." He's looking at my eyes, which reflect his grin.

"*Pancake,*" I enunciate. "One word."

"I didn't quite catch that." His tone is mockingly formal. "Come closer." Mykal motions with a few fingers.

I near, eyeing his mouth. "*Pancake.*"

"I heard nothing," he teases and motions again.

I'm about to repeat myself, but the kitchen door bangs shut. I flinch back from the sudden noise, my head swerving. My muscles tighten.

Mykal squeezes my shoulders.

I remember what he said before—his question: *Why has he not seen pancakes since today?* "Pancakes are usually eaten with syrup," I tell him, "and there's been a shortage. Until now it seems."

"Where's the syrup?" He scans the table, and then his eyes flit to me with a smile.

My heart skips a steady beat. "Here." I set the porcelain syrup dispenser by his plate. I doubt he'll like it.

My gaze travels to Franny again, her lips too rushed to read. I focus. The anger flaring in her eyes is a front. I feel no real hostility, but as her voice escalates, I catch her words.

"So now you don't believe me after I've told you my word?"

This has happened before. *Tree* apparently seems too simple to other candidates, and without an indigo card as proof, they doubt Franny.

She scowls darkly, shoves her half-eaten toast at Gef and rises with a haughty façade. "You're liars and cheats." At this, she stomps to our table and plops down across us like nothing transpired.

"That was *dangerous*," I snap.

"So you said yesterday and the day before that," Franny says with less bite than the day before. "You should find a new word for *dangerous*, at the very least."

Mykal chimes in, "Predictable as always."

Rolling my eyes, I watch him drown his pancakes in syrup and then I steal the dispenser. "You'll hate every bite."

"Let me be the decider of that."

"Fine." I wave him on, and he cuts into his pancake stack, the fork alone dripping in dark syrup. As he eats, the sweet flavors hit our tongues all at once.

Mykal gags, about to spit on his plate.

I put a napkin to his mouth and he spits into the ivory fabric. I remind him, "You're twice as predictable as me."

Mykal downs his water, not disagreeing.

Franny makes a face. "Gods that's sticky." I can tell this is her first taste and touch of syrup, and it's through Mykal.

My mind reels back to Franny and her attempt at spreading Raina's word. "Is that your last time?" I question. "It's not working anymore."

"It is," she says. "Even if they doubt me, maybe they'll still use the word if they need one. We can't quit before we've tried."

I nod. I'm grateful that Franny chose Raina's card among all the candidates. I'm even more grateful she's taking the risk, but I can't shut off my worry.

I should thank Franny instead of chide her like a child. I should say so many things, but I just stare.

She no longer stares back, not even expectant of gratitude. Because I rarely give her any. It's my fault. I hate that I combat with the simplest kindness when she deserves more, *so much* more.

Say thank you. I open my mouth.

Say it. I close my mouth.

"Any guesses on what the next exam could be?" Franny heaps sausage on her plate. Whether knowing or not, she offers me an out to my internal battle.

I take it like a coward. "Something difficult," I say, "and with a hundred still left, it might expel half of us at once."

TWENTY-EIGHT

Court

In StarDust's indoor training pool, all one hundred candidates wait on edge. Triangular country flags of Maranil, Orricht, and Altia are strung in rows high above an iced pool. Crystallized fruit is scattered across the completely frozen surface.

Barefoot, we stand on damp violet tiles in identical onyx and gold-trimmed swimsuits: briefs for boys, and briefs plus a high-cut swim top for girls. Candidates shiver and hug their arms around their bodies.

My pulse is in my throat, but not from the cold. For the first time at StarDust, I bear my ink and scars openly.

Ninety-seven pairs of eyes claw along my back and thighs and arms. Some dart to Franny at my left, her arms crossed, two tattoos visible. Whispers escalate all around us.

"Gods, her tattoos are so atrocious."

"Is that Mal's . . . tree?"

"Have you ever seen someone with ink on their thighs?"

"Why does he have so many?"

"Are those scars?"

Don't look at them.

I remind myself that we're not the only ones with ink. Several Influentials tattooed significant dates on their arms. Like the day they graduated university. Others have snowshoe hares that they deem *adorable* and even more etched their country's insignia on their skin.

We attract unwanted attention because of the poor handiwork of our tattoos and the sheer amount that I bear.

Don't look at them.

I can't help but watch my father as he speaks to a few StarDust directors. Huddling around a clipboard, their gazes cast back to us. To me. Their judgment scours my skin up and down, back and forth. I stand like stone.

I can't move. Can't think of anything but the worst outcomes. I barely hear Mykal growling at me to breathe deeper.

"I'm fine," I murmur distantly.

When my father saunters to us, his smile cradling kindness, I tell myself to relax—but my shoulders barely loosen.

As though reciting the weather forecast—*snow, snow, and more snow*—he says very simply, "Half of you will leave StarDust today. I may be the Director of StarDust, but I cannot run the world's aerospace department alone. Likewise, just one candidate cannot execute a space mission. We need *five* of you. Five who'll work in cohesion as a team. That's what today's exam is about. Be ready, be prepared, and we'll begin calling the first group of ten. Five candidates will be expelled from every group."

The second he says this, I think, *Split us up.* We have far better odds if we're all in different groups. Tauris says he'll give instructions once the first group makes their way to the middle of the iced pool.

"First group of ten, when I call your name, walk forward. Winrock Bolcastle," my father reads from a predetermined list of candidates, what all the StarDust directors must've been nagging over. "Zimmer Creecastle."

Zimmer ditches the crowds and crosses the ice barefoot. His wily grin sits uncomfortably with me. No tattoos decorate his tall, scrawny body.

He's been bedmates with Franny for a while now, and when she caught me scrutinizing him, she said, "Besides me hogging the quilt, we've been fair to each other. He's not a threat."

"He's another candidate. Therefore, he is a threat," I refuted her more frostily than I meant. As her guards lower, mine skyrocket. I always hesitate to admit my theory: That Zimmer is at

StarDust with the intent to take over the Saga starcraft, all for entertainment and thrill.

It sounds too outlandish in my head to even speak aloud, but a small portion of belief eats at me.

"Odell Petalcastle," my father continues, "Mykal Kickfall . . ."

He tears from my side. Mykal walks across the ice like he's impervious to the chill, not tiptoeing or slowing. Odell slips onto her knees, and he lifts her up with one strong arm before continuing his course.

"Evers Zucastle, Gem Soarcastle . . ."

After squeezing through candidates, Gem approaches the ice, her swimsuit too small for her round shape. More than anyone else, the fabric cuts into her wide hips, shoulder straps digging into her soft flesh. If the swimsuit hurts, she never lets on. Confidence radiates off Gem as though she's already victorious.

"Seifried Newcastle, Joi Plycastle." My father lists the last two in quick succession. "Court Idlecastle and Wilafran Elcastle."

All nine candidates and I clip metal bands around our ankles, chained in a circle to the ice. Feet numb the longer we stand. Everyone quakes and trembles but Mykal.

My breath smokes the air.

Suddenly, glassed walls rise and rise from the edges of the pool. I crane my neck, watching the glass meet the ceiling. Confining us like we're in a room. The directors and other candidates observe us outside the enclosure.

Beside me, Mykal kicks a frozen strawberry, skidding across the surface. We were already informed that once the exam begins, the atmosphere will change. Low oxygen, higher levels of nitrogen, and zero gravity.

We're told to hold our breath for as long as possible. In minutes, maybe even seconds, we could pass out.

Between all ten of us lies a single purple mask. One that will continuously supply oxygen. There's only one other way to obtain oxygen. By our feet, each candidate has a box, bolted into the ice. As soon as you unclip the ankle bands, an oxygen mask will pop out.

The exam seems simple: *First five candidates to unclip themselves will be expelled.*

Once the atmosphere changes, there's no incentive to share the purple oxygen mask. In my mind, whoever grabs it first will put everyone else at risk.

Franny mutters, "Gods be with us."

"We have to rely on ourselves," I remind her.

She shoots me a glare that fizzles into fear. She mumbles, "A hundred and thirteen."

While the other candidates are frightened of being expelled, Franny is afraid she'll die from nitrogen asphyxiation. A fact that I now regret pointing out to her.

They cannot die today, but we can. It's just the harshest parts of our reality.

Franny chokes down acidic panic.

I must be caging breath *again* because Mykal grunts at me. Irritations spiking. *Measured breaths,* I tell myself. *Measured breaths.* And then our numb feet begin to lift off the ice. Zero gravity takes hold, our bodies weightless in the air like we've begun to fly.

Our chained ankles restrain some movement, but Evers laughs and somersaults. I fixate on the purple oxygen mask that floats with us along with the frozen fruit. A crystallized apple bumps into Franny's ribs.

I wince, the cold like a knife.

Franny winces more and swats the apple away. The fruit sails toward Odell.

"Heya!" Odell swims in the air, dodging the apple.

Joi, the youngest candidate, flails and starts crying, auburn hair drifting wildly around her. Winrock pushes out his chest and makes a concerted effort not to rotate midair. Staying motionless like a statue.

Zimmer swings his head to each candidate, sizing us all up.

Ten of us are here and five will be expelled. I know all their names. I've seen their faces during seminars, classes, and simulations: Seifried, Odell, Gem, Joi, Zimmer, Winrock, and Evers. Then there's the three of us.

"Candidates," my father says. I can barely hear him from outside the glassed walls. "Hold your breath in three . . ."

I start to flip upside down, but I kick out to right myself.

". . . two . . ."

"Don't panic," I tell Franny, her widened eyes darting every which way. "You're fine. *You're fine.*" But this is something that can't be willed away by repeating *one hundred and thirteen.* This isn't fear from a creaking ceiling or a violent winter storm. We are about to be deprived of oxygen.

". . . one—"

I suck in a deep breath before closing my mouth. My lungs constrict and Franny squeezes her eyes shut. Black hair whirls around her face, freckled cheeks puffed out.

Joi's big, frantic eyes aim for her box. She opens her mouth, inhaling nitrogen, and she clutches her throat before fumbling with the band on her ankle—*beeeeeep.*

A scarlet oxygen mask pops out of her box. The little girl swims through the air and catches the mask. In seconds, she fits it over her mouth and breathes deeply. Tears of regret spill from her eyes, the droplets sailing off.

Nine of us are left.

Mykal flips backward, coping with the lack of oxygen better than Franny—and even me. My throat is tight and what air remains in my lungs feels infinitesimal. Like it will disappear at any moment. Struggling, my heart beats violently in my chest.

Hurry. I reach for the purple oxygen mask, but it drifts much closer to Seifried. With the easiest stretch, he grasps it.

Frozen blueberries brush and prick my skin like bullets. *Hold your breath.*

After Seifried takes a breath from the mask, he passes it to the candidate on his left. Odell. I narrow my eyes, watching her devious expression take shape. *How do I win? How do I end this quickly?*

On the other side of Odell, Zimmer frantically extends his hand for the mask. Veins protrude in his neck as he loses oxygen. He starts to spin backward, the zero gravity disorienting him.

Odell yanks the mask out of his reach. Shaking her head, she returns the mask to her mouth.

Gods be damned.

Zimmer screams at the little girl, openmouthed and furious. He jerks forward, but Odell again leans back. I watch him lose air during his bout of rage. He wavers between Odell and his ankle cuff, seconds from quitting.

I thought I'd be relieved by him leaving StarDust. But all I envision is a future where Zimmer has lost incentive to keep Franny's secret. He could easily and spitefully tell the StarDust directors that she's a Fast-Tracker. She may trust him.

But I don't.

I have no more time to think.

I just act.

Crouching down to my ankle, I unclip myself from the ice. *Beeeeep.* Lights flash around the enclosure, indicating that I've quit.

I haven't. Not yet. I convince myself of these lies. And I don't touch my scarlet mask that floats out of my box.

I swim through the air toward Odell as she clutches the mask to her mouth. She shrieks at me, eyes widened in horror as I near.

Woozy, I fight my eyelids that try to drop, my head that tries to be heavy. I curl my fingers around the mask, stronger than this little girl of ten years. I forcefully tug and rip the mask off Odell.

Instantly, in her hysteria, she gasps and gasps, lungfuls of nitrogen. Aching for air. She feverishly reaches for her ankle. And Odell unclips herself, greedily placing her scarlet emergency mask to her lips.

My body protests, maddeningly dizzy, all air gone, and I try desperately not to take nitrogen into my lungs. But I see Zimmer's fingers descend to his ankle chain, and I veer toward him quickly, tossing the mask in a soaring arc.

He catches it and confusion morphs his face. But he doesn't hesitate. Zimmer takes a long deep breath before he returns it to me.

I press the purple mask to my face, and I inhale strongly, my splitting lungs grateful for each breath. It doesn't calm my panic, which I begin to realize belongs to Franny.

Eyes still tightened closed, she doesn't see what's happening, but her fear remains. Suffocating. Dying. *Here.*

I slice through air to reach Franny, and I place my hand to her cheek. As the link heightens by the touch—her sense in clear focus—my stomach knots and coils, frightened to the bone. Tears leak from the tightened corners of her eyes. Droplets drifting midair.

I rest the mask against her mouth. Franny instinctively breathes and then I hand the mask to Mykal. He fits it over his mouth with trembling hands. His face reddened, neck muscles taut.

So quickly, one of us could hyperventilate and pass out. *Die.* Both of them struggle. *I* struggle. This isn't simple or easy with the link. Their panic is mine. Mine theirs.

All I can think is, *This needs to end now.*

Evers and Winrock fight for oxygen, but they both have begun pinching their nostrils closed, determination gripping their faces. They know they won't die here and so their resolve is un-paralleled.

I make a decision that ices over the last warmth inside me.

I remain unchained, and with a kick against the glass wall, I propel myself toward Evers. His distrust mounts higher and higher the closer I near. Then I aim for his ankle.

He doesn't process what I've done until my fingers unclip him. Lights flash around us.

Evers screams, face paling and eyes heaving. Focus lost and desperate for air, he seizes his scarlet emergency mask and sucks in oxygen.

Zimmer, Seifried, Winrock, and Gem are left. Two have to go. *End this.*

I will.

My lungs tighten with each stroke toward the blond girl, my energy being used on swimming through zero gravity rather than caging oxygen. Despite the pain and the incoming cherries and rare peaches that scald my skin, I'm hollowed out like a bottomless pool.

I grab Gem's ankle cuff. She tries to shove me while concentrating on breathing. Weak effort. The second I'm about to unclip Gem, she rams her knee into my chin.

My teeth batter together and Franny's eyes snap open.

I force my lips shut, but my brain rattles, lightened. *I need air.* Mykal and Franny ingest enough from the mask, but they can't physically give me oxygen.

The moment my fingers skim Gem's ankle cuff again, my insides light up in panic. I feel Franny fully. She jerks against her chain, trying to slice through the air, like she means to come toward me. The metal band digs at her ankle, restraining her body.

Alarm mounts and mounts and mounts until I have to back away. Franny eases for a second, her body going still.

I don't question her emotions. I float away from Gem and unclip Winrock, his face painfully reddened. I expect him to fight me. I expect him to grab my shoulders and try to knock my head against the glass wall.

But his bloodshot eyes just rip into me like serrated knives, full of unbridled hatred. Even as he grabs his scarlet mask and gulps air.

Last one.

I swerve to the freckled boy. Seifried.

His little hands try desperately to shove me away, but he's small and young and fragile. And I'm too numb to care.

I can't even think of an apology. I do what needs to be done.

It has to be this way. I unclip Seifried. He fights me for a second, grabbing at my arms. I push him with the flat of my palm, and before he ingests nitrogen, he finds his emergency mask and pushes it against his mouth.

Beeeeeep.

Suddenly, gravity returns and gently lowers all of us to the ice. Oxygen filters into the enclosure and I'm on my knees. I choke for air. Coughing hoarsely while the glassed walls groan on their descent.

My ears ring, candidates shout over one another. I rub the frost residue off my face and brows. My eyelashes crystallized.

The walls disappear completely. I just stare at the ice beneath my knees.

"He should be disqualified!" Evers yells to the StarDust directors.

Winrock chimes in, "I was forcibly unclipped by a madman!"

"Shhh," someone chastises.

I breathe so heavily that my ribs jut in and out.

"This is undignified and unfair!" Winrock exclaims.

I turn my head to meet Franny's darkened scowl and Mykal's hostility. For a moment, I believe they're meant for me, but they direct their riled emotions at the candidates.

"Disqualify him!"

I flinch.

"Please, be calm. We need time to review what happened," Amelda says hurriedly. "We'll have a decision later today. Thank you for your patience."

Slowly, I pick my inked and scarred body off the ice. The remaining candidates gape at me, shock and horror emblazoned in every wide eye.

TWENTY-NINE

Mykal

Hours ago, Tauris announced that Court showed an uncharacteristic amount of selflessness by saving Zimmer, but also a heaping dose of ambition by unclipping other candidates. Two qualities StarDust apparently admires for a team.

More than that, he never used his emergency mask. Meaning he never disqualified himself like the others wished he had.

Tauris ended the speech with, "The remaining fifty of you may relax in the city tonight. Remember secrecy and do not mention StarDust or your affiliation with the Saga 5 Mission."

So we did just that.

Fortmont Tavern is louder than three hells. Court said he had special "criteria" for our hangout spot, and the dank, boisterous tavern fit his three standards.

One: filled to the brim.

Two: housing Influentials and Fast-Trackers alike.

Three: playing iceling on the lone, fuzzy television. (Though he won't admit that one, but his attention wanders to the aired game nearby.)

I wait for the bartender to slide over three mugs of ale. And I grunt at a damned Fast-Tracker that pokes my arm for no other reason than to feel my muscle. "If you pester me once more, I'll be launching my boot up your ass."

The boy snorts. Then jabs a finger again.

Gods bless. I hate everyone.

Thankfully I collect the mugs before my temper boils over and I return to a rickety corner table where Court and Franny sit.

"I swear to the gods I heard the ceiling crack," Franny says to Court, not very hushed, but commotion from rowdy Fast-Trackers and talkative Influentials grants enough privacy.

I look up. The ceiling is a bit stained, but our flat in Bartholo appeared much worse, and the tavern's leafy green wallpaper is in perfect condition.

"You *heard* the ceiling?" Court is disbelieving. "I can barely hear my own voice."

True. I plop in a chair between them and dish out the mugs.

"Maybe my hearing is greater than yours?" Franny recoils at nothing in particular, eyes pinging to the wall. A pang of nauseous fear roils in her stomach. "I hate this."

"You're safe," I say. Ever since we left the iced pool, Franny has been jumpy, and her little "one hundred and thirteen" trick is working less than usual.

I strain my ears to catch her muttered words. "I don't feel safe."

My bones hurt to hear that, but more so to *feel* the truth of her statement. I sense how badly she wishes this world didn't scare every bit of her. I have no answers to give, so I elbow her side and nod to her ale.

With a tight breath, Franny cups her hands around the mug.

Court is gripping his ale so firmly that my own knuckles ache. He's been as unbending and rigid as ever.

I cut our thickening silence. "Should I be calling you Court Idle*fall* from now on?" He rolls his eyes while I add, "You're the luckiest gods-damn person in all of Altia, you realize." With so many candidates hollering for Court's expulsion, Tauris could've easily sided with them.

"It wasn't luck." Court's grim grays look humorless tonight.

Franny raises her brows and teases, "Is succeeding considered *bad* luck in your eyes?"

"That sounds just like our Court." I clink mugs with Franny and she flinches a bit but takes a swig to wash away the trepidation.

Court groans out, "Shut up." But his lip tries painfully to tic upward. I scoot closer to Court and tap his cheek twice.

His lips twitch.

Almost a smile, little crook.

I can't stifle a bright grin that nearly overtakes my mouth. I hold his jaw for a long beat before dropping my hand to his knee.

His heart skips. "It was coincidence," Court tells us, clearing his throat. "Nothing more."

I follow his gaze to the television again. At first I was surprised by a television in a tavern, but Yamafort's electricity has outshined Bartholo. Lights remain lit in buildings much longer here. Sometimes I wait for a power outage like the Bartholo shops endure, but none ever arrive in Yamafort.

Most Fast-Trackers play table games toward the farthest back corner, and Influentials flock around the high-top wooden tables, drinking wine and ale. Some Influentials and FTs chat together by the iceling game.

"Is that girl waving at you?" Franny asks Court.

By the bar, a lady most surely waves at Court. Glittering sapphire jewels weigh down her ears and cover her whole collar.

I squint and tilt my head. "Maybe she's confused."

"No," Court says, "she's familiar."

"How so?"

"The black curls," Franny says with a sip of ale. "I remember her too. I think she's from . . . you-know-where." *StarDust.*

My chair creaks as I lean back. "How'd someone find us?"

Court releases his grip on his mug. "We're only five blocks from you-know-where. She could've checked multiple restaurants or parlors before stumbling on this one."

A fleeting smile from Franny touches my lips. Court used her phrase without hesitation, even if it's not proper sounding. We all latch our focus on the StarDust candidate.

After the lady snatches a goblet of wine, she sidles up to our table. I rest my feet on the free chair. Not letting her grow comfortable.

She frowns at my unwelcome but remains standing. "Heya,"

she greets to Court only. "I'm Trix Nortacastle." Stretching out a hand to Court, he reluctantly shakes it.

Trix gloats as though he invited her to a grand ball. "I know that you know me. I know you, and I think it's best if I join your alliance." *A what?* "My family owns Maranil's Jewel Emporium and all the jewels in Altia are outsourced from us." Her rouge-painted nails skim her necklace. "A strand of sapphires is worth over twenty thousand bills."

Even I can see that she's bribing him with jewels. For something called an *alliance*—I don't like the sound of that word. *Alliance.* All I imagine is a baby alligator.

"Why do you want an alliance with me?" Court asks, deepening my confusion.

Trix looks to sit, but I refuse to move my boots. Sighing, she says, "Tauris obviously sees you as a potential leader for the mission. It's quite clear you're in the running to fill the captain's chair and they're seeking a *team*. I can be a part of your team. We use one another to reach the finish line and we'll be hired together."

I understand a bit more. Already sensing Court's reply, I have fun. "What sort of sapphires are we talking about?" I ask. "Big? Tiny? Cut in the shape of a butterfly?"

Court's laughter dies in his lungs, but I grin enough for all three of us.

Trix scoffs. "I'm not offering *you* anything."

"No," Court says immediately.

"What?" She gapes.

"I said *no*. I reject your offer of an alliance."

Steam blows out of her ears. "*Fine*. I'll see that you fail then." With that feeble threat, she trots off—only to be replaced by a constant line of StarDust candidates looking to bribe Court.

"Thirty thousand bills."

"The best liqueur in all of Altia."

"A jar of honey from an indoor greenery in Orricht."

"Front-row seats to an iceling match."

"A night in my bed."

I choke on ale, my body freezing up like I've been struck by an ice demon. Franny coughs into her fist, sensing me fully.

"No," Court rejects easily and as another wave of bribes start, he shouts, "Enough!" Our area of the tavern falls to silence.

"But—" someone says.

"*No* to all of you. I don't need to hear your offers. I'm accepting *nothing*. In fairness to everyone, we let the directors decide." Maybe he's afraid if he agrees to them, it'll be ruining Franny's chances and mine.

At his declaration, their respect for Court only grows. It's not like he accepted some and blew off the rest. He denied them all, so nothing has really changed.

Except for one thing. "It's now fact," I whisper to him. "You're the most valuable candidate."

I wait for the eye roll, but he's too fixated on the candidates. Watching as they shuffle to other tables and the iceling game. Mumbling to themselves. Farther out of view.

Court barely relaxes, but Franny tries by chugging a good portion of her ale.

"Court Idlecastle . . ." We all jerk at the sound of his name.

Padgett Soarcastle sneaks up on our table. Dropping the magenta fur hood of her coat, she acknowledges the three of us with a nod. I'm as wary of Padgett as I am every other candidate. Maybe even more so.

Her brain is forever turning.

"I'm not taking bribes," Court says with bite.

Padgett never eyes the chair occupied by my feet. "Bribing you? I'm not here for bribes. I don't need help to be hired for the mission. I can do that all on my own."

"Then why are you here?" Court wonders.

Padgett knots the pink ribbon in her dark hair. "To say *thank you*. You could've unclipped my sister, but for whatever reason, you chose not to." Sincerity wells in her eyes. She even drops her head to hide the emotion.

Franny frowns. "Why do you care so much? I just don't know if many would . . ."

Padgett lifts her intense gaze. "In Maranil back home, Gem and I assembled a G5 electronic computer from old manuals. We built the computer from scratch, but a week later our president confiscated the machine. She enacted a law that forbade Maranilans from creating new tech that had no agricultural purpose. 'A waste of our resources,' she said. 'You should've invented high-tech fishing gear.' We were chastised in Maranil, but I was certain we'd thrive in Altia."

Padgett shakes her head in remembrance. "Gem didn't want to leave. She felt as though she had something to prove in Maranil and the gods wanted her there. I stayed right by her side." She steps forward. "I didn't leave my sister behind then and I certainly won't abandon her now. We weren't right for Maranil, but we belong on that starcraft. *Together.* That's why I care."

"Does this mean you won't be asking for my indigo card today?" I question.

Her lip hikes. "I won't hassle you anymore."

I pick my words carefully. "It's fine. I wouldn't want the winds to change now. It might create a storm."

"Can I have your card?" Padgett asks.

"No."

"Well then." Padgett bids us farewell and then exits as discreetly as she arrived.

Franny presses her lips to the rim of her mug. "Gem told me something last week and I didn't think it mattered much. Now, I don't know . . ."

"What?" Court and I say together.

"Padgett and Gem have the same deathday," Franny says. "It's rare, but not uncommon for family, I've heard."

Court's worry mounts like bricks compacting on his chest. "It matters."

"Why?" I scratch at my rough jaw.

"Oftentimes, when family has the same deathday, they die together in the same place and the same time," Court explains, his voice strained and tight. "Which means that if Padgett is on the Saga when she reaches her deathday, then Gem is more likely to be with her sister. It only leaves three open spaces for the mission and no room for error."

I watch Franny's face fall. "We'll be all right," I say. "Maybe they'll die apart."

"Unlikely." Court snuffs out my optimism.

"Mayday," Franny curses beneath her breath, but not at Court or me. I catch sight of an angered little lady with silky russet pigtails. With accusations on her round face, she weaves through the congested tavern.

Raina Nearfall charges toward Franny.

THIRTY

Franny

Raina smacks her palms flat on the tabletop. "You *thief*."

I startle. "*Thief?*" Of all the names she could've called me, I wasn't prepared for this one. "I stole nothing of yours." I even *gently* returned her indigo card to its original place. The details make me feel less like a wart.

Stretching over the table, she sneers, "You know what you did. I heard you spread my word to other candidates this very morning."

I grow hot and lean close, our noses nearly touching. "I did what I had to." In my journal, I even scribbled, *Telling candidates Raina's word—owed to Raina.*

"It wasn't fair or right," Raina retorts. "I worked hard to be here. It's all I've ever wanted in life and you're stealing my dream. *It's not fair.*" Every hurt syllable punctures my spirit.

Guilt douses my fiery demeanor. "What do you want in return?" I ask.

Court stiffens, but Raina quickly snaps, "Nothing. There is nothing in this world that can replace what you've taken."

"It wasn't yours," Court interjects.

"Excuse me?"

Court combats the little girl with only a shadow of remorse. "You haven't earned anything yet. You say she stole a dream, but you're forgetting that we all have dreams."

Our dreams don't align with anyone else's, I remember.

"You would rather succeed by cheating then?" Raina asks me. "Is that how you really wish to be hired?"

I force down any regret. Not wanting to turn back the days. Every time I share the word *tree*, I help Mykal and hurt Raina. *I know.* Our survival depends on leaving behind disasters and broken hearts. And my morality fissures little by little. Yearning for me to mend the cracked pieces.

I can't. I know I can't.

If I want to survive, then I need to destroy her chances and better ours.

"I wish to succeed by any means," I tell her with a heavy heart. "I'm sorry."

Raina growls between her teeth, then captures Mykal's mug and douses my face with ale. *Fyke.* I pinch my burning eyes shut.

Mykal stands and hollers, shooing Raina away, and Court quickly passes me a stack of thin paper napkins. Burying my face in them, I soak the auburn liquid and groan in defeat. "I deserved that."

"No you didn't," Court says sternly. "We're enrolled in Star-Dust and some of us won't be hired for the mission. You don't see other candidates starting food fights when they're expelled."

Mykal collapses to his seat and starts squeezing out my drenched hair. "And she hasn't even been expelled yet." I hear the underlying question. *What if she still beats Mykal?*

I ball the sopping napkins. "Raina is worried. Otherwise she wouldn't be this mad."

Court nods in agreement.

When I chug the last of my ale, I expect wooziness or giddy feelings, but the effects never touch me. I frown and size up my mug. A drink this large usually bangs at my head and lightens my body, but I feel no different. *What a day.*

And of course, the night becomes stranger.

Zimmer appears. Instantly, Mykal puts his boots on the only free seat, but Zimmer yanks the chair away and spins it backward. Sitting with his legs spread, he invites himself to our table.

"You're not wanted here," I tell him easily, Mykal and Court's displeasure clear on their faces and in my body. I consider Zimmer as good of a Fast-Tracker friend as any, but there is a level of mistrust that I try not to ignore.

"That's never stopped me before, orphan Fast-Tracker," he says, then swings his mop of brown hair to Court. "Influential, *obviously*." To Mykal, he clucks his tongue and snaps his fingers. "Orrish Fast-Tracker. Possibly."

I kick the leg of his chair. "And you're a nosy Fast-Tracker."

Zimmer drags himself even closer to the table. "*Wise* Fast-Tracker." He flashes a self-satisfied smile. "I fixed it for you."

"*Wart*. I fixed it better—"

"People are around," Court cuts in, severity blanketing his grave eyes.

Zimmer plucks napkins out of the steel dispenser. "And we'd have to yell for anyone else to hear us. You seriously haven't noticed how loud it is?" He chucks the napkins at my face. "You're dripping."

I shoot him a glare but gather the napkins and pat the ale off my temples. "Someone threw a drink at me."

"I saw."

Mykal runs his tongue against his molars. "Is that why you're bothering us?"

"No. For one, I thought I'd maintain appearances. Seeing as how I'm in an alliance now." Zimmer reaches to pat Court on the shoulder and Mykal slaps his hand away. "Holy hells, all right—I won't touch without asking." Zimmer balances on two legs of his chair. "Everywhere I look, more and more candidates are coupling. It's turning into a fykking dating show."

I toss my dirtied napkins at him, but he blocks more than a few with his hand. "Why would you be in an alliance with . . . ?" I trail off because the answer hits me. Court aided Zimmer in the pool. Therefore the other candidates must believe Court is protecting him.

"I didn't help you because I like you," Court says bluntly.

"And I'd be a chump to believe you did." Zimmer raises two

fingers. "And two, I'm here to announce that we're *even*. You got me fired and now you helped me through an exam."

My brows crinkle. "Wait, *wait*. You're sleeping in *my* bed to erase that debt. We don't owe you twice."

Mykal grins wide as Zimmer gawks, befuddled for a moment. His neck flushes red.

"So you do owe Court for saving you," I tell him. "Unless you'd rather leave my bed."

Zimmer rips apart the soggy napkins. "How about I just write an *I owe you* in a journal? That seems to work so fantastically for you."

I glare.

"You told him about your journal?" Court scolds.

"Not really." While writing in my journal one night, Zimmer asked for a blank page. Strangely he likes *reading*—he said he taught himself in the boring hours at the Catherina—and even more than that, he enjoys drawing his favorite scenes from classic fantasy novels. As I tore a page from my journal, he caught sight of my scribbled words.

Under the covers, he asked me, "You can't really expect to repay everything you've ever taken."

"I will." I glowered, about to shut off his little handheld light and ignore him completely.

He jerked the light out of my grasp. "You're bound to disappoint yourself, and I'd rather not be around when you meet the truth."

I had to ask. "What truth?"

"That your journal is a placeholder for all your bizarre remorse." Zimmer then described how half the people on my list would probably die young. And no one would dwell on the dead the way that I did.

Maybe I am avoiding the full impact of all the wrongs I've made and all the debts I've incurred, but right now I need the journal to be more at peace with my decisions.

"What do you mean by *not really*?" Court asks the both of us.

"I accidentally saw her journal one night," Zimmer says with a shrug. "It's not as big of a deal as you're making it out to be."

Court begins to boil, disliking Zimmer's snappy tone, and before a stew starts, I reroute the topic. "Unless you want to leave my bed, you do owe Court," I tell Zimmer.

Mykal straightens up at this news, pleased that Zimmer will most likely sleep in his own bed now.

Zimmer licks his bottom lip, thinking and thinking. "All right, what do you want?"

"You like her bed that much?" Mykal clutches his empty mug with whitened knuckles.

Zimmer shreds more napkins into piles. "I like the company."

"The *company*," Mykal spits out like it's a foul word.

I try to keep focused, but their heat swelters my skin. "We want to see your indigo card," I tell Zimmer. "Then we're even."

Once I tried to make another swap: his indigo card in exchange for my Juggernaut. He immediately rejected me. "I hate drugs," he said, and before sleep, he whispered about how he took Hibiscus, fell unconscious, and woke days later. I heard how addictive Hibiscus could be, and I didn't have the bills for that kind of constant pleasure. So I never tried it, but the loss of time scared Zimmer enough to stay away from all drugs.

Zimmer digs into his pocket. "Only because I wouldn't be here if it weren't for Court, but know, if you spread my *word* around, I'll come after all three of you."

Court swiftly plucks the indigo card from his fingers, digests the word, and then slides it back. "It's an *icicle*."

"And three." Zimmer raises three fingers. There's a third reason for why he's at our table? "I should look past this—hells, I've looked past a ton already—but it's eating at me. So I'm asking *you*." He zeroes in on Court. "That day at the Catherina, I let you through the back door with a passed-out and bruised Fast-Tracker. I asked no questions, but I'm asking now: What's your relation to Wilafran?"

Frost nips my veins. I hadn't even thought about Zimmer's perspective. How he saw me being carried in Mykal's arms: battered by the Fast-Trackers in rags who fought to steal my clothes.

Mykal grips the table. "I was with him, you realize?"

"You're not the Influential." Zimmer holds Court's narrowed gaze. "I've seen enough of them take advantage of strung-out, unconscious FTs. *They're going to die in a few years anyway*, right?"

Court ices over. "It's not like you stopped me."

His throat bobs. "Just tell me. What is she to you?" Zimmer did ask me this before and all I said was, "We're not married." I should've been more specific, but what is Court to me? If there's a precise word, I don't know it.

Court's eyes soften on me. "She's my dear friend."

I smile weakly. I like how he tenderly cradles the words. To Zimmer, I add, "Some Fast-Trackers tried to steal my clothes off my back. He just wanted me to be warm."

After Zimmer settles with the truth, he asks if I can speak alone with him. I don't mind. So I rise and stumble. Woozy. I grip the back of Mykal's chair. *Gods.*

My lips part in realization. The ale I chugged, I must've been more homed in on their senses. Not my own. My vision blurs, but I blink and blink.

Zimmer stands right in front of me.

"When did you get there?" At least I'm not slurring my words.

Court asks if I need help, half rising out of his chair—and I bet he's seconds from suggesting I sit. I assure him that I can walk on my own and I do just that. Albeit, not very gracefully, but my gait has never been very sweet natured.

We wander into the back of the tavern. Where the lighting dims and vibrantly clothed Fast-Trackers play dice, swig ale, and laugh raucously. I spot orange braids, pink and lavender chopped hair, intricate tattoos, and silver piercings.

I wobble into the wall and lean for support.

Zimmer props his shoulder next to me. "How do you go from being coherent to sloshed in seconds?"

The link. "Maybe I'm a Wonder," I joke.

"Wonders have more sense than you. And me." Zimmer never presses for a real answer. More thoughts nag at him and he lets them out quickly. "Remember what you asked me yesterday night?"

I do. "I asked when you're going to die." For a silly moment, I believed he dodged his deathday too. But without citing myself, I mentioned the theory, and he laughed so loudly that he almost woke up Gem.

Zimmer has a deathday and while every candidate in StarDust will live beyond a hundred years, Zimmer will die much sooner than that. He bought a fake identification to enter StarDust as an Influential.

All I know for certain is that he won't see past twenty-nine.

No one's deathday has ever saddened me before, but I often find myself wishing Zimmer had as much time as every other candidate.

"I said that I'd think about whether or not I'd tell you my deathday."

"I remember that too."

"I decided." Zimmer nods to himself. "I'm not ever telling you, and I don't want to hear yours either. When you look at me, the last thing I want you to see is an approaching deathday. I want to be *more* than a dying Fast-Tracker in everyone's eyes."

I can live with not knowing his deathday much easier than I can live with not knowing my own.

The noise escalates, half the FTs cheering, the other half groaning and booing. "Is that why you're pretending to be an Influential?" I ask quietly enough.

Zimmer shrugs. "It's a . . ." I can't hear the last part.

"A what?!" I yell over the commotion.

He dips his head toward my ear. "A bonus!"

"A bonus to what?!"

He wears a dazzling grin. "I want to see the stars before I die! Don't you?"

I can't help but smile. What a Fast-Tracker goal. Zimmer is in StarDust with the sole hope to see the stars. "I guess so!" I shout back.

Zimmer plucks a deserted half-eaten basket of chips off a nearby table. He tosses the bitten pieces on the floor and then offers me a few. In the dark depths of the tavern, he acts more like a Fast-Tracker, and I realize that I can too.

I eat more than the few offered chips and then he shakes the crumbs into his mouth.

Several feet away, a girl in orange braids chucks the dice at her friend's head—he ducks with more laughter.

As I watch, I expect and wait for *yearning*. To be welcomed and accepted into their Fast-Tracker folds like long-lost friends. But longing never arrives. With Court and Mykal, I have real fealty. Strong enough that ancient battalions couldn't raze it.

"I hate that game," Zimmer says, drawing my attention toward four Fast-Trackers playing Pull the Trigger. Loaded gun in hand, a young man pushes the barrel hard against his temple.

Fear knocks me farther against the wall. I stand too close to that gun and their game.

The man tries to pull the trigger, but the gun jams, not even clicking. The corner cluster of FTs erupts in loud cheers. He takes a measured bow.

"Let's go," I tell Zimmer, clasping his wrist for balance. As we push through the congregated Fast-Trackers, a girl with spiky blue hair wraps the barrel around her lips.

Finger on the trigger—*boom*. The violent gunshot rings out and shock electrifies my body, zipping through my limbs. Something wet splatters my shoulder. I glance to my left—*gods*.

"Are you all right?!" I shout at Zimmer.

His whole face is sprayed in crimson blood. Like a deathday scene. He swears some of the nastiest Fast-Tracker slang and uses his shirt to wipe off the splotches. "Today's not my deathday," is all he tells me.

I'm running. No, I'm not. Court and Mykal are trying to find me. Racing through the masses and uproar. The Fast-Tracker girl cries in pain, twitching on the floorboards. Half her cheek is blown off.

"Don't move, kid!" the bartender yells from afar. "You're going to bloody the entire tavern!"

People argue over the angle of the gun and how her injury will look after it's healed, but no one aids her now. *She'll live*, I predict what most people are thinking.

And then some kind of wetness drips out of my nose, sliding down my upper lip. I touch my face and inspect my fingers.

Blood?

My blood.

My mind drifts off into terror.

THIRTY-ONE

Franny

I'm dying."

My words hang unpleasantly in the chilled air. We walk across an empty stone street, snow fluttering gently. Like it hopes to blanket our worries for the night. I button my brand-new coat—soft blue wool—tight to my collar.

Our boots crunch ice, shattered glass of broken bottles, and other fallen debris. Court asked to take the long way to the museum, a detour he remembered from his childhood. The three of us aren't fighting to return to StarDust anytime soon, so our pace is slow and heavy.

"You're not *dying*." Court blows hot breath on his gloved palms.

"You can't be that sure." I wipe at my nostrils *again*, but the nosebleed stopped after ten minutes. Court pinched my nose and then instructed me to tilt my head forward. We left Zimmer and the tavern so quickly—it's all a blur. The effects of the ale even wore off, since I was so alarmed and panicked.

Each step, my fright carves scars into my lungs. I'm one brutal moment from crying and wailing out in guttural frustration.

We pass a coat shop, lights blinking off, the store closed. "You don't know why this is happening," I add, fire scorching my voice.

While Mykal trudges forward, breaking slick ice with his heel, Court slows to my side. "I may not know *why* you have a nosebleed," Court says, "but they're common. I promise."

I heatedly rub tears that prick. "If it doesn't mean I'm dying, then why did I have a nosebleed so close to my deathday?" I wasn't even linked to Court and Mykal when the first one began.

I feel Court suppressing the urge to roll his eyes. "What I mean is that a nosebleed isn't always serious. They can happen because the air is too dry."

"I was just *inside*," I snap. "The air was warm!"

"Franny—"

"*No*," I nearly yell again. "Don't *Franny* me." Fear seizes my heart in an iron fist. I hate the unknown. *I hate this.* My voice rattles with every bit of life inside of me. Every piece of Franny Bluecastle I wish to keep safe and alive. "You've had over two long years to come to terms with not knowing. Mykal has had *eight*." I point at Mykal, who is stopped a few feet ahead of us. Waiting with his hands stuffed in his wool coat. "I've had nowhere near that time. I need answers."

Court whispers, "A hundred and thirteen."

I want to scream at my own awful trick. "Why?!" I spread my hands toward the sidewalk as though the answer is there. "Why are we still alive? Why do we share as many commonalties as we do differences? None of this makes any sense." *None of it.*

None of it.

I want none of it. I kick the closest stone building. My toes throb, but I kick again.

Court pulls me backward and I spin on him. Shoving his chest. He grabs my wrists.

"I'm dying," I cry angrily.

"You're not. You're *right here*," he says strongly. Court cups my cheeks. "You're right here. I can touch you. *You're alive.*"

My hot tear slips down his glove. "What about tomorrow?"

"What about tomorrow?"

"Will I still be alive?" I breathe burning breath. "What about the next day? What about a year from now?"

"I have no answers," Court says.

I shake my head profusely. "There are answers. You just can't find them."

Jaw muscle twitching, his hands drop from me. "We have no *time*. We've been through this."

My chin trembles with fury. With despair. "I can't shut it off like you two. I thought I could, but I can't. I *care* about what happens to me, and you both feel like the unknown is normal because you searched and searched for answers and found none. I wasn't with you. I never had time . . ." He's been saying I still have none.

I distance myself from Court. From Mykal, who stares at me like I'm the girl who put an iron rod at Court's throat. Who only trusted herself. Back to the very beginning again. His sadness pools deeply, painfully, and my body quakes as though I just dodged my deathday again.

The onslaught of emotion tries to rush back, so I ask them, "When we have more time, will you ever search for the answers with me?"

"No," Court says the same time Mykal tells me, "Yeah."

I *loathe* every part of Court and he must feel that because his face cracks.

"Franny—"

"I hate you," I say through gritted teeth. "I've been here for you. I've done all that you've asked and you can't even spare a single second for me in return." I leave him and walk down the street.

Court runs after me. "There are *no* answers," he says to my back. "You shouldn't spend your life on an aimless search. You'll be stuck in misery."

"I already am!" I spin on him. "Can't you feel me?" My hands hover over my body like I'm afraid to touch my own skin.

He inhales a staggered breath. "I'm—"

Sirens blare, so near that all of our heads rotate toward the sound. I rub at my face again, realizing that my time is up.

It's always so short, isn't it?

When will I have longer than a moment to process what's happening to me? I stifle my contempt for Court and all the ill feelings and fear. I stomp every darkened sentiment so far down that I grow numb and uncaring.

We hurry toward the museum, a path that follows the sirens.

Louder and louder, they roar. Our street suddenly opens to the largest city square and we skid to a stop.

Altia Patrol swarms the outside of the stone Bank Hall, but all their lights rain down on Yamafort's most treasured marble statues: three skyscraping silhouettes, made to represent the three gods.

They're not how I remember. "Good gods," I breathe, horror-struck.

Court sways backward and Mykal catches him.

Someone chipped out the marble eyes of the first statue. The second: a gaping hole is where a heart would lie. The third is missing a head completely.

Stolen family photographs are taped to the arms and legs, a little boy's face scratched off the pictures. What chills me from toe to head: the name painted in a deep bloodred on every marbled chest.

Etian.

THIRTY-TWO

Court

Cemented in a malevolent, cruel nightmare, I thrash and thrash.

I see Bastell the instant I shut my eyes. His sinewy frame clothed in a crimson Vorkter jumpsuit, his ash-brown hair flying madly in high winds. The graying rough stubble on his jaw and that feverish gaze, which devours all the purities of my soul.

His full weight bears agonizingly on me. Two daggers puncture my chest. And I scream and scream. A bloodied pickax lies a few feet away, my jumpsuit and skin torn to shreds. Bleeding, I pat helplessly at the snow. Ice splits beneath my back while I lie on a frozen lake. And I try to add more pressure. I would rather drown than feel this torture.

I want to quit, but somewhere, someone is tugging at my aching muscles and arms. Yelling at me to fight.

To live.

"Is it your blood?" Bastell asks, his voice melodic. Tranquil, almost.

My first months at Vorkter, his voice soothed me to sleep. In my dreams, I recognize the tone for what it truly is. *Sinister.*

Bastell licks my blood off his fingers. "If you refuse to give me your gift of life, I will just *take* it." He slices my ribs in a quick movement as if conducting an orchestra. I kick and cry out and my actions are met with a blow to the face. My vision fades while he brings the bloodied blade to his mouth and tastes the glistening tip.

"I'm not . . . ," I choke. Cold twists through my naked body, fabric torn terribly, flesh ripped even worse. All around me, the snow is red.

I'm not gifted. He searches for the meaning to why I dodged my deathday. He searches for more life that I cannot give.

Bastell appraises me like I'm a stranger, not his cellmate of five long years. "I don't think it's the blood either." Digging both daggers, he severs my inked snake and I wail, vision blurred from tears. Snot running down my chin, I sob from the pain.

He cocks his head. "Maybe the heart, then?"

The daggers pierce my flesh deeper and deeper. My world erupts in violent colors and then bleeds out altogether. My mind clatters. Vibrates. Reroutes. Pressure never releases from my chest and I hear that sickeningly silky voice again.

"Maybe the heart, then?"

I jolt. Waking upright in thick sweat and coughing hoarsely into my fist. My sheets are tangled, pillows smacked to the floor. Canopy tied back. The other four beds lie empty, all my roommates expelled, but Mykal is truly here.

He sits beneath the askew covers, awake beside me.

With a shallow breath, I ask, "Franny?" I've been trying to protect her from this terror. I can't stomach dragging Franny or Mykal down with me every night. And I'm afraid to focus on her and sense a wide-awake, quivering body.

"She's still asleep," Mykal assures me.

Good.

Good.

Tears rise.

As soon as I start shaking, Mykal wraps his arms around my sweating build, my shirt suctioned to my chest. I tuck my head against the crook of his neck and shoulder.

"You're all right," he coos. "You're all right." His gruff voice contrasts my nightmare.

I hold on to him. Terrified to let go. My eyes leak, my nose runs, but he just clutches tighter and whispers in my ear. "You're all right. You're all right."

I grasp the base of his neck—his soft hair between my fingers. My pulse begins to slow and breath begins to strengthen.

The nightmare always ends the same. For some reason, my mind never relives the parts where I survive. In the quiet, I think about the very next moment.

I sensed Mykal swinging his head—it *felt* like my head—and the forceful motion overtook me. Mimicking Mykal, I banged foreheads with Bastell.

I knocked him backward.

Scrambling weakly to my feet, I subconsciously focused on Mykal's strength to stagger and run out of harm's way. Others had tried to attack me before Bastell. Three people: the rest of the prisoners who escaped Vorkter with us.

Bastell had stabbed and hit two men unconscious. Wanting me for himself. The young woman, Nattala Icecastle, had been stripping the men for their clothes and boots. The second I detached from Bastell, she clocked him in the head and scavenged his jumpsuit.

I ran faster. Until she was so far out of sight, I believed she'd fall through the ice trying to catch me. Crimson droplets trailed my every step. I stumbled. Tripped. And I sensed someone screaming at me to *never quit*.

I rose. And trudged onward.

Using a thorn from a ricket bush—buried under sheets of ice—and wispy tendrils of its shaved stem, I sutured my cuts. Stitched, I began to walk once more. For days and days and days.

The rest of the story—where I find Mykal, where I race into his arms—calms me.

You're all right. You're all right.

After a while, my heartbeat levels. I lift my head off his broad shoulder, my bloodshot eyes meeting his reddened ones. "To think," I whisper, "there was a time where I called him my mentor, my friend." *It sickens me.*

"You couldn't know he'd maul you," Mykal reminds me. "I would've killed him myself."

"You can't kill him," I say. "He'll die at eighty-five." He's in his thirties and still, Bastell desires more time to live.

"I'd injure him until he *wishes* he were dead," Mykal always rephrases. It's a thought that eases him, not me.

"I don't want you near him," I say. "Promise me, if he finds StarDust—"

"He won't," Mykal growls. "He won't be finding this place. He won't be finding you. Not *ever*."

I want to believe, so badly, that I'll only meet Bastell in my nightmares, but the maimed statues said, *I'm close, Etian. I'm coming for you.*

Bastell knew me as Court, but he chose to call me Etian. The maddened boy who believed he could save lives that would soon die.

In another whisper, I tell Mykal, "Of my names, I know which I like the best." A prisoner scratched a quote into a hallway wall from a novel called *While the Wind Sings*. I was entranced back then and I'm more entranced now.

> *Rest all passions at your heart's highest court.*
> *There, you are the authority of your own soul.*

"Which?" Mykal wonders.

"The name I had when I met you," I say assuredly. "The one I had with Franny."

Nodding, Mykal begins to smile wider and fuller. "Court Icecastle."

Yes. That name is mine.

THIRTY-THREE

Franny

The final exam to determine the most qualified thirty candidates arrives out of nowhere. Amelda wakes everyone in the early morning. Then she orders all fifty candidates to dress in their best formalwear, then line up outside of the dining room and remain completely silent.

We linger in the marbled hallway and, one by one, candidates enter the dining room but never return. I'm ahead of Mykal and Court.

No mathematics, no mathematics, I pray. I've only passed classes with multiplication because I cheated. To my dismay, Gem has speculated that the indigo cards may involve a mathematical equation.

I must be the tenth person in line. Before I even fantasize about what exists beyond the door, I'm stepping through it.

Motionless and untouched, the dining room appears like a preserved museum exhibit. Rows and rows of tables sit varnished and shiny, as though no bodies have ever sat on the tufted chairs, no one has ever spilled syrup and goat's milk. No chatter has disturbed these walls and no feet have scuffed the carpet.

I spot one difference to the usual dining layout. An onyx StarDust cloth cloaks a long table where an ornate golden box waits for me. Quickly, I close the distance and walk urgently up the aisle.

I hear my own anxious breath, and if it weren't for Mykal drumming his thigh and Court rubbing his lips nervously, I'd feel all alone.

Once I reach the table, I exhale deeply and scan the items. A stack of blank paper sits beside the box, then a black pen and very tiny, hand-painted directions on a slab of polished wood.

Peering forward, I read the directions aloud, " 'Congratulations candidate, you've proven your aptitude in sciences, quick-learning, history, flight, and teamwork.' " I smile at the word *flight*.

Of all my classes and simulations, I enjoyed flying the most, and toward the end, I even excelled without cheating. Court wasn't surprised since piloting the starcraft shares a few similarities to driving.

I lick my lips and read on, " 'Now you'll prove how well you can keep a secret.' " The bottom of my stomach drops, but I shouldn't be scared. I dodged my deathday and never spilled the truth to anyone. So I'm a confirmed secret-keeper, aren't I?

My reading skills have improved so much that I read all the directions out loud, hoping Court and Mykal can sense my lips, but then I skim them over a second time and digest the fine print.

Your task: List three words from the candidate cards.
(You may use your own.)
You will be expelled for the following:

1: Listing a stolen card.
2: Listing a card from a candidate who has already been expelled.
3: Listing a card that does not exist.

And lastly, if you shared your card with many others, here is your disadvantage: the candidates whose words are most frequently written will be expelled.

I mutter, " 'After writing your three words and your name at the top of the paper, slip your answers into the slit of the box.' "

THE RAGING ONES   311

My pulse races as I uncap the pen and procure one sheet of paper. I wish we could've discussed this with one another beforehand, but I guess that's the point.

I scribble *Wilafran Elcastle* at the top and then list the two words that I'm sure are true.

Tree.

Icicle.

Tapping my pen, I worry a little that if all three of us write Zimmer's word, he'll be gone. We have no way of gauging what *frequent* means. Frequent could be as much as a word appearing ten times to as little as two.

I have to leave *icicle* because I won't risk writing Court or Mykal's word. I add my own at the bottom.

Bear.

Folding the paper and depositing it into the box, I'm about to return to the hallway, but Amelda appears at the kitchen door.

"This way," she calls.

She ushers me through StarDust's kitchen, out another hallway, and then into the main classroom auditorium. Eight other candidates already wait here. Winded from my nerves, I thud onto a front-row velveteen seat and turn my head.

Several chairs from mine, Kinden sits poised and confident, arm stretched, heel kicked up leisurely on his thigh. He checks his wristwatch.

His nonchalance could be a front, but then again, on the night of the vandalized statues, Kinden never hid his frustrations. He shut down whispers and side-glances left and right. Candidates theorized that Kinden and Tauris were being targeted for Etian's wrongdoings, but only we know the truth.

Too curious, I have to ask Court's brother about the exam. "You aren't worried at all?"

"No." Before I question why not, he adds, "Because I never shared my indigo card with anyone."

I sink in my seat and wonder just how many other candidates sheltered their own cards.

"Listen closely," Tauris says, paper in hand. The rest of the Star-Dust directors line the auditorium stage beside him. Beaming, Amelda clutches a glass bowl with triangular emblem pins.

What I've deduced: *every* candidate believes they've made the final thirty. It worries me. I'm somewhat comfortable knowing that Court, Mykal, and I each jotted down *icicle*, *tree*, and our own words. But I don't like how candidates smile. They're elated, *happy* before the results are even announced.

Twenty candidates are about to leave StarDust stunned. If I could speak to the gods now, I'd tell them that I may botch everything in time—and I may not be the worthiest or most deserving—but I'll put my whole heart into my future. Just guide all three of us through StarDust so we'll have the chance to be free.

Tauris continues, "If we expel you, please exit. If you've made the final thirty, remain seated. These cuts will be quick." He unfurls his paper. "No one listed a card that was stolen or a card from a candidate that has previously been expelled. However, eighteen candidates listed a card that *does not exist*. All eighteen will be leaving—"

Chatter explodes, drowning out Tauris.

My face starts contorting. Court goes rigid and Mykal cranes his neck over his shoulder, searching furiously for Zimmer.

I bristle at the thought of being betrayed by him. I'm all right with looking like a chump, but I trusted him above Mykal and Court. I *vouched* for Zimmer.

Now I'm questioning everything.

I question his glimpse of my journal. Zimmer mentioned that he lacks my kind of remorse, so maybe he could ruin our chances without batting an eye. Too sick to my stomach to even search for him in the auditorium, I cross my arms and listen to the Star-Dust directors quiet the flustered candidates.

"This is as hard for us as it is for you," Tauris says loudly and sincerely, no microphone needed. All fifty of us congregate in the front rows. "We can't alter the exam, so the results stand. If you're expelled, please be courteous and respectful." With another deep breath he begins reading the names of all eighteen candidates who must leave.

Bodies pop up from chairs, fuming. Crying. Some shuffle out without another word, but the majority stay standing.

Tauris reaches the end, "Gef Zucastle, and lastly, Trix Nortacastle."

We're safe for now. I let out an even larger breath. Zimmer showed us his real card after all. In the group, I spot him biting his thumbnail. He's nervous about his own chances.

After the results settle, the air thins.

Trix, the girl who tried to bribe Court with jewels, speaks out. "My words were not fake." Her voice is rushed and upset. "I would've known. I had everyone show me a card."

Amelda takes a step forward. "I apologize, but the word *goat* does not exist."

Every standing candidate casts a scathing glare at someone seated. I pop up slightly to see their hatred directed straight toward Padgett Soarcastle. Dressed in the prettiest raspberry-colored gown, collar made of tawny fur, she sits casually, fingers to her lips.

Gem glows in satisfaction beside her older sister, chin upward. Smile expanding. *Proud.*

They're both so proud of their achievements.

"What card did you show me then?" Trix accuses.

Padgett unclasps a velvet purse and flashes an indigo card. From my view, the goat with gray and white paint splatters definitely looks real.

"I made this card," Padgett tells the candidates. "Gem did the lettering."

"I did." Gem crosses her ankles.

Groans of defeat ring out, followed by incensed shouting. Tauris has to usher two lingering candidates through the exit.

Amelda addresses us, "Only two more candidates will be expelled. The first candidate that I call had their word written twenty-two times."

Most mutter, "Gods."

"The second and *last* candidate sadly leaving us had their word written four times."

Zimmer. We lock eyes and he shrugs at me like *What happens will happen.* Most would say that it was impossible for a Fast-Tracker to reach this far. If others could see and hold and feel the truth, they'd realize our perceptions are not the entire sum of a person.

That we are all *more* than a word.

He's a smart Fast-Tracker. As brilliant as any Influential. If this is our last time together, I'm glad to have known him.

Tauris exchanges the paper for the bowl of pins that Amelda is holding.

"Oh and the rest of you . . . ," Amelda says. "Your words were written three times or less. So you're the thirty that will be hired for a position at StarDust and you'll be eligible for the Saga 5 Mission. But I'm jumping ahead." With a big breath, Amelda pulls back her shoulders. "Raina Nearfall, I apologize, but you're no longer with us."

Raina shoots up from her seat, cheeks blotchy red. "I hope you know," she fumes to all the directors on stage, "that *Wilafran Elcastle* can't be trusted. *She* did this to me." Raina jabs a finger my way and I don't shrink.

I glower and sit straighter.

"Oh please," Gem says. "You're just upset that she outsmarted you."

Raina lets out a high-pitched noise, and her father, a StarDust director, leads her out of the auditorium. I bet he hates me as much as she does.

Mykal mutters under his breath, something about defeating a mountain lion. Court breathes a little easier. I guess we made the final thirty already and I should celebrate now. A lump sticks to my throat. I can't smile yet.

Amelda waves the paper. "Last candidate to be expelled."

Zimmer clutches his armrests like he's ready to push himself to his feet.

And Amelda announces, "Zori Daycastle." While the young woman retreats, Zimmer falls into his chair and laughs once, surprised.

"We made it." Mykal elbows my arm.

I elbow back. "We did." My lips rise with his, but Court is still grim. Right as candidates begin to cheer, Tauris raises his hand.

Shushing us.

"The thirty of you," Tauris says, "will carry the secrets of Star-Dust. What we are about to say, very few in this world will ever know. While you have achieved what a thousand before you could not, this isn't a time to celebrate."

THIRTY-FOUR

Mykal

There is no true ceremony or banquet or any sort of lavish Influential ball. No one places crowns of river reeds or gold upon our heads. They pin an itty-bitty StarDust emblem to our collars and tell us to follow them down the hall.

No celebrations, they say.

I've been complying all right, but I'd like to cheer.

I, Mykal Kickfall—the no good, useless Babe—have been hired by StarDust. I want to imagine a river wreath nestled in my hair. Rugged winter wind stroking my cheeks.

Smiling because I never ruined Court or Franny's chances. Then I'd like to take a pause and thank the gods. To sing songs of valor and victory. To feel wholeheartedly proud for one final moment.

But I have no time for fantasies. The Saga 5 Mission is in arm's reach now and Court would be the first to say that's all that matters.

StarDust directors guide us through a narrow hallway I've never walked. Then to a door I've never seen. We slip inside a pitch-black room that shadows everyone in pure darkness.

The door bangs closed and Franny twitches, fear of death like needles pricking my neck.

Sensing her presence nearby, I grab hold of her hand and squeeze. She squeezes more fiercely. Court is behind me. I'm sure of it. Before I reach, he plants his firm hands on my shoulders.

Candidates murmur about the "spookiness" of the room and their chills. In Grenpale, children are teased for being frightened of the dark. But I understand the fear all right. Anything can attack, and if you're not alert, it'll be injuring you before you injure it.

In our case, it could kill us.

Suddenly and noiselessly, an orblike device glows in the very center of the dark room. A luminous white light bathes Tauris. His hand skimming the iridescent surface.

In a sharp blast, the orb projects tiny flashing lights against the walls. Even the air. And they touch the faces of the candidates, their bodies . . .

I glance at my palms and then jerk back into Court's chest. These fluttering lights blink midair and on my skin like a living pest. I scrub at my arms.

Court seizes my wrist. He holds the back of my head to whisper, "It's an illusion." *An illusion?*

Franny must understand that too. She stands awed, not fearful. As I calm, I start to recognize these shining twinkles from textbooks.

They're stars. The kind only seen in space.

Candidates gasp in wonder as the stars spin and dance and float. I question whether we've been transported to another galaxy.

"What sort of illusion?" I whisper to Court.

"A hologram."

Thinking I heard him wrong, I ask again, but he repeats the same word. "I thought you said they were gone." *Extinct.* Along with phones and other technologies.

"They are . . . were . . ." His mouth turns down, the beauty of the stars blanketing his grave face. "StarDust has more tech than any other place. It's not a surprise."

I dunno. "Tell that to everyone else," I mutter. Candidates start pointing at the hologram, whispering eagerly, and Gem crouches near the orb like she yearns to discover its mechanisms.

Franny has lost a bit of the glimmer, brows bunched, thinking hard.

"Our history is remarkable." Tauris's voice silences the chatter.

"It is also fraught." Tauris skims his palm over the orb. The hologram stars recede into the device.

Another hand motion and a spherical globe appears, airborne and engulfing the room.

Translucent light shimmers to form iced rivulets, jagged mountains, and woolen clouds over thick lilac smoke. Snow white and purple.

"This is our world," Tauris says. "Saltare-3." The globe rotates and then shrinks as the universe expands. "And these are our sister planets." Sun glowing in the farthermost left corner, planets scatter in a descending diagonal. Our Saltare-3 lies low, near the right floorboards.

I squint more. Textbooks are gray, no colored pictures, so surprise strikes me at the sight of our sister planets shaded in different colors: yellows, greens, blues, oranges, and Saltare-5 is deep red.

"You must be wondering," Tauris continues, "how did Star-Dust acquire the starcraft and all of this advanced technology?"

No one nods vigorously but me. So I stop myself, neck roasting. I'm sure they share my feelings, but they're just too proud to display that emotion.

Tauris places a hand on the orb. The hologram zooms to the largest planet of the five, robust greens and blues melding together.

"Saltare-1," Kinden says aloud, but he shifts his weight, questions riddling his features. I suppose his father never muttered these secrets to him. He's as unaware as us.

"Yes." Tauris gazes at the hologram. "When our people landed on Saltare-3, StarDust has had one purpose: maintain contact with our sister planets. This hologram is a gift from Saltare-1."

A few candidates groan. More than several start fuming. Chatting angrily.

I have no ill will toward a planet I know nothing about. I never even heard of Saltare-1 until StarDust.

"We don't need or *want* their gifts," someone says.

"Saltare-3 has thrived on its own."

"Return the hologram," Kinden declares.

"Yes!" a huge number of people advocate.

Court is watching the StarDust directors who line the wall. All of them appear uneasy, throats bobbing, wiping sweat off their brows.

Tauris raises a hand to silence the commotion. "After we were wrongfully cast out of Andola, Saltarians made a commitment to remain unified, especially while we're separated on five different planets. We *cannot* uphold that commitment by shutting ourselves off from Saltare-1, despite all of your opinions."

Candidates huff, but no one raises their voice.

Tauris takes a heavy breath. "Now, everyone is here for a reason. StarDust hasn't considered space travel in centuries, but that has all recently changed. We were contacted by Saltare-1 to aid them."

"Has a natural disaster hit their planet?" Kinden asks, heat in his stance. "I recall our history well, and they never came to *our* aid during the Great Freeze of 2501."

Now everyone starts nodding. I don't understand people, but I'm trying to follow their logic as best I'm able.

Tauris speaks mostly to his son. "You can despise Saltare-1 for as long as you want, but your hate will not change the facts, Kinden."

"What are the facts?" he asks. "Tell me."

"Saltare-1 is planning to start a war with Andola. To reclaim what we once lost—what is ours. *All* our sister planets, not just Saltare-1, have asked us to send an army to fight in the war."

My jaw unhinges. Chatter immediately reigniting, loud enough to drown Tauris's pleas for silence. Padgett curses and Gem looks disappointed.

I feel Franny touching her parted lips, and she mumbles beneath her breath, "How are we supposed to fight?"

Body rigid, Court's hands drop off my shoulders. Sickness burns his throat, and I wrap a rough arm around him, but he's unbending.

"It's all right," I tell them both. *Is it?* We're supposed to find safety after we leave Saltare-3, not fly into a war.

Franny angles toward us, her voice hushed. "They never taught us to punch or . . . shoot anything."

"This doesn't sit right," I agree and Court nods dazedly.

Tauris slams the orb, and stars burst around us. "*Be calm.* You're all representatives of Saltare-3 now, and you need to act with grace and refinement."

"How?" Kinden points at his father. "You're asking us to lose arms and legs for them. There is no grace in war."

"Kinden—"

He angers forward, a foot from Tauris. "We shouldn't even be in communication with Saltare-1, let alone flying their starcrafts and using their radios. Don't you see, Father? They're clutching Saltare-3 by the neck for their purpose alone."

"As hard as this is to hear," Tauris says pointedly, "we were never meant to stay on Saltare-3. Our goal—as a people—has been to strengthen our numbers and resources so we can reclaim our home on Andola."

The orb swirls so fast. Dizzying almost everyone. I rub at my eyes.

"Our sister planets asked for a quarter of our population, but after the Great Freeze, we can't afford to lose that many."

Padgett slips into the conversation. "What about sending the entire population of Saltare-3 to space? You said the goal was to reclaim Andola, which means that in time, we'll all desert this planet anyway."

Tauris nearly smiles. "StarDust and the four presidents of Saltare-3 had a similar idea. We asked our sister planets for more resources to send the entire population to space—they said *no*." He speaks over the complaints. "We're not asking all of you to physically fight. None of you are trained in combat for a reason."

The room quiets wholly.

"Our sister planets asked too much of us. If we send a quarter of the population, our theorists and mystics estimate a disastrous future. One where newborns on Saltare-3 will have earlier and earlier deathdays. We'll produce more *Babes* instead of Influentials. Lineages will die out, and the planet will soon follow. We will not risk the peace and harmony of our planet."

Then what do they want us to do about this war?

"Which means . . . what?" Kinden questions.

"Which means that the Saga 5 Mission is extraordinarily important. Out of the thirty of you, we're choosing the five boldest and brightest." Tauris strolls around the orb. "Convince our sister planets that Saltare-3—*your home*—needs to remain out of the war. We'll join them at Andola after it's been won, but not a minute before."

Amelda chimes in with a short wave and smile. "For this initial launch, our sister planets believe we're sending our leaders, but instead, we're sending ambassadors of peace."

Peace. I mull the word. All I've ever wanted was peace, but I'm feeling more like a mountain lion held beneath an ax. Sacrificed for someone else's needs.

"Saltare-1 will be furious," Padgett says.

Gem frowns. "What are we to do then?"

"The Saga 5 will have ample time to plan and strategize," Tauris explains. "After one-on-one meetings with me, we'll announce the five candidates. You'll have over three months to prepare and bond as a team . . ."

I tune him out as wetness leaks from my nostrils. I wipe roughly at my nose. *No.* It's not me.

Franny.

Blood streams down her lip again. Cupping her hand over her nose and mouth, alarm and fright slithers into her body.

Gods bless.

THIRTY-FIVE

Franny

T he air must be irritating your nose, everyone tells me. *It's not like you're dying anytime soon.*

At three o'night, I lie wide awake on my bed, forehead to my bent knees. Pinching my nose with a bloodied cloth. My mind wanders to fretful places. Sudden, unforeseen deaths. Gory and gruesome.

I shudder.

Zimmer sleeps soundlessly and peacefully beneath my quilt, and I think I'd really, *really* like to trade lives with him. Gods, let me be Zimmer. I wish I were that assured and certain. And safe.

Shaking my head, I mutter, "Stop. *Stop.*" Self-pity does nothing but cramp my stomach. I sniff and shut my eyes. So terrified that I'll start crying blood next.

When is my deathday?

Tell me, gods. When will I die?

Boots suddenly cover my feet. I freeze, brows furrowing. Court has slipped on shoes. He rises off his mattress and then walks to the hallway. *The library,* I guess. Sometimes he reads late at night. If he planned anything serious, I'd like to think he would've told me. Instead of creeping around alone.

But maybe he prefers keeping me in the dark.

I shake my head fiercer. "What are you doing?" I mutter heatedly to myself. I'd never let anyone shadow my life, so why am I letting Court?

Because I feel him.

I know him.

I trust him.

And I hate him. My chin quakes. It hurts to loathe someone that's so much a part of me. Someone I understand entirely. Their flaws, their quirks. Their ups and downs. None of us are near perfect, and if I condemn him for every imperfection, then I might as well condemn myself.

Yet, I can't change what I feel. I can't replace the bitter resentment with warmth and kindness. So I sit here and blister.

Not descending stairs, Court just . . . stops. I frown and concentrate harder. He clasps a doorknob, turns, and steps—*I hear him.*

Court is in my dorm.

"What?" I breathe, my voice muffled in my bloodied cloth.

Never—not a brief second or moment, not one single day—has Court ventured into my room. Kinden sleeps here and he wanted to avoid his older brother.

After learning StarDust's secrets, it's possible that's changed. He's here for Kinden. To speak to him about their father.

My thought vanishes right as Court draws open my canopy. Surprise sways me backward. Too bewildered to speak, I stay still, but Court carries no hesitations. No reluctance.

He stretches out his hands. "Will you let me help you?"

I inhale a sharp breath. *Will you let your hallucinations help you?* I hear his smooth voice from our first meeting. "Am I hallucinating?" I ask with pooling tears. "Am I dead already?"

His chest collapses like I impaled him with words alone. *I did.* The knife drives shrilly into my gut as well as his. "You'd sooner believe you're dead than believe I'd help you?"

Yes.

I can't bear to say the truth aloud, but my silent affirmation swells an awful pain between us. "Did Mykal force you to do this?" I wedge another blade in our ribs.

Court grips the canopy so strongly. The phrase *I will not quit tonight* is embedded in his features and body. "This was my idea, not Mykal's."

Choked on doubled emotion, I rub my neck.

Court extends a hand again. "*Please.* Let me help you better this time."

Listening to my gut, I ball my bloodied cloth in a fist, blow out a mangled breath, and say, "All right." I'll let him try.

Court brings me to the empty clinic. Doors are unlocked for personal all-hour use, but almost no one has had an injury. So it's quiet, warm lights dim.

"Sit on that bed." Court nods to the center of the room. A protective thin sheet of paper lines a partially reclined bed. I've only been here for a physical, but without the glaring white lights turned on, the room is somewhat more inviting.

As he shuts the door, I climb on the bed, legs hanging off. I sniff constantly, even when my nosebleed ends.

I watch Court open and close cabinets. Searching. He piles a few instruments and jars onto a rolling tray.

I slip further into my thoughts. "It's not important." I freeze us.

Court slowly faces me. "What's not important?"

"*This.*" I gesture all around the clinic. "What's important is StarDust . . . and Bastell. We don't have time—"

"*Stop.*" His nose flares.

"Why?" I seethe. "Why do I have to stop? I'm saying *exactly* what you've been telling me. So you're allowed to utter the words, but I'm not?"

"I was wrong!" His face breaks, but he pushes forward. "I've made you believe that you're unimportant, and I hate myself for it." Tears well, but he breathes out, suppressing the waterworks with me, and then he wheels the tray to the reclined bed. "Look up."

I meet his gaze.

"Your health is important," he says powerfully. "I'm *so sorry* for acting like it's not."

I'm overwhelmed, not prepared for these emotions at all. My

nose runs, not blood. I wipe and then nod and nod. I can accept his apology, but . . . "Why now?" I question. I can name and list many other days or weeks he could've reached out, but why this moment?

"Feeling how lost you were tonight, I just . . . cracked." His dark brown hair shrouds his eyes. "My silence has been more unbearable than speaking, and I realized that we may never find more time. But we have to *make* time for what's important. Mykal made time for me after I dodged my deathday, and I denied you that."

Every figurative door that Court had shut, he starts whipping open, giving me the chance to cross the mountains we've constructed. Just to meet him. I remember how I stopped expecting this moment. Now that it's here, I can hardly believe it's real. Rock in my throat, I swallow. Nodding and nodding.

I sniff loudly. "Now what . . . ?"

"Now I run a few medical tests on you."

"For my nosebleeds?"

"And your deathday."

I almost burst into tears, but I clutch the bed beneath me and fight this onslaught of emotion. "Really?"

Towering above, Court stares straight into me. *Feeling me.* "Really." He's pained again.

My brows scrunch. I watch him grab a rectangular purple device: two prongs on one side, a tiny screen on the other. "Why are you already upset?" I have to ask.

"Because this is where you believe you'll find hope."

I don't understand. *If it's not that, then what is this?*

Court rakes a hand through his thick hair, his torment staking daggers up my spine. "Hold out your arm for me."

I stretch my limb.

Gently, he cradles my wrist. "This is a Death Reader."

I straighten up. Court is retesting my deathday. My pulse speeds at all the deathday possibilities that'll now shrink to one truth. After wiping what he calls *antiseptic* on my skin, he places the prongs on the inside of my wrist.

"This'll hurt."

"I don't care." I gaze fixedly.

Court pushes a black button, and the needlelike prongs puncture my flesh. *Mayday.* I wince, Court winces, and then after a long moment, the strange greenish-blue prongs retract. Paper crinkles while I shift nervously.

He displays the screen-side of the Death Reader. Numbers flash and scroll rapidly.

Before I ask, he says, "It's normal. Give the Reader a second to process."

"What is it processing?"

"Your blood."

He's being more considerate than ever, but his stomach clenches twice as much as mine. Like he foresees the tragic end already.

The numbers halt. I gasp before reading the actual date. *1-23-3525* is clear. My old deathday. I blink and blink, my body numb. "Maybe . . . maybe the Death Reader is broken."

I wait for Court to say, *It's not.* But he returns to the cabinet, finds another Death Reader, and retakes my test. Retreating into my mind, I tune out when the prongs prick my skin.

We wait for the results, and I breathe shallow, hurried breaths. "Maybe . . ." I shake my head at a theory that has already been squashed.

1-23-3525.

Court tests me for a third time. I don't even have to ask. He just knows what I want and need.

1-23-3525.

Gods. I process this news with a faraway gaze, and Court examines my body for the cause of the nosebleeds. Tucking my black hair behind each ear, he peers in them with a medical instrument. Then looks up my raw nose.

"Open," he says.

My mouth. I fall into a daze as he massages my neck with two fingers. I think he mentions something about "glands"—whatever those are.

Maybe an hour passes before he finishes. Court rolls the tray aside.

"And?" I ask.

"And besides the nosebleeds, you appear healthy, Franny." He stands strictly. "I'm diagnosing you right now, and telling you, these nosebleeds are *not* life-threatening."

I ease only a fraction. A wave of heartrending realities slams at me. My voice is stilted. "I'll never know the day I'll die."

I've met this truth before, but never with this much permanence. It claws at my throat. Suffocating me. I slide off the bed and pace and pace.

Court studies me, his quiet intensity hard to ignore.

I swerve to him and place a hand on his chest. I halt, uncertain. Unsure.

Of everything.

He must feel me battling tears. "You're allowed to cry," Court says. "You're allowed to scream and hate everything that's happening."

My whole body shakes. "Is that what you did?"

Drawing toward me, Court clasps my cheeks, bare hands on my flesh. Sensing me fully as though to say, *I'm here for you. I'm not afraid to experience this pain with you.* "I bawled," he says deeply. "I cried until there were no more tears to shed."

I rest my other palm on his chest. Like I could shove him away any second.

I push Court, and his hands fall from my face. "It shouldn't hurt this badly. I feel like . . ."

"Your heart is trying desperately to escape your body. Your lungs are banging against your ribs." Court steps into my palms. "And you stare at yourself and you wonder if you're even real."

"Am I?" I lick my trembling lips. "Are we real?"

Court raises my palm to his heart—his knotted, callused scars beneath my hand. "That is real." *So real that someone tried to steal it.* He places his hand over my heart. "This is real." I feel my own heartbeat thud and thud.

For some reason, I shake my head.

"What?" His grim eyes bore into me, trying to help me find the words to my feelings. Letting me process and think and understand.

My face twists. "Am I the same as I've always been?" *I don't want to change. I don't want to change.*

Please, gods. I don't want to change.

"No," he says bluntly. "You're not the same."

I shove him back again, harder, but Court only sways, his dark brown hair skimming his eyelashes.

I shuffle backward to add distance. Growing hot, sweat builds, and I waft my woolen shirt. "I'm *exactly* the same," I say with as much certainty as I can. My stomach twists like I lie to myself. Somewhere inside, I buried uncomfortable truths that I haven't had time to meet.

That's why Court brought me here.

To cry and scream and cope.

His squared jaw tightens as he repeats, "You're not the same."

"I am," I sneer, digging a finger in my chest. "I am *Franny Bluecastle*. I am my good-natured mother. I am my long-lost friends—"

"You can be everything you once were, but you're still *not* the same."

I groan into a scream. *I hate this.* "Why?!"

"Because your life no longer ends at seventeen!" he yells back, pumped full of my indignation. "Because you'll have tomorrow and a year and another year to change and be someone better or worse. We grow. The three of us will *grow* beyond what we believed."

I can't catch my breath. "It makes no difference . . ."

"Deathdays are a part of our identity. You can still feel like a Fast-Tracker, but you're other things now." Court walks stringently toward me.

This time, I don't push him away. "What other things am I?" We've never shied from the heat of our gazes, so he seizes mine as forcefully as I seize his.

"You are compassionate. You are loving."

My lips part, but I have no impulse to shake my head.

"Franny Bluecastle has questioned reality. She's someone who was left nearly naked in an alley. Who felt hands rip senselessly at her clothes when she wanted them to stop."

I shed a maddened tear. "That's not who I am." I'm angry because I know it exists inside of me. Those people touched me and changed pieces of me without my permission.

"I know." He clutches my arms as my legs weaken. "*I know.* I'm plagued by the weight of a man on my chest. I *feel* the weight of yours. I feel his knee digging harder. I feel the scream dying in your throat, and I tried desperately to scream for you."

My ribs heave, and I start to cry hard. He's chipping away the wall he constructed since we met, but I didn't realize how much agony would be on the other side. How much we'd have to share. I wish for a simple life. *Easy* and weightless.

Shielding my face with my hands, a guttural sob rips through me. My legs slacken. Before I sink, Court tugs me close. Arms wrapping around my frame. Hugging me.

Our hearts pound at the same ragged pace.

His knees almost buckle. I hold him upright. Giving and taking each other's senses.

Court dips his head to my ear, his voice raw. "Franny Bluecastle is more."

"What else is she?" I ask so quietly.

"She's a girl who asked to die but found strength to live."

I cover my face again.

"She is *loved*," he says. "More than she ever dreamed. More than she ever asked."

My hands fall, and I look up, his palms encasing my tear-streaked cheeks again. I almost believe I misheard him.

Court reads the challenge in my features, asking him to say it all again. Unwavering, he tells me, "You are loved by two boys."

"Just two?" I joke with a tearful laugh.

Court rolls his eyes, but there's a smile attached. Their friendship is the strongest I've ever had.

"What . . . ?" My thought flits away, and I impulsively touch his lips. He lets me feel his smile beneath my fingers.

And then he hugs me again.

We hold on to each other, our pulses descending off a terrifying mountain. I've been split open, but somehow I can breathe better. Stronger.

I remember how Court struggles to touch his own memories. How they plague him whenever they involuntarily surface. *He was right,* I think. Silence can be more unbearable, and breaking it can be even harder.

I'm glad he did.

Court whispers in my hair, "There's something I've been meaning to ask."

I draw back just to see his face. "Is it about Star—"

"It's about you."

My chest swells because he never asks about me. Not really. Not unless it has significance to StarDust and our goals.

His hands slide down my arms into my palms, clasping warmly. "What was stolen from you," he asks, "that ignited your hate for thieves?"

I smile sadly. "The most beautiful shawl you could ever imagine." I describe my mother in vivid detail. I tell him the story of how she revealed the garment from a fancy bag. How she spread the fabric across my tiny shoulders, and how she used every bill of her Final Deliverance check for this gift. For me.

Court listens intently, our gazes reflecting a thousand striking sentiments.

The door suddenly creaks open, and my lips shut quickly. Our heads whip to the left.

THIRTY-SIX

Court

Swiftly, I attempt to pull Franny behind my back, but just as determinedly, she tries to shove me behind hers. We're side by side, emotionally spent but jolted in panic. I have no time to really think.

The door swings fully open and Kinden saunters into the clinic room. Dressed in khaki night slacks and a loose shirt like he snuck out of bed.

"You followed me?" I say between clenched teeth, irate that my past is jamming itself into this moment of all fucking moments. Just as I breathe, just as she breathes, we're being choked again.

"So what if I did?" Kinden replies.

I laugh an enraged, disbelieving laugh. Out of nowhere, I remember Mykal. If he senses me, he'll storm the clinic. I turn my head. Concentrating for a split second.

He's sound asleep. Unaware. *Good.* I can only protect Mykal by leaving him out of this confrontation.

Arms crossed, Franny simmers. "Were you listening through the door?"

I go rigid. If he heard anything about Franny being a Fast-Tracker, I'll snap.

Kinden stalks forward. One step, two steps. "Why? Do you have something to hide?" Unblinking, resolute and raptly focused, he looks disturbed.

"No," Franny nearly spits, but she must recall etiquette because she straightens, arching her shoulders.

Kinden is perceptive of every tiny shift she makes. His lip tics upward, as though vindicated. "Lie all you want, but I know the truth."

"You know *nothing*," I sneer and call out his bluff. Without question, I'll protect Franny over the starry-eyed idea of a relationship with my brother. He wants Etian, and that boy died inside of me at Vorkter.

Kinden studies my every facial movement. "I heard you talk about her deathday."

"No," I instantly deny while Franny scans the clinic for a weapon.

"You said that she should've died at seventeen."

"You're unhinged, Kinden," I snap, causing his gaze to drop. Questioning himself.

Franny freezes, but she nudges my waist and tilts her head slightly toward the . . . Death Readers.

Gliding discreetly to the left, I block the medical tray with my body. I try to calm myself, but my voice is layered with frost. "I understand the toll the thief must be taking on your family, but stalking me won't solve anything."

"The thief . . . ," Kinden muses before wandering to the cabinets. "Altia Patrol spoke to my father yesterday. They revealed an interesting detail about that thief and my brother." Facing me, he grips the medical countertop behind his tall build. "Apparently they'd been cellmates and escaped Vorkter together."

Franny speaks before I can. "Your brother *died*, Kinden. His deathday already passed."

"That's what they said, but they didn't find a body."

Franny groans in frustration. "He probably sunk beneath ice."

"Says the girl who has the handwriting of a child, who has Mal's tree inked on her shoulder, who fears an insignificant nosebleed, and who Court referred to as Franny Bluecastle—not Wilafran Elcastle. So pardon me for believing nothing you say, *Fast-Tracker*."

I charge my brother and fist his shirt. "Leave us *alone!*"

He fists mine, pulling me closer. Ignoring my wrath entirely. "You have his eyes," Kinden says. "His lips, his skin. His hair."

Sickness scalds my throat. Ill at being this close to him—where he dissects my features with so much fervor—I release my clutch and fight to pry his fingers off me.

His grip fortifies. "You're taller than him, but you would be. It's been eight years." *Let go of me. Let go of me.*

Franny senses my desperation and alarm. "Stop, Kinden," she spits, trying to break us apart. Wedging her body furiously in the tight space. "STOP!"

Kinden elbows her jaw—my head swerves with the throbbing blow, and she stumbles backward, holding the reddened spot.

Remorse touches his eyes briefly, but his curiosity has annihilated any common sense. So zoned in on me, I doubt he even realizes he hit Franny. Kinden jerks me closer. "Please . . . just tell me you're Etian."

I can't.

I taste blood. Her teeth must've split her gums. "Calm down, please." I raise my hands in surrender, but he still clenches my shirt. Like if he lets go, the answers will soon follow.

He cringes at himself. I've made him believe he's losing his mind when he's entirely, completely correct. I drove him to this distraught place. I fractured my older brother.

"I've tried quieting my suspicions," he breathes.

"You have," I say, placating him a little more.

Franny lingers close . . . a scalpel gripped in her fist.

"I talked to Father about you," Kinden says. "He said, 'Your mind is playing tricks on you, Kinden, wishing for a result and causing you to see impossible things.' I tried to push the madness out of my mind, but if she's a Fast-Tracker, then what's to say you're not my brother?"

"Logic," I refute.

My shirt stretches as he winds the fabric around his knuckles. "I've given you evidence."

Franny nears, but I shake my head once at her, worried about my brother's mental state.

She stops.

"You've given me banal similarities, Kinden," I say. "No one dodges their deathday. It's fact. You're being delusional."

Hot tears prick him. "I'm not. You're just frightened. *Please.* Tell me you're Etian."

I can't. "I'm sorry."

He hangs his head, his grip releasing, tortured. Two deep breaths and his resolve strengthens. "You want logic?" His gaze drifts to the metal tray of Death Readers.

I back up. Instantly. Obstructing his path to the purple Readers.

Franny lunges at Kinden, not baring the scalpel, and instead, she rips the collar of his shirt to disorient him. She lands her boot against his calf, cracking his ankle, and he thrusts Franny out of the way—her temple strikes a cabinet corner.

Breath ejects from my lungs.

The collision knocks Franny unconscious, body thudding limply to the floor.

I fall backward, crashing into the metal tray. Mykal is running. I shake my head, vision sputtering out. "Franny," I breathe. *Franny.* I try to pick myself up to reach her, but my legs quiver.

Kinden isn't aware of what happened to Franny, barely even acknowledging his broken ankle or his torn shirt. He nears me and grabs a Death Reader from the floor.

"You're right," I have to say. "I'm afraid. I'm *terrified* to tell you the truth. You could spill our secrets to Tauris."

"I won't," Kinden says, riled tears slipping. "I wouldn't."

"I can't know that." My gaze flits beyond him. I need to reach Franny, her breath too shallow inside of me.

Mykal descends the stairs, his blood pumping furiously.

Kinden won't stop, so I think quickly and reclaim what little control I have left. Picking myself up off the floor, I seize another Death Reader and place the sharp prongs to my wrist.

"I'm trusting you," I tell my older brother. I broke him, and part of me wishes to piece Kinden back together. But in the same breath, I can't be what he wants. I'm not Etian and he'll realize that in time. For now, I have to quiet his mind.

"I promise you," Kinden says with a pained breath. "*I promise you.*"

I try to believe him. The prongs puncture my skin. Without a wince, I wait. They retract. I toss the Death Reader to Kinden. He feverishly stares at the rolling numbers.

Not another second wasted, I kneel by Franny and lift her limp body into my lap. "Franny," I say, tapping her cheek. "Franny."

My vision recedes, darkening, but I concentrate harder, checking her pulse. Listening to her breath like she's a patient in the trauma unit. This is my fault. All my fault.

"You're my little brother."

I strain my neck over my shoulder. Kinden is crying, the Death Reader in hand. Reality finally catches him, and he notices his tattered shirt and his bent ankle.

He staggers to the reclined bed. "What . . . did I . . . ?" Horror and guilt assaults his features. "Did I hurt you?"

"Yes," I say. "Because you hurt her."

"I wouldn't . . . I didn't mean to . . ." His eyes widen at Franny. "If you dodged your deathday, did she dodge hers too?"

I nod tensely. "She can die today or years from now. Just like me."

At the thought of almost killing Franny, he vomits to the side, but I grasp his remorse like a lifeline. Maybe he will keep our secrets. Right now, I can only hope.

The door flies open.

Mykal roars, "I'm going to rip your pitiful lungs out, you rotting—"

"Mykal." I stand and thwart his advance, a hand on his chest.

"Get out of my way, Court." He slaps my hand aside.

"He's my older brother." I finally acknowledge that something—a glimmering piece of what once was—still exists between Kinden and me. Strong enough to cause all of this.

Mykal drills his hard-hearted eyes into me. "You've lost your damned senses. He knocked out Franny."

"I didn't mean to hurt her . . ." Kinden covers his face, bowed forward. Silently sobbing.

Mykal grimaces at him, understanding me. "All right."

I go to lift Franny in my arms, but he's faster, cradling her unconscious frame.

"Will she be waking?" Mykal asks, his fear palpitating my heart.

"Yes."

She's not dead, and for one bitter moment, I could look up to her gods and thank them for her. What she'd do. What she'd want.

For Franny, I do just that.

THIRTY-SEVEN

Court

Ice pressed to her pounding temple, Franny sits on the armrest of the common room couch. Mykal leans his weight against the back, smoking a cigarette, and I stand like the *sternest stiff* beside them. Her words. Only a few days have passed since the clinic, but her headache persists.

She called out my "hovering" the other day and added, "There's nothing more you can do for my headache, so you may as well relax with us."

I can't relax at the moment. Not when I have a StarDust meeting with my father soon. Mykal and Franny had their one-on-one interviews with Tauris yesterday. In and out of his office in two minutes. So brief that neither Franny nor Mykal feel hopeful about their chances to be picked for the mission.

Franny eyes me suspiciously.

"What?" I snap.

"You aren't going to scold me for slouching?"

It's six o'morning. Only a few candidates, huddled by the fire-place, could possibly notice Franny slightly hunched and seated on an armrest. For another, everyone's aware that she "slipped and fell" with Kinden. Hence, his broken ankle and her poor posture.

And lastly, if anyone else suspects she's a Fast-Tracker, they would've said something already.

Smoke slips down my lungs thanks to Mykal. I try not to take the cigarette away from him, but I cough a little and say, "You don't feel well."

Franny glowers, not appreciating the coddling.

"Stop slouching," I chastise.

"No," she rejects me, smiling as Mykal laughs.

I roll my eyes and soak up the bright rumble in my lungs.

"Wilafran?"

At the exact same time, our heads turn to Kinden. He supports his weight on a wooden cane and approaches us with softer determination. We don't flinch or recoil. Partly because he carries a bouquet of pink roses. The fifth bouquet in three days.

From the fireplace, the young candidates ogle Kinden and giggle. Everyone believes he's been romancing Franny.

In reality, he's been apologizing.

"For you." Kinden stretches the bouquet out to Franny.

Mykal leans forward and slaps the bouquet from his hands. The flowers flop to the rug. It's so expected that I have no reaction anymore.

Kinden glares. "Must you do that every time?"

Mykal just fits his cigarette between his lips.

I collect the flowers and hand the bouquet to Franny. She aches to sniff them, but Mykal sneezes uncontrollably every time, so she'll have to wait until we're not in my brother's presence.

"I already forgave you," Franny reminds him. She said that he owed her nothing because she broke his ankle, but Kinden hasn't forgiven himself yet. "You'd do better gifting Mykal something, but not flowers." She cranes her neck to Mykal. "What do you want?"

"A hare's foot."

"He's joking," I lie.

Mykal wears a crooked grin.

Kinden studies Mykal for the shortest second. "I don't care about him." I hear the unsaid words: *Not like I care about you, Etian.*

Mykal grunts. "Likewise, you little—"

"I have to go," I interject. "So please . . . be civil." I say goodbye to Mykal and Franny, and as I leave, Kinden follows me. I'm used to this. It's like he's trying to regain all the time he lost with me, but our conversations have been mostly stilted.

Still, Kinden tries. He's as persistent as Etian Valcastle.

We enter a hallway, his cane clapping against the marble. It'd be a lie to say that I'm not wary and paranoid. Only three days have passed and he can run to Altia Patrol or our father with these secrets at any time. So I choose my words more carefully when I speak to him.

After pushing through the dining room, we enter another hall-way and I tell him, "I care about Mykal *deeply*."

Kinden gives me his classic *I know it all, I'm the older brother* look. One I recall more fondly. "You deserve so much more than Mykal Kickfall."

"No." I shake my head. "Mykal Kickfall deserves so much more than me."

Kinden has missed the pieces of my life that define me, and even though he's always seen me as a fragile boy, he thinks less of Mykal, someone who hasn't exactly excelled at StarDust.

"I'll think on that," he says seriously. Despite his arrogance, he's always been thoughtful and critical. Free thinking and believing.

Hells, he believed in the impossible.

He believed in me.

Kinden captures my arm, slowing my lengthy stride to a complete halt. "Just once more, I need to ask something."

I stiffen. "No." I lower my voice, candidates in black and gold StarDust garb passing us. "I said yesterday was the last we talked of Vorkter." He asked if anyone physically hurt me. I think Kinden recalled my scars and the fact that I can die at any moment.

"I'm better now," I told him.

He didn't believe me, but there's not much more I can actually say.

"No," Kinden says, "it's before that." *Before Vorkter.* "I just want to know why you did what you did. Father questioned your reasoning more than Mother and me, and I believe, in part, he applied for a position at StarDust to forget about you."

My gaze drifts out the hallway windows. To the Saga starcraft. *My father tried to forget about me.* I asked Kinden yesterday if he lied to us about being a physicist, but he said no, Tauris just changed careers after I went to prison.

I struggle to speak aloud. To tell Kinden the truth. I'm still afraid.

Even without a link, Kinden sees this. So he braces his weight on his cane beside me, both of us side by side and gazing out the window.

When the hallway clears, he speaks. "My little brother once tried to breathe life into a young girl when she was already dead and gone. Years passed, and I started to understand. Because there was only *one* theory that made sense. That could belong to Etian. I knew him well."

Chills bump my arms, but I wait. I listen.

And he says, "He was fighting for more than the young girl. My brother was fighting for all of us. For hope."

I shut my eyes. The words warm every inch of my soul. Bathed in light. And all I ever dreamed, all I ever desired, was a world where lives could be saved.

Where no one quits on people the moment we learn their deathday.

In his warmly lit office, Tauris offers me tea and an Altian cookie, but both sit untouched on his wooden desk, my insides coiling. Tea is rare, the leaves unable to grow outside of a greenhouse. As a child, I liked the taste and my father often made me tea and sweet bread on my birthday.

I can't bring myself to sip the drink. So I hold the armrests of my leather chair and watch Tauris on the other side of the desk. He peruses a maroon folder and thumbs the grayed hairs on his dark brown chin.

"You're eighteen years of age now?" he asks.

"Yes." I sit perilously upright.

Tauris flips through a few papers and then shuts the maroon folder. Clasping his hands together, he stares attentively at me. "You're one of the quickest studies I've ever personally seen at StarDust. Your ability to adapt and attain new skills is remarkable."

"Thank you," I say flatly.

"But I'd like to be frank with you, Court. I have concerns."

I edge forward. "Whatever they are, I'm certain that I can ease your mind."

His dark eyes dance across my golden-brown cheeks, my smooth, squared jaw, the thick dishevelment of my rich brown hair, and the starkness of my gray gaze. My father absorbs my features with a sorrowful smile.

Do you see me?

"Is something wrong?" My biting voice scalds my throat.

My father exits his stupor and smiles politely. "It shouldn't be a surprise by now that you resemble a son of mine. I'm aware that Kinden has confronted you about the similarities, and for that, I apologize."

"It's—"

"Unacceptable," he finishes. "StarDust wants to find the most compatible team of five, and with your aptitude, we'd like you to lead the team." My father speaks too quickly for me to think. "My concerns: Kinden is highly skilled at language and communications—a standout for the Saga 5 Mission—but with his obsessions, I'm concerned that you two are not well matched for a team."

I blink a few times, processing.

My father scoots closer and pushes my tea aside. "We're willing to remove Kinden from the Saga 5 Mission if that makes you more comfortable."

I hold his assured gaze, my nose slightly flaring. My heart breaks for my older brother. He could never surpass Etian in wisdom in our father's eyes, and even as Court, I trounce Kinden. I leap beyond him and steal our father's attention.

Forget about your brother. I flip over the lavender-glazed cookie. "I work best with Mykal Kickfall and Wilafran Elcastle. They're who I'd choose as teammates first."

My father sighs. "I'm sorry, but it's just not possible. Mykal is not qualified for any position on the starcraft. He ranks in the bottom tier in communications, and mid-to-bottom tier in engineering and piloting. There are no roles for him."

I go cold. I can't imagine a world where Mykal isn't by my side. "And Wilafran?"

"We're still discussing. She's grown to be a good pilot, but there are more well-rounded candidates that would better serve a team."

I'm hollow.

"We need your answer about Kinden. Do you want him on the Saga 5 Mission with you? Yes or no?"

Yes.

No.

The two choices haunt me. Glare at me. And wait for me.

Yes.

No.

I thought I'd have to face my father's suspicions this morning, but he has none. I'm deciding the fate of my older brother. I'm determining where he goes.

What he does.

His dreams, his life.

It's all in my hands.

THIRTY-EIGHT

Mykal

Six rows of metal folding chairs line the launchpad. *Finally a celebration of sorts,* I first think. Nearly everyone seems to be present for the Saga 5 Mission announcement: StarDust directors, remaining candidates, even a few starcraft technicians.

Bright-eyed and formally dressed StarDust directors face the audience, and next to Tauris, the hologram orb device is perched on a round table. Blazing spotlights show off the freshly buffed Saga starcraft. Reminding us why we're all here.

Well, not all of us.

"He's late," Franny mutters, peeking over her shoulder again. From the concrete launchpad, we can see into every hallway and no one parades through a single one.

What in three hells are you doing, Court? I crack a crick in my bones, straining my neck as much as Franny. Court would say our glances are pointless because we can feel his whereabouts without looking. I can and he's nowhere *near* the launchpad.

Since his interview two days ago, a pit has sat in his gut like a pile of rocks. Court wouldn't even spill the details. Just said that it went poorly.

I focus my mind on his senses for a bit. His fingers fumble with the StarDust pin on his tux. Anxious.

"He'll be coming soon, little love."

Franny reties the silky bow of her dark blue blouse. "Why do you call me *little love*?" she suddenly asks so softly that I almost mishear. She's seated at the end of a row. While we talk of private matters, I keep my voice as hushed as hers.

Months ago, she could've questioned me, but maybe it's a good distraction from Court. Or maybe she just now found the courage to ask.

Little love.

I extend an arm around her shoulders, my lips curving upward. "My pa talked a lot, and he'd often tell me"—my mouth brushes her ear—"'Beyond the mountains, Mykal, the old say that those who die young find little love. No time for more, yeh see, but if that's so, then I'll be surrounding myself with a little love over a great big love any day of the week.'"

"A little love," she whispers, smile spreading. "I wish I met your pa."

"I wish I met your mother." I pause, thinking. "But I feel like I sort of know her through you."

Franny elbows my side, a bit happy, but her smile fades at the empty chair next to me.

We return some of our attention to the directors. The ceremony has not yet started. I lean into Franny again. "Promise you'll be sending me a letter from space."

I feel the heat of her scowl. "You're joining us, even if I have to pack you in my satchel."

"There's no luggage that'll be big enough to hide me."

Her face falls. "You're supposed to say '*We're more than all right.*'"

The likelihood that I'm chosen for this mission is slim. I've always known that, but I'd say anything to see her smile. "We're more than all right."

Franny mutters, "Gods," after feeling my lie.

I sense Court again. Still in his dorm, he sluggishly ties his polished shoes. After all the work we've put into StarDust, you'd think he'd like to be here, but he's slow. Slower than he's ever been.

"He wants to miss this," I realize.

Franny cringes. "He's afraid to face us if the outcome isn't in our favor."

I nod. "He'll be blaming himself."

We know him. We're linked, so he can't exactly hide, even when he wishes to.

Good effort, but we feel you, Court.

Our focus veers to the directors as Amelda waves in greeting. The crowd begins to clap and whistle. I join them at the right time.

Tauris places a palm on the orb, and a hologram sparkles to spell out *The Saga 5 Mission.* The applause intensifies, but then weakens altogether, Tauris raising a hand for silence.

"On behalf of StarDust," Tauris says, "the directors would like to congratulate the five candidates who'll embark on a great mission in a few months' time. Without further wait, here are the Saga 5."

The directors step aside. Beneath *The Saga 5 Mission* the orb projects a full-bodied image of Court: posture strict, seemingly motionless, but the glittering hologram makes his grim eyes sparkle.

My grin bursts and I clap heartily with the audience. Franny is smiling from ear to ear. The directors share the applause, but their gazes flit every which way. In search of Court. He's missing his celebration.

The second image pops up next to Court's. Brown hair blowing, lips in a mischievous, bent smile—I recognize the lady.

Padgett Soarcastle. Two rows ahead of us, Gem hugs her older sister, but Padgett stares fixatedly at the hologram, concerned about her sister's chances. She has nothing to fear. They'll be dying together. Same place, same time, most likely. Gem has to make the mission.

As the cheers quiet, the third image appears. "Who's that?" I ask Franny. Never noticing this little boy, his big ears drawn forward and eyes a dazzling green.

"Arri Lowcastle," Franny says, worry crinkling her brows. "He beat me in a couple pilot simulations. Not all, but some . . ."

Gods bless.

The fourth candidate's image floats next to Arri's face. I can't place this lady either, but her deep red hair spools around fair cheeks, her stretched smile a bit forced.

"Evie Lowcastle, Arri's older cousin," Franny says with fingers pressed to her downturned lips.

One spot is left.

"It's yours," I tell Franny, and I'm happy for it. She deserves to be on that starcraft with Court. I'll be finding a way to them eventually. In time. It may take me years, but I can't just . . . I can't—I hunch forward, winded.

I rest my forearms to my thighs and hang my head. Not able to paint on false hope anymore. Defeat crushes me inside and out.

Franny curves her arm around my taut back. "It can't be me. It has to be Gem."

"Last candidate," Tauris calls.

The applause resounds, somewhat weaker, but Franny's low gasp forces me to look. The striking, camera-ready features of Kinden Valcastle stare back at me. If I could spar with a damned hologram, I'd tear off his arrogant grin.

We sit like hardened cement. Even when the hologram blinks away and Tauris says, "Wine and cocktails will be served in the dining room. Please, everyone, join us in celebrating Court, Padgett, Arri, Evie, and Kinden. Our Saga 5."

After polite applause, people start filing out of the launchpad. Only a few candidates seem disheartened. If the mission had been to colonize a new planet, more might've been glum.

"How is this possible?" Franny murmurs, watching Padgett and Gem speak rapidly to each other. I catch a couple of phrases like *you must go* and *not without you.*

Zimmer sighs heavily when he stands, stuffing his hands into his baggy slacks. On his way out, he shrugs at Franny and says quietly to her, "Now I understand why they tell us not to make lofty goals."

Franny grimaces as he trudges away.

All the chairs soon empty, but Franny and I stay rooted, dazed. The pitter-patter in the hallways fades to silence, leaving us alone— and suddenly, my head, her head, *our heads* careen forward, a swift excruciating blow.

Again, a blunt object slams the back of our skulls, obliterating my sight into tiny shards. Pain blossoms and ripples through my hard bones . . . but it's not her. It's not me.

It's Court.

"Mykal?" Franny's panic drifts away from my mind.

Court's hands are my hands, reaching to the back of his head. His fingers wet with blood. I scream from the core. In agony. In despair.

His terror pierces me like a thousand daggers, and I try to rise for him. *Get up. Get up.* I need to find him. To hold him. But I'm weighed by his senses. I collapse off the metal chair. Landing on my trembling hands and knees.

Franny yells but her voice is nothing but a hurried whisper of "Mykal, look at me, focus on me, hear me, feel me."

Tearing myself away feels impossible.

Someone fists his thick hair and slams his head to the floorboards. I gasp for air, my lungs flaming. Scalding, enraged tears crease the corners of my eyes.

My senses. I bear down hard on my teeth, growling out frustration and hatred. A quick, malicious hand clutches his ankle and wrenches Court to his back.

My spine shrieks. I'm on my back. *Get up.*

Get up.

I try to rise again. "Court!" I scream.

Then I feel my name on his terrified lips, yelled in desperation.

His back bumps against the hardwood. Dragged forcefully. My head—his head bangs the ground, and I scream violently, "GET UP!"

Veins bulge in my neck. I scream and scream; his pain shredding me. *Get up.*

Franny wraps her arms around my bare chest, after stripping off my shirt. Skin to skin, our link heightens to where her pulse pounds over Court's, and on the launchpad's concrete ground, I sit up. Through blurry vision, I try to claw the hands off his ankles. *Mimic me. Mimic me.*

Court struggles.

He can't sit up.

His cry rips through my throat.

"No!" I yell, my eyes wet and burning. "Don't you quit!" *Don't quit.* His fright cuts me in half, and I keep heaving for breath. I'm being dragged faster.

I kick and kick. "Get away from him!"

My fingernails dig into floorboards, splinters slitting my skin—*his skin.*

Fight.

Sharp nausea roils, but Franny supports me to my feet. I wrap an arm around her shoulder. "We have to . . ." *reach him.* I stagger, my blood boiling. I should've protected him. I should've been there for him. I promised him for years that I'd never let anyone touch him with malice.

I failed him.

When he was battling in the Free Lands, I had more focus, more awareness. Now I can hardly make sense of where I am. *We heightened the link.* So many emotions course through me. Disorienting. Our senses jumble, but his horror stomps on most everything else. Like a widespread, inextinguishable wildfire.

Franny's voice flits far off.

I grunt, a hard boot striking my ribs. Air escapes my lungs but never fills up again. My shoulders pound against harsh stairs, dragged farther and farther. I'm a sack of weight, but I fight. *Don't quit.*

I sit up to seize the hand on my ankle and a blade slices my thigh.

Another scream dies between my clenched teeth.

Franny slaps my face. Twice, maybe thrice. Until I blink and see her wide eyes and freckled cheeks. I see where I am. *Court's dorm room.* We must've stumbled hurriedly here while I drowned in his senses.

My body numbs at the pool of crimson blood streaking out the door.

"Mykal!" Franny clasps my arms, shaking me. "We have to find him. Focus!"

Focus on what? I don't understand . . .

"Focus harder," she urges, voice rushed. "What do you feel around him? What kind of floor? Where is he?!"

I'll be returning to his senses then. I can't see or hear him, but I can feel and taste and smell. "You may have to slap me again . . . to wake me."

"I will. Just go, *go*."

I shut my eyes and immediately kneel—and retch, his emotions tangled and marred like diving into a bitter nest of twisted thorns. Puncturing every part of me.

Blood floods my mouth, gurgling in the back of my throat. I cough. My scratched fingers grip a substance . . . not wood. Something else. I roll onto my side. Choking for air. *What am I grabbing?* I kneel to my hands and feet, sore muscles wailing. Then a boot crashes against my lower back, forcing my stomach down.

The floor is soft.

Not carpet.

Not snow.

Not marble or tile.

What is this? Dry and coarse. Gluing to my bloodied mouth. I peel the parched strand off and my palm flattens on the ground.

Then I know.

THIRTY-NINE

Court

Golden straw adheres to my mouth and chin. I'm enclosed in unnatural dried grasslands. Surrounded by fake brush, fake blue skies, fake animals—and the back of my head hammers jarringly. Vehemently. Reminding me that I'm not fake and that reality is ten paces out of reach. Where velvet ropes section off this museum exhibit.

I spit out a wad of straw, blood, and bile. A heavy sole is grinding into my back. My energy depletes, struggling to scream and claw myself to a stance and thrust his boot away.

Breathing rapid breaths, I spit again. And again.

I don't need to see his sinewy build or his ash-brown hair or his feverish eyes to know whose boot bears on me. Who has dragged me mercilessly to the closed museum. Who has tormented me for much longer than just today.

Bastell. He crept into my room so lithely that as soon as I noticed the door ajar, he was behind me.

And struck my head.

Now Bastell frees my body, removing his boot from my back. And he glides around my battered frame like a cold shadow. Somewhere in the exhibit, he watches me pant helplessly and struggle to my hands and knees with quivering arms.

Pain clouds my vision. I pinch my eyes—*No* . . . Mykal pinches his eyes. I think. Is that him? Or is it me? I reach for his enduring strength, for his love, for all of him—his senses beating and beating next to my dying heart. If we hadn't kissed, if the link wasn't this strong, I'm certain he'd be as lost to me as Franny.

"Mykal," I choke out.

He stands. He's yelling, screaming at me to follow. *Get up!* I can almost see him. *Get up!*

Bastell slashes my ribs, his sharpened blade dripping with my blood, and my jaw locks, face twists, a moan mangled in my throat. I lose *all* sense of Mykal.

He's gone.

Fear capsizes my stomach and I puke and spit again. Exhausted tears haze my sight, but I turn my head to see honey-brown fur and a reddish mane.

An enormous lion is mounted on a low fake boulder. Teeth bared and anger lancing his glass eyes, the extinct animal roars a noiseless roar. As though knowing his last breath would be one of unbridled rage.

Is it possible to empathize with something that's already dead?

I'm not a lion. Franny and Mykal would scream out their dying breath, but I only ache to slip away and shut my eyes. And let this end.

Then I think: If that were true, I wouldn't have fought for Star-Dust. I wouldn't have tried so hard and put my heart into something so impossible.

I have fight left in me.

I'm not decayed and gone. I'm here. I'm still breathing.

He hasn't killed me yet.

"Do you not recall the thief's dance?" His saccharine voice sickens me, and his frenzied gaze latches on to my every action. Pacing around my fragile body, Bastell twirls a dagger, his plum trench coat dusting the yellowed straw. "Be effortlessly unseen."

My glazed eyes lose track of his swift feet.

"Blend in so not a soul spots your mischief." He speaks of how he snuck into StarDust by following a group of candidates who kept yapping about *flying exams* and *aerospace*. He also heard that Kinden and Tauris worked at StarDust, and he thought I'd be here to see them, unaware of my desire to leave the planet.

Then he waited for a quieter day and slid into the museum's

private elevator, only accessible to StarDust. A porter rode down, oblivious to Bastell standing behind him.

"So be lithe," he adds, "and imperceptible."

Suddenly, Bastell crouches by my face, the tip of his dagger perilously close to my eye. "Never cower like you are now. Never be so pathetic," he says, clucking his tongue in distaste. "I taught you how to *move*. So move."

Bastell yanks my ragged body to my feet and right as I stabilize my weight, I swing. He ducks and sinks his dagger in my hip.

Gods be damned.

I elbow his jaw, but he wrenches the dagger out—the pain blazing through every vein and organ like glass has shattered in my body. Cutting me, slicing me inside.

Every time I try to combat him, I fall ten times farther than before. Breathing hot breath through my nose, I stumble backward into the lion. And I throw my arm around its soft mane. Bracing myself upright.

I clutch my wound on my hip and watch him stalk me.

Bastell is not the same as he was in Vorkter or even the moments after the escape. Age and hunger darken his eyes, and his sallow skin hangs like its repulsed by him.

While my body bellows at me to just *sit*—legs threatening to buckle, blood dripping from fresh wounds—I stay standing.

He may've dragged me, kicked me, and slit me, but I'm stronger than when I trekked through the Free Lands at fifteen. And much stronger than when I was ten and trusted a man who'd come to betray me.

"You spent three years hunting me, is that it?" I sneer, hatred flaming my face. "For what?" I remove my soaked hand from my hip, palm stained red, and I jab at my heart. "For this?!" I cry furiously. "You want this?!" Spit spews off my lips. "YOU CAN'T HAVE IT!"

Bastell storms forward, blade to my sternum but not breaking skin. He snarls, "That's not up to you."

I wrap my fingers around the blade. Cutting into my palm.

"You can carve out my heart and squeeze it between your hands, but you will *never* truly have it."

My heart exists within Mykal and Franny. I hope they will live fearlessly even when I'm gone.

Bastell loathes how I grip his dagger. He wrenches the weapon back to his chest, slicing my hand deeper, blood gushing, but I'm beyond the pain now. I'm hot with fury.

"I cannot believe," I seethe, "that there was a day I revered you or listened to you." I just wanted my brother. Older, wiser—a Kinden who was *honest*. I thought Bastell could be him, but my love for Kinden shrouded my judgment. People are self-interested and self-involved.

Bastell taught me all he knew, but that didn't mean he loved me. It just meant that he could finally escape Vorkter. Because he needed two sets of unseen hands.

So he used me.

"Oh come on, Court." His lip curls. "Your life was supposed to end at fifteen. I should be the one feeling betrayed. If you were really *my* friend, you would've given me your heart. You would've let me poke at you and understand why you dodged your death-day. Who gods-damn cares if you die then or now? You aren't even meant to be here. But *I am*."

He'll die in his eighties.

My fingers tighten on the lion's mane, my shoes slick against the pool of blood. I try to staunch the stab wound on my hip, pressing my palm harder.

"Stop fighting me," he says. "Stop making me chase you. This whole ordeal could've ended years ago if you just let go. You're causing your own pain, Court. You're the one dragging out the inevitable."

"No," I sneer.

His fist flies against my jaw, and before I react, he stabs my shoulder and rips the dagger out, blood seeping through my tux. I crumble onto the boulder beside the lion. I start to bleed out, but I choke for breath and clutch the wounds tight to keep myself alive.

Bastell stands over me and then squats down, blade to the hollow of my throat. "Is this all you are?"

I breathe and breathe and say, "I'm more than you'll ever be."

"Is that what you tell yourself? You're *less* than me, Court. You're the protégé, the student. There is nothing that you have that I don't already have."

"I have friendship that's deep in my soul," I say. "You have no one."

"And where are these soul mates of yours?" He mockingly looks around.

They're running. Unseen and swift, I steal his blade out of his hand and spin it onto his throat.

He laughs. "And what? You'll cut me?" Bastell shakes his head. "You've already forgotten how to hold it."

He's right. I grip the hilt loosely like someone clawing to stay conscious.

Bastell adjusts my clutch, firmer. "Like this."

My nose flares. He's not frightened because he knows I can't kill him. My palm is too wet with blood, and the dagger already slips out of my grasp, clattering off the boulder to straw below.

"Pathetic."

I'm not stronger than him. I'm not faster or smoother, but I am smarter. And I say, "I can kill you today."

"I won't die—"

"I dodged my deathday, Bastell. Anything is possible." I force myself to believe these words, my confidence like my natural skin and not manufactured clothes.

I believe.

I can kill him.

He can die right now.

I sit up on my elbows and he bears his knee into my ribs. Biting down, I say, "You've tasted my blood. Ripped me open in so many different ways. You're searching for more years, more time— for immortality—but what's to say you haven't already found the trick? What's to say that you haven't already changed the course of your own deathday, Bastell?" I lean forward. "What's to say that you can't die right now?"

His face reddens. "You know nothing."

"We're all uncertain," I say, my vision fading to black, but I dig deeper to be present. "We're all wading in the unknown. You think cutting out my heart and testing it will solve the riddle, but you made that up on your own."

Bastell breathes heavily. "You can't trick me, Court."

My lips lift because I see the fear flicker in his eyes. Uncertainty creeps into his veins like poison. I gain some of the control that he stole from me. Warm peace blankets my dying body. My elbows weaken, and I collapse back onto the boulder, staring up at the painted baby-blue sky.

FORTY

Franny

amafort's Museum of Natural Histories & Figures is always closed to the public on the last day of the week. When I hear noises rebounding off the archways and high ceilings, I know they belong to Court and Bastell.

I race down deserted, darkened hallways, flying past extinct habitats. Mykal staggers not far behind, clutching his body like blood leaks profusely from his hip and shoulder. We only share the feeling; not the actual wound.

Court's pain has tried to overwhelm me too, but I chant, *Focus on yourself, focus on yourself.* I concentrate on my boots thudding marble and my black hair whipping backward as my legs pump faster and stronger.

We'll find you, Court.

I quickly read a few signs and veer to the savannah exhibits where we'll find dry grass. Mykal winces and starts lagging. I capture his hand and tug him to my hurried pace.

"I'm not leaving you behind," I pant.

Mykal growls out in determination and keeps up, step for step. One more turn and light shines on golden-wheat grasslands. Life-sized replicas of wild leopards and panthers pounce on a dead gazelle. Crimson drips off a boulder where Court lies next to a roaring lion.

A few feet away, Bastell paces in ankle-high brush, a silver handgun in wary fingers.

Gods. I boil deep. "Move away from him!" I scream, crashing through the velvet ropes. Bastell flinches, a little flustered for a man with a gun.

"Court!" Mykal barrels straight for him. "COURT!" We rush through the grasslands, my skin scalding every place that Bastell stabbed and cut Court. I expect him to charge us. To stop us. A dagger glints in the tall grass beneath the boulder.

I grab the weapon while Mykal climbs the low boulder and draws Court gently onto his lap. His gray eyes roll into the back of his head. *Court.*

No, Franny.

I can't think of him right now. Only one of us can concentrate on Court at a time. My sight is so fuzzy that Bastell and the leopards blend together. I blink and blink and focus on my boots, my hands, my arms. I bite my own tongue, and my vision returns, not in full, but enough that I distinguish Bastell's unruly hair and plum trench coat.

He mutters to himself.

"Court, look at me," Mykal growls, tapping Court's cheeks. "You better be looking at me." Mykal frantically pulls off his shirt and presses the fabric to the wounds. "Franny—" I'm already peeling off my blouse before he asks. I chuck the garment at him, my shoulders tensed.

I tighten my grip on the dagger's hilt, not understanding why Bastell lets us near Court. Without another pause, I shuffle forward and guard the low boulder. He'll need to cross my path to reach them.

Much more perplexed and anxious than I imagined, Bastell fiddles with his gun, unsure of himself. How can this be the same man that dragged Court ruthlessly up to the museum?

Bastell shifts uneasily and finally notices me watching. "He said that I could die at any minute." And then Bastell pushes the silver barrel to his temple. Chin raised and chest caving in a fearful breath.

My mouth drops. What is he . . . ?

"We'll see if he's right." Bastell hesitates for a second.

Mayday.

I take a sweltering step forward. "I hope it works. I hope you *die* right here." *Right now.* I've never loathed someone this terribly, this coldheartedly—and it's all my own. It scares me because I feel like I could do anything to him without remorse. Without guilt.

I could snap the little bones of his neck. I could break his ankles and poke out his eyes. I want to do it all. I want him to die.

Bastell shifts. "If I live, then I'll do worse than kill Court for tricking me . . . and I'll let his soul mates watch."

I scream and brandish my dagger in threat—just as he squeezes the trigger. I flinch but no *boom* arrives.

The gun jams once.

He presses again.

Jams.

And again.

Jams.

Again and again, in quick succession, the gun locks on Bastell. *Fyke.* Confidence and certainty returned, he points the barrel at me.

I yell and run at Bastell with impulse, my lungs splitting open and fear abandoning my senses.

If I die, I will die hard.

And fast and full.

I'm within arm's length, the cold gun pushes against my chest, but I don't slow. I use my speed and strike his forehead with the heel of my palm. His brain rocks in his skull, staggering back, and the gunshot rings—the bullet grazing my shoulder. I wince but waste no time, smacking the gun aside. Clearly, it won't harm him.

Still disoriented, he holds his rattling head. I jab two fingers behind his collarbone. He screams out, but the pressure point forces him to his knees. I'm not finished. I move as fast as possible, leaving him no room to retaliate.

I throw my hardest knuckle into his sternum. He moans and gasps for breath. *Punctured lungs,* Court said would happen. Then

I chop at his neck with my hand. Gurgling, he clutches his throat and falls to his back.

I hover over him with the dagger and crush his windpipe with my boot. I single knuckle-punch the soft spot by his ear. Bone cracks and his jaw dislocates. Not able to speak, he wheezes.

I hate you. I spit on him, my eyes glassy with fiery tears.

"I know I can't kill you," I say, "but you'll never hurt him or us ever again." No reluctance inside of me, I stab Bastell repeatedly, crimson spraying my chest. I see my own hatred staring back. Not a body. Not a man.

When his eyes flutter shut and his limbs sag unconscious, I stop driving the blade in his chest. He'll eventually wake and live, but for now, he's harmless.

I drop the dagger and teeter backward before turning around altogether. By the time I reach the boulder, Mykal finishes tying his shirt and mine around Court's wounds, already soaked a deep ruby red.

Fighting to stay awake, Court's heavy-lidded eyes droop open and closed.

"We have to go," I say hurriedly, worried that someone will find all of us and Bastell together. Then they'll start asking questions. "Can you carry him alone—?"

"No," he immediately cuts me off. "I keep fighting consciousness by being this close."

"All right."

Court may be too tall and muscular for me to carry by myself, but I'll try. While I stand off the boulder, Mykal places Court's limp arm around my shoulder, and I support his whole body against my side.

"Let me . . . I'll try . . . walking," Court sputters, his feet weak beneath even flimsier legs.

"No *thank you*," I snap and flex every muscle in my body, walking forward with this added weight. I bear hard on my teeth. *I can do this.* Even if he outsizes me.

Mykal just now notices my shoulder, skin seared off in a

scorched, bloodied line. "What the three hells . . . ?" He swings his head back to Bastell, unmoving on crimson-stained straw. Mykal's eyes grow and grow. He's seen more gruesome sights, but not by my hands.

We exchange one short look, knowing that I've hardened. For better or for worse, I don't know yet, but I'm not the same as I once was.

On our elevator descent to StarDust's common room, we concoct a plan that Court has always said, "Is full of impossibilities." So we never tried before, but as long as Bastell lives—and he'll live a long, *long* while—he'll hunt Court.

And with the gory museum exhibit and Court's wounds, we don't have a good explanation to tell the StarDust directors. Tauris isn't a chump; being exposed by them or Bastell is almost a certainty. There are no more choices left but this impossible one.

We're stealing the Saga starcraft.

And if we succeed, it'll be the largest thievery of Court's life.

Elevator doors spring open and, with Court supported between us, we run through the common room. *Empty.* Everyone must still be celebrating in the dining room.

Mykal blinks hard to stay coherent, his head lolling more than once. I can only sprint this fast with his help. We keep sharing tough glances. Mine saying, *I need you.*

His replying, *I know it.* And he moves forward like he is pushing through hellish winds that slap and shove. Not stopping. Not pausing.

Court often talks about Mykal's impervious nature and fortitude, but I never saw him in the Free Lands. I mostly saw him flounder and slowly pick himself up at StarDust. All of today, right now, I completely and wholeheartedly understand what Court meant.

I see and *feel* the magnitude of Mykal's iron will. Trekking through three hells, he could be shackled with weight, punctured with a hundred arrows, and I believe he'd still find a way to move. His strength breathes fire inside my lungs.

I kick the door open to the hallway and spot a violet code box beside a window. While I quickly type in the most recent code, Mykal stares out the windows.

"Launchpad looks about empty," he says.

Court, unable to support his own head, sinks in our arms. Mykal growls out a Grenpalish curse and then adjusts Court's weight on his side.

I finish entering the code and the door to the launchpad slides open. We struggle with bracing him and walking, and by the time we reach the rows and rows of metal chairs from the ceremony, Court faints.

Wooziness brings us to our knees and we crash into chairs, spreading blood everywhere.

My side cramps from the collision and I roll onto my back. Wincing, I look to Mykal. He's hovered over Court, tapping his cheek. Trying to wake him.

I force myself to my feet. So light-headed that I sway and clutch Mykal's broad shoulder.

I say, "If one of us splits apart from Court, maybe our minds will clear."

Mykal nods. "Go." He motions with his head to the starcraft. "Run. We'll be catching up."

My exhausted jog morphs into a quick sprint. Up the boarding ramp, I reach the locked entrance. *Mayday.* "I need a keycard," I mutter. I've only ever seen Amelda and Tauris use them.

From up here, I have a good view of the entire launchpad and hallway windows. I scan the technician areas, but what's the chance someone left a keycard lying around?

I freeze in panic.

Clutching goblets of wine, a group of candidates exits the dining room. They meander through the marbled hallway. *Don't look out the window. Don't look out the window.*

Only one person turns their head.

Padgett Soarcastle instantly spots me on the ramp. Gaze narrowing, mind clicking, then she snaps her attention off me. Padgett speaks to the other candidates, but no sound filters into the launchpad. At first I think she'll snitch on me, but the candidates nod and disappear into the common room.

She lingers behind and then runs back into the dining room.

I try to return my mind to the keycard, but out of the corner of my eye, Padgett appears in the hallway again. This time with her little sister.

Gem.

The Soarcastle sisters type in the code and enter the launchpad.

Mykal curses at them, but he can't leave Court. Padgett barely glances their way, and she never slows, headed straight for me. Gem skip-walks to keep pace with her sister's authoritative stride.

I may know them, but I can't trust them. Balling my fists, I stand tall and ready.

The ramp shakes as they step on. "Whatever you're thinking about doing with that starcraft," Padgett says confidently, "we want in."

"What?"

"I'm *not* leaving this planet without my sister," Padgett says. "Do you understand?"

Just as I nod, shock thieving my voice, Gem slips beside me. "Oh Wilafran . . ." She blushes and then pales at my blood-splattered bra. I'd forgotten that I gave my blouse away.

"It's fine," I say firmly.

Gem focuses. "Let's see." She drums her lips and then pries off the casing of the keycard device, revealing tangled blue wires.

Mykal lifts Court to a chair, awake but barely, and he combs back Court's sweaty hair, trying to inspect his head wound.

Gem risks a glance at them and loses more color in her face. "Shouldn't have looked." She blows out a controlled breath. "Blood has always made me squeamish."

"Hurry," Padgett tells her sister.

In haste, Gem plucks the wrong wire. An ear-splitting alarm blares and yellow lights flash in the hallways and launchpad.

"Gem," I say.

"I have it." Gem tugs another wire and twists the ends together, sparking—and then the starcraft door grinds open.

While I hesitate to wait for Court and Mykal, Gem and Padgett push inside, passing me. People start filling multiple hallways.

"Mykal!" I yell.

"We're coming." He supports Court, whose feet find better footing. "Go! Go!"

I see Court holding more of his own weight, his eyes opened, so I run into the starcraft. Not about to let the Soarcastle sisters fly away without us.

Bolting through metallic corridors, I remember every lesson and exam about this vessel. Quickly, I reach the bridge. Pass the captain's chair, the communications and MEU station, and race down the few steps toward the cockpit.

Before Gem settles in the second pilot chair, I push her out of the way and claim the seat as mine.

Padgett shoots me a look from Pilot A but doesn't start a stew. Harness buckled, joystick between my legs, I have control of the direction. Padgett controls the speed.

Gem clips herself into the MEU chair and types on the pad, screens lighting up.

Padgett flicks buttons, and the starcraft rumbles, air expelling from the base valves. Prepping for takeoff protocol.

Where are they? I concentrate—their boots aren't even on the ramp yet.

"Collapsing ground wheels," Padgett announces. "Preparing for hover module." That includes retracting the boarding ramp.

"Wait," I say, panicked. "We have to wait!" Court staggers. Mykal hoists him up again. Through the windshield, the yellow lights keep flaring, and more bodies swarm the hallways, some leaking onto the launchpad.

I lose breath at the thought of leaving them behind on Saltare-3 while I fly off to space.

Padgett grips her joystick. "If we don't launch now, they'll lock the sky port. Then we'll never be able to fly out."

"Wait!" I shout. "I'll fly us in the sun if you don't wait!" My threat does nothing but darken her glare.

"Padgett," Gem calls out, tenderness in her gaze. They can leave now. They're together. They have everything they want, but I think of all the months I've lived with Gem. Of the dances and laughs we've shared, and I wonder if that means anything at all.

Padgett shakes her head.

Gem nods. "Wait. *Please.*"

FORTY-ONE

Mykal

Sirens burst my ears, the hollering even louder. "Do not climb that ramp!" people yell from all sides, but, with our arms over each other's shoulders, we're already climbing this damned ramp together.

We're not the only ones.

Candidates start racing up behind us, but Kinden suddenly sprints ahead, bowling their bodies backward and shoving them off the metal grate. No one attempts to rush on again.

Gods bless.

His eyes meet mine. "Help my brother!" As though that's not what I've been doing.

My features grow harsher, and I do even more—I *heave* Court's body into my arms, cradling him. He complains instantly.

"Set me down . . . ," he pants. "I'm better—"

"Shut up," I growl, "that's what you've always told me. How about you listen to your own unkind words?"

Court coughs instead of laughs.

I stagger once because of the link, not because of his weight or height, but I trudge forward into the starcraft, leaving behind the infuriated yells and demands to cuff Kinden Valcastle.

FORTY-TWO

Court

Retracting the boarding ramp now," Padgett announces.

I'm slumped in the captain's chair. I reenergize from Franny and Mykal's senses, just enough to remain coherent and shift my head and arms. Anything else might cause me to faint again.

I had to have been half unconscious to agree to this impossible plan.

Franny casts looks of concern from the cockpit, but I mouth, *I'm fine.*

She mouths, *Liar.*

We both try to smile, but we equally struggle to produce one. She confronted Bastell and risked her life. My gratitude and admiration floods me with warmth. I can only nod at Franny, and she nods back, knowing what I feel and everything I'd like to eventually say after this is all over.

We're not safe yet, but to strengthen them, I have to heal. I inspect the sodden makeshift bandages on my hip and shoulder. "Needle and thread," I tell Mykal.

Kneeling at my feet, he rummages through a med kit. His guilt is a silent and cold passenger inside him, and every second or two, he balls his blood-stained hand into a fist. Anger contracts his muscles, and if we had time, he'd yell and yell, veins popping from his neck.

"It's not your fault," I whisper. "You did more for me than you're accepting."

His eyes redden and he nearly chucks the med kit. He must remember what I need, so he clings onto the white box. "I promised you—"

"To hells with that—"

"Leave it alone," he cuts me off all the same. "You're the one we need to be fussing over." Then he tosses gauze and pill bottles— I point.

"That." *Pain meds.*

Mykal doles out a few. "Open your mouth." He gently places two pills on my tongue, and I swallow while he digs through the kit.

"Auto-locking the starcraft's entrance." Padgett's announcement seizes my mind.

I think of my brother. "Did Kinden . . . ?" I trail off as Mykal shrugs. And then I think of the worst. Kinden jumped on the ramp and protected us from candidates and StarDust directors who would've thrown us off, but by guarding the entrance, they'll send him to Vorkter for aiding our crime.

My face grinds into a wince.

Don't think about him.

I focus on Mykal. On his fingers threading a needle. He'll stitch me. He's sewn enough clothes to do well.

"Heya, did you all really believe you'd fly this starcraft without me?"

Our heads whip up.

Kinden slinks onto the bridge. *My brother made it.* My chest swells. Up close now, he cringes at my beaten state and inhales sharply.

"Ugh," Gem complains. "Not you."

I'm thankful for the distraction. Kinden removes his concern off me and mimics Gem, *"Not you."*

"Take a seat, Saga 1," Padgett calls, lip quirked.

"You're on comms," I add.

"My specialty," he says, sinking into the silver communications chair and fitting on a headset. "Though I'm great at everything."

"Problem," Franny calls out, and the air strains. "They've locked the sky port."

FORTY-THREE

Franny

"Father, open the sky port!" Kinden shouts into his radio headset.

My sweaty palm cements to the joystick, my other hand on the keyboard. We're running out of time. Through the windshield, more and more bodies flood the launchpad.

"I told you this would happen," Padgett says from her pilot's seat, more frustrated than I've ever seen her.

I crane my neck over my shoulder. "How are you doing, Gem?"

Gem types feverishly in the MEU station. "Manual override of the sky port may take another ten to . . . fifteen minutes."

Padgett shakes her head. "We don't have that long."

"I can't force the processors to run any faster than they're capable of," Gem huffs. "Technology has limitations, and a system reboot would take *hours*."

"Father, listen to me!" Kinden yells and slams his hands on his station's desk, partially standing.

Burning pain blooms in my hip and shoulder. Without looking, a needle pricks me—or Court, rather. Mykal sews up his deeper wounds.

We need to leave now and my mind races like I push my whole weight on a gas pedal.

"Father, Etian is here," Kinden says frantically. "He's hurt. He's *dying* and this is the only way to save him. Do you hear me?! Don't you want to save your son?!" At the static silence, he pounds his palms again.

Padgett and Gem exchange an unreadable look, but they're both too concentrated on leaving to ask questions. I breathe through my nose. *Think, Franny.*

I haven't botched everything yet. I can plan. I can even *execute* one, so I think hard.

And a voice booms through the starcraft's intercom system. "All of you must calmly evacuate the Saga starcraft," Tauris commands. "If you do not cooperate, we will have no choice but to charge you with high treason." A capital punishment.

Court licks his cracked lips. "They'll charge everyone regardless."

"We're not going to Vorkter," Padgett says adamantly. "Gem!"

"I'm trying!" Then Gem balks. "Oh Holy Wonders . . . something or someone triggered a sensor in the east wing. They're headed to the bridge."

"That's impossible," Kinden combats, yanking his headset to his neck. "I saw the entrance auto-lock, and I'm the only one who entered after Court and Mykal."

"It's still closed," Gem verifies. There are no weapons on the starcraft since we're supposed to be ambassadors of peace.

I'm about to unbuckle and check the bridge door, but Padgett clasps my wrist. "We need you here," she tells me.

And then Mykal pushes to a stance.

FORTY-FOUR

Mykal

Ten meters away," Gem calls.

I guard the bridge door, needle between two finger-tips. Ready for whoever believes they're gonna imprison us. With my last dying breath, I'll be ensuring we're all free.

"Four meters . . . two . . ."

The door slides vertically open, and instinct propels me, not thinking long. I push the lightweight body up against the wall. *Thump.* I jab the needle at an eye and the tip pierces and slides into . . . an apple.

I register who I grip by the throat, his half-bitten apple raised to protect his face. I let go instantly.

"Zimmer?!" nearly everyone yells. I dunno what to think. He's not someone I'd toast with ale, but he's better than all the other people outside.

Zimmer spits out a chunk of apple and coughs once, lifting his hands in surrender. Just noticing the needle. "Dodged that one." He bites around the needle like nothing happened. "Heya." He waves. "Thought I'd drop by." He pats my arm, and I shove him hard.

Zimmer stumbles toward the comms station.

"Where'd you come from?" I growl.

He gawks and catches sight of Franny, both nodding in rec-ognition, and then he flashes a wily grin at me. "I stole a keycard about an hour ago, boarded the starcraft, and hung out in the sleep-ing quarters. I was going to fly away with the Saga 5 whether they wanted me or not."

"Wait." Franny scowls. "You planned to stow yourself away like luggage and wait around for three months before takeoff?"

"Yeah, that sounds about accurate. Wise, aren't I?"

"Fool."

He touches his heart and mouths, *Chump not fool.* Not many see his lips move, busying themselves with the sky port problem.

Intercom crackles. "This is the last warning," Tauris says. "Remove yourselves from this vessel *now*."

FORTY-FIVE

Franny

hat is the sky port made of?" I ask Padgett quietly.

"Plexiglas." Hope glimmers in her eyes. Plexiglas is breakable. Maybe not by my blistering Fast-Tracker fists, but a vessel of this size and power could shatter clean through.

"Preparing for vertical lift?" I ask, about to shift the joystick, but one pilot can't function without the other.

"Preparing for vertical lift," Padgett agrees.

We both work fast, the starcraft engines heating. Bodies bolt toward the hallways and off the launchpad, realizing that we plan to take off, regardless if the sky port opens or not.

"Shut off all comms with Saltare-3," Court tells his brother, both slumped in their chairs. "You have to . . . Kinden? We can't let any of them track us."

Kinden fits on his headset again.

The starcraft begins to tilt. "Everyone strap in for vertical lift," Court commands. Mykal and Zimmer unleash two jump chairs by the bridge door and buckle in. I hear the med kit sliding as the vessel angles upward.

From the windshield, the sky port slowly skates into view. Lilac smoke clouds the Plexiglas dome. No one on Saltare-3—not a Babe, not a Fast-Tracker, not an Influential—has ever seen what exists beyond the haze.

Now all three kinds of people will.

Kinden hesitates for one second to cut all ties and the intercom booms again. "Kinden," Tauris calls. "I'm ordering you, son, to disengage right now. *Please.*"

"No." Kinden speaks into his headset.

"Don't be a madman!" Tauris yells, panicked. "Don't be like your brother!"

Court barely flinches. He left his father behind long before this day, and after his interview with Tauris, I sensed closure that has no reason to open again.

"Amusing," Kinden breathes, tears surfacing, "considering all you ever wanted was for me to be *just like him*." The starcraft reclines, almost completely vertical.

"Kinden!"

"It's you who's mad, Father. Not us." Fingers to a switch, he says, "May the gods be in your spirit." The intercom silences, static vanishing.

We're on our own. At ninety degrees. "Engaging the thrusters," I say. "In three . . . two . . ."

Padgett wrenches her joystick toward her chest, and I drive mine outward. Violent streams of fire roar from the triple-barreled engines.

"Engaging acceleration," she announces. We coordinate our movements like we were paired from the very start, and in seconds, the starcraft ascends. The windshield is so vast—it stretches from my feet and toward Gem and Kinden. I feel like I'm floating and flying all by myself. No massive starcraft beneath my boots.

I smile, thrill screaming in my lungs, and we speed faster and faster. In one *boom* and rumble, we break through the dome. Plexiglas rains down on the Saga starcraft, but we never decelerate.

"Vessel is intact. No harm," Gem reads off her screens.

The sheer force of the starcraft splitting through the atmosphere overwhelms all of us for a moment. We fall to silence, the rush of power pressing on our chests and thundering around us.

Lilac smoke slaps the windshield. Bulleting through, we suddenly breach the smoke, flying through bright blue sky, and then we accelerate into blackness. As gravity alters, I tilt the starcraft upright, a flat saucer again, and the pressure ekes from my shoulders and chest.

My lips part and I reach out and put my fingers to the cold windshield. In the calmest moment of my life, I feel three hearts beating peacefully against my ribs. I hear only awed breath and the unclipping of seat buckles.

Is this our universe, gods? Our stark white and purple world falls behind us, and I stare out at endless darkness lit with hopeful, glittering stars.

I dreamed of beauty once or twice—maybe a thousand times more than I've admitted. I dreamed of an oil-painted sky and rich tapestries and woven rugs. They said I dreamed big—but if a room at the Catherina was big, then this view from this very seat must be absolutely, breathtakingly limitless.

Nothing compares to the beauty of the universe.

I hear the pitter-patter of boots, and then Zimmer sidles to my chair, propping his elbow on the top.

"Look at them," he breathes in soft wonder.

Look at the stars. "I see them." I wipe a slipping tear. It's not my tear.

I touch my lips. It's more than just my smile. Feeling their happiness, I burst into a much greater one.

FORTY-SIX

Mykal

I sit on the armrest of the captain's chair, entranced by Court's overcome smile. I hardly even stare out the damned window. Truth being, space is maddeningly dark—but that smile . . . *Gods, that smile.*

It brightens my whole wide world.

Tears drip down all three of our cheeks, and Court looks to me, searching my eyes for the name to my expression.

I lower my forehead to his and clutch the base of his neck, breathing in the warmth of our bodies, and he clasps my jaw between bandaged palms.

I whisper, "You've stolen my heart, you little crook."

His smile only stretches further and brighter. "My most valuable theft."

We shut our eyes, love and peace washing over us. But not for long—fear spikes, and our eyes snap open again.

Franny notices the interior bridge lights flickering before we do, and in one quick moment, we're all plunged into darkness.

FORTY-SEVEN

Court

The power cuts out and I muster strength to yell the protocols that rip through my brain. Emergency grav shield and air pumps kick in so we can breathe at least. Everyone moves. Even me.

I bear my weight on my good leg, but mostly, I lean against Mykal's chest.

"Sit," he growls in my ear.

"Later. We have no time." Bridge lights flit in and out. Screens flash but then fade to black. Gem huffs loudly, and Kinden flicks switches left and right.

And then the starcraft lurches away from Saltare-3 like an invisible rope lassoes our vessel and *pulls*.

Franny and Padgett fall back into their seats, checking their controls. "It's not us," Franny says. "It's . . ."

"Someone else," I finish, my gaze narrowing at a massive starcraft that looms in the distance. Outsizing the Saga by ten times. Our starcraft matches the mass of its docking port.

"It cut our power," Gem proclaims.

"Comms are down," Kinden adds. "I can't alert or connect with it."

The weak navigation of the Saga starcraft only detects incoming objects or vessels. No extra details, no information about what or who is on board. Other starcrafts probably have more advanced systems than ours, and I can only hope this is another Saltare ship.

Our sister planets are the only ones nearby in this galaxy, so it's the most obvious answer.

Mykal holds me upright. "We don't have any weapons."

"If it's a Saltare starcraft, we shouldn't need them," I say.

Padgett stands, her velvet gown from the StarDust ceremony sweeping the floor. "So what are we supposed to do? Pretend to be ambassadors of peace? The moment they hear our decrees, they'll call us cowards and throw us out the port window."

I hang my arm around Mykal's waist, a stabbing pain radiating from my hip bone. I stifle a wince and say, "If this is Saltare-1, then they believe we're here to join forces with them. We don't argue. We take the path of least resistance."

Kinden rocks backward. "That is beyond treason, little brother. It will put our entire world at war."

I'm the enemy.

I've always been the enemy of our world. I'm not a martyr. I won't sacrifice my life for hundreds of people on Saltare-3. Hundreds who recognize the exact day they will die. The last time I tried to save them, I was called a madman.

My heart will not bleed for the people of Saltare-3. I'm sound and clearheaded, and I choose to survive with Mykal and Franny. Even if that means starting a war.

I meet Kinden's indecision. "Our father will contact Saltare-1," I tell my brother. "He'll let them know that seven outlaws just commandeered the Saga. Unless we align with Saltare-1, we'll be seen as adversaries."

The bridge quiets, air vents humming.

Gem is the first to speak. "I suppose we're the Saga 7 then."

Zimmer peers out the front windshield. "And what if that isn't a Saltare starcraft?" To me, he asks, "What then?"

"Then you all stay silent and let me talk."

"You can barely stand!" Padgett shouts like this is the worst idea.

"Then I'll speak," Kinden says.

"Maybe if our goal was to be loathed," Gem says pointedly.

"Let me." I release my hold on Mykal. Standing on my own accord. My confidence is not just a front this time.

Either they all take pity or they recognize why StarDust named me their leader, but everyone nods in agreement.

Franny and Padgett unbuckle their harnesses, no longer needed in the cockpit. As Padgett retreats to her sister's side, Franny joins ours.

She crosses her arms. Blood speckles her bra, and we need to bandage the bullet-graze on her shoulder. A third erratic pulse belongs to Mykal, and my stiff body refuses to bend.

Franny takes a deep breath. "We're a mess."

"We're together," I murmur.

We're together rings through us, but we look out at what we face. With the universe at our window and the unknown roping us in—we become one maddened pulse. Raging, raging.

Raging.

FORTY-EIGHT

Franny

After they tether and land our Saga starcraft on their dock, they board and say they're the commander and cadets of the Romulus. Principal starcraft of Saltare-1. So we enter their vessel willingly, and we're led to a viewing bay.

The room is nothing more than a long metal railing and an enormous window overlooking the universe. Several cadets linger close, hands cupped by their waists. Their sleek burgundy uniforms contrast the onyx and gold slacks and cloaks that all seven of us found onboard the Saga. We changed clothes before landing so they wouldn't catch our lies in our bloodstains.

However, there is one similarity between the Romulus and Saga. We all wear identical StarDust pins.

I'm not so much a chump that I believe the StarDust emblem makes us friends, but maybe it'll let them realize that we're not foes.

The twentysomething, brassy-haired commander appraises us, pleasantries slowly waning. He carries a kind of brisk authority that puts me on edge. *Anything can happen.* In one moment, he could snap and decide to eject all of us into space.

I swallow an anxious pit at the sight of his eyes, so black the pupils are lost.

"Stand in a line," he instructs. Court told us not to dispute any of their requests unless they were self-harming, so we listen. Arm's length apart, we form a horizontal line. Court braces some of his weight on the metal railing.

"You're the Saltare-3 crew that stole the Saga starcraft . . . that *we* gifted to your planet. Correct?"

All seven of us tense, but Court is the only one who speaks. "Yes, but we had reason that tips in your favor."

"And what's your reasoning?"

Court inhales strongly. "Saltare-3 wanted peace over aiding our sister planets, and when we asked to stay loyal to Saltare-1, they threatened us. We took the starcraft because we believe in your mission to start a war with Andola."

"Hmm," the commander muses, his reaction unreadable. He scans each one of us from toe to head. "It's hard to believe people I don't know. On Saltare-3, you all may take one another at face value, but we're smarter here." The commander motions to a cadet who approaches with an ivory device, shaped much like a Death Reader.

I go numb and try not to flinch. My nails dig into my arms.

Mykal grits his teeth until his jaw throbs.

"What is that?" Court asks in a seemingly calm voice. His pulse thrashes as vigorously as ours.

"A Helix Reader," the commander says. "Stay still and everything will be fine."

We have no choice but to listen.

Starting at the right of the line, the curly-haired cadet puts the double prongs to Gem's wrist. She winces, but the screen never reveals numbers. It just lights blue.

The cadet moves on to Padgett.

Blue.

Kinden.

Blue.

Zimmer.

Blue.

Then me. Court cages his breath, and I try to expel mine through my nose—wetness drips and drips. I rub and examine my fingers. Another nosebleed.

"Gross," the cadet says.

I pinch my nose and scowl. "Just do it."

The cadet presses the prongs to my wrist. I wait.

And wait.

The screen blinks orange.

"What . . . ?"

I'm jerked by the cadet into the group of Romulus crew.

"HEYA!" Mykal roars and punches a cadet who tries to seize him.

Hands grab at me, and I shove every direction, disoriented. Confused. *Stop! Stop!*

"What are you doing?!" I hear Zimmer's angered voice in the background. I hear befuddlement from Gem, Kinden, and Padgett. Three cadets restrain Mykal and they stab him with the device.

Orange.

I stop fighting and he goes eerily still. His huge eyes pop out, horror-struck. What does this mean?

Court willingly lets them test him.

Orange.

"Take those four into the bridge," the commander orders. "Leave these three here for a second. Call the security team in, Brewer, thank you."

Cadets restrain us, their hands gripping our arms and shoulders like we've already wronged them. "What's going on?!" Mykal growls.

"I don't understand," I mutter beneath ragged breath.

Court is lost, drifting in his own mind.

Facing us, the commander scrutinizes our frames once more and then begins speaking in a language that causes my frown to deepen and brows to furrow. What . . . what is he saying?

Court shakes his head, just as unsure.

Mykal looks incensed, like he could topple all of the cadets over with one blow, but he stays still and listens as keenly as us.

"Commander," a cadet says, "it looks like they don't know English. Maybe try another Andolian language."

Chills rake my skin.

Court lifts his grim gaze. "Why would we know an Andolian language?" he asks in Saltarian's native tongue.

The commander cocks his head. "They planted you well. I almost believe you don't know who you are."

Words blare in my head and scald the tip of my tongue. Longing to be yelled.

Who am I?

Who am I?

Who are we?

"How'd you even survive?" the commander wonders. "Your deathdays would be inaccurate. Did you already think you dodged them?" He absorbs our shock. "You really don't know, do you? You're not even aware that deathdays don't work for you."

Why?

A cadet speaks up. "Maybe they don't know the planet as Andola."

The commander says to us, "Your people call the planet something else. They call it *Earth*."

I've never heard of Earth before, and no recognition sparks inside my soul. The commander studies our features closely.

Court keeps shaking his head.

"My people?" I say. "I'm Saltarian. *We're* Saltarian."

"No," the commander says with so much more certainty than I've ever held. "You're human. All three of you are human." And then he raises his voice. "Take our new prisoners to their cells—"

Mykal's violent scream pierces the air and tears through me, buckling my legs, and cadets instantly swarm us. Grabbing at our limbs. Pulling us away from one another. We reach out. *Stay together.*

Stay together.

Court elbows and jabs cadets with the last of his strength. "Mykal! Franny!" He tries desperately to clasp our hands. I stretch and stretch, my fingers brushing his, but someone hoists me up. I slam the heel of my palm at a forehead. My own blood flows from my nose.

I reach for Mykal.

He's being dragged backward by twenty people.

"FRANNY!" Mykal hollers, face reddened with ire. He shoves and screams.

Court slips, his knees banging to the floor, and a cadet presses their boot on his back.

No! "NO!" I cry out for Court. I fight to reach him.

He fights to stand for us.

"Humanity," the commander says in the background of our struggle, "what a tragic thing."

ACKNOWLEDGMENTS

GREATEST, LIMITLESS THANKS TO:

Our heroic agent, Kimberly Brower, who has changed countless lives with her passion and dedication to so many brilliant authors and strong women. You are a wonder, and we are so lucky to have you in our corner. We're deeply grateful for how much you believed in this book and us. It wouldn't exist without your encouragement and love.

Eileen Rothschild, our editor, for loving Franny, Mykal, and Court enough to give them the biggest shot, and for giving us the greatest chance of a lifetime. You've made our childhood dream come true.

The Wednesday Books team for championing this book when so many exist in the world and for helping make a lofty dream turn into a vivid reality. You've made a pair of dorky twins happier than happy.

Our mom, who is the embodiment of kindness, family, and fierce strength; our dad, who is thoughtful, witty, and loving—thank you for teaching us compassion and empathy. For instilling a kind of persistence and determination inside of us that has no deathday. For believing we're extraordinary, even when we're ordinary. We love you both endlessly, terribly, and wholeheartedly.

Alex Ritchie, our older brother, who is the true space explorer as a SpaceX engineer. Thanks for all your knowledge, help with StarDust, and every chat. We're proud to call you our brother. You're contributing magnificent, incredible things to society, and we're in awe of you.

Jenn Rohrbach and Lanie Lan, our shining sea stars and literal superhero sweethearts. You both were with us at the beginning of it all. Our favorite movie growing up said the secret to the success of life is finding something you love, but if you're not good at it, you'll probably fail—and the only way to truly know whether or not you're good is if people tell you. You two were the first ones outside of family to tell us we were good at what we love. You believed in our success before we ever knew what success was. There is not enough thanks in the world to repay all the love and support you've given us throughout years of time.

Some of the loveliest people in the whole universe, Lex Martin and Kennedy Ryan, thank you for your friendship over the years; it has meant so much to us. We're geeky introverts, and you both always bring us out of our shells.

Julie Cross, for helping us in immeasurable ways when we were starting out. We're great believers of fate, and years ago, one of us (Krista) decided to read your book instead of studying for the MCAT. With that decision, Krista realized she loved books and writing more than she could ever love medicine. So in a small but big way, you had a hand in leading us here.

Thanks to our grandparents, Grandpa Pat and Granddad Ritchie, who are no longer with us—who almost made it to see this book on shelves. For thinking we're the smartest girls on the planet, as grandparents often do. They're both subtly in this book.

The rest of our family—our grandma, our aunts and uncles, and our amazing cousins—for their overwhelming love and encouragement. We write about family because we love family. Thank you for always believing in us.

To the Fizzle Force family, you are powerful. And rare and beautiful. Your excitement for our work and our characters is a thing of purity and beauty that never goes unnoticed by us. You've helped us defeat doubt monsters and believe strongly in ourselves and climb over mountains and kiss the sky. We feel your love every day, and we wouldn't be where we are without passionate, loving humans like you. An infinite thankyouthankyouthankyou.

Thank you to every single person who has read this very book. For taking a chance on Court and Mykal and Franny, for opening your hearts to this world, for reaching this acknowledgments section—we're so honored that you've chosen to read a story that we've written.

Lastly, to every teenager at home thinking, "I want to do this, I want to be this"—you can. We were the young girls scouring the acknowledgment section thinking, "Maybe one day." Your one day will happen. Maybe it won't be in the way you expect. Maybe your path will be different from the one you imagine at twelve, thirteen, fourteen—but you can and you will. Hold on to your passion. Seize the day, and the moment will come when you may still be ordinary but you'll feel *extraordinary*.